IGNACIO DE LOYOLA BRANDÃO was born in 1936 in Brazil. He began a career in journalism at the age of sixteen writing reviews for the films that played at the only cinema in his hometown. At twenty, he moved to Sao Paulo, where he worked for the principal newspapers of the state capital until 1979. ZERO was finished in 1969 but was not published until five years later, when it was accepted by an Italian publisher. Not until 1975 was it published in Brazil, bringing considerable scandal, but extraordinary praise and a number of literary prizes, including the Brasilia Prize, a national literary honor. In 1976, it was banned by the Ministry of Justice. Following a national protest in 1977, the ban was lifted in 1979 and ZERO immediately returned to the bestseller list. This is the first English language edition of this international bestseller.

ZERO

IGNACIO DE LOYOLA BRANDÃO

Translated by
ELLEN WATSON

 A BARD BOOK/PUBLISHED BY AVON BOOKS

ZERO is an original publication of Avon Books. This work has never before appeared in book form.

AVON BOOKS
A division of
The Hearst Corporation
1790 Broadway
New York, New York 10019

Copyright © Fianfiacomo Feltrinelli Editore 1974
Copyright © 1979 by Ignacio de Loyola Brandão
Translation Copyright © 1983 by Ellen Watson
Published by arrangement with the author
Library of Congress Catalog Card Number: 83-91043
ISBN: 0-380-84533-4

First Bard Printing, October, 1983

BARD TRADEMARK REG. U. S. PAT. OFF. AND IN
OTHER COUNTRIES, MARCA REGISTRADA, HECHO EN
U. S. A.

Printed in the U. S. A.

OP   10 9 8 7 6 5 4 3 2 1

FOR BIA, DANIEL, AND ANDRÉ

fear's going to have everything
almost everything
and we will all
almost all
each by his own road
become mice
yes
mice

from ''A Slightly Original Poem of Fear''
by Alexandre O'Neill

Somewhere
in Latíndia-America,
tomorrow

José kills mice in a dingy movie theater. He's an ordinary guy, age 28, who eats, sleeps, pisses, walks, runs, laughs, cries, has fun, gets sad, screws, keeps both eyes open, has a headache every now and then but takes Anacin, reads books and newspapers regularly, is always going to the movies, doesn't wear a wristwatch or lace-up shoes, is single, and limps a little in the presence of strong feeling—good or bad.

Lately, José has been troubled by the Pope's declaration that Christmas is in danger of becoming a purely secular holiday.

EVERY MOUSE HAS ITS PRICE

Nine o'clock, and José puts on his overalls and rubber boots and rigs up his contraption of barrels and plastic tubing. He starts the crank and yellow smoke pours out the holes. The mice run around and fall down dead. He stuffs them in a sack and dumps them down by the river.

NAME: cosmos or universe.

CHARACTERISTICS: includes the celestial "bodies" and the space that surrounds them. All together it contains 10^{76} (10 elevated to to the 76th power) protons.

WEIGHT: (in grams) 10^{56}.

SIZE: according to Einstein, the entire universe has a diameter of 8 million light-years.

AGE: (probable) 10 to 12 billion years.

FORMATION: the celestial "bodies" are principally stars, planets which move with their satellites around the stars, comets, and matter which appears periodically among the stars.

HALF-LIFE OF A STAR: 10,000 million years.

NUMBER OF STARS: each galaxy contains on the average billions of stars.

FORM OF LIFE: 1 planet in each group seems to offer conditions favorable to life.

1

José has a daily quota of mice. He knows that when he's exterminated all of them he'll lose his job. One day there weren't any more mice. So he paid two kids 50 cents apiece and they each brought him three mice. That's how José kept on working.

SIZE OF OUR GALAXY: length—100,000 light-years; width—30,000 light-years; thickness—15,000 light-years.

SPEED OF OUR GALAXY: 150 to 330 kilometers per second.

THE SUN: weighs 330,000 times more than the earth.

THE EARTH: weighs:.......
6,000,000,000,000,000,000,000 tons.

JOSÉ: weighs 154 pounds.

AFFECTIVE MEMORY

He was ten years old, it was at a party one night at Chola's house, with a bonfire in the back yard, the time of the year for cherrybombs, firecrackers, pinwheels, sparklers, but none of the kids had any money, they just made bonfires. Everyone in front of the fire, Chola holding a string with a mouse on the other end, he threw the mouse into the fire, the thing sizzled and squeaked, Chola gave it more string and it ran from the coals.

FREE ASSOCIATION

Father defending penniless whores and Mother with soapy scrub brush in hand washing the obscenities off the walls of the city, she and a whole group of ladies collected stamps for the Catholic missions in Africa, and at home José read *Christian Family* and *Little Missionary* and the good families of the city didn't even enter Father's office, not even you my son can ever go there.

MEXICANS FROM THE SOAP FACTORY

For six months Mexicans had been arriving in the neighborhood. There were more than forty of them and they slept in an empty warehouse. José had gone to see it: an ancient soap factory, the vats were still there, immense, half full of black sludge. The smell of fat. The first Mexicans had already opened a shop for reupholstering armchairs and fixing transistor radios. They spoke a comprehensible Spanish and the smallest girl, with dark and oily skin, ran through the streets asking for charity, food, and sweets. There was one girl about thirteen who'd screw anyone in the neighborhood (she liked it with her legs closed). She'd even do it at the boardinghouse, right there in the room with the others watching (there were five in a room). José had asked her to go to the movies, to screw there. She wouldn't go. José suggested the movies because in the boardinghouse he slept in the top bunk and was afraid of falling out.

BLACK EYES

As he turned the corner, José saw the black woman. She was staring straight at him. She was very old, you could see from the wrinkles circling her eyes, forming big pockets underneath. But the look in her eyes was so alive, it made José uneasy. The whole street went yellow for a second (it's my empty stomach, I need a drink).

INTRODUCTION OF JOSÉ'S FRIEND ATILA

Atila took a teaching degree in the same city where José was born. But he didn't get a teaching position. A supervisor asked him for a "contribution"—to make it "easier" to get him an assignment. Atila defecated on his diploma and threw it at the door of the Department of Education.[1] He went to work fixing tires. He met Carola the day the first billboard was set up in front of the tire place. She was the model for the advertisement. The nickname Atila comes from the habit he has of breaking everything, demolishing places when he gets drunk.

WORKERS HEATING UP LUNCH PAILS

At the boardinghouse José washes at the water tank (the landlady locks the bathroom in the morning so they won't use the hot shower). He grabs coffee at the corner. Workers

---

[1]Afterward he regretted it.

already heating up lunch pails around a fire. They have blank looks. Construction: the city covered by planks. Telephone lines, water pipes, sewerage, wires. Holes down the length of the streets. A slow bus in congested traffic. José's daily headache begins. The theater opened at 10:30. The same audience every day. They didn't come to see the film, they came to sleep. They'd spent the night in bars. People who came from housing projects, brothels, the lock-up, a park bench. The smell of alcohol, marijuana, grime, shiftlessness, neglect. They went to sleep, two movies in a row, and woke up three hours later for the five-minute intermission. Then they went back to sleep for the rest of the day. Atila had a reserved seat.

YOU CAME, I WAS ALONE

José has always wanted to be a singer. American. Like Ray Charles, Nat King Cole, Paul Anka, Frankie Lane, Billy Eckstein. Ever since he was fifteen years old he wanted to go to the United States, to sing, be famous, give out his autograph, have fancy clothes. He walks around singing *Temptation, you came, I was alone.*

TO SEPARATE ME FROM ME

Atila only smoked pot when he was down in the dumps. "To separate me from me." With his girlfriend, a brunette named Carola, too skinny for José's taste. Atila liked skinny women. He was really hooked on Carola. She was timid. Quiet. She had a little snack bar, left to her by her ex-husband, dead of tetanus. Just a tiny counter on a school patio. She got by selling soda pop, cups of coffee, fruit, cheese, sweets, and sandwiches. Carola spent her whole day there. Atila told José why he was so crazy about her. They never did it face to face.[1]

THE LIFE OF THE SERMONIZERS
(Coming Attractions)

—Come on, let's go. It's fantastic the way he reads palms.

-----
[1] Carola only exists in ad photos. Atila makes everything up.

4

—Maybe tomorrow.

—But the police are practically on top of him, he could be gone by tomorrow.

—Liar.

—Come on, let's go.

—Why don't you go by yourself?

—Shit, you know I don't do anything by myself.

(The police are going to kick out the sermonizers?)

THE RING OF SAINT BARBARA

Rosa was seven years old. She had been playing in a vacant lot in Salinas when she stepped on a black stone and cut the bottom of her foot. The stone was translucent. Rosa's father had a ring made. As soon as she put on the ring and went out into the street, Rosa found money on the sidewalk. "Never take that ring off your finger," said her mother. "It's good luck." Everybody began looking for stones there. Fifty years ago on that spot there had been a slave house.

CURFEW

With the repression that's going down around here, nobody wants to leave the house, the streets are empty, they revoked the passes to be out after 9:34 p.m.

THE WELL OF SOLITUDE

José was called to be a witness. The owner of the boardinghouse had thrown himself in the well, citing misery. He'd invited his wife along, but she didn't want to. She said: "Go by yourself." The police were suspicious. In just one week three people had thrown themselves into wells, citing misery. A psychologist declared: "Psychosis. Normal. There probably was no foul play—after all, everyone who died was really miserable."

THE MIRACULOUS ONE
Frankil, the biggest fakir in the country, will
try to bring us the title for world champion of
fasting, remaining without food for 111 days.
Come encourage Frankil to give us another
world record.

José paid a dime (son-of-a-gun, the dime's so he could go
eat later), and came through a green plastic curtain. The
long glass case lay in a whitewashed vestibule. Posters,
photos, newspaper clippings, crepe-paper pennants. A
television cameraman was there, too, and a fat photographer in a tattered three-piece suit.

DAYS WITHOUT EATING: 55
STILL TO GO: 56

Nasal recordings: tango, bolero. The fakir reclining on
nails. Blue-and-yellow streamers, a little flag in the corner,
snakes slithering on the tormented body, a figure imitating
Christ. José scraped his nails along the glass. The fakir
seemed to be asleep, it didn't bother him.

A skinny guy, bald, big smile, came in with the photographer and two others carrying note pads. Frankil opened his
eyes, seemed to recognize the thin one, gave a ravenous
smile and thumbs up. The thin guy came over to talk with
José.

—Look, I'm making a film about fakirs and hunger. I'd
like to know what you think of this. I'm going to tape it,
okay?

—Sure.

Gilda Valença was singing "Coimbra." José spruced
himself up—the shutter clicked away.

—You can start.

—What's your name?

6

—José Gonçalves.
—Profession?
—I clean the movie theater.
—Why did you come here today?
—I wanted to see this guy.
—Do you often come to things like this?
—Always. Every day.
—Every day?
—Yeah.
—So what do you think?
—I think he's a jerk.
—Well, then why did you come?

The fakir was watching. The thin guy asked if he could film the interview. José curled the corner of his mouth, like he was going to spit. His cold sore was bothering him. It was a chronic problem, no one had been able to come up with a remedy. The men went on filming and the loudspeaker played "Ave Maria Lola." A short man with glasses and blue eyes arrived, along with a slender girl who also had blue eyes: Glora, the queen of striptease at the Santana Theater.

José saw the fakir was looking at him. He took a sandwich out of his pocket. He chewed and watched, the fakir kept looking straight at him. José ate, screwing up his mouth. The director was getting it all on film. Glora protested: "Oh, no, Fernando, don't let him do that!" José showed the sandwich to the fakir. He swallowed the last bite. Looked straight at the camera. As he was turning to leave he noticed a strange mark. On the top of the glass case there were two yellow lines which formed an incomplete triangle, with a half circle drawn inside. A sign that became engraved in his head.

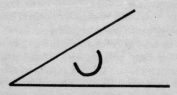

Even outside in the sun, José continued to see the two yellow streaks. In the street, from one side to the other, hidden behind opposite windows, two men were shooting telescopic rifles while people passed by.
SCCCRRREEEEEEEUUUUUUUUUUUU, blam

—Look at that old woman!

BRrrrrrrruuummmmmmmmmmmm (the guy was revving the motor to take off)

—Get him, get him!

VVVRRRROOOOOOOOOOMMMMMMMMM

—Let's get her to the hospital. How awful . . .

—Did anyone get the plate number?

—Ah, aaaaaaaaaaaaaaaaaaaaaaaaa, Ige-Sha was groaning. Devil, you demon, you just don't want me to have the Stone of Xangô. Aaaaaaaaa.

She got up, she didn't feel a thing. That's the way it was, the demons hit her, they beat her down, she shouldn't have come to the city, she left beaten every time. It was their fear, aaaaaaaa how it hurt. The daughters never let me come to the city, but I'm stronger than the demons, aaaaaaaaaaaaaaaaaaaaa.

BYE, BYE

After having his entire library confiscated and burned by Government #1, sociologist Carlos Antunes, who was researching the origins of national underdevelopment, accepted an invitation from Yale to lecture at that famous North American university. He should be leaving in ten days, if the lawyers release his passport.

THE DOORS

Jag, jag, jee, craaazy, rolacola, *baby, baby, love me, baby*, tic, toc, tic, hooter, tooter, my love, I love you, I am a black cat, *Stop, Mr. Judge*, my dear, there there, here, I oooooh, *pills of life, from Doctor Ross, they're good for the liver and for all of us*, Kasham, boomboom, *I want to hold your hand*, the Beatles, fuck, I forgot to talk to Atila about the gypsy women, give me some fried shrimp please, with lemon, and a fanta, today's special is: chick-pea soup, Chinaman arrested for frying *empanadas* in diesel oil, Big Record Sale, why doesn't everything just go to hell, *love, take good care of this love*, nighttime soaps more sensational than ever on channel 9, that store has good-looking salesgirls, I'll go back in, pretend I'm shopping, get a load of the legs on the brunette with the red shoes (Odete, my Portuguese teacher in high school, wore red shoes, she was a hot number, wonder where in the world she is now, we ran down the stairs behind her, and everybody was jealous of Shorty 'cause he danced with her at the Town Hall), larali, grofrgst hgtfyuj, 7869504, boom, boom, outta here. Some legs. Miniskirt and long legs, curvy. In the middle of the crowd. As she walked, men turned around, she walked with a zig-zag. José following along. She turns the corner, he stops. (She's coming back, I know she's gonna come back, that's what I want, *I want it real big here inside me*, and she'll come back.) It's happened before. He'd seen her once and was sure he'd see her again. And always did. Like now, the girl in the leather miniskirt and the red sandals. She was coming back, looking around, distracted, maybe wondering why she was coming back. And while José was watching the girl, an old woman laughed nearby. She laughed (shit, is she old!) and said *Na, na, not yours yet!* (Not mine? My what? Crazy old hag, she doesn't even know me. Funny. This sun, so yellow all of a sudden.) He kept thinking. (The number of sick people in this city!) Crippled, blind, missing an arm, missing a hand, missing feet, pigeon-toed, duckfooted, cross-eyed, twisted mouths, no nose, hunchbacked—always with a mess of kids running behind to touch the hump, for luck—senile, no ears, crooked necks, women with elephantiasis, gigantic legs, breasts that look like bags, making them walk tilted forward, lepers, people covered with pimples, with crust, faces that are one big wound, stained faces, heads of living meat. José ran down the sidewalk, crashing through people (I have to get out of here, it's making me crazy). He ended up in an alley of car repair shops, no people, just mountains of automobile carcasses. They were gleaming in the sun (yellow). They were missing windshields, had broken windows, full of dark holes, like toothless mouths, or with broken teeth, torn out headlights (eyes), front, sides, and back smashed, wrenched apart, engine compartments empty. Old cars piled one on top of the other, a tower of multicolored, peeling tin. José went into a passageway lit by mercury vapor lamps. There were doors and doors—car doors. He tried them one by one. He opened and closed them. Until the last. (I would close the book, I never read the end of that story, I didn't want the girl to go in, she's not supposed to open it. So I wrote another story where she'd stay frozen in front of the last one, and she'd die there, obstinate, desperate, but scared.) José had his hand on the door latch and was trying to make up his mind.

> ## WILL HE OPEN THE LAST DOOR?
> ## WHAT WILL BE INSIDE?

Another bank robbery in Vila Clemencia.
Wounded: 1
Stolen: $14,000
Total number of bank robberies to date: 64
Total amount of money stolen: $12,546,786
Total wounded: 56
Total taken prisoner: 4
Total dead: 13

SEVEN ITEMS

1) José did not go see if he'd lost his job as mice-killer at the movie theater. He doesn't feel like it. He doesn't feel like anything.
2) He thinks it's just not worth it. He's got enough money to last a little while longer. Tomorrow, someday, maybe he'll go see about it.
3) If he needs to, he'll make an excuse to the manager, say that he was sick.
4) You can dock me (bosses love to dock you) for my missed days. I swear to God it won't happen again.
5) It's only kissing ass a little bit. That's what they think it is, but it isn't. It's lying in their faces. They go nuts for asskissing.
6) What I like is staying in bed, just thinking. I don't want to have to worry about anything in life.
7) This morning the police came and arrested the guy in the front room. He wasn't a criminal or anything. Just a student. Something to do with politics. They tore his whole room apart, wrecked clothes, books, turned the closets inside out.

O TEMPORA, O MORES

"Either we join together or the world will explode in a wave of chaos, sin, and immorality." The President was speaking in a park in the capital. In front of him, thousands of people listening. Each one held in his hand a fat candle, which made a fantastic spectacle: a fire that illuminated everything (but for him, the fire consumed; that very night a reform of the civil code was scheduled to be instituted). Microphones carried his words to all the town squares in the country, to every house. Below the rostrum was a platform on which were seated the dignitaries of the Church, government ministers, Supreme Court judges, Attorney Generals, the Supreme Chief of the Repressive National Guard, the Commissioners of Order and Morals, the Crusaders, the Order of the Knights Templar, Defenders of the Family, the Avengers. Each represented hundreds of associations and organizations that had been formed all over the country in defense of decent customs, the family, good conduct, liberty, and propriety. These hundreds of groups represented millions of members. "Let us throw ourselves into this great campaign, this gigantic undertaking, so that sobriety becomes the fashion, so that skirts go back down to the ankles, so that licentious magazines are burned, so that swearwords cease to exist in our beloved and beautiful language, so that young people lead discreet and decent lives, so that the term prostitution is abolished once and for all from our vocabulary, so that there is no 'pill' and we all procreate for the greater good of the nation. This is why we strive to change things so completely, to reform the laws to protect society, and thus to protect you from yourselves. Our wise legal advisors have completed drafting a new constitution, based on trustworthy documents from long ago, from the golden legislative store of humanity. And we are going to apply these laws from this day forward, so that instead of hastening man's demise, his total decomposition, his utter negation, our time and our land shall shine in history, an emblem of the ennoblement of man." The people applauded, and lifted up their arms.

11

LEAFING THROUGH MY NOTEBOOK

What's going on with José is—in his own words—this: today, when I went to take a shit, the turd was really light-colored. You know what that means? It's proof that I'm getting cleaner inside. The day it turns white I'll be in a state of total grace. I was crossing the street to catch a bus, and I had to stop on the island in the middle. On the ground in front of me was a long-stemmed yellow rose. It was pretty, I stood looking at it. I don't know why, it was just a rose thrown on the median strip at 6:30 in the afternoon, congested traffic, ads on the newsstands—such and such a magazine offers free plastic surgery, win a house, a bedroom set, come see who the beautiful people are, millionaire throws himself out ten-story window. The rose's stem branched into two small shoots, forming a V. I missed the bus on account of the rose. The rose, a rose, rose on the island (I was thinking). People think nonsense all the time. I like to think about senseless things. Because sensible things don't make sense. With yards to spare, the bus took the corner too wide, got clipped by a truck, and turned over. It looked like an elephant doing a somersault. People died. I don't know if I would have died because I don't know where I would have been sitting. I think I saved my life. Galaxies, astronauts, astronart, atronart. People looking at the sky: look, is it a star or a sputnik? is that Apollo 8 or 9? Buses bringing us home at seven p.m.—home to the table set with rice and beans, tomatoes and onions, home to the sitcoms on TV. Everyone forgetting the sky, the satellites, rocket ships, astronauts (except the women, they think of them at a certain moment). And I always have this headache. I wish it was an aneurism. The other day I read a report on aneurisms that said you can have one and not know it; it bursts all of a sudden, and you kick off. Maybe I've got one, but I'm not going to a doctor, let it burst, it's easier that way. Still. It's been like this for two months. She says it's because her mother's sick. Some custom of theirs. Could be. Mexicans are really funny, we're always noticing the odd things they do around the neighborhood: like uplanders except they speak Spanish. They're even starting to get jobs in construction. I'm going to call a meeting at the grocery of all the guys who are screwing her. Everyone can chip in a little money, the doctor will come and cure her mother, and then we can go back to fun and games. What do you say? Don't say. What a drag. Something else . . . Something elssssse . . . You hear that all day long around here. Something else. I should say: sorry, but I never did screw the Mexican girl. Only by myself. I think about her, and screw her. The way I want to. She told me:

—If I get pregnant, I'm not having an abortion. And I don't want to get pregnant by a cripple.

She said it all in her language. What a bitch! 1, 2, 3, 4, 5, 6, 7, 8, 9, 10, 11, 12, 13, 14, 15, 16, 17, 18, 19. I can't stop counting, wondering why 1 and 1 make 2. The guy who invented this! Why isn't 1 called 2 and 2 called 9? That way I could say: 2 and 2 make 9. But it doesn't work that way. The whole world thinks alike, they've accepted it, it has to be that way. If some guy came along—me, for example—and proved that 1 isn't 1 but really 3, it would screw everything up. They might arrest me, they're arresting people all the time. Just read the papers. I get pissed off that people accept things like that, just to accept it, because it's ready-made, no need to lift a finger. Not really pissed off, but *perturbed*, I get all confused. Sometimes for me something is four and not seven, but they can't see it the way I do, can't see that it's four. Somewhere inside me I sense the language of things telling me: I'm not this, I'm that. And I have to believe them, whether they're rocks, sticks, plastic, iron, paper, flowers, whatever.

And here I take my leave, awaiting your attention in the following pages. I hope to have pleased you thus far. Greetings to you and yours.

THE REVOLVING RESTAURANT

"Palm trees grace my native land, and warblers by another name. The warblers warble here as well, but somehow they don't sound the same."

(I wonder if the Mexican girl is coming over, I wonder if she'll come over and make it with somebody. It's about time. I need to screw a girl like that, a nice piece of ass, really sexy. Shit, she's sexy!)

13

At the tone, the time will be exactly seven o'clock.

Stay tuned for our next attraction, News Update, in thirty seconds, brought to you by Puratek.

(Who cares what's happening in the news. It's all a bunch of junk. You get sick of it. I'm up to here with it. Why don't they talk about *my* life, *my* prison? I went to the radio station to complain but those guys didn't even pay attention. They just looked at me, they thought I was nuts. But I already know what I'm going to do.)

Cold water in the bathroom, he forced himself under the shower and scrubbed with the gray soap his aunt had sent from the interior. He rubbed his skin raw. The day he'd crawled on all fours pleading to get his job back he'd needed to take the biggest bath. He stayed in the bathroom for hours, the landlady came to see if he'd died. When she saw he was alive she complained about all the water he was wasting. She yelled a lot. It didn't help, he couldn't come out yet, he needed that water on his body. He wanted to live like Marat, inside the bathtub, continually refreshed. But Marat had a woman to take care of him. At least in the movie he did. Bread, medium dark. The Mexicans drink cheap rum and tell stories about Mexico. One of them swears he's Pancho Villa's grandson. Someday he's going to go back to his country and take power. He stutters, you can't understand what he's saying, he fixes TVs and radios, understands transistors, has customers all over the neighborhood. He spends the whole day sitting on a sack of potatoes, smoking cigarettes (the owner of the place swears it's marijuana by the smell) and chewing tobacco, without spitting. He's never spoken to José but he looks friendly.

400 kilometers from here, Dona Osvaldinha is fit to be tied, telling her husband that one of these days she'll call the police, those neighbors are unbearable. Now they're throwing dirty water in the yard, making puddles that bring mosquitos and bad smells. Osvaldinha lives on a 24-acre farm. The neighbor's farm is 36 acres and full of trees.

José's afraid of him, though. It's the only place around to get coffee in the morning or he wouldn't go in. (People

14

scare me. I always think someone's going to attack me. I spend my life preparing to defend myself. If someone suddenly raises an arm nearby, I jump. I treat other people good, even when I don't want to, because I think: what if that guy doesn't like my attitude and jumps on top of me? When I get home at night, I expect someone in the hall, behind the door, or someone lying in my bed saying that it's not mine anymore.)

José saw a preacher on the street. No one listening, but there he was, preaching away. At eleven a.m. Book in hand, greasy black suit, spittle in the corner of his mouth, gold-rimmed glasses held together with adhesive tape.

Atila arrived and sat down at the lunch counter with José.

—How's it going? Did you lose your job?

—They lost it for me.

—Why?

—I took off a few days and when I came back there was another guy killing mice. You know something funny? They arrested a student from the boardinghouse. He wasn't really a student, I guess. They say he was holding terrorist meetings. What baloney. Some terrorists. Meeting there, no less. How can a guy overthrow the government with meetings in a shitty boardinghouse like that?

—Who knows. It's crazy these days. They're setting off bombs all over the place. Any day now the whole city's going to blow up. I don't even kick tin cans in the street anymore, there could be a pound of gunpowder underneath. Come on, let's go. You won't believe all the people! If we don't get moving, they'll be gone before we get there. Any time now they'll start taking down the tents.

Business Lunch

Specials of the Day:

Codfish Portuguese-style
Baked Codfish
Codfish w/ oil & garlic
Steak & fries
Vegetable omelet
Barbecue Beef
Fruit & Ice Cream
Coffee

Come on in—
Fast & Clean
The Most Popular
Restaurant in Town—
No one can resist
our prices!

—When?

—How should I know? They have their own rules. They stay a while, then they go.

The lunch counter was rotating slowly, but Atila discovered his stool was moving even slower, so that his plate was always a little ahead of him.[1] The smoked fish smelled strongly of oil and bay leaf.

—Think I'll manage to finish before we get to the other side?

None of the customers looked at the person beside him. They ate, watching the curve of the wall, measuring their progress by the food left on the plate. A black guy who was coming around the final curve suddenly whipped out a plastic bag and scraped all his leftovers inside.

José was getting near the far wall where there was a triangular hole in the tiles. He saw the cook, or the cook's helper. Or whoever it was. A chunky girl, with her thick arms squeezing out of the sleeves of her dress. She was dark and had a yellow kerchief around her head. José forgot his hunger. She had an ordinary face, an almost ugly nose, a pimple on her chin. She moved from side to side, and as José's seat moved along his view of her was cut into half a triangle, he kept looking at the yellow kerchief, he saw nothing else, only yellow. His stool came into the home stretch.

HE EITHER EATS OR HE DOESN'T EAT

I went to see the fakir. He gave me a great idea for earning some money. Next to the glass case there's this sign—you know how proud the fakir is of his honesty—well, he promises a bundle of money to anyone who can prove that he eats. So that's what we'll do.

—Prove that he eats? How, pal?

—Oh we'll figure out some scam.

—Oh yeah, what about his friends? What do you think they're there for?

—I went by at night, there's only one guard. Every night

---

[1]The Revolving Restaurant was inexpensive and quite popular, and worked like this: the counter and stools revolved around the center where one employee handed out the plates of food and another took the plates away after the customer had completed a full circle.

16

it's the same. Shit, man, I already spent ten bucks this week, just to observe the guy. That money is ours, you'll see.

—You'll see, nothing. You're crazy . . . the guy doesn't eat.

—He eats.

—He eats, nothing.

—Wait till you see what he eats.

—What about the guard?

—We'll give him a piece of it, just to look the other way. He can be bought.

THE COMING OF THE SERMONIZERS

In Agua Baixa, back behind the zoo and the woods, there's a series of terraces on the hillside, like a giant staircase with steps thirty feet high. Each step has an enormous surface, no one knows what they were made for. One day at dawn tractors appeared and started working, stayed for months, and then disappeared, without even a sign to say whether it was a government project, a new industry (there are machine shops on either side), or a land developer.

The earth there is made up of bands of various colors, so that each of the steps is light red, dark brown, yellow, or grayish. To get there, you take the road to the zoo, and when you get to a grocery named Moraēs with the "s" written backward, you turn right and go up a dirt path.

In the early days of the Sermonizers you had to climb from the grocery on foot. Later, with all the activity, some company bought old cars and started an unofficial bus line up to the encampment. Atila drove one of these "buses" and was paid by the trip and the number of passengers, packing them in like a cattle car. He and the ticket taker made a deal to overcharge people and split the difference. The company didn't care, they bought the cars cheap, no upkeep, no taxes. Atila worked from noon until closing. The drivers of the four cars were always at war, trying to sabotage one car or the other, disconnecting wires, siphoning gas, deflating tires. The buses kept running, though. There were no seats. The windows had no glass, the paint had disappeared. They were skeletons propelled by half-drunken motors. Even so, not a car went up without being full.

The terraces divided the encampment into sections. There were nine tents on each, first one color, then another, until you got to the last, the big brown one (the color of the earth—to which we aspire—from whence we came (seeds)— the only truth, mother earth, said the leaflet which called the people to the truth of the future). There were long lines. Wooden stairs led from one terrace to another.

The big brown tent had a sign made of painted tin with neon over it. The words had designs in them; the designs were symbols (Each symbol has a significance for our people, said a gypsy).

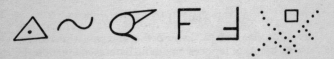

Looking at each character, José had the impression of Egyptian writing, hieroglyphics, dozens of little symbols in a row piling up to form yet another, larger symbol. Images added to other images in order to reach a definition. As if it were painstaking, Chinese script. Or an enigmatic letter.

"Our people's origin got lost over the ages. African? Chinese? Hindu? Russian? Who knows. Maybe a mixture of them all. Our people are nomads," said the chief of the clan on TV. He was a tall man, not too old, swarthy, with dark, straight hair, gold teeth, colorful clothing, necklaces, flowers, boots, and a whip (the traditional image of a gypsy in the movies, of Carmen, filmed in Hollywood). He appeared on all the talk shows, he liked photographs, movies, newspapers.

"There is definitely some Black influence in our heritage, a little of their skin, their wisdom, we've received teachings and abilities and preparation, we keep in touch."

Slices of honeydew and pineapple, sweets made of squash, coconut, and milk, chewing gum, mocotó jelly, hot dogs, everything in little booths, carts in the sun, on top of packing crates, newspapers spread out on the ground, wooden trays hung from the vendors' necks. Skewers of meat dripping grease, beef or cat or whatever else could be found in the the woods nearby.

—I really like this stuff, said José.

—Gonna have your fortune told?

—You bet—my fortune, the future, I love all this strange stuff you can't explain.

—Take a look at all the people! Someone told me the other day that the governor's wife came. At night, under cover. I was about to make the last trip, waiting for the car to fill. A cop came and rounded up everybody who was hanging around. He got in the bus and ordered me to go down the hill. At a turn in the road there was a car with official plates waiting. The next day they said it was the governor's wife, spying on him, trying to find out if he was fooling around. She's the one with the money, you know. When they met, he was good looking, ambitious, and completely broke. She made his career. And she demands absolute fidelity in return. Yeah, and they say he's terrified of her, that's why he's loyal. You know what else? I heard that every time they screw he runs into the bathroom and vomits. Heaves up gall, that's how sick he is of the broad.

The sign on the booth where Atila had brought José:
I READ: Hands—Heart—Eyes—Messages in Oil—Soles of the Feet—Coffee Stains—Tea Leaves—I Decipher Burned Cotton—I Tell the Future by Footprints in Sand or Plaster or Mud or Flour—
I read all the lines of the body.
I interpret the voice.
Coded reading of private signs: scars, birthmarks, warts, wrinkles, pimples, and moles.
Urine analysis to indicate present and future diseases, with a retrospective of past illnesses and all existing tendencies.
—This is worth more than a checkup, said Atila.
—I doubt it.
—This guy's the best. It's only that he's humble, he's not like a manager, always promoting himself. He never leaves this tent, day or night. He just studies, meditates, talks to people. The world comes to him, so why should he go out? He knows the world through other people. You should have seen the anatomy class he gave to some medical students the other day! Those kids left with their mouths hanging open. Even the professor.
—He cures people?
—No, he doesn't cure them, he just talks. Later the people cure themselves, or look for a doctor to cure them. You

19

know why people don't cure themselves? Because doctors don't believe in it so they tell them it's impossible. But that's just because they're doctors.

—I'd like him to tell me about my bum foot. Think he would?

—Who knows? You realize who meditated with this guy? The Beatles.

—Sure, chum.

—No, really. There are pictures and a newspaper report. In the best London paper. No lie.[1]

—So how come there's so few people here?

—They're just the ones he's accepted. You need to send in an I.D. first, and he chooses who he'll see. Give me your driver's license.

There were crepe-paper streamers, colored banners, loud-speakers radiating boleros, tangos, the twist, and in between announcements of those lucky winners there were people reading palms, discovering the future in a thousand ways.

After lunch it got more difficult to wander on the terraces, it was like a church fair to which the whole city had been invited. The woods and roads above and below the terraces were full of people walking, eating, waiting in line, meeting in groups, talking endlessly about the wonders they were about to see.

At three José went in: a tent, plain and airy, made of white fabric, full of light. Flour sacks had been patched together to cover the floor. José felt like taking off his shoes, so he did. The Man was standing there, radiating calmness. Somehow the noise from outside didn't penetrate the cloth tent. But inside José's head there was a tumult: packing crates being opened, wood planks being cleared away, nails being pulled out with a hammer, all the compartments

---

[1] In spite of being the type of character who makes up his girlfriends out of pure imagination, Atila seems to be right about the meeting between the Man and the Beatles. It was just before Epstein's death, when the Beatles disappeared for three days. What's odd is, the Man had advised them that they needed to split up in order to survive. After the meeting, the Beatles forgot everything that had happened—this is characteristic of the Man: his advice remains, diluted, in the subconscious, still active, but you don't remember it clearly. You just feel a little anxiety when you go against his prescribed advice.

being transformed into a great room, open to view, where almost everything could be seen with clarity. The Man had his hand on José's head.

—My friend, you must use your whole head. It's a good head, ready to receive a lot. You don't do anything, my friend. Nothing for yourself, nothing for others.

The uproar was beginning.

—Nothing for nothing, what's useful is useless, what's good is wasted. You should be yourself. There's someone calling and you aren't answering.

That uproar José knew so well.

It got louder. Teeth.

—Do you remember? There were many closed doors in the room. You were able to enter all of them but one.

—No one said I couldn't open it.

—Ah, but you knew that you couldn't open that one, my friend. That you shouldn't.

—How could I know?

—The message was in the glove compartment of one of the cars.

—But there were so many.

His teeth were chattering.

—What about the sign?

—What sign?

—Friend, your head is only working ten percent. *There are signs* all around and no one sees them. Signs and symbols everywhere. Open your eyes, wide, to the present. And you'll have the future nailed, all put together. Don't look down like everybody else. Least of all you.

—What sign?

—When the car came *toward* you, in the middle of the street, the numbers on the license plate were different colors. Someone had retouched the plate. Was it a kid's joke? Apparently. But the car bearing those numbers was the one with the message in the glove compartment, for you to not open the door which opened into where you should go out.

—I don't remember, after I went in.

—At the right time you will remember, my friend.

—Who sent the sign?

—Who?

The Man took his hands from José's head. In the bottom of his brain there were sealed compartments with luminous inscriptions whose letters José couldn't make out.

21

THE EDUCATION OF JOSÉ ACCORDING
TO THE MAN

Ten days passed.

Ten days with the Man.

The first day José learned that the body should be free and satisfied.

The second day, that the mind should dominate and that strongly willed thought succeeds.

The third, he got to know each muscle in his body.

The fourth, he was introduced to the sky and the stars, the name of each one, visible or invisible, their power, how they influence man; he learned about the sun and the moon, the planets and their cycles, the signs of the zodiac.

The fifth day the Man reproduced José, gigantic, projecting him on the ceiling of the white tent, transformed on the infinite screen. José saw himself: the Man opening up his body, like an anatomy professor, showing him the inside. He was made up of corridors leading to other corridors, one inside the other, a room inside the corridor, clear, bright, illuminated. A zigzag of labyrinths, rooms, alcoves, great halls. (How monotonous a man is inside, there's nothing there.) The projection took up the whole tent and it was as if he were inside himself (but I don't feel inside myself, not at all, I'm always on the outside). And the Man tilted the lantern and showed his body, its passages, arteries (mesenterics, hypogastrics, carotids), cavernous veins, pulmonaries, aorta, alleys, bones, trap doors, lymphatic system, skylights, entrails, hatchways, ventricles, nervous system. José felt like running around inside himself, running loose across the fields which extended from his stomach, up the hills of the kidneys, that white light shining in his eyes (white flash, that flash of white that's hitting me in the eyes). Then he saw a triangular opening with nothing behind it, and he felt such pleasure that he had an orgasm. He was hungry but didn't feel like eating, he was hungry but got nauseous at the thought of food. At midnight on the fifth day he saw inside himself. What pleasure. No prohibitions. At midnight he needed to leave (Don't forget your shoes on the way out. No one will come looking for you). But he didn't have everything he needed for traveling. (How can I tell the Man I haven't seen all of myself?) He decided not to say anything about leaving.

The sixth day he was introduced to the sensations and explorations of touch, taste, smell, sight, and hearing, and the effects of taking them away.

He touched himself.

He listened to himself.

He saw himself.

He tasted himself.

He smelled himself.

Find out who you are, said the Man.

And José, thankful, kissed the Man on the mouth. Not sensually, not passionately, not emotionally. Just gratefully.

And the Man thanked him for the kiss with a punch in the ear, which made him deaf.

The seventh day José stood naked while the Man invited people in:

men, women, children. José wasn't embarrassed. The people didn't matter.

The eighth day José remained standing for twenty-four hours. First on one foot, then the other. Three times he stood on his tiptoes for half an hour. He was pricked with needles, smacked across the knuckles with a ruler, he walked on live coals, dove into hot water.

He was mastering himself. He had learned.

On the ninth day José was strung up by his arms, with his head high, to listen to the devil: then he was hung by the feet, with his head down, to talk to God; last he was hung by the waist, with his head in the middle, to listen to the middling dieties. He didn't hear anything. Is it that they had nothing to say to him, or that they don't exist?

On the tenth day the Man rested.

And then, the following morning, he called José and took off his clothes. He loved José and let himself be loved by him, he hated José and let himself be hated by him, he desired José and let himself be rebuffed by him, he rebuffed José and made himself feel desired by him. They rolled on the ground / punched each other and shouted / like animals / they roared / and they howled, wanting to find each other.

23

EJACULATORY PRAYER: "Jesus, Mary, Joseph, ex-
pire in peace, come into
my soul."

INSCRIPTION IN THE PRIVY (Graffiti)

to shit is the law of the land
to shit is the law of the sky
George II shit, same as you
& speaking of shit, so do I

On her farm, Osvaldinha is still nagging her husband to get even with the neighbors. She's sure they've been stealing eggs.

BARBED WIRE IN THE THROAT

José walked around the terraces with Atila. The sermonizers were leaving. Only one tent was left to be taken down. No more crowds. A few vendors were still selling roasted meat (cat). José stood on the spot where the white tent had been.

(I know who I am and what I can do. But I only wish he had taken away this anger, this barbed wire that's stuck in my throat. He helped me, but the wire is still there.)

Low clouds. José noticed that behind the clouds the sky was (egg) yellow. He felt like he was being watched and stuck his hands in his pockets, but it didn't help.

Didu

A little bird peeped in the woods. Twice.

Didu

It was a yellow bird that looked like a parrot. In a nearby tree.

—Don't move, I'll grab him! said Atila.

Didu

The bird took off, flew right up to José, let out a cry, then flew off again.

That day at four p.m. Atila took his last bus trip up the hill. The sermonizers, or whatever they were, had left tent marks in the ground and all sorts of debris. There was an awful smell at the edge of the woods where people had been relieving themselves. Kids arrived and started to rummage through the trash. Scabby dogs came along with them, or nosed around on their own. The kids got into fights, the dogs got into fights, and so did the women who came looking for scraps of paper. Garbage-pickers were setting fire to the stuff, and the smoke just added to the stench.

—So what now, Atila? We're both out of work.

—Something will turn up, don't worry. That's what it's like these days. Jobs, jobs. Don't have one and don't want one.

—But I do. I get nervous without a job. It makes me feel funny.

DANGER

The next day in the boardinghouse, José was woken by the racket two of his pals were making as they screwed the Mexican girl. She was screaming real loud. One tried to cover her mouth while the other was still inside her. After it was over, José asked if she had some time for him.

—No, no time.

—Because of the kid?

—Yeah, that's right, I doan want one like you.

—You're a fucking bitch. If the kid was born like the father it'd just be a little lame. And what if it was born like the mother?

—The mother is beautiful!

—The mother is a whore. Isn't that worse?

—No, is better. Much better. Today is better to be a whore.

That's what she said, the one who was unlearning Spanish without learning Portuguese.

(I feel like murdering that girl. The Man taught me not to hate, but I still haven't learned. I can't do anything without hate. Nobody can. This girl makes me feel lame. And I'm not lame anymore.)

Yellow light, in a band, shining in through the door, it annoyed him. He jumped

DRAMA,
ALMOST MELODRAMA
(To be read to the bolero "Anguish") Rosa Maria Lopes's father, who was dark and had black hair, was a fanatic for the Taquariti Soccer Club. He took Rosa Maria to the game every Sunday. Her mother had made her a special

25

out of bed, ran over to the Mexican girl and began to hit her. She didn't make a sound, she bit hard on the pillow. When his friends came back from the bathroom, José stopped hitting her. They jumped on top of him and held him down on the bed, and he saw the girl bring the pillow down on his face. She pushed harder. To suffocate him. He needed air.

IS JOSÉ GOING TO DIE? P.S. José stayed on at the boardinghouse because he had always been punctual with the rent and the owner liked him. ("There are still some good folks in the world.")
—Does anyone have their doubts?
—No, no one.
—If so, go get fucked.

dress in the team's colors, with its emblem on the front. At the game Rosa yelled whenever her father did. She laughed whenever her father laughed. She swore when he did, too. Rosa liked him, she liked his lap, his smell: sweat, cigarettes, booze. Or grass, when he came back from the stadium on training days. In those days Taquariti was in the second division and was supported by fatcat landowners. In the playoffs against Catandu the home team couldn't lose. Catandu started a big fight and Taquariti closed the gates, it turned into a massacre. Rosa Maria still had the dress she wore that day, stained with her father's blood, ripped by glass from beer bottles. She was seven years old. And she was *not* traumatized.

SENSATIONAL: THE DENTURES SAVE JOSÉ, RESCUING HIM FROM THE CURSED DOCTORS' CLUTCHES

They took the stretcher to the courtyard of the clinic and left it there. Nurses and more nurses passed by. Quite elegant men arrived in late-model cars (they were the doctors, filthy rich, all of them), they didn't even look at José's stretcher abandoned in the sun out in the courtyard. When it started to get dark, an old man pushed the stretcher along a corridor. He passed through a door, down another corridor, across a gigantic room full of beds, up into the elevator, and finally shoved the stretcher into a green cubicle containing a white bed, a skylight in the ceiling, and a

Rembrandt—anatomy class. José was unconscious. The old man went back downstairs. He searched among the people in the hall.

—Is anyone here a relative of the boy on stretcher 13?

Everybody was asking questions, what the devil is this about stretcher 13? The old man repeated his question, walking up and down the hallway. He found the young man who had brought José in.

—What's wrong with him? asked the old man.

—How should I know? That's why I brought him in here!

—You just brought him in like this? For no reason?

—What do you mean, no reason? This *is* a hospital, ain't it?

—It's a clinic, my boy. A clinic. There's a big difference.

—Well, he's here now, so let him stay.

—Why did you bring him in?

—Look, pop, I brought him in because I've been roaming around with him like this for two days. The government hospital didn't want him. I dragged him all over São Maulo. At the Municipal Hospital I had to use force just to get him a stretcher, but the creeps there threw him back out onto the sidewalk. They said he was dead, there was nothing they could do. I put my ear to his heart and it was still beating. So I walked and walked. There's just no room, one doctor said. Too many people are getting sick. The government ought to do something about it, no kidding. (The doctors have nothing to do with it, they weren't made to take care of this stuff.) Then I ended up passing this place, and I came in and left him there.

—Does he have any money?

—Look, Jack, I don't know anything about him. I saw the guy get hit and the car sped off. Nobody paid any attention to him. I waited a little, and then carted him off, looking for help. If you want to take care of him, fine. If not, okay too. I've been hauling him all over creation, I've had enough! I already spent more on taxis than I can afford. Now he's on your bill, okay!

—That's some job. I can't take it on . . . no, I'm not getting involved. I'm a doctor, and I can't assume any responsibility for a person's life or death.

—Fuck you. I'm leaving.

The doctor met with the directors of the clinic. They

talked and talked, and finally a decision: we'll treat him. If we save him, he'll have to work here to pay the bill.

"Do the average treatment, but write it up as the most expensive kind," said the director of the clinic. (That way he'll have to work longer for us. That's what we need! A dozen cases like this and we'll be all set for help without spending a dime for payroll . . .)

José had been conked on the head violently, he was unconscious, in a coma. Every once in a while he'd show some response, move his foot, a finger, or a leg would start to tremble. He was being fed intravenously. And for cleansing, various enemas: tea, beef broth, milk, and scrambled eggs. He was getting 2,000 calories a day.

Injections, trepanation, heart massage.

The wait for a reaction. The paperwork piling up. Blood tests, serum, plasma, too many medications, American and Japanese drugs.

"Don't exaggerate it *too* much," said the Director.

José responded. "This guy is showing signs of life," said a nurse as she administered distilled water and recorded it as some expensive medicine.

He lived, he got up. He remembered a door opening. He remembered a car coming in his direction (I could have gotten out of the way but I didn't want to, I think at that moment I wanted to die. The door: from a '51 Ford, milk-colored. The latch was hard to open. But I got in. There was the car. The wheel went right by my head, it was really cold on the ground.)

Blood test, urine test, x-rays. You were lucky, the accident didn't leave a mark. Didn't affect anything. You're healthy as a horse!

A door, a corridor leading off into other corridors. The one on the right forming a square and leading to another corridor (the same one?). A door into a room with two doors. High windows, you'd need a ladder to see out of them. Zig-zagging hallways, operating rooms, labs, a strongbox, open, full of money, stretchers with the patients covered up.

—How do I get out of here?

—You weren't discharged. We need one more blood test.

—Just one more exam.

—What about that new technique they discovered? Let's do another test.

—An x-ray.

—An x-ray from the left side.

—From the right.

—From the top.

—From underneath.

—From inside.

—Through the mouth.

$1 + 1 + 2 + 4 + 7 + 6 + 4 + 2 + 1 + 3 + 1 + 5 + 2 = $ Total:

Dialing the telephone, the operator comes on:

—Who did you want to speak with, sir?

—I want to talk to Atila.

—What's the number?

—Maybe you could find it for me?

—What's the last name?

—I don't know. Look, he's called Atila.

One corridor inside another, rooms inside rooms, everything white, doctors, nurses, everything white. Crucifixes on the wall. The Lord's Supper.

—Let's do a biopsy.

—A peritoneoscopy.

—Immunofluorescence.

—Feces.

—Urine.

—Wasserman.

—You're sick, extremely sick.

—What do I have?

—Nothing.

—Then I'm not sick!

—People who have nothing wrong with them can be sick. We're worried. We can't figure out why you have nothing wrong.

—I don't because I don't. I'm healthy as a horse. My father was very strong.

—Your father was very strong . . . that's it, my friend! We've discovered that he had syphilis.

—Syphilis? My father! Only if he knew your mother. My father is a bull.

—*Was.* Your father died.

—My father died? Are you crazy? Check to see if it's really my father.

—We already did.

—José Gonçalves?

29

—That's right. The lawyer. Some fella. Bohemian. A great guy, that's what everyone says!

—That was my father, all right. But he died? When? While I was here?

—It was a year ago he died. You inherited his syphilis. But you don't have anything. That's what has our team of doctors intrigued.

—Can I go?

—No, you need to work to pay off your bill. We saved your life, kid. You were dead. And now, well, here you are!

One day José managed to get a spool of thread. He didn't know if it was morning, noon, or night. The corridors were lit by fluorescent lights, anonymous. He tied the thread to his doorknob and started to walk. The spool ran out and he didn't arrive anywhere. He came back, following the thread. Whenever he tried to run away, leaving his floor without the thread, leaving the limits the head nurse had imposed on him, he got lost. They always had to bring him back to his room.

One day, morning, noon, or night, he heard a lot of noise behind his bed. They were digging behind the wall. It was a rhythmic scraping. A hole was opening up. Outside it was daylight, and gigantic dentures were eating the tiles, opening the hole. He didn't waste a minute, he left at a run, jumped out from seven feet up, ran some more, looked behind him (still afraid to be turned into a pillar of salt). The clinic was a building under construction, with this sign:

THE LARGEST HOSPITAL IN LATIN AMERICA

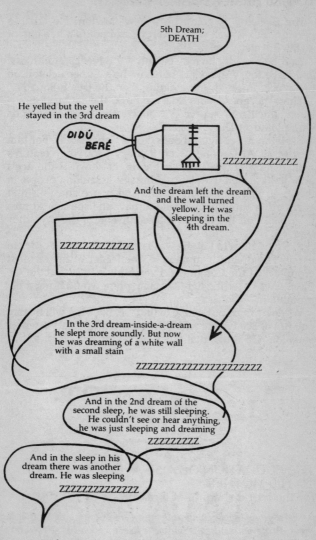

JOSÉ DREAMT THAT HE WAS SLEEPING

PRESENTING THE SKELETON:
YOU'LL HEAR ALL ABOUT HIM

The Skeleton is going on a new mission. He crushes pervitin, mixes well with dexamyl, and pours it in a cup of distilled water. Skeleton pricks a vein.

And he's ready: he may be only 4'9", 104 lbs., toothless, and have lousy eyesight, but now he's Superskeleton on the attack, intrepid, more daring than the Death Squads.

There he goes, alongside his boss, the fat, well-nourished, intelligent supercop who created (and commands with pleasure) The Avengers.

Skeleton never figured out who Al Capone was. For him they're all Al Capone. Even if they're starving creatures with fishing knives in their hands, or down-at-the-heels poor jerks armed with blunderbusses, assaulting people in the dark, guys full of marijuana and booze and pills and every other thing people take to have the courage to turn their backs on the hunger and confusion of the lives they lead.

Skeleton likes to kill, he was issued a .45 and an order to use it. His dream is to nab Gê, the leader of the terrorist group called the Communs. Everybody's talking about Gê these days, a terrific fighter: nailing him would bring a big promotion.

When he finds out where to find Gê, Skeleton will fill that guy full of 300 bullets and walk away ready to face a whole battalion. Gê is his, that much he swears.

STAY TUNED

THE EDUCATION OF JOSÉ ACCORDING
TO HIS MOTHER
(or the moral shaping of a man)

We're going to take communion now, son, Come with Mother to mass, Bring your missal, You went to confession like a good boy yesterday didn't you, We must be good Catholics, You're going to

32

be a good Catholic now aren't you, yes, so good and pious. I want Jesus in my heart. (Serious faces, heads bowed in reverence, said the catechism teacher: first communion is the most important moment in a Catholic's life. After that, only death.) The hand bringing the Host (will it turn into chocolate?), the silver plate flashing brightness, light reflected through the Host. A white blaze of light-and-Host, swallowed by José, pleasure, eternity, the ice of heaven, Jesus descending to the stomach, later he'll find the right channels to the heart. Masses, prayers, ave marias, litanies, creeds, rosaries, how many indulgences, the vesper benediction, saints on the altars, that deathly church smell, morning, afternoon, and evening, sanctuaries opened and closed, crucifixes, candles, flowers, bells, gloria in excelsis deo, gloooooooooooria in excelsis deeeeeeooooo, the censer burning incense, pro nobis this, pro nobis that, tantum ergum sacramentum veneremur cernui. *My brothers, ours is a Catholic nation, the largest Catholic country in the world, which is why ours is a good people, pious and good.* Pulpits, priests, monks, orders. *The Barefooted Carmelites are forming a legion to dominate the world with goodness—taking the word of God to every hearth—wiping out the dangers of the devil.* It's my birthday, Mom, I don't want to go to school, I don't want to do anything today. *We must thank God, son, that you're so big and healthy, so grown-up, thank God that you're good and pious.* But what about my foot, Mom, why did God make it all bent like this? *To test you, son, we must always accept God's will, He knows what He's doing.* Priests in black cassocks, threatening in their pulpits, solemn voices with the organ behind them. *God punishes—Look at Hell at your side—brothers in our Lord Jesus Christ. Our nation will be saved from final damnation—We're the most Catholic nation in America, not Protestants like the Americans—or even the English, Praised be our Lord.* Holy Oil, Holy Water, badges, blue sashes, medallions, rosary beads, little statues, *Bring your son to be altar boy, thus will God look after your home, since your husband isn't looking after it very well, I don't mean in the material sense, in that way he provides well, but what do material things matter when God provides us with everything?* Processions, Corpus Christi, Holy Week, Saints, the Day of Our Lady, of the Sacred Heart of Jesus, crossing yourself in church and in the cemetery, genuflecting in the center of the nave, because He is there in His sanctuary, *always say an ejaculatory prayer, to get indulgences, to get to heaven.* Boys, thousands of young boys dressed in white, candles in their hands, walking slowly behind the litter, Christ died, there He is in front in that coffin, the catechism teacher passing by. *My children, you are the future of the country, good and pious boys, Laudate Dominum omnes gentes: et collaudate eum omnes populi. Quoniam confirmata est super nos misericordia ejus: et veritas Domini manet in aeternum.* They ran, ran, ran to the Lord. The pile of them, priests in black, nuns in black and white, the brothers of the Eucharist with their red surplices, the women with their yellow sashes (St. Joseph), red sashes (Heart of Jesus), blue sashes (Daughters of Mary), flying down to the street below, closing their eyes and yelling. And his mother, fallen on the ground, dying of shame, sobbing *son, oh my son, come down from there this minute,* and the children in white shouting and laughing, and running toward him, without looking back because if they did *they would be transformed into a pillar of salt.* And José, naked, glorious on top of the litter that the men had been carrying, and the whole city looking. Three cheers for José, good, pious, and pure, naked as he was when God brought him into the world, *naked, before the expulsion.* Get out! Go home José!

BYE, BYE

Scientist Marcondes Reis has managed to leave the country, with the help of friends. He's on his way to Patrice Lumumba University, where he has been promised the necessary conditions to continue his research. Here Professor Reis first lost his lecturer's chair, and then his house was ransacked twice by the police, who confiscated all the books in his personal library and threatened his children.

The President made a declaration: "When science subverts and corrupts, it's better to have a country without science, a little backward."

THE END OF DANGER

In the last chapter, José tried to screw the Mexican girl and she refused again, thinking he was still lame. He started getting rough with her, and only stopped when two roommates came back from the bathroom and jumped him. They held him down on the bed, and he saw the girl bring

34

the pillow down on his face, pushing it hard to suffocate him. She was pushing it down, and he needed air.

(When people are dying they remember their whole life, everything. That's what they always told me. Am I remembering because I'm dying or because I think I'm dying and I'm making myself remember? I could let them kill me, end it all right here and now, my dream of the electric chair, the gas chamber, the guillotine. But I don't want to die such a puny death.)

The girl was getting tired of holding down the pillow, and the other two were watching José's legs, which still struggled. They hesitated.

(Death is yellow and awful.) He needed air, it seemed like he was all bruised inside. He swooned and went in . . .

. . . went in, after having thought about opening the door. It was the door to an old Volkswagon (Had someone told him not to go in? Like Bluebeard said to his wife: don't go in).

The light was a beacon in the fog, even though there was no fog anymore. José was walking. Was he awake? Sleeping? Dreaming? Actually taking steps?

(When I went in I saw that I was walking toward myself. It was me, myself, trying to leave by the door I had entered. At the same time, I was seeing myself come in. The me that was coming in wanted to say to the me that was leaving that he should stay. And the me who was leaving tried to tell the me who was coming in that he should leave. But neither of the two could talk. It was as if there were glass between us. The me who was coming in passed through the me who was leaving, so that I didn't know anymore if I was coming or going and inside my head was a terrific confusion. There was no one to help me and at that moment I really needed someone. The room was empty, and it took me a long time to notice that there was a body suspended by ropes from the ceiling. The body lowered, I saw the girl: pretty, real pretty, a little fleshy like I like. Nude, perfect, she was sleeping or unconscious. There was a rose on the floor and when I picked it up I saw a petal on the old woman's face. She must have been about 300 years old. I'm dreaming, this is silly, none of it makes any sense, it's not true, I kept thinking.)

—Ay, que me voy!

The Mexican girl let the pillow up, looked at unconscious José. The two guys who were holding him let go. The girl opened José's fly, looked at his cock and laughed:

—Bueno, muy bueno.
—Hah! You're a real cow, you know that?
She punched him, with all her strength, in the groin.

He was in the hall, right next to the bathroom.
And his cousin came running, all set to go . . .

JOSÉ AT THE WAREHOUSE

José left the boardinghouse and went to live with Atila in an apartment near Estrela Verde's soccer field—they were the most famous suburban team. Every Sunday he went to the game. The apartment was a temporary warehouse for books belonging to a publisher who had been closed down by the government.

José would spend all day reading.

---

70 DAYS AND NO ONE
HAS YET PROVEN
THAT THE FAKIR EATS

2001: the odyssey of Carlos Lopes, textile worker. On April 21, 1964, Carlos Lopes's son wasn't feeling well. He was coughing a lot and having a hard time breathing.

THE STONE IN THE INTESTINE

The taxi stopped. They heard shots. The driver said: "Probably a bank robbery or some terrorist. Maybe it's the Communs." The shots were getting closer. A man appeared with a double-barreled shotgun in his hand. His leg, both arms, and one shoulder were bleeding. He ran from one side of the street to the other and people ducked for cover. He shot out a window, glass shattered everywhere.

The driver put it into reverse: "If we don't get out of here we're gonna get blown away by this fucking maniac." Another group of cops arrived, already shooting. The man fell. People gathered around. The man was yelling: "It's okay, it's all right now. I shot them up good. I had to. I had to give it to you guys, there was no other way. You just gotta shoot up this shit of a life. So what if I killed a couple? At least I got rid of the rock in my gut. There was a rock in there, pushing down on my intestine, it was making me crazy. But the shoot-out made me shit out the rock . . . just look at all the blood! Oh my poor intestine. It's okay now. If only I'd known, I'd have done this a long time ago."

---

90 DAYS AND NO ONE HAS YET
PROVEN THAT THE FAKIR EATS

THOUGHT FOR THE DAY:
Today's little bugger
will be tomorrow's mugger.

EJACULATORY PRAYER: Jesus, Mary, Joseph, my
soul is yours.

AFFECTIVE MEMORY

She was sixteen but said she was eighteen: Rosa Maria won the Miss Armando Prestes contest. Her mother made her a white satin dress with lace trim, she wore a gold belt and red patent leather shoes. Her hair was teased and sprayed, the mayor presented her with the sash. She had short, thick legs. Her mother, a widow, dreamed that Rosa would go to business school. She even thought that Rosa might end up marrying the oldest son of the owner of the school, and become a rich and virtuous girl, a good housewife, with a car, an account at the National Bank, a membership at the Tennis Club and (no, no, that's dreaming too much, I don't want to even think about it) manage to get her husband elected president of the Rotary.

WATCHING THE GOVERNMENT
NEWSREELS

José grabbed an armful of books on his way out the door, sold them to a secondhand bookstore, and then went to get something to eat. He'd been living on ham and cheese sandwiches, yogurt, oranges. He was dying to get into a fight. It had been ten days since he'd been in a fight. He felt apathetic, far from himself. He needed to steal a pair of shoes, his were falling apart. He stopped at a record store, stayed an hour and a half listening to music. Which bugged the salesman. The music from the store mingled with whistles / screeching brakes / towtrucks / hammering / other music / slamming doors / street hawkers / a pattering of feet / typewriters / gears changing / poles being sideswiped / swearwords / broken glass / voices: Where are you going? To look for a job. I'm headed for the red-light district. He went in the movie theater, there was a gong, the curtain opened in front of him. (Where I come from they clack a pair of nutcrackers before the movie starts.) The sports short, the coming attractions, the European news, the government newsreel proving how the country is developing, the Raquel Welch movie. Lights up, the government newsreel full of inaugurations, more coming attractions, a French news report showing Rockefeller's visit to Latin America, another government short about how they were resolving problems in education and about the wonderful production climate in all sectors, and how scientists who had emigrated were coming back with big salaries and opportunities for new research, then the feature with Raquel Welch opening her blouse, a peek at those firm breasts. Lights up, the out-of-focus short, the coming attractions, the French newsreel of the picket signs that greeted Rockefeller, the police butchering people, and Rockefeller in another country and the police butchering people, and Rockefeller in a third country, Yankee Go Home, Latin America Doesn't Want Charity, and the police butchering people, and the newspaper talking about the wonderful aid the U.S. gives Latin America and eulogizing the success of Rockefeller's mission: here in our country his visit was received with order and peace, showing the high level of civilization of our people, and Rockefeller arriving in a closed car, crossing lines and lines of guards / military cordons / helicopters above the streets / hidden tanks / Military Police / shock troops from the state / and the movie with Raquel Welch and her tits hanging out, and that angry mouth she has (that mouth gives me a big fat hard-on), lights up, the theater filling, the tired men (out of it) waiting anxiously for Raquel Welch and seeing the inauguration short, the coming attractions, an incomplete striptease (oh, don't cut it!), the French news report, the government newsreel. Until Raquel Welch appears on the screen and down go their hands.

THE END, and José's eyes were burning, he had a headache, the theater smelled bad. He stopped at a bar, sugarwater please (I had a big shock, was almost run over, I need to calm down a little). Sugarwater kills hunger, now he'd be able to sleep if he hurried home. He got on the bus, then remembered he had no money, hey, can I get off here, I've already gone three stops. The ticket man let him out the back door. José waited for another bus, jumped on, hey, I don't have any money, can I get off here? He waited for another, four stops later, another, this time he managed five stops without getting off. With just two stops to go, he got off and walked home. He curled up in a quilt on top of a heap of books. And noticed the magazine he'd picked up at the movies when the girl next to him left it behind. But it wasn't a magazine—it was a fat pamphlet:

WHO SAYS YOU CAN'T GET MARRIED?

OPERATION ENCOUNTER

MORE THAN 100,000 HAPPY PEOPLE

TO OUR CREDIT ALREADY

SO WHY BE LONELY, WHY STAY SINGLE

JUST BECAUSE YOU'RE SHY?

THERE'S SOMEONE OUT THERE FOR YOU

DON'T MAKE THAT SPECIAL SOMEONE WAIT

"THE HAPPY HEART" MARRIAGE AGENCY

José read a book a day. Every two or three days he'd choose a dusty stack and go sell it to the secondhand store. He read novels, essays, grammar books, textbooks, politics. He got a job. At an export-import firm. On the Street of Flowers (and iron, and tools, and lathes, and machines, and metal fittings, and steel).

A WEEK WITH JOSÉ GONÇALVES

employee, jacket and tie, shined shoes.
Monday:
I get up at seven. I brush my teeth, wash my face, and shave. (Atila got a plastic pail, every night we fill it with water from the bar next door. The warehouse has no water.) I go to the bar for coffee, bread, and butter. I walk two blocks, wait for the bus. Get off at Largo. I go up to the office and punch in, 8:30 sharp. I go to my desk, take the cover off the typewriter, open the drawers, and start working. The faces in the elevator, in the office, on the street, are the same, I work alone among a million mirrors.
Tuesday:
I get up at seven. I brush my teeth, wash my face, and shave. I go to the bar for coffee, bread, and butter. I walk two blocks and wait for the bus. Get off at Largo. I go up to the office and punch in, 8:30 sharp. I go to my desk, take the cover off the typewriter, open the drawers, pick up my letters, and start working.
Wednesday:
I get up. Walk two blocks. Go up to the office. Take the cover off the typewriter. Start working.
Thursday:
I get up, walk, go to the office, work.
Friday:
Get up, walk, go in, work, leave, sleep.
Saturday:
Every Saturday I get a whore.

"I DREAMED YOU
WERE SO PRETTY"

VOMIT & VOMIT

Carlos Lopes got off the first bus, got on the second. The son on his shoulder was screaming. And drooling. Carlos Lopes got off the third bus. Walked ten blocks and arrived at the Clinic of the National Welfare Institute. Closed. The boy was crying. Carlos Lopes went to the bar on the corner. Coffee, regular. The boy threw up all over his clothes. The bartender asked: "Is the boy thirsty?" They gave him some water, and he vomited some more. There was still a half hour until the clinic would open.

NOTES FOR THE DUST JACKET

Banks, gas stations, motels, bars, stores: none of them escapes being robbed. Generals die in Russia. Blacks say there's racism in Cuba. France is on the road to the extreme right. Student demonstrations curbed with violence in the U.S. People are dying in Biafra. India doesn't want to kill sacred cows. Here, droves from the northeast continue migrating to the south. Firing squads for all those picked up for subversion.

> JOSÉ:
> SOMETHING IS HAPPENING IN THE WORLD
> AND YOU DON'T KNOW WHAT IT IS.

Tangos, day and night, Valentino and Theda Bara movies, Clara Bow, Gloria Swanson, the warehouse filling up with old 78's from secondhand stores.

INTREPID FIRE FIGHTERS CAN'T
PREVENT CATASTROPHE

On Tuesday morning there was a bank robbery. With machine guns. A Japanese in command. In the afternoon they hit another bank. With revolvers and a carbine rifle. Wednesday, three robberies, two of them led by a Japanese. Thursday, a small stickup at lunchtime at a downtown bank. And Friday, to make up for the weekend, five robberies in different, far-flung locations. The victims swear there was a Japanese. Millions stolen. The police are sure the money is destined for "political ends." The banks don't have sufficient security.

—I don't know anything about it, said José, I didn't know the guy. He lived there in his room, me in mine, we never even met.

—He had your name on a list.

—I don't know anything, I swear.

—Maybe you need some reminding.

The cop worked him over for five minutes.

The cop worked him over for five minutes.

The cop worked him over for five minutes.

They put ammonia under his nose. He came to.

—If you don't start talking soon, you're gonna be here a long, long time.

—Then I guess I'm staying, 'cause I don't know anything.

—Wait, I think I know your mug from somewhere. You been brought in before, haven't you?

—No. Never.

The cop roughed him up a little more, so as not to get out of practice. He left and came back.

—Well, you don't have a record. At least not here. I'm sending out to have it checked.

He left and came back.

—I was here to be a witness once.

—A witness. For what?

—My landlord killed himself, jumped in the well. I was here to answer some questions.

—I'll check on it.

He left, was gone a while, and came back. A gray light (daybreak) appeared in the slit of a window. The room turned yellow a tenth of a second, a vehement yellow. (There must be something wrong with my eyes, with this yellow. Or maybe it's hunger.)

—Come with me.

—Name?

—José Gonçalves.

—Profession?

—I work in the movies.

—Actor?

—No. I kill mice.

—What? You playing around with us?

—No, that's really what I do, at the movie theater.

—How long have you been living at the boardinghouse?

—Two years.

—Did you know Walter?

42

—More or less.

—They say you were a friend of his.

—I knew him by sight.

—I think you knew him pretty well.

—I knew him by sight.

—And if I prove the contrary?

—No, sir, I only knew who he was.

—You want me to have you roughed up some more?

—Please, for God's sake, don't hit me. I don't have anything to do with this.

The cop worked him over for five minutes.

—You were in their group. You were going to meetings in his room. Were you or weren't you, creep? Did you or didn't you, you shitty Communist?

—No. I didn't. I'm not a Communist. I don't have anything to do with this. Let me go. Please don't beat me anymore, for God's sakes don't hit me.

—Then confess!

—I don't have anything to confess. Nothing, I don't know anything.

The cop worked him over for five minutes.

—And now? You going to confess?

They took him outside. The Organization for Political and Social Change was located in an ugly, red-tiled building, an English castle in bad taste plopped down near the railroad tracks. They got in a black and white van and went to the Department of Investigations. José handcuffed, poor bastard, people looking at him, not looking at him. In the file room, the cop looked at photos, records, called people in to recognize José. He took José's I.D. and went to check on something else. They looked up the case of the guy who jumped in the well.

I've seen this guy someplace before, said a detective at Investigations. He was known for his good eye, he always recognized people and remembered things. He checked the papers and magazines every day, searching carefully through the crime pages, looking at faces surrounding the body, curious. He registered everything. His nickname was "Photographer."

—Okay, we don't need to keep him here. But he's gotta stay in town. Next week, come down here, hear that? Report to me. You can go.

—Huh?

—You can go.

—What about my stuff?
—What stuff?
—A watch, my I.D., papers I had on me.
—You didn't have anything.
—What do you mean? They took them, over in the other place.
—No, sonny, no one took anything, remember that. Now get going or you'll never get out of here. Shitty little Communist. We'll get you, don't worry.

THOUGHT FOR THE DAY:
The city is getting more and more civilized.
Children are raped in broad daylight.
Thieves assault women on afternoon shopping trips.
Thieves fight other thieves,
and kill each other, get themselves killed.
A new squad, The Avengers, is being formed.
A group that existed years ago. In heroic times.

THE DISINTERESTED FRIEND (Tribalization)

José reading away, he's finished all the novels, that leaves politics. Lousy. He doesn't understand it all, but he reads, he likes to look at the words. José is starting to get tired of words, added-up letters: why do these letters together mean a certain something? What if I join letters like this: clutgrf. Is that a word? He gets tired of sitting around on top of piles of books. He'd like someone to explain the political stuff. Atila didn't want to hear about it, he wasn't interested, just smoked pot all the time, eating boiled eggs and listening to tangos. One day Atila disappeared. He left his records, a dozen eggs, his hot plate, and some marijuana. That same day José looked out the window and saw three crooks assaulting a man, beating him up, while the Victrola played "El Choclo." Right afterward, a radio patrol car came along and ordered him to come downstairs. José told it this way: he'd seen an armed man assaulting three guys and the three had resisted. The man was in the back of the patrol car and started to cry, and the cops had a good laugh (a smart aleck on our hands, ha, wait till we get our hands on you at headquarters, we'll see how smart you are).

José turned on the radio he'd stolen (it's easy to steal when you're not really intending to . . . when you're not scared of being picked up, and it doesn't really matter if it works or not). He was thinking about stealing a television, that way he'd be with people he could see. It was a drag just listening to the radio, not getting a look at who was talking, never knowing what to expect. Suddenly they would all be right there. Friends who would be there, no questions asked.

Meanwhile, he had his radio. Years ago he would listen to the radio, the big radio in the shellacked wood shell. His mother didn't let him listen much, this is something for grown-ups. She would listen to the Voice of the Nation, and there was that ad, sung haltingly by the P-A-L-M-O-L-I-V-E girls, letter by letter, and there was the advice to the lovelorn. His mother sitting next to the radio— the whole day slowly leafing through weeklies and fashion magazines and stories about actresses—and the meals were never on time, she didn't even straighten up the house, it was always a mess, a pigsty, and of course she didn't take care of the kids. But wait a minute, what kids? José couldn't remember having a brother or a sister, but he remembered his father always saying "take care of the kids." So there must have been another one. But where was he? And where was his father?

José's mother collected magazine covers and one day he ripped them out of the album, set fire to photo after photo (those actor friends of his mother), burning up Tyrone Power, Linda Darnell, Douglas Fairbanks, Jr., Maureen O'Hara, John Hall, Maria Montez, James Cagney, Xavier Cugat, José Iturbi, Cary Grant, George Sanders, Lorraine Day, Robert Young, Susan Hayward, Bette Davis, Joan Fontaine, Olivia de Havilland, Clark Gable, Jane Powell, Ricardo Montalban, Loretta Young, Judy Gar-

Carlos Lopes waited all night for his son to feel better. He didn't feel better. As soon as it was light he carried the boy to the bus stop. It was very early, there weren't any buses yet, so Carlos Lopes started walking along the path that led to the paved road two kilometers below—where there would be more traffic.

land. Burned, twisted, black ashes he blew through the air to the bathroom and flushed down the toilet. Drowned.

The radio. Glued to his ear, it brought him the world, *Reach Out I'll Be There*, Herb Alpert, Aretha Franklin, *He Wore a Striped Shirt When He Went Away*, the news, soccer, with each goal, we'll be back in 30 seconds with our next program, government-approved National News, small craft warnings (there are no small craft warnings), at the tone the time will be, the best and worst records, Merilee Rush, an umbrella for your financial protection, friendly folk who offered you money, the chance to buy houses, cars, furniture, appliances, clothing, people who told you where to go and how to go, what to eat or drink, or which medicine to take (Wave bye-bye to your cold: 700 oranges in just one little box!). He was getting sleepy, so he kissed his little radio good night, thanks for the company, loyalty, support. He kissed the antennae, the case, the dial, the buttons. He turned it off and drifted into a contented sleep. One more day, happy to have done nothing, absolutely nothing, in life.

IN THE BEGINNING

Rotted steps, windows with the glass missing, paint chipping off. A floor full of holes.

—Hello, can-I-help-you?

An employee smile, complete with blackened bridgework and bad breath.

—I saw your ad. I'd like to know more about it.

—Yes, indeed, have a seat. Just-one-moment-please. I'll bring you all the forms. Do you know how our agency operates?

—No.

HELP WANTED

"Carpenters. Metal workers. Mason's assistants."

—Soy carpintero.

—Argentinian?

—No, de Costa Rica.

—You have experience?

—Sí.

Costa Rica: 50,000 km², population approximately 1,500,000. Bananas (United Fruit), coffee, cocoa, cotton, rice. Monetary unit: colon.

Every day workers arrive looking for jobs. There are always openings at the national monuments. They say (it's not confirmed) that workers die in accidents almost every day because of the lack of safety precautions and because the government is rushing the job in order to commemorate the Tenth Anniversary of the Revolution that took the country out of the hands of the communists.

The Costa Rican got the job because he accepted the Minimum Third.

Which means, my dear, if you'd like to know: foreigners' salary. It's gone down a lot in our country lately. What's it like over there?

The Minimum Third: one third of the minimum wage.

VISION

the giant eagle to take José to his nest in the head of America

THIS AGENCY IS DESIGNED TO SELECT PEOPLE WHO SINCERELY WISH TO BUILD A HOME LIFE WITH SOLID FOUNDATIONS AND WHO FOR VARIOUS REASONS OR LACK OF OPPORTUNITY HAVEN'T SUCCEEDED IN DOING SO.

A mimeographed magazine discussing the definition of marriage and demonstrating its necessity as the basis for the family, the foundation of society, the root of happiness and the future. A contest for "Most Elegant Bride and Groom"—who will win a trip to the renowned honeymoon spots of Lindóia and Poços de Caldas? Articles on venereal disease.

PROPOSALS: Ads, all the same size—code number, age, race, religion, height, weight, profession, appearance. I'd like to correspond with. I want to initiate contact with. In order to marry. No obligation.

—First, sir, you have to make up an ad.

—One of these?

—Uh-huh. Like this, or with a photograph.

—How does it work?

—You pay by the month as the ad comes out. With a photo you pay double.

—I guess I'll do it. To see what happens.

—It works. Sometimes just one ad is enough. Our agency is the best, the most efficient. In just two years we've already arranged 7,000 marriages.

—Should I say in the ad that I'm lame?

—Lame?

—Just a little bit.

—Let me see.

José walked for him.

—No, I don't think you need to. You can hardly notice it. After all, you've got a good face, nice body. Probably intelligent. What the heck, no problem. You going with the photo?

> #789786
> male, age 35, mulatto, Catholic, 5'1", 137 lbs., businessman, good-looking, wants to write to a 20-year-old woman also of mixed blood, good-looking, and Catholic. For future meeting.

> #8765789
> male, age 69, white, Catholic, good moral principles, 5'3", 165 lbs., wants to correspond with foreign widows in good financial situation. No obligations. Will exchange photos.

—No, I don't think so. Maybe next time.

The employee wrote up the ad.

—Have you read Scott Fitzgerald?

—Mmmm. But I didn't understand it too well. (The impatient functionary)

—Scott Fitzgerald? You mean you've read him?

—No, actually I haven't had the pleasure. Is he good? Gee, I'd like to.

—He's fantastic.

—Well. If you like to read, we have some good books right over here that we published ourselves. All about marriage. Written by good people, too. Professors, priests, lawyers, psychologists. Would you like to have a look at the catalog?

Scrap iron
QUIT READING THOSE BOOKS, JOSÉ / YOU'VE AL-
READY READ MORE THAN 1,000, YOU AREN'T THE
SAME JOSÉ WHO FIRST WALKED INTO THAT WARE-
HOUSE / IT'S STUPID TO READ THAT STUFF, IT ONLY
COMPLICATES YOUR LIFE / DON'T LET THE REPRES-
SIVE MILITIA KNOW THOSE BOOKS ARE THERE / YOU
WERE ALREADY HAULED IN TO INVESTIGATIONS
ONCE / THE NEXT TIME IT'LL BE THE END OF YOU
/ YOU'LL DISAPPEAR LIKE SO MANY PEOPLE DO
EVERY DAY / BUT HOW WOULD YOU KNOW ABOUT
THINGS LIKE THAT, THEY'RE NOT IN PRINT, THEY'RE
NOT ALLOWED TO BE IN PRINT / STOP, JOSÉ / STOP
READING THOSE BOOKS: scrap iron

THOU ART PEDRO

They opened a nightclub across from the warehouse.
Green and yellow neon flooding the whole block.
—You want a whiskey?
—Well . . .
—So have one.
—Costs too much.
—Hell, it's on me.
Pedro:[1] at 42, he's stoop-shouldered, has shriveled, scaly
skin (not from aging),[2] sores on his arms, hair falling out,
bad teeth, bleeding gums, poor vision—the world looks
dark to him because he sees in only two colors: light gray
and dark gray. He hears poorly, sees poorly, is indifferent
to everything. Pedro: inheritor of illnesses and hunger and
slavery since time immemorial.[3] (Check the resemblance between this description and the medical diagnosis at the end
of the chapter on the Astronomer.)
José and Pedro:

---

[1] ". . . and upon this rock I will build my church." Matthew 16:18
[2] In certain parts of the North and Northeast, premature aging is
brought on by hunger, malnutrition, lockjaw, profound anemia,
and vitamin deficiency.
[3] Immemorial: that's over and above the four hundred and seventy-
four years of attacking the Indians in the middle of their green and
peaceful villages.

—You mean it, kid? You wanna be a working man? How come?

—I need a job, pal. Any kind of job.

—Workin' a factory—you call that a job? You crazy, chum.

—A job is a job, man. I need a job. No luck at all lately.

—But you went to school, you know things. Read and write. Don't forget you studied, son, don't fall into a trap.

—Sure, I studied, but I've got no job. So what good did it do?

Atila and José:

—Pedro's all right, you know? Now he's working construction—a building with 178 floors. Know what it's for? They're going to make an atom bomb there. But nobody knows about it yet. A big secret. That's why they want to bring back all those scientists who went . . . who escaped abroad. Hey, Pedro take off that hat!

—Aw, come on, guys, I'm used to it—on top of that building the sun really gets to you.

He was smoking a hand-rolled cigarette (strong enough to kill a rat) and sitting there watching the girls in miniskirts go by with their asses hanging out.

—Excuse me, your name please?

—Pedro Rodrigues.

—Where were you born?

—Up north.[1]

—When did you come here?

—Ten years ago.

—Married?

—Yes. Eight children.

—Salary?

—Minimum wage.

—Do you work overtime?

—If they got the work, I work.

---

[1] The migration from the North and Northeast to the South continues nonstop, people looking for better living conditions. The majority intend to farm, but they end up in cities where the unskilled workforce is growing and the number of jobs shrinking. Civil construction has attracted a large percentage of these migrants, but the rate of construction fell sharply after 1965, causing a great wave of unemployment.

—And do they?

—Most of the time, twenty hours extra. But they take a lot out.

—Do your children work?

—Three of them.

—Where did you work before?

—Machine shop. I was always in a machine shop.

—What position?

—Burnisher.

—Did you participate in the union?

—Sure. I got into everything. In the last election I even got voted an advisor.

—How many strikes have you been involved in?

—Five.

—Why?

—I was for the raise in salary and the only way we get it is a strike. But now you're not allowed to have strikes no more, doesn't matter why, they call the police and take you in. Last year we tried to have a strike and a lot of guys got arrested, lost their jobs and everything. And these guys who were thrown out, they can't get no job anyplace. It's tough.

—Do you read the newspapers?

—Sometimes. Nothing in them.

—How do you keep up on what's going on?

—Television. They got everything you need.

—Are you interested in politics?

—No. What for?

(End of Interview)

SACRIFICE TO THE GREAT DICTATOR

They didn't remember how they got to the Astronomer's house in the first place. They were drunk. Or even how many days they'd been there, because they didn't know when they'd arrived. As they left, a demolition crew was beginning to work on the place. Already the verandas, which had encircled the house, rows and rows of glass doors, were scattered on the ground. The flower boxes, shrubs, and lawn looked like they'd been abandoned for a hundred years.

But what about the Astronomer himself—where could he be?

Signs:

For Sale: Material from Demolition Call: 456-7289

Associated Building Wreckers, Inc.
"Any structure, large or small"

And more signs:

COMING SOON—Luxury Apartments
one per floor
Take advantage of our easy credit terms

Had the Astronomer gone away, had he died alone in his little room at the top of the tower?

José was really hungry. He'd gone to the kitchen to look for something to eat, but the kitchen was all dusty, full of crumbling books and note pads. The battered refrigerator, its door hanging open, was a rat's nest, and there were spiders in the freezer. He had walked around the house trying to look in the rooms, but all the doors were locked except for one at the end of the hall: a sitting room with yellow stained-glass windows and walls covered with mirrors. So José saw himself opening the door and coming in, and afterward walking toward himself. Except that the other José was dim, the mirrors were old, the silver was peeling off. Each stained-glass window had a title: "The Intimacies between Mme Joanna and Helen"; "Voluptuous Love in the Virgin Forest (and among the Virgins)"; "Paradise"; "Mother, I Love You"; "The Satyr Meets the Virgin Donzela." The windows were broken and falling apart: men without members, women without breasts, strange figures, deformed.

When the Astronomer pointed out the star "Atik" he said: They came and stoned Madam Moçinha. They surrounded the house for days, hidden in the garden. Not because of what she had done but because of what they thought she had done. They didn't know she was pure and virginal and ill. She was a virgin, all right, in spite of being a grandmother.

52

A NECESSARY NOTE

Actually, according to those who knew Madam Moçinha (and there were many), she was a whore who had behaved scandalously right there in the garden. The stained-glass windows all bore her face, the same face on all the women. And it was Madam Moçinha who stoned the windows, which had come all the way from Brussels. Out of sheer rage toward her father.[1]

BUT THE TROLLEY CARS STOPPED RUNNING A LONG TIME AGO

El Matador left without his shirt, he couldn't manage to remember where he'd left it or even why he'd taken it off. He didn't want to go back inside that house full of rooms, he'd get lost again. And Atila wanted to run out to the street to see if they'd changed the billboard on the corner. The night they'd arrived with the Astronomer (when was that?), there were men on top of the scaffolding with paper and glue. Maybe there was a pretty new model for him to fall in love with. Atila was already getting tired of the girl in the black bikini who advertised the Leather Fair. But when he got out to the street and met José, he was confused, he was sure he'd never been there. And there was no billboard on the corner, just another villa in ruins, and woods (full of small coffee saplings), and trolley cars going by (but hadn't the trolley cars stopped running a long time ago?). José figured maybe they weren't in the same city anymore, they just needed to get their bearings. They should go back inside, maybe they had come in through a different gate. Wandering in the garden, they separated. There was the greenhouse, no—it wasn't really a greenhouse but a giant construction of glass with the roof made into a map of the stars. I was here last night, thought José. The stars of the first magnitude: Sirius, Canopus, Tolimanos, Vega, Capella, Arcturus, Rigel, Procyon, Achernar, Altair, and ten more. The Astronomer had named them all, explaining the constellations, and he brought out a map, wanting them to

---

[1] A romantic touch of ancient history, a light flavor of four-hundred-year-old things.

learn: man will only be great the day he conquers the stars. Which Atila thought was nonsense, because man had already gone to the moon and soon he'd be on the stars and not even that would make him great. Man would only be great the day hunger disappeared from the earth, then the festivities would go on and on.

THE STORY OF A MATADOR

El Matador wants to be a toreador very badly. And go to Spain. He doesn't have any money, or a job. Once in a while he's in some Sunday rodeo promoted by television. He goes up against cows with their tails in their ears who don't have any idea which end is up. El Matador came from the interior where he learned to work the bulls in the pasture. One day he joined a circus and ended up in Jaco, where he fell in love with one of the famous Tininha daughters. It didn't work out. So El Matador went looking for other circuses, other bullfights, looking to die on the horns of a heifer.

SACRIFICE TO THE GREAT DICTATOR
(continued)

José walked through the house and into a greenhouse with a glass roof so dirty that it looked as if it were barely dawn. The potted plants had grown wildly, all tangled together. In one corner there was a tub of green sod. José went into the kitchen: red tiles, with a stoked-up wood stove, iron pots and pans. On the walls were wooden shelves of preserved sweets: banana, orange, pineapple, mango, guava, jaca, cashew, raspberry, papaya, strawberry, squash, fig. Each jar had a label handwritten in round, careful letters. The Astronomer was on the back veranda, which faced the garden full of wildly sprouting grass and plants, all twining around each other. José looked out over the garden, which was bounded by a high wall, and saw a tomb, or what seemed to be a tomb, in the middle of the yard. A pond of putrid water. In the middle of it, an island of stones, and on top, a construction made of rectangular pieces of granite. On top of the rectangles were cylinders, sharp-pointed triangles, spheres, and above them, a life-size portrait inside a glass box. It was an official photograph of the Great Dictator. The country's first, whom many had venerated, oblivious to the tyranny, despotism, and egoism of the legacy he had left the country: his family—who were trying to climb to the top government positions (clingy folk). In front of the tomb, lighted candles flickered on a mountain of old wax.

—I am meditating on my master.

It was the Astronomer, with a knife in his hand. Suddenly he lunged at José, José jumped out of the way.

—The master is waiting for a sacrifice. I haven't sacrificed anyone in months.

—A sacrifice?

The Astronomer sat himself down on the edge of the pond and puffed on his cigarette.

—I think, I imagine, I trust, I conclude that he needs blood. They say—I don't know, I didn't see, I didn't suffer under his regime—but they say that he used to need it. I'm not positive. If they press me, I'll deny it. But I think that if he needed blood then, he must need it now. He didn't die, his body died. His soul goes on. I'm Catholic, my friend. Apostolic, Roman. I obey the Holy See, I go to mass every Sunday, take communion at least once a year, do my devotions. The Great Dictator still needs blood. From those who believed in him, who followed him. Like I did. I proudly belonged to his Police Squadrons. What perfect organization, my friend. Take it or leave it. Spare the rod and spoil the child. Everything runs according to the rules. I found out—I'm not sure, I can't guarantee anything—that when he died he asked that they make sacrifices in homage to him. He was a god, my friend. A generous, paternal god who cared about the poor people. He was almost a father to them. He left a whole lot to the poor. Everything he had. Whether or not it got delivered, I don't know, it seems like his family had a hand in everything. You know how families are.

LOUD-SPEAKERS[1] HIDDEN IN THE FOLIAGE BEGIN TRANSMITTING SECTIONS OF THE GREAT DICTATOR'S SPEECHES:

---

[1] Loud speakers or loud-speakers. Some people use the dash, some don't. Obviously the word doesn't appear in the great classics.

*We must concern ourselves with our nation's
security. Only very poor countries have nothing to lose and need not worry about matters of
security. We will reform the laws to give more
power to the army, we will increase mandatory
enlistment and the total number of troops, and
we will honor military uniforms and the colors
of the flag.*

The Astronomer was listening with his head bowed. As if
he were praying. Or receiving the voice of God. When he
raised his head his eyes were filled with tears.

—He was a magnificent man. He didn't have the least respect for the human condition. For him, no man had rights.
Only obligations. No nonsense. Behave yourselves, or it's
the back of my hand you'll be getting. He was a man, my
friend, a macho man who didn't like conventions. It was
wonderful to live under his regime because there was no
liberty or licentiousness or amorality. They say—I don't
know, I can't say anything about it since I don't know the
world out there, just people who come to visit me—they say
that there is a new regime, good, hard, cruel. If it's not
cruel, if it doesn't make us suffer, if it doesn't crush what
good a man has inside him, then it's not a regime to take seriously.

ANOTHER SECTION FROM
THE SPEECHES:

*The cycle of development is beginning. The
past is still inside us and an obstacle to progress. It could be said that we have so much
strength, so much real strength, that our
strengths turn into weaknesses. When we
learn to control these strengths they will give
us energy, which is why, my people, we cannot, even for a minute, or a second, or for just
one instant, stop believing in ourselves or
doubt the destiny to which we are being elevated.*

The Astronomer was sobbing. The tears ran down his
reddened face. A silvery robe, ridiculous slippers, deep cir-

cles under his eyes. José had the impression that the Astronomer was emerging from a Carnival costume competition that had been going on for centuries, where he had wrestled with plumed transvestites, disputing first place by biting and pulling hair. As if he were just stepping off the runway, looking tired, drained. The loud-speakers scattered around the garden were playing old-time waltzes now, and the Astronomer looked at José, and turned the knife in his hand.

—You understand. I need a sacrifice.

—But why me?

—Someone must be sacrificed.

(An idea occurs to José.)

—Couldn't it be someone else?

—It could be anyone.

—But didn't you say the Great Dictator was a sort of father to the poor?

—He was, yes.

—Then I think he'd prefer a laborer or something.

(What kind of idea is this, José?)

—Maybe. Could be. Who knows.

—There's someone in my crowd who's a genuine working man. He'd be the perfect sacrifice.

(José, José)

—Who knows. Could be. Maybe.

—Sure. Of course the Great Dictator would prefer the sacrifice of a working man.

—Yeah. He probably would. I accept.

(Oh, what complete lack of moral fiber, José!)[1]

José went back through the garden, noticing for the first time the heaps of human bones in the shrubbery. Ribs, thigh bones, skulls. The loud-speakers were quiet now, and instead the plastic birds with little records in their bellies were singing on the plastic branches of the artificial trees.

("Gloomy Sunday"— they say that song caused more than thirty suicides in New York alone. People

THE DOCTOR'S DECLARATIONS ABOUT PEDRO THE WORKING MAN

---

[1] When the going gets rough, moral fiber doesn't exist—except in tales of social and civic zeal.

threw themselves out of windows. Some helluva song.)

There were flags and portraits of the Great Dictator all over the place. On doors, on windows, in bathrooms, on coffee pots. José went looking for the working man. It so happened that Pedro was looking at a star, listening to the Astronomer explain: that's Kaiten from the Pisces constellation. And suddenly he collapsed. The Astronomer fanned him, slapped him across the face, dumped a bucket of cold water on him. Nothing from Pedro. José thought maybe it was the booze, he just wasn't used to it. They lay him in bed. Then they took him out in the street. He kept passing out. Look, he's as good as dead, said Atila, it's better to leave him here. Or maybe he's not dead, and we'd better try to save him. They took Pedro to the doctor.

He needs proteins, vitamins, salt, minerals, and medicine to fight infection. He needs a minimum intake of between 1,300 and 2,000 calories per day. Without all of these things people become indifferent, rejecting any kind of sensation. This man's children are worse off, no doubt, and his grandchildren will be worse yet. They will die, little by little, mentally and physically deficient. The lack of vitamin A means they will go blind; without vitamin D they'll become paralyzed; lack of calcium will result in rickets; and without vitamin B the nerves will lose their capacity to react. Iron deficiency makes the formation of red blood cells difficult, diminishing the flow of oxygen to the heart: fatal suffocation. Their skin will become white and wrinkled, their bones will be fragile, and their hair will fall out. They'll become immobile, unable to laugh or cry, with fixed and frightened eyes.

DIAGRAM OF PEDRO THE WORKING MAN

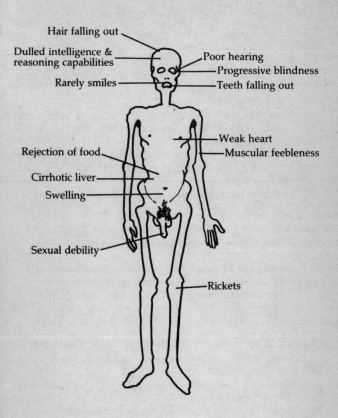

Hair falling out

Dulled intelligence &
reasoning capabilities

Poor hearing

Progressive blindness

Rarely smiles

Teeth falling out

Weak heart

Muscular feebleness

Rejection of food

Cirrhotic liver

Swelling

Sexual debility

Rickets

CULTURE IN A BOTTLE CAP

José is thinking about the loud-speakers which are being installed. From now on they'll be transmitting the pronouncements of the government for everyone to hear. It will be impossible to turn them off, José, like people used to do between seven and eight p.m. These loud-speakers will roar at top volume, and the people will hear, even if they use cotton, wax, earmuffs. They're being installed everywhere, you know, even in villages with only one or two houses, even in Indian settlements (wherever there may still be Indians in this country).

José is getting ready.

Announcers with monotonous and solemn voices will spell out the government's latest decisions, the ones you'll have to live with tomorrow.

Remember, José, that the movie theaters will be closed during broadcast time—churches, theaters, television, too.

His Master's Voice

Listen: time to synchronize our watches, José:

Eight o'clock sharp.

José, age 28, black hair, Catholic, reasonable financial situation, is looking for a girl for future arrangements.

What a Show / Amazing / Sensational / Never before seen on the screen / A super-reproduction in Cinerama / 70 mm / Brand new prints, bold new colors /
A fabulous cast / The best group yet brought together since the birth of the cinema /
Wildly provocative scenes / Uncut by the censors /
A fantastic cinemagraphic conception / The man who never pardoned an enemy / The most entertaining comedy of the year / Mastroanni and Ursula: the battle of the sexes in the 21st century / Tarzan lives—a new and spectacular adventure / An eloquent scream against accommodation / If you think you've seen everything, you *must* see this /
Suspense, violence, and love

—Zé, I've got a job for you.
—A good one?
—A cinch. You're always reading all the time, it's just up your alley.
—Tell me more.
—At Coca-Cola they need people to write bottlecaps.
—What?
—You've had a Coke before, right?
—Yeah. Ice cold.
—So? Doesn't the cap always have something in it? Like: it was Edison who discovered the light bulb in who knows what year.
—Yeah—
—So that's what you'll do.
—Okay. Listen, have you read Scott Fitzgerald?
—No. I've never read a single book in my shitty life and I'm not going to start now.

Here's what the bottlecap
says (José's notes):

The country was discovered in 1400
Independence came in 1748
The width of the Suez Canal is
Suez, Gaza, the United Nations . . .
soldiers

> "So proudly we roam
> these lands far from home.
> God keep us from falling,
> *so young and alone.*"

Soyoanal:

a cap with a prize, another with "culture"
(more culture than prize)
this Coca-Cola was a guzzle to remember!

KCL Detergent, Casas Biancamana—the discount chain
where everyone shops, Aron gives out lots of prizes,
clothes

window displays, buy on credit, shirts,
colored underwear

/ the latest /

ooooooooooooooooonnnnnooonnnnooonnnoooonnnnooon
nnnooooonnnnnnnnnooooon
bee, bee, bee, bee, bee, bee, bee, bee, bee, bee, beeeeeeeep,
fonnn
blem, blem, blem, blem, blem, blem
buuuuuuuuuuuuuuuuuuuuuuuuuuuuuuuuuuuuuummm
mmmmmmmmm

Carlos Lopes waited for the clinic to open. His arms ached from carrying his son. An employee came to the door, Carlos Lopes started in. What are you doing? asked the man. I'm going in to wait for the doctor, answered Carlos. Fine, but you have to wait for me to open up first. But if the door's open, why can't I go in? asked Carlos Lopes. Because we're only open after I open all the doors. But this door is open, said Carlos Lopes. Yes, agreed the man. It's open, but we're closed. Can't you see that we're closed?

. . . police did not capture any of the terrorists, flies were still flying, fans stopped dead, the air heavy, people stopped dead, heavy stares staring. They'd come to see the Man. He'd been on television but the Church banned his program. The TV station, so as not to lose money, had rented a corner and was exhibiting the Man. During the first days the only spectators were people coming out of the striptease who wanted something more.

THOUGHT FOR THE DAY

It's terrible to be poor

Buy Money Certificates today

I.D.E.M.:

The ones that double your money overnight!

BLACKOUT (preparatory to conversion)

Outside the warehouse the noise was so loud it was as if a thousand cars were honking their horns. José, perched on top of a tower of books, couldn't (or didn't want to) get involved. He just stayed where he was, watching the yellow light pour in the window. The luminous yellow (from the bar), made up of a million volts. Inside of him there were rats tearing around, cockroaches, leaf-cutter ants, eating everything, ripping everything apart. No pain. Just the sensation (unpleasant) of being gnawed, feeling his own meat picked at, shredded. José began to realize that something else was happening—new parts were being substituted for the gnawed ones, in a sort of transplant. Until he fainted, conscious only of the yellow light (so bright) that crossed the walls of his body, focusing on a point in his stomach.

CURIOSITIES OF LIFE

The Church decided to intervene a second time, this time trying to get the Man arrested as an assassin. The plan did not succeed, however; it just added to his fame. All day there was a line down the street. They needed to begin organizing the entrances—exits—duration of each visit—ticket windows—loud-speakers—music—announcers—snacks for employees—rest periods for the Man—organization of caravans from the interior—public roundtables—commemorations—lectures—anniversaries. The police cordoned off two square blocks, the mayor's office demanded that they move the Man to the outskirts of the city, but the promoters didn't want to, of course. It was a permanent party—popcorn men—plastic souvenirs for sale—8 × 10 photos of the Man—medallions—rosary beads—necklaces—shreds of his clothes—posters—biographies—little pamphlets telling his whole story in verse.

At the end of the first month, the bar next door rented a

back room to *The Girl Who Transformed Herself into a Gorilla.*
A week later, *The Scientific Wax Museum* arrived, with exhibits of syphilis—gonorrhea—hemorrhoids—the dangers of
smoke in the lungs—cancer in various parts of the body—
eye diseases—mouth diseases—people stabbed to death—
shot—blown up—burnt.

Then came *The Jungle Museum,* a busload of stuffed and
mounted animal oddities.

And *The Monsters of Nature:* chicken with three feet—pigs
with two heads—a goat with the head of a dog—a child with
the head of a fish—a snake with fur—a woman with three
breasts—men with paws—an elephant with the head of a
marmoset.

Rarities of Life: the bearded woman—the man with only a
torso, who sat propped on a tray all day long—the man with
both male and female organs, all of them in working order—
the woman without an ass—the child without a face, just
two holes for mouth and nose—the man with eyes on his
fingertips—the living arm, complete with a little head and
everything—the ball-man all rolled up inside himself.

The Museum of Charity
An Exposition of the Curious Life of an Earthworm
A Live Ant Colony Behind Glass
The Humping Dog
The Woman and the Mule
The Man Who Gets Off Alone—no woman, no hands
Cockfights
Fights Between Pigeons and Calves

People came, rented rooms, corners of cafes, small plots
of land. They put up loud-speakers (yes, more), played records, made an infernal racket. In a year's time, none of the
original residents were left. Anyone who owned a house
rented it for an astronomical sum. By the end of the year
there were ten blocks chock full of all the curiosities in the
world—phantom trains—a hall of mirrors—cabarets—secret
bordellos—and a multitude of people twenty-four hours a
day. The Man was still the toast of the town. Lines to get in
to see him grew by the day, there was publicity overseas,
pamphlets in several languages.

José, Atila, and Hero, walking along. José is carrying a
suitcase full of books he rescued from the warehouse before
the Political Police came on a raid and confiscated everything. Books he needed as writer for Coca-Cola bottlecaps.

And also: *The Diary of Ché Guevara, Quotations from Chairman Mao Tse-Tung, Guide to Marx's Capital,* and *China in the Year 2001,* by Suyin Han.

The three go to the back of the bar and sit down awhile. People are crowding in to get out of the rain, the floor is a trench, the stink from the urinal cuts your nostrils and makes you want to puke.

THIS MAN
DEVOURED AN ENTIRE EXPEDITION
OF MISSIONARY PRIESTS IN THE JUNGLE

HE ONLY EATS HUMAN MEAT

—COME ON IN—

THE BIGGEST CURIOSITY IN LATIN AMERICA

THE MAN WHO EATS MEN

> In this lonely place
> every smart-ass squats
> All bravery forgot
> every hero plops
>
> (Inscription in the privy)

WANTED

—Look, sir, the computer is never wrong, it's never made a mistake. It's, well, perfect. It truly delivers matrimonial bliss. We call it the science of servicing the heart.

And then, with a flourish, the employee with the bridgework punched a button and the computer spit out the relevant statistics: how many people had been married, how many still were, number of children, etc.

100, 345678, 768590, 13456278, 176895, 1456.º789, 123456H-89u

Don't know why, but it's true, my heart beats when I see you, parala-la, parala-lay, tooky teeky tooky tootooky, gorogogo gorogoga, elephant stampedes a great many people, two elephants stampede a great many more, oooooo bah tatatatatatatatatatata, oh juicy, juicy festival of striptease.

—Run the ad another month, okay?
—Sure. Don't lose hope now. I think the computer is saving something really good for you.

OCTOBER
—Run it another month.

THE DISCOVERY

As he held out his hand José felt the yellow exploding. And he felt as if he were spinning, looking at a triangle in the wall, behind which was the kitchen, and framed in the triangle a dark-haired girl with thick arms squeezing out of her sleeves. An ordinary face, an ugly nose. A yellow kerchief around her head. It was the same one, the girl from the Revolving Restaurant. The first time he saw her he had lost his appetite.

You are my destiny, Paul Anka was singing suavely over the agency's loud-speakers.[1]

(This is the girl I wanted that day. Such a long time ago.)[2]

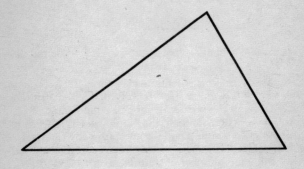

---

[1]The employee with the bridgework always put that record on for "atmosphere."
[2]What a coincidence. Seems like something from fiction, literature, comic books.

AT THE AGENCY:

—This is Miss Rosa Maria, said the guy with the bridge-work.
—Pleased to meet you, said José.
—My pleasure, said Rosa.
—Shall we go have a cup of coffee?
—Let's.
—Sure is nice to meet you.
—Me too.
Silence.
Silence.
Silence.
(Fuck, I need to say something.)
—Mm-hum.
—Good.
Silence.
She was:
Dark-haired, kind of short, full face, full body, little round thighs, her whole body tilted forward (ready to be fucked, he's thinking).

ATILA AND JOSÉ

—So you really like this girl Rosa?
—You bet.
—Funny. She's chubby, and cheap-looking, and kind of tacky. Did you see what she had on?
—So?
(*Love is blind, sees only perfection, Love wants no advice, refuses protection:* sings Dulce Garcia.)

EJACULATORY PRAYER: Dear God, shelter me in your heart for all eternity.

FIRESIDE CHAT

—Age?
—18.
—Specialty?

—Huh?

—What's different about you?

—Uh, I'm eighteen but I look like ninety.

—Too bad, my friend, but we have about twenty from your area already. All that way. We already chose a boy of eight who looks a hundred.

2

—Age?

—Fourteen.

—Specialty?

—What do you mean, specialty?

—What do you have to show for yourself?

—Look here, I got no eyes. I was born that way, but I can walk and do stuff good as anybody else. I can even read.

—Okay, report to the group of Blind Readers.

3

—Hey, fella, give me a break, will you?

—What is it?

—I gotta earn some money. Took me twenty-eight days to get here . . . on foot.

—So? What's your thing?

—Hey, look, no feet or legs, see? But I run. I can beat any good runner you got, I jump along like this . . .

—Where do you come from?

—The south.

4

—You. What do you do?

—I read.

—Anybody can read.

—But I'm illiterate.

—Where are you from?

—Up north.

5

—Hey, Mex, what are you doing here?
—You know me?
—From Santana. You used to fix radios.
—Yeah, right. Hey, amigo!
—Hey, so what can I do for you?
—I'm lookin' for work.
—What do you do?
—I can go with no water for like two months.

6

—You four, what do you do?
—We're not four, we're just one.
—You come from out east?
—Uh-huh.
—There are lots of groups of "four in one" from out there. Go on in. We've got a candy company that can always use you guys.

7

—You from the backlands?
—How'd you know?
—Eight "rolling balls" have already come from there.
The soles of the man's feet were stuck to his head. His body formed a circle. He got the job.
—Firestone sponsors the show. They've made a truck and you fellas will be the wheels.
—Thanks, pal. Thanks a lot. Finally, a job to support my family, my kids.
—You married?
—Seven children.
José just got an idea.

WHAT COULD JOSÉ'S IDEA BE?

The line was a mile long. José had two counters next to his table. One with blank forms, the other with forms already filled out. Two secretaries would come pick up the ones with a red stamp and take them to the Extravaganza Team. All kinds of people. From Argentina, Bolivia, Peru, Guatemala, Colombia, Venezuela, Chile, Uruguay, Brazil.

By the end of the day, the yellow sun was beating down into the small room filled with mud, cigarette butts, paper, and sawdust, and José felt dizzy. He remembered the afternoon when he was walking along downtown, the woman in the unbelievably short miniskirt and the long legs went by, what white, shapely legs. He froze. *Na, na, not yet.* The black woman had passed his table today. With her moldy smell, her smell of herbs—rue—wormwood-mint-lemon balm. He had seen the truth that day: cripples, blind people, deformed mouths, diseases, crossed eyes, lepers. But he'd been seeing the insides of people, and now it was the outsides passing by, he couldn't see inside. And these were people from all over the country and from all over Latin America, lining up in front of him. He was used to it by now, spoke ''portugnol''—everybody understood, it was all one language.

GIANT DENTURES CONTINUE TO CHEW BUILDINGS—THE POLICE REFUSE TO INVESTI-GATE: THEY SAY IT'S A PROBLEM FOR THE DEN-TISTS. THE DENTISTS SAY IT'S BECAUSE OF AIR POLLUTION, ACCORDING TO INFORMA-TION FROM MARA, A SCIENTIST WHO IS RE-SEARCHING STRANGE APPARITIONS SIGHTED ALL OVER THE COUNTRY.

—Honey, no . . . only after we're married.
—That's stupid.
—Stupid, nothing. Get your hand out of there, come on.
—Where'd you ever get that idea?
—Nowhere, silly. It's just that I like you. So with you it's got to be different. It's got to be, you know, *right.*
—Stupid, really stuuuupid.
—Or else what will you think of me? That's the way it's got to be for now. If you like me, you'll put up with it.

70

ALL BECAUSE OF A DOILY FOR THE WATER FILTER

They had their picture taken by an old photographer set up on the street corner. Their arms around each other. Seated on a bench. Looking straight at the camera. José planting a kiss on Rosa's cheek. The man came out from under his black cloth looking forlorn: I've run out of paper, they'll be ready tomorrow, I promise. You can stop back here or pick them up at my house.

At the house, the guy's wife produced an envelope. Rosa didn't even open it—she was on her way to the seamstress to have her wedding dress made, then she had to stop at a friend's house, and later she went to buy a crochet needle and blue thread (she was planning to make a little doily for the water filter). When she got home, she spent some time recopying recipes. When she opened her purse, there was the envelope. But the man had made a mistake, these were just pictures of some thin-faced man who looked only vaguely like José. She stuck the pictures inside a book, figuring she'd complain the next time she was in the neighborhood.

OFFICIAL NEWSFLASH

The official herald mounted the platform: From now on, government clerks will only register children with names which are on a list furnished by the government. Outside of that, there will be no recourse. This measure is meant to put a stop to the proliferation of given names which are pagan, wacky inventions, an embarrassment to the individual and to the nation. Ordinance 6574893456Yhg.

> *Siempre que te pregunto / que quando, donde y como / tu siempre me respondes / Quizás, quizás, quizás, quizás, quizás, quizás . . .*

IN SEARCH OF THE GOLDEN FLEECE

The blue and white and yellow bus rambled dully along the street, past dull scenery, carrying its dull passengers.

DRIVER: OBEY THE TRAFFIC SIGNS—THEY ARE
YOUR SECURITY.

On Sundays they used to have dances at the social club
and José would sit outside on the cold, granite benches
watching the girls who stood near the window between
dances and you couldn't go in, José, that's why you're
thinking about the city and those empty Sunday nights and
your buns feel cold.

No passing on curves or hills.

José, do you remember the tenth day in the Man's white
tent?

Rosa was talking with the guy in the next seat because
she didn't like to travel without talking and José didn't like
to talk when he was traveling.[1] She had brought along a
portable record player and put on a Connie Francis song until a sullen-looking passenger complained.[2] Rosa had bobby
pins in her hair, with a fancy new hanky over them, and she
wore a pair of Cuban sandals for maximum comfort.[3]

Obey the traffic signs and have a safe trip.[4]

José and Rosa were traveling to the interior so José could
ask for her hand in marriage. As per the established norms
of society.

FILHODA CITY LIMITS

IN FILHODA BE SURE TO VISIT
YOUR AUTHORIZED FORD DEALER

COME TO BERTO'S LUNCHEONETTE
FOR THE BEST BURGER IN TOWN

NOW ENTERING FILHODA:
THE MOST PROGRESSIVE CITY IN THE
    COUNTRY
BIRTHPLACE OF SIX PRESIDENTS
HOME OF TOP MEDICAL AND LAW SCHOOLS
WELCOME!

---

[1] "The recipe for a happy conjugal life includes mutual understanding," said my great-aunt.
[2] Your freedom extends only until another's begins.
[3] "Straps that really hold—leather that doesn't smell"
[4] Rosa to José on the bus: "Honey, wouldn't it be good to have traffic signs to follow through life? It would be so much easier. All
you'd have to do is follow."

CHECK OUT OUR VOLKS 1600
HORSE-DRAWN CARRIAGE RIDES THROUGH
THE PARK
VISIT THE COLOSSAL BAZAAR, SPONSORED
BY SAINT ANGEL OF OUR LORD CHURCH
BUILDING FUND

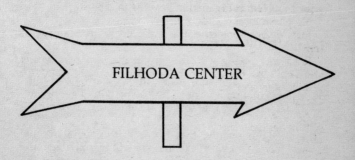

FILHODA CENTER

In the living room: woven straw chairs, hatstands with mirrors, the father and mother seated among portraits of grandparents, aunts who have died, Rosa dressed up for first communion (a hand-colored photo), Rosa in a bathing suit wearing the Miss Armando Prestes sash, Christ and Our Lady enthroned.

The father in a jacket and tie, the mother in a Sunday dress.

The father wanted to know:

full name, age, profession, salary, savings, possessions (house, car, what brand—Volks 1600? Corcel? Galaxy?—any real estate?), what's your family like, and where from, what did your mother die of, did she smoke, drink, how's your health, your politics, would you let my daughter take the pill, do you intend to have children, did you go to school, did you participate in demonstrations, what do you think of the government, of communism, are you Catholic?

José told the truth.

José lied.

The old man embraced José.

The mother, too, gave them her blessing.

"Well, then, son-in-law, it won't be long before we have grandchildren running around the house, eh?"

The mother's eyes shining: "Children are the happiness of a home."

So, expounded the father: you should know that we're locals, here in this town for 150 years, that's to say my family has been here these many, many years, I belong to the Rotary, the Lion's Club, the Business Association, the Tennis Club, the Yacht Club, I have a little rental property, we're involved in organizing benefits for charity.[1]

CALL ME, SWEETIE

This town reeks of sex. It's in the air, on the walls, on the people. It's sex, I'm sure of it. I don't know how, but I know. Rosa told me I have an odd sensitivity, I get premonitions. A sensitivity that sees inside of things. And into the future.

It's at night, mainly, that sex is in the air, above the houses, hovering over rocks that are still warm, above the groups conversing on the sidewalk, walking down the street. It's there, glued to the girls in miniskirts or tight pants, their bodies smelling of Ivory, Lux, Palmolive, Phebo, Eucalol, OK, Carnival Brand, their bodies loose inside summer dresses. They walk past the boys, and want them, and the boys want them, too, and a current is established, and the girls are terrified thinking about being alone in the bushes, in the cemetery, on the tennis court at night, along the shortcuts around town, by the sides of the road. Grabbing and letting themselves be grabbed. And the excited boys push hard on the accelerators and the Volkswagons roar and the ones without cars put their hands in their pockets.

I've been here for days without doing anything besides looking, feeling, smelling the sex, the perfume, the sweat,

---

[1]The truth about Rosa's family is quite another story. Her father died years ago and the widow moved away and married an Italian-Turk, atheist and owner of a bar. As the city expanded in the direction of the bar, the neighborhood became more and more middle-class, and the bar became a busy restaurant. The Italian-Turk opened a luncheonette, bought a chain of fabric stores, and a hamburger concession at the high school (where he exploited the students). After that, he turned Catholic, respectable, got a good credit rating, and managed to be admitted to the Tennis Club.

the hot earth. Studying the nightly game: nervousness, frenzy for contact, the lunge, desire doubling and redoubling, screams circling the town, the town enveloped by frantic fucking, girls burying themselves in boys' cocks, while their mothers (happy) watch television (soap operas), pray and dream for the future: houses, cars, grandchildren, church on Sundays. My daughter and the doctor's son (famous doctor), my daughter and the engineer's son (rich engineer). And they, the daughters, are out fucking in the woods, in cars, standing up in the garden. They're biting the boys—biting themselves—moaning—shouting and flinging themselves on the ground—

—on hot nights in that town.

A grid of orderly streets and trees, a big hotel and an ugly church under construction, a social club in the middle of the park, a concrete bus station next to the open market, a tall, homely tower with a square clock, the old railroad station, silent electric buses, businesses closed up tight, empty, washed-up stores (the poor sales clerks), vestiges of the decadent age of the city, faces who pass, who greet each other, the town that lived on farming and today is nothing, no industry, just did not understand change.

Banks, banks, banks, one after the other, dozens and dozens of them, where does so much money come from?

"Would you believe it? That boy was writing letters to my daughter! I called him and ordered him to stop. I asked politely: Will you please do me the favor of not writing to her anymore? She's still a young girl, he was writing, well, strange things. Bad things. He said it wasn't really important to get married. That's just an example. She liked it. But I put a stop to that, all right. After all, what's a mother for? To make her daughter happy, that's what. So I phoned and said: Do me the favor of not writing to my daughter anymore, *please*. Look, these fellows talk like they're so smart, so mature, but they're milquetoasts. He stopped. Right away. Well, it made sense. Here we are, minding our own business, and these degenerates come and put nonsense into our daughters' heads. Wanting her to leave town someday, huh. Look, my daughter is fifteen, has a perfect boyfriend, the son of a college president, she'll get married, she'll be happy. But once in a while she writes something or other, says she's going to be a writer. And I put a stop to that, fast, such silliness. I'm keeping my eye on her, it's for her own good.''

A neighbor was talking to Rosa's mother. The woman must have been pretty when she was young but, like all the women in this town—I don't know why, maybe it's the dry air, or the sun, or maybe it's from staying in one place, waiting for the nothing that's supposed to happen tomorrow—her skin was stiff, stretched taut, expectant. Her eyes shone, but with a hard brightness. To me she was not just herself, but all compulsive people, hating to be bothered, irritable, not wanting anything to change. I didn't even know her, but I knew that she had done something terrible to her daughter and the boy who was writing her. You could see she had a knack for spying happiness and finding a way to snuff it out, it made her happy.[1] After she left, Rosa's mother said:

—Such a nice woman, nice family. They live up past the gas station, you pass it on the way out of town. Funny, though. Now, I don't want to be a gossip, but isn't it odd—she acts like she's forgotten that she couldn't get married with a white dress and all. She was in a family way.

I let her go on talking—what I wanted to do was leave, but Rosa said no, let's stay a little longer, my father's taking a liking to you.

So José spent the afternoon in the town library, full of books with red spines and students copying things out of the encyclopedia. There were three librarians. He was keeping his eye on the one who had arrived the same time he did. She had gotten out of an MG, and had enormous glasses with blue lenses. She was small but densely packed (once in a while she would go up the stairs and José could watch her shapely legs), that's why he spent the whole afternoon excited, without leaving his chair, without even glancing at the Jack London he had in front of him.

—Have you read any books by Scott Fitzgerald?
—Uh-huh.
—Do you have any here?

---

[1] A popular singer once introduced the song "Maria, Maria" by saying: I'd like to dedicate this song to all those who think of other people's love as an unpardonable sin . . . my contribution to everyone who compensates for their own unhappiness by wishing unhappiness on others.

—Not a one, said the little brunette who had gotten out of the MG.

Her face was a little broken out. José wanted to hang around, who knows, maybe some day he'd go out with the little brunette. She was called Sylvia.

JOSÉ RECEIVES A PHONE CALL

Four p.m., motionless trees, houses closed up tight, an open hydrant, a woman singing, a horn, a cough, a rooster. The telephone rings.

—Is this Rosa's fiancé?

—Yeah.

—Listen, I've got something you should know. You interested?

—That depends.

—Depends on what?

—Who is this, what do you want? Do you know me?

—I'm a friend. Listen, ask Rosa something. Ask her if she remembers the little cabin near Britos. Or the Bezerro curve on the road to Matão. Ask her about Alberto's farm. Or the bathroom in the public garden, at midnight . . . Hello, hello?

—I'm here.

—Ask her about the bullfight at Betinho's house. Or the two queers, the Turks, who were dancing with her, naked, in the middle of the road. See if she remembers anything about the striptease at the war memorial. Hello? Hello?

—Go on.

—Why aren't you hanging up?

—I'm listening.

—Ask her if she remembers when the drain at the Tennis Club got clogged up, it was full of underwear. That was a fuck festival if there ever was one. Forty men and four women. Rosa and the numbers runner's wife, and the bookseller's wife, and the woman from up past the gas station.

—Go on.

—See if she remembers down the cellar at the high school, where all the girls would read dirty books. See if she remembers how she liked to kiss the other girls on the mouth.

—I'll ask her.

—You're a horned wonder, you know it? What you need is the shit beat out of you.

—You gonna give it a try?

—Hey, this is Olguinha you're talking to. Rosa knows me. From the dressing rooms at the Municipal Theater. When they had the ballet school. Too bad they tore down that place, it was creepy all right, we'd sneak downstairs to the dressing rooms and hang out, smoking pot and getting hand jobs. After that, Rosa would get it on with everybody, one by one, while the rest watched. God, did she love it— the bigger the prick the louder she'd yell. One day—you wanna hear this? really?—we put on a show. At dawn. We filled the fucking theater. Men got out of bed in the middle of the night and came, paid a shitload of money. A real sex show, Mr. Horns. What a show. We had everything. A swearing contest between the girls, fucking, striptease, pissing, shitting, sucking, ass-fucking, fist-fucking. The place ended up reeking of come. The next day they had some meeting there, the Crusaders of the Eucharist or something, and they thought it was mold, but it was sperm, Jack, the sperm of five hundred men. You know what else? More than ten guys discovered their daughters there—what a scene that was! The biggest scandal ever in this town's 150 years, what a fucking scene. People talked about it for ages, even longer than when they lynched those guys.

—Somebody got lynched?

—Yeah, a while back. People around here don't fuck around. You'd better not mess with us, uh-uh.

—I'm not.

—Hey, Horny! (a new voice) Did he tell you we climbed the wall of the club and went skinny-dipping in the pool, and Rosa took off all her clothes and ran around the garden completely nude?

—Got your horns on yet, buddy? (another voice) You know why Rosa would only sit in the balcony when she went to the movies? So she could jump up and down on the guy's tools, that's why, jerk-off.

—Did you know she never wore underpants?

—So?

—So, you still gonna marry her?

—Yep.

—Asshole. Cocksucker. Faggot. You'd better hit the road.

JOSÉ TELLS ROSA ABOUT THE
PHONE CALL

—Well, now what? said Rosa.
—Now what, what?
—You're going to fight with me, aren't you? It's all true.
—No, it doesn't change anything.[1]

JOSÉ UNDERSTANDS

They stopped me before I got to the corner, under a big tree, in the dark, near the Funeral Parlor.

They piled out of four Volkswagons and surrounded me. Still kids, not even twenty years old I bet.

They put me up against the wall and stood around, nervous. Looking at me, at each other.

They looked at the empty street. Then one guy came up to me. A little unsure of himself.

—So, you're a faggot, huh?
—Who's a faggot?
—The guy who's gonna marry Rosa.
—I'm gonna marry her, if that's what you mean, but I'm not a queer.
—Fella, we told you the whole story. Only a faggot would take it.
—What if I didn't believe you?
—He didn't believe us. Hey, gang, he doesn't believe us. Me, a judge's son, and that one over there—the mayor's nephew. And *his* father's the D.A. His is a cop. Hey, João, isn't your uncle a priest? Yeah, and the guy in the fancy jeans, his mother is the president of the Ladies Rotarians. This guy, Cross-eye, is related somehow to the founding father himself. What do you think, gang? This dude just doesn't know the score.

(Christ, what's all this stuff? Seems like an American movie, or a bad novel.)

—Why are you guys wasting your time on me?
—We don't like you. That's why.

---

[1]What explanation can be given: A generous soul? Neurosis? Moral defectiveness? Sexual aberration?

—Yeah, you've got twenty-four hours to get out of town.[1]

—Hey, listen, maybe you can order your little flunkeys around like that, but not me.[2]

—When I give the orders, everybody listens. Me and them, we do what we want. We have ourselves some fun. You're tonight's little entertainment.[3]

—Let's do the same job on him as we did with those college boy commies that time—

—Ha! Know what we did?

—We beat the shit out of them. Remember that little black guy who was going around preaching agrarian reform? Boy, did we do some agrarian reform on him. We took him out to the Blond Devil's farm.[4]

—What a night! We tied him up in the orchard and sprinkled ketchup all over him and left him under the orange trees. By morning he was covered with leaf-cutter ants, a perfect feast, aaaah ha ha ha—

—Ha ha haha ha hoo

—Oh hooo ha ha

—Hahahahahahahahahahahaaaaa . . .

Their laughter filled the street. Without closing my eyes, I tuned out (the way the Man taught me the second day), and I thought: if they beat me up, I won't feel a thing. It would be my first time trying it out. I knew that I'd have the strength to win—I just needed to bring together the teachings of the second and ninth days and that gang could do whatever they wanted. It was a chance to test myself.

So I kicked the creep in the stomach, a strong jab with the point of my shoe. They jumped on top of me, held me down, punched me, kicked me, smacked me in the face, in the chest, I tried to steady my legs and fight back, I fell down, rolled over, they rolled on top of me, they let me go, I tried to get up, they pushed me down again, you crazy

---

[1] Like sheriffs say in westerns. Or Al Capone's thugs to the honest young kid.

[2] Typical honest young kid answer.

[3] Life in the interior is monotonous, there's just not much to do: movies, television, a couple of church festivals a year, the social club on Sundays.

[4] The Blond Devil is actually a gigantic brunet who a) is crazy for blonds and b) bleaches his pubes because the blonds (he says) think that's really sexy.

fairy, get out of here, who do you think you are? And there was a giant yellowness in the sky, egg yellow—but how could there be? It was one o'clock in the morning. The yellowness was inside my mouth.

I hated those guys, I hated what they were, and it wasn't just that town, they were the whole country, and I hated them because hate is love and you need to hate and not love, you need to break and violate the world if you want to start something new and good, something better. If something good, something better, exists. I only know it couldn't be worse. I let myself be hit and I didn't feel anything, not a thing. I understood then that I was ready. I located the guy with the brass knuckles and tried to climb all over him but they didn't let me, they punched me and kicked me and sat on my stomach.

THE PEOPLE OF FILHODA
HOPE YOU HAD A NICE STAY
COME BACK REAL SOON

(Municipal Committee for Tourism)

THE POLICE ASSURE US: "No one will be free until the turn of the century."

("It can't be helped," added the Secretary of Security.)

SPACE ODYSSEY

Carlos Lopes waited an hour. When the clinic opened:
—My son is sick.
—You need to prove he's sick.
—What about the doctor?
—Have you contributed to the National Health Fund?
—Of course, they take it out of my pay.
—Then all you have to do is bring in your driver's license, birth certificate, proof of signature card, social security number, payroll stubs for the last six months, I.D. card, 3 x 4 photos stamped with the date, voter's registration proving that you voted in the last election,[1] a photocopy of your running file

---

[1] There haven't been elections in the country for twenty years; José's voter's registration was a blank card protected by plastic with a picture of the flag on the front.

with the police department, proof of residency, declaration of acceptable conjugal conduct, marriage certificate, your son's birth certificate, baptism, and dependent child tax voucher *(What is this thing called love)*, proof of income tax payment and discharge from military service.

EMIGRATION

    —My name José, I from Colombia.
    —I'm José, too.
    —Please to meet you.
    —What do you do that's different?
    —Nothing. Work on farm.
    —Then how can I give you a job?
    —I doan know.
José, the Colombian, left without a job.

GEOGRAPHY LESSON (Elementary)

COLOMBIA: 1,283,400 km², coffee, cotton, and sugar cane; wheat and corn, United Fruit, petroleum; official monetary unit: the peso.

BYE, BYE

Scientist Carlos Correia, the country's leading authority in electronic communications, just left for the University of Michigan. Since he had been earning a salary only slightly above minimum wage and was not provided suitable conditions for research, Mr. Correia decided to go abroad for a while until the situation here improves.

FREE ASSOCIATION

The Odeon Theater, in the balcony, "Robinhood" with Errol Flynn, Canoe perfume (by Dana), peppermint drops, fumbling for the girls' tits, Tim Holt, Hopalong Cassidy, Bill Elliot, Roy Rogers, Ken Maynard, Zorro, bang-bang, Clelia.
bam shebam, rataplam, shooooooooeeeee, pffffttt (a fart), *begin the beguine*, the big stars and piiinnk, ping, ping, ping, ping, ping, clap, clappety clop

LIVING LIKE A LOONY

José and his friends: (reflections)
(formerly THOUGHT FOR THE DAY: bad with her, worse
without her)
José:

(I'd like to live like a complete lunatic, without paying attention to my life, non-stop living, dying of so much
living,[1] instead of leading the life I lead, skipping along without doing anything, without knowing what I dreamt last
night, or whether I dreamt—I don't even know what I want)
(José is drunk)[2]

Government Proclamation:

CITIZENS! BEWARE OF THE COMMUNS!
A NEW TERRORIST GROUP HAS BEEN DISCOVERED:
  THE COMMUNS
THEIR AIM IS TO CONFUSE THE PEOPLE, DISTURB
  PUBLIC ORDER,
OVERTHROW THE GOVERNMENT, & SPREAD AN-
  ARCHY.
IF A COMMUN APPROACHES YOU, DENOUNCE HIM!

The post office delivered this handbill house to house. Every
magazine, newspaper, book, and journal carried the official
proclamation. Every day, during the Official Newsflash hour,
the government broadcast the warning.

Suddenly, the Communs were part of the life of the populace.

(Legend) They were commanded by a skinny, bearded
guerrilla who smoked a cigar. His people called him Gê,
though his real name was Geraldo. His father had been a car-
penter, and Gê had graduated from medical school before he
gave it all up to join the cause.

THE AMERICAS UNITED,
UNITED THEY WILL WIN

Civil and military leaders from all the American countries
met with the Europeans in Geneva and founded LIVARG

---

[1] cliché

[2] José doesn't have an attitude because he doesn't want one. His
problem is that he just won't define himself, and he lets himself be
walked all over without even screaming. I'm mad at José.

83

(The League of International Verification and Repression of Guerrillas). It was decided that a united effort is increasingly necessary to combat guerrillas who are organizing in rural areas of Latin America, in North American cities, and in a few European countries as well. (There is a fledgling movement in Spain, and also—even further developed—in Greece, Yugoslavia, and Czechoslovakia.) LIVARG will be a paramilitary organization, subordinate to LIVARS (The League of International Verification and Repression of Students), whose greatest activity will be concentrated in the U.S., France, Italy, Poland, Hungary, Brazil, and here.

FREE ASSOCIATION

After dinner, people chatting in the living room, people who had all died, uncles, aunts, priests who visited the house, older cousins, mother. Children shouldn't listen to grownups' conversations, children should go play outside. He was in the closet near the bathroom and he saw his cousin come running, in a hurry, he hung back in the shadows, she grew in the light. He stood there breathless, his mouth hanging open.

BLACKOUT

—He's out cold, all of a sudden he just fainted.
—It must be exhaustion. Goddamn life really wears you out.
—What exhaustion? Zé had yesterday off.
—But he's been real nervous lately, don't you think?
—Sunday he blew up at a guy looking for a job.
—I don't get it. Usually he's so nice and easy-going. Everybody likes him.
—Did anyone call a doctor?
—What for? He just blacked out.
—But it's the second time this month.
—It's exhaustion, that's all. He needs more time off. Needs to get married. He's been real nervous ever since he got engaged.

The next day José kept fainting. They took him to the clinic. Hospitalized him. Gave him oxygen. In three days he was himself again. Healthy. He got out of bed, said good-bye to the nurses. Went back to his interviewing table.

There was a whiteness in his head. Once in a while José had the impression that it was lightning.

There was a great peace inside him. He had been there. A bluish desolation.

Crack, crecka CRACK

Once upon a time, those were the days, taquetatiuqueg, frigndhtg, 67859, caracaracaracaracara, naked women, turd, shit, ass. José rolled over in bed, his arms shook lightly, his legs jerked, he was singing for an audience of thousands, in English, he autographed thousands of records, was presented with awards, gold records, 1,2,3,4,5,6,7,8,9,23456789, 98765432, 543276789, and he heard the sound of a piss, loud like a waterfall. It got him excited, he felt the pleasure coming, he heard the piss, louder by the minute, intolerably, intolerably exciting.

José is depressed. He thinks:

(I told Rosa it didn't matter, that I didn't believe what those guys told me. But I think maybe I believe it, and it does matter. I get mad at myself, I keep thinking: that's stupid, Zé, really stupid. There's bigger stuff in life than that. I can't help it, though, I want it to be a lie. But what difference does it make, I don't even like her, I don't know why I'm getting married. I just know I've got to get married, I want to join myself to her, I want to stay with that fatty forever. I *like* her thighs, her thick waist, those meaty breasts. Sure, there are all sorts of reasons to stay with Rosa. There are. Or there aren't. I'm being dumb, I should break up with her. I'm not breaking up with her, I don't have the nerve.)

IMITATING VALENTINO'S SPIRITUAL WIDOW

No one appeared to carry the convict's coffin, so he was taken to the cemetery in a police car. They say that every night someone leaves a yellow rose on his grave: the bandit of the yellow rose.

DELILAH

A little drop of blood, galigabigala, police novels one after the other, he was going to grandmother's house, she had a green agate mug, big, big, big, it was raining only halfway down the block, from there on it was sunny and beautiful aaaaahhhh, he ran from sun to rain (a widow's wedding), from rain to sun (a Spanish wedding), hey you, come in out of the rain. Boom ratatatatatata, boom ratatat. Bang-bang, you're dead, no more kidding around, you're a big boy now, José, grfthryu, grtsugfrdf, rerer, laguaraleri, A is 1, B is 2, C is 3, D is 4, bregtd, bregft, bregft, rfegrt, the green mug is still around, in a million pieces, that night they all went out, they went to a play about a sailor, and I stayed home, in the front room waiting up for my father, Tom Jones singing *my, my, my Delilah*, everyone in the club was dancing, but José had cold buns, his mother had cold buns, too.

HOLY RESOLUTIONS

Five new prohibitions:

1) Overtime hours will no longer be permitted, in an effort to save money for the employer.

2) Newspapers will not be permitted to publish pictures of nude or semi-nude women.

3) The use of the national standard[1] on clothing, houses, cars, and the like, will not be permitted.

4) Public hand-holding will not be permitted, even between married adults. Kissing, embracing, and other such demonstrative behavior will be punishable by six to twelve months in jail.

5) Loafers will not be permitted. The official footwear will have laces and the permitted colors are brown and black.

With these, the number of official prohibitions has risen to 114: little strokes fell great oaks.

CONJUGAL TOURISM

—As soon as we get married, I'm quitting my job.
—No, don't do that. It's a little extra money at least.
—But a married woman . . . working?
—What's wrong with that?
—It's not right. It's just not right.

---

[1] i.e., the flag.

—Rosa, look. It would be silly to give up your salary. I don't make all that much.

—Well, then you should. If you want to get married.

Three days ago José gave Rosa a tour of Boqueirão.[1] Of course she had heard about it, like everyone else in the whole country, but she had always been scared to go there alone.[2] The government had recently decided to provide official support. They built pavilions, painted houses, put up billboards,[3] there were ads on television, promo shorts in the movie theaters.[4] Boqueirão was getting organized, abandoning its early chaos; the streets were cleaned daily; repossessions would probably be necessary in the future to accommodate growth. Boqueirão was already enormous. It was a neighborhood that families avoided.[5]

José and Rosa walked along. They saw the calf with seven heads, the golden mule, the automobile with human feet, the turtle which expectorated light, the dinosaur,[6] the pirate's skeleton, the poorest woman on earth,[7] the richest woman in the world,[8] paintings that talk, the mule with

----

[1]Since there already were neighborhoods called Boca do Lixo (Mouth full of Trash, or low-class prostitution) and Boca do Luxo (Mouth full of Money, or high-class prostitution), people nicknamed this new neighborhood Boqueirão (Big Mouth, or, mouth full of everything). The name stuck.

[2]That girl Rosa makes me want to hit her.

[3]Welcome, Bienvenu, Bienvenido.

[4]The quick-thinking entrepreneurs made a fortune.

[5]Obviously. Families avoid everything.

[6]This live dinosaur was found in the most primitive area of the country, in an egg which was inside a priest's head. After the egg was broken open, the dinosaur popped out and immediately grew to an enormous size. They figure there must be others like it, because there are many priests in the region, converting Indians, teaching civilization (sinful behavior, moral attitudes), bringing in clothes, food, and medicine, and organizing the Traditional Indigenous Family.

[7]She was so poor, so astoundingly poor, that she had no house, no clothes, no body, nothing.

[8]She kept getting richer exhibiting herself there, and this made her happy. It takes money to make money.

white wings, the basketball game for men without arms, the boy with a knife in place of his cock, the marching beans, the trained fleas, the race of the paraplegics.

They stopped in front of the Biennial Pavilion. It contained the exhibit of the worst deformities of nature from all over the world, the human aberrations, the zoological curiosities, the strangest diseases. Items from this country alone filled eight floors (the largest representation). Applications had been taken simultaneously all across the nation and lots of political infighting had erupted. The hunchbacks accused the government of unfairly protecting the people without asses, just because the government considered the representation of hunchbacks subversive. Some of the most extreme cases were considering a boycott, which could possibly diminish the prestige of the Biennial.

José and Rosa went inside.

—There's a room I've got to show you. It's incredible.

—Yes, well, let's talk about getting married.

—It's all settled.

—For when?

—I'm still thinking about the date. A couple of months from now.

—Two more months?

—I've been really busy, Rosa, you know how it is. And there's a few things I have to take care of before we get married.

—What you need to take care of is a house, furniture, clothes, all the legal paperwork, you need to get a suit. Just look at you. You've been wearing the same jeans and T-shirt for two months. You need someone to take care of you, honey.

They got up to the top floor, there it was, completely white. They went down a corridor leading off into two other corridors. The one on the right formed a square and led to another corridor (the same one?). A door into a room with two more doors. High, wide windows. Zig-zagging hallways, tables covered with white tablecloths.

—This is weird. I don't like it in here. It looks like a hospital, even smells like one.

—This is going to be the most important part of the Biennial. The most famous exhibits will be here.

Rosa counted the little rooms, all the same.

$$1 + 1 + 2 + 4 + 7 + 6 + 4 + 2 + 1 + 3 + 1 + 5 = ?$$

She was trying to do it in her head: who could add it up?

They walked in a straight line and doubled back, she didn't know if they were coming back to the same place or if it was a different one, let's get out of here, honey, there's nothing to see, come on, I want to see the rest of downstairs. But José seemed hypnotized, walking through one hallway after another, in a room within a hall, the tables covered, everything white.

—I want you to read Scott Fitzgerald.

—Sure I will, sweetie, I'll read anything you want. To be the way you are.

—I'm serious, the guy is terrific.

—Come on, let's go.

—Don't you like it here? It's so calm.

—Calm? This place sucks, if you want to stay, stay.

—Okay, leave.

—I don't know how.

—That's the thing, the hard part is leaving. You'd like to, but how?

THE HUMAN WHEEL

José sent for the man with his feet stuck to his head forming a wheel.

—I've got an idea. A show just for you, your wife, and your two oldest kids.

—Just us?

—Uh-huh, the four of you on stage. Look, I'm having a truck special-ordered, made out of light wood. We'll put you in place of the wheels and you'll tool around the stage. It'll be a great success.[1]

ROSA COMPLAINS

—Honey, this is no job for someone like you. It makes me feel bad just to come here. You need something decent, with a future. Where you can get set in a career and we'll have some security.

—Mmmm.

------

[1]This was José's idea, months before, when he first saw the human wheel.

—You've got to quit this and start looking for something nice, that pays well. This is small fry, just for low life.

—Huh?

—Oh, honey, you don't like me anymore, I know it.

An old black woman was looking at them. José felt a little dizzy, a yellow flash (I know that old woman, but from where?) He pulled Rosa toward him. Embraced her. She started to get excited, she was breathing heavy and rubbing against him. (Hey, today I'm getting somewhere!) José kept kissing her. She had thickish lips. He squeezed her breasts. Such firm breasts, just beginning to get flabby. She breathed hard and said: my love.

THE OFFICIAL COLORS

They have established colors for each social category. The rich will use red, blue, pink, lilac, wine, bordeaux, and all the variations thereof (variations determined by computer, according to income tax returns). Next come the less wealthy, the upper middle class, the middle class, the lower middle and lower classes, which will range first from orange to peach to yellow, and all the variations, and then blue, green, brown, and ending in black, which is for those who have nothing, nothing, nothing. In addition to houses, the decree covers clothing, which will be designed by specialists, and will be either a military uniform or a Mao-type suit (in polished cotton for summer, wool for winter). There will be just these two styles and no possibility of choice.

ROSA DOESN'T COMPLAIN

Such firms breasts, beginning to get flabby. She breathed and said: my love. (Today I'm getting somewhere!) José put her hand down lower. (That girl in the library would have been good at this.) Rosa didn't want to, she pulled her hand back. He placed it on his crotch again. No, don't, that's not nice, it's vulgar. But you want to. I want to, but it's not right. José opened his jeans and pulled everything out. She ran down the stairs. He took advantage of her leaving and pissed on the wall, he had to go really bad.

Boy Scout, Boy Scout / cleaning out the can
What's gonna happen / when the shit hits
    the fan?
I'm gonna take a crap / I'm gonna take a
    piss
Let's just hope that I don't miss

CARLOS LOPES RETURNS

Let's not forget Carlos Lopes.

Remember him? The man who took his son to the clinic? Here he is back again, more sensational than ever. In the last chapter, the employee at the clinic told him to bring in all of his documents and Carlos went off to get them.

Carlos Lopes walked up to the first window, carrying a suitcase full of documents, and stated his case.

—Go to window number 7.

So he did, and explained his case again.

—That's at window 12.

Carlos explained.

—Number 32 is over there.

—You should be at number 31.

—I'm closed. Come back tomorrow.

The next day:

—No, it's not here at 31. Try over at 56. That might be it.

—They're crazy sending everybody here. Go to number 2.

—He said it was here? No, it must be at 13.

—That should be at window 7.

—I was already there.	FREE ASSOCIATION
—Then it's 12.	
—No, it's 14.	Dawn, the bar at the club,
—15.	after the pre-carnival party,
—67.	and they were singing *the*
—Go upstairs to window	*distance that separates us,*
131.	a big hit from "Mondo
—No, not here, should be	Cane," and he was nodding
154.	off, holding his girlfriend's
—It's down at number 43.	hand, and later they left, he
—Up at 108.	didn't kiss her goodnight,
—107.	he got on the train for home,

91

—103.

—Ah, I knew it, it's 897.

—The people downstairs are crazy, this case belongs at 567.

he always took the train at dawn, until one dawn when he thought: why?

765, no it's 435, yeah, it's further on, go down, go up, turn to the right, 657, 6547, 23456, on the floor below, 789, around the side, 987, go up two more flights, 198786, go down four, look for Aristides at #3728, it was never here, 433, 555, 666, 888, 999, 665, you've already been here three times, look, how many times do I have to explain these things to people, go to number 198767898767656, ah, sorry, this window is closed, better go to 78654663425, or no, how about 657483954637, or to any one which ends in the series BG56.

REFLECTION

Rosa is depressed. She thinks:

(I told José it was true, what those boys from my home town said, but I was lying. I just felt like testing if he liked me. I'd be able to tell by his answer. But he was so quiet I couldn't figure out if he understood or if he just didn't care. Oh, it doesn't matter, all I want is to get married, I'm sick of this single life. Girls can't stay single, they go daffy, just like my mother said.)

HOLY RESOLUTIONS

Now the government wants to close down Boqueirão. The justification: people are having too much fun.

"People need to stay home with their families and spend more time with the wife and children."

Holy Resolution #34567659f

THE DEVELOPMENT OF BOQUEIRÃO

Seated at his table, José is selecting candidates for Boqueirão. The line in front of him connects far-flung parts of the country like a dot-to-dot in a coloring book. And José notes: yes, no, yes, no, yes, no, yes, no, yes. He goes on making his recommendations, apathetic by now, tired of these people and their stories, vaccinated against them.

—And you, sir.
—I'd like to be considered for a position.
—But how? You're handsome, clean, healthy . . .
—Uh-huh.
—What's your distinction?
—I'm a normal man.
—There are thousands of them.
—You're wrong. There are very few.

José sent the man for medical exams: completely healthy, not even a cavity. He sent him to psychiatrists, psychoanalysts, and psychologists: perfect. He sent for the man's records: good, honest, a clean slate.

—You're so normal you don't exist.
—What do you mean? Give me a job.
—You're hired.

INTERMISSION / INTERVAL

In a city in the interior, fifteen years later, a group of thirty-five-year-old men meets at the club every night, and every night they reminisce about what they did in their youths.

Beer bellies, graying hair, wrinkles appearing—because of the dry climate, the hot air, the sun, and the tedium, which make everything decompose faster.

—You have to say one thing, the guy had nerve.
—Yeah, he stuck it out, all right. And got a few bull's-eyes, too. The SOB kicked me in the balls.
—I really gave it to him, though, didn't I? I was so fucked up that week, I hardly remember a thing.
—Ha. You're always fucked up.
—No, cut it out, it was that woman from up past the gas station, that's what it was. She was busting my balls. You know, the one who got her kicks spying on her daughter.
—Shit, it was her all right. I'm just beginning to put it together.
—What ever happened to them anyway?
—They got rich, Mac, and moved away.
—But what about that guy, that sure was a laugh . . .
—You think he really believed us?
—What if he did!
—If he only knew, poor fella.
—We sure suckered him, huh?

93

—I just said what I knew.

—You didn't know a thing.

—I did so. Pedro told me he'd screwed the girl.

—Pedro died lying.

—I only said what I'd heard. I didn't even exaggerate.

—Oh, come on. Did anybody here ever actually screw that girl?

—I didn't myself, but I know a guy who had a real orgy with her that night at the theater.

—Oh, you're full of shit, that orgy at the theater never happened. Hell, it was just a myth. Those two brothers invented it. Two goddamn Turks, the bastards. One a conquistador and the other a retard. What happened at the theater was no orgy.

—What was it then, smart ass?

—It was when I was a kid, maybe five, my father talked about it at the dinner table. And my father wasn't about to tell the family about some orgy. It was a political congress or some stupid party meeting, the Integralist party convention, something like that. Some guy started a rumble, so they punched him out and threw him in the fountain.

—Yeah, I heard about that. But that was something else, big deal. The orgy was at dawn, nobody knew about it. And the gimpy guy's sweetheart was there.

—She was not. Nobody even remembers that girl.

—She was an armful, all right. A real cow.

—And rich, man. That Portuguese guy had a lot of dough.

—He was Turkish.

—Italian.

—Wasn't it him who screwed the mayor's wife and pissed on top of her?

—No, the mayor pissed on *him* the day he found out. They were both fat.

—You think he really married her?

—Who knows?

—You think he told her about it?

—Well, she disappeared. Never came back here.

—That was a good one, huh?

—I'd just like to know one thing. I'd like to know if it's true what everyone said about her.

—When I first got the Volks, I tried to make it with her.

She was working at the Post Office. But she didn't put out. And I'd heard, too, that she was good for a tumble.

—Boy, I was loaded for bear that night. I was crazy to kill that guy. Would have been easy.

—Yeah. We were getting a little sick of the Blond Devil routine.

—Oh, come on, we didn't get that serious. He lived to tell the story, didn't he?

—That guy was weird. We should have wiped him out.

—Fuck off, you asshole. I didn't wanna kill anybody. Not now either. I just want to have a good time.

—Don't wanna kill anyone, eh? How many abortions has your wife had, count 'em.

—Go get fucked.

Quien será la que me quiere a mi / quien será / quien será / quien será la que me de su amor / quien será / quien será

In a city in the interior, thirty-five years later, a group of seventy-year-olds meets at the club every night and reminisces about their youths.

Does any of this matter?

100,000 VISITORS THE FIRST WEEK

COME SEE THE GREATEST RARITY IN HUMAN
  NATURE:
THE ONE AND ONLY NORMAL MAN

ANOTHER EXCLUSIVE ENGAGEMENT
  BROUGHT TO YOU BY
BOQUEIRÃO—TO SHOW HOW MUCH WE
  APPRECIATE
OUR DISTINCTIVE CLIENTELE

The lines stretched way past the boundaries of Boqueirão, like in the good old days when everybody had come to see the Cannibal. The crowds came streaming in, loaded with folding chairs, sofas, beds, thermoses, sandwiches. They bought photos, figurines, medallions which had been touched by the normal man. The people pressed forward in a procession, as if to kiss the feet of the Dead Lord during Holy Week.

ATILA'S NEW LOVE

—Oh, Zé, she's fantastic. What a girl![1]

—What girl?

—The one from Holiday on Ice. I stole the poster last night. Take a look . . .

It was a huge section of a 10 × 5 meter billboard, which had been peeled off in strips and then pasted back together.

—I spent two hours putting her back together. Isn't she terrific?

A blonde on ice skates, with feathers on her head. Her arms thrust above her head like a real star.

—Another heartthrob, Atila?

—Just look at my pretty American. The Champion.

He was practically drooling on the poster.

—And that's nothing, Zé. This one likes me back.

—What?

—Yeah, when I saw the poster and fell for her, I decided to go meet her. I pretended to be a reporter and just kept babbling in my phony English, you champion, beautiful baby, talk to me, honey, come on. The words came out sounding all funny, and she laughed, and said my English was real good, better than her Portuguese. Then the interpreter came and I interviewed her and told her the article would be out on opening day. I came back the next day, and the next, and the show opened, and I sent a rose inside an ice cube with this card: "To my Queen of the Skates." Oh, Zé, you'd like her. She knows Scott Fitzgerald.

—She does?

—I took her out to dinner, I didn't have much to talk about, so I asked: Do you know Scott Fitzgerald? She said she did. She'd read everything. She went on naming all the books, my tongue was all scrambled, I just let her go on talking. She's crazy about that Scott of yours.

—Give her a hug for me.

—You know, Zé, there's just one thing. I found something out. I mean, I think I like her better on the poster. Really. She's more beautiful, happier, I can say what I want, even in Portuguese. It's nice, her on the poster, quiet.

---

[1]A badly translated subtitle from a foreign film. Nobody says: "What a girl!"

That's the way I fell in love with her, that's how I want her to stay.

A SPACE ODYSSEY

Carlos Lopes climbed stairs, got on and off elevators, walked through lobbies full of benches full of people from the clinics, knocked at windows, asked questions, asked for help, ran all over the place. For two years he forgot about everything else, he never went home again, he gave up work, life, the only thing he wanted was to save the son in his arms. His clothes were frayed, his shirt was gone, shoes worn out, imagine, a good suit in shreds. But Carlos Lopes was strong above all else. He wouldn't give up hope. He just knew he'd find the right window.

—Go to 177.
—178.
—175.
—179.
—174.
—1774.

He got the numbers all mixed up, went back to 174.

—You were here five minutes ago. Go to 1111.
—This is 11111.

At 1111 they sent him to 2222.

—No, it's at 3333.

Carlos Lopes persevered. He was unshakable. He believed in the good in human nature, had hope for the new destiny. He climbed the stairs soothed by visions of triumph. He wanted to find his window, he wanted to save his son. He shouted out loud, a superb shout of

FREE ASSOCIATION

I gave you the Jorge Bem record and we had so much fun but you were looking for a rich guy who could set you up for good you talked funny why did you disappear?

faith. The window, the window is about to open in front of him, it's opening its little gate over our heads! *Through the battle and the storm, your voice is my strength and inspiration . . .*

Early one morning, in the ruby flare of dawn, a naked man climbed the stairs to the clinic.

In his arms he carried a little white skeleton.

—Window 9.

—He's dead? Then it should be window 7.

—What lunacy to send the dead ones to me! You belong at window 14. Oh for the day I get some respect around here, they treat me like dirt.

—That's at number 12.

—1.

—22.

—Yes, that's right here. Let's see.

But in wars, in supreme trouble, you will see us struggle and win.

—You want to see the boy?

—No, your documents please.

The bulging suitcase was passed through the window. The clerk examined it.

—There's just one problem.

—What?

—You're no longer entitled to anything.

—Why?

—You left your job over two years ago.

—I had to take care of the boy.

—Wasn't the boy dead?

—No, he was alive.

—Then you killed him.

—No, it's just that it took so long.

—You killed him. You killed your son.

He called the guards and they took Carlos Lopes away. He goes to trial the 7th of December and it's almost certain that he'll get a life sentence.

FREE ASSOCIATION

That familiar grate and the priest behind it, Rosa always thought of priests as prisoners. All you could do was listen to that voice coming from the depths, from some place where they could see everything you did ("No, Mom, I'm not going, I hate it, I don't want to go." But she was going, and not going, she ran off to the plaza instead, or to where the boys would be flying kites.)

The priest: No, I do not absolve you.

(Ho-hum, who's listening . . .)

I cannot absolve you, my daughter.

(Wait a minute, what's he saying?)

Fornication is a great sin, permitted only in sacred matrimony, and only to have children.

(What if my mother knew?)

That's why God delivered us from uncleanness, from the lustfulness and defilement of our hearts and bodies.

(What if they knew at school?)

Don't you know that your body is the sanctuary of the Holy Spirit?

(I have fled from impurity.)

Come, return and be purified. Then you shall be absolved.

Conversation in a taxi:

Sweetheart, before we get married I want you to have a prenuptial exam. And also I want you to take a preparation course with Father Adamastor. It's really a good course—all the men are taking it, all the good ones, at least, and I want so much for you to do it, too. Marriage is a big step, we need to take it seriously. Promise me, sweetheart, that you'll do it . . . promise.

ROSA GIVES A PRESENT

First Prize: 200 million (after taxes). 01187.506. Drawing number 9. Twentieth block of tickets. Series B. Federal Lottery. There are two series, A and B, with 50,000 tickets each, and the winner will be decided by one single drawing. Winning tickets which are defective or torn will not be paid, and tickets must be presented within three months of the drawing. Decree #204.27.[1]

---

[1]Rosa said: "I don't have any money to buy you a wedding present, so I'm giving you this lottery ticket. If you get lucky and win, that will be my present, a pile of money for you. If you don't win, it can be a memento." (What's happening is that José, not having found another job, went back to Boqueirão where Atila and a new friend of theirs, Hero, were still hanging around. One afternoon José got married without telling anyone, not even us. He did it on a whim, he was scared but he thought it was now or never. He thought he half liked Rosa and half didn't, but he wanted to see how it would go. José has been married for one day.)

99

SOUTH AMERICA IS THE WILD WEST

Robert Panero, planner for the Hudson Institute, said yesterday at his conference at the Copacabana Palace that there are three distinct countries inside the countries of Latin America:

—Country A, or the urban area (which occupies less than 5% of the total), with twentieth-century cities and all their modern trappings: luxurious taste, big buildings, higher prices than Geneva, and even psychiatrists.

—Country B, or the rural area (which occupies less than 30% of the total), which is just emerging from feudalism and still needs Country A in order to survive. In Country B, if a child breaks his arm he will probably grow up with a defective arm because no one will know how to set it.

—Country C is the "wild west," another planet. The hero of the area is the pilot who arrives with the newspapers. Panero defended his thesis that in order for Brazil to assume leadership on the continent, the construction of lakes and dams in the Amazon area is fundamental. He also thinks that one of the factors impeding faster development in Latin America is the out-of-date moral code.

"Everything stays as it is. Other things may change, but not Latin America. And regionalism is a negative factor in all this. Countries are actually not even understood by their own citizens because internal tourism doesn't exist."

Continued pages 13–15 . . .

WHERE THERE'S A WILL THERE'S A WAY

The Minister of Security went on television and asked for the people's collaboration in fighting the recent wave of assaults. "We need all of you to react instead of remaining passive, note the assailants' facial features and apparel and denounce them, help the police to counter this wave of assaults, prostitution, smuggling, and narcotics traffic. Let's make every citizen a cop."

WHO COULD UNDERSTAND?

Remember the seesaw with respect to those stories about Rosa in Filhoda, her home town? I didn't want to tell you before, but I need to make it clear that José is still confused. He doesn't know if they're true or false. If they're true, he doesn't know if he should fight with her about it or accept it. If they're lies, then why didn't she say so? José doesn't know what to think, but he thinks it's kind of exciting not to understand people.

> A HONEYMOON IS A WONDERFUL THING
> There is
> in the city of Filhoda
> an ancient belief
> that the husband,
> if he really enjoys his bride,
> will be able to see her
> transparent
> the first night.

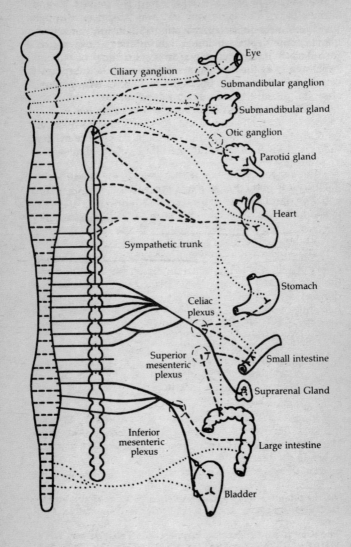

Eye

Ciliary ganglion

Submandibular ganglion

Submandibular gland

Otic ganglion

Parotid gland

Heart

Sympathetic trunk

Stomach

Celiac plexus

Superior mesenteric plexus

Small intestine

Suprarenal Gland

Inferior mesenteric plexus

Large intestine

Bladder

José touches Rosa, she wants him to, enjoys it, and shrinks back. The same way the Man had seen through José, José sees Rosa. Heart, stomach, lungs, intestines, glands, suprarenals, bladder, mesenteries. Rosa naked, José excited. José naked, Rosa getting excited.

They couple, glue themselves together. She thinks: now I can. Now he's my husband. Before it was wrong. But I shouldn't like it. Women aren't supposed to.

—Rosa, let's make love. I want you to really feel it.

Rosa is silent, she knows she shouldn't. It's the husband who's supposed to like it, the man, the mister, the master, the boss.[1] She should be his, for him to use and abuse.

—I need it lover, just you and me.

And Rosa thinks: I've already gone so far, I enjoyed it once before, that was bad, I should be my husband's, that's why I got dry, now José is my husband and wants me for himself.[2] He can do what he wants, that's what I'm here for.

—Smooth, delicious skin.

His hand on her thigh, José crazy with desire, feeling layers of cellulite, skin, a system: epidermis, stratified epithelium (variable thickness), nourished by the lymph—the dermis, connective tissue, structure, hair, follicles, pilus, hair bulb, sebaceous glands, sacs, fat, sweat glands, glomerulus, pores, sweat, nails, corneal epithelium, constituent parts, root, body, matrix.

José caresses, Rosa trembles, a longing coming from somewhere, trying to avoid it, desire, a fierce swelling going on down there, and José there at the door, hard, the need to be fucked, to suck (but I can never do *that*, it's not something for a married woman to do).

José sucks her breasts, Rosa moans, wants more, all over, his fast tongue at her ass, pink-colored, velvety skin, short black hairs with a red spot in the middle, José crazy to give it to her in the rear.

Rosa draws back, she advances and retreats, gets in-

---

[1] All the primitivism of the Latin American woman conditioned by traditions—religious, moral, social, political, conservative, Puritan.

[2] She went to confession and the priest didn't absolve her. WHY? WHAT COULD ROSA BE HIDING? IS THE STORY FROM THE INTERIOR TRUE?

volved and stops, opens and closes, like a guerrilla who attacks and slips away, shows himself and hides. They throw the sheets on the floor, José howls, screams, moans, bites.

(I want to kiss his dick, I want to)

Female Genitalia

External organ or vulva

Mound of Venus—large and small lips: furcula and mucous membrane—clitoris

Vaginal area: urinary canal and vaginal opening

Internal or reproductive organs

Vagina: mucous membrane, hymen, Bartholin's gland—viscous substance

Uterus: triangular form, located in the pelvic cavity

Ligaments

Ovaries

—Fuck, fuuuuck, son of a bitch, what a hard-on, shove it up your honeypot

(Say it, baby, talk like that, talk dirty, men can say what they want to, me too, fuuuuuck)

''the husband gives his wife what she is due''

Rosa extended her hand, took it back. Ten times she extended it, and ten times withdrew it. There was his prick, big, red, its smooth head, the opening wet on top. Her hand stopped, petted his belly and came back up, grabbed his ears, she was moaning, hearing her own noise and stopping, she shouldn't be doing this—while José was a festival of movement, running like a horse on a rough track, sweat running down, his body inflamed.

José's tongue was working, he felt what Rosa needed, wanted, asked for, she was getting wet, ''the mucus found in the vagina originates from glands in the uterine cervix. The epithelium of the mucous membrane is stratified in design, its cells presenting a certain quantity of keratin.''

(But why isn't she cooperating?)

His head buried between her legs, a wonderful strong-smelling place, her thighs squeezing his ears, fleshy vulva, Rosa groaning, like this, I like it, like that, do it more, do it, dooooo it, I shouldn't be talking, this isn't something to do with your husband, not for married people. José coming up from the valley (so green-black-red-brunette, my valley with its stream of come flowing through the middle) and putting his tool there, hard, and Rosa swallowing it whole

104

with the thrashing of her ass, and José coming and going, an excavating tool, opening, as men open the well to look for water, and Rosa seeing fire over her head, a yellow fire that consumes her toes, goes up her legs, and she's paying attention to the fire, forgets the pleasure, which had been violent at first, had passed, and now she scarcely feels the excavation in her valley, not pleasure or pain, nothing.

"Erection is not merely a local phenomenon experienced by the sexual organ but an extremely complicated process involving various glands and the nervous and circulatory systems. The first indispensable condition to erection is the stimulation of the cerebral cortex by hormones secreted by the sex glands. Also important to the process are the erectile nerves, leading from the erectile center to the sexual organs and ending in the veins, particularly the veins in the corpora cavernosa of the penis.[1] Normally these veins are constricted; under the excitation brought about by the erectile nerves they dilate, and blood streams into the spaces within the *corpus spongiosum,* thus causing the swelling of the member."

The cock (swollen) penetrates and withdraws. Rosa opening her mouth. Can't get enough air. She feels like biting José (they said I stood naked on the stage at the Municipal Theater, everyone looking at me, at my pubes, and I was ashamed of my black pubes, thought only *I* had them, that's why I begged the other girls to show me, and even when they showed me I didn't believe it, I thought we were special, our hairiness was ugly, I was never going to be naked in front of a man, until I found out men have them too, and that our pubes meet when we screw, but I was never going to screw in my life). She feels like crying, crying forever, because a beautiful thing is happening below her, but it's not hers, Rosa's, it's not something she wanted, it's like a prize (but a prize? for what, what did I do, I never did anything, this pleasure is in the wrong place, the wrong woman, it's too good for me).

—I want you to enjoy it, sweetie, can you feel it? Come on, baby, come on.

(Everybody says the same thing when they screw. The same things)

---

[1]Rosa read Fritz Kahn. Her mother gave her the book.

—Come on, Rosa, I'm holding back so we can come together. Let's take off . . .

(How do I know what they say? I just know. I'm taking off, all right, but forever, far from this bed, far from this prick, far from these screams on top of screams, yes, scream in my ear, suck me whole, eat my ass, imagine if I said these things out loud, what would he think, my husband, *whore*, that's what he would say, he wants me to have fun so he can explode later, insult me, think what of me, of my mother, daughter-of-a-whore, of a hard-on, that I liked to be screwed, laid, fucked, banged, a prick the size of a Mack truck scraping everything, a crane to wrench pleasure from me, a crane, because it'll take a lot of muscle, if I stop to think and let him go in and out, going in and out, if I stop this is what happens, if I yell, prick, prick, dick, big prick.)

/ the penis is essentially constructed of three cylindrical layers of erectile tissue wrapped externally by skin /

oooh, good, tasty, more, hard, stick it in me

/ the *corpus spongiosum* and the *corpus cavernosa* in a resistant membrane of dense connective tissue, the *albignea* / don't stop, stop, stop, I'm not ready, you can't do this to me, I like you, oh stop, but I wanted it.

you go away, on a summer day, if you go away

Male Genitalia

Testicles or gonads—scrotum—epidermis—deferent canal—seminal vesicle—ejaculatory canal: deferent canal, seminal canal—prostate—Cowper's gland—urethra—penis (cylindrical body, root, body, gland, prepuce)—sperm or semen.

if you go away

Larulagrape, trgodfr, cocobutto, plumbumpum, dawarekingdo, gdreooeyjjooi, juuuiooeo, adorable, fuckable, widawfg, snatchable, snatcheon, duffable, bluffeon, foblotto, grun, grun, grun, riguiriguiriguiriguiriiguiriguiertroertoriet rogrtujihnfgtyuoirriijjnagrerrrrerrrdohtuio.

—Was it good, lover?

—For me?

—Yeah . . .

(He's gonna trip me up. Right now.)

—Say it, go on, you liked it.

—You wore me out.

(What do I say? You're supposed to like it)
—Come on, talk to me. Or I'll be worried.
—Well . . .
—Was it good?
—Oh God!
(What to say, what to say?)
but if you stay
Then José hit her.
First, with the backs of his hands (like his father did). He hit her in the face, on the ass and thighs. He hit her breasts, her stomach.

After that, José used his belt. And Rosa moaned, she yelled, jumped up and ran to the other room, pissed all over herself. The hot piss ran down her legs and she cried and José hit her and Rosa ran and the piss ran down and the belt left welts and José smiled and Rosa smiled and José lay down on top of her on the floor and fucked her, feeling her wet thighs. And he took and licked Rosa, he licked her piss, cool now. And he fucked her again, and hit her in the face, and she cried and laughed, laughed and cried, in spite of not knowing if she should like it or calm herself down, wanting and not wanting it.

if you go away, on a summer day
Summer wine
Excavators exploring the valley, opening a hole in the red earth, the perforators going in and churning and coming out full of earth and suddenly that noise and the black oil coming up with a roar booooooooooooooooooom, all that black oil, thick, held thousands of centuries under the earth, roaring up and exploding there, spraying and falling like rain on the earth and the men, black mush diluted into droplets, while José yells and moans and screams and makes all that noise, what's this, my god, what a delicious cock, I'm going to like it, fuck everything, fuck what he's thinking, no, stop the music, if you go away, I hate Brenda Lee.

And José came out from inside her and hit her one more time. With his belt, with the backs of his hands. He picked up a book, hit her on the head, gave it to her in the nose, stood watching the blood flow, not even all the violence in the world resolves anything, it's not violence or anything else I need, what's necessary and inevitable is that I start to kill, to destroy, to tear everything to pieces.

107

(Almost. If I say a dirty word, if I tell everything I know, he'll like it, and I will, too, he'll see that I like it, need it, and it will be a good fuck)

—Laralaralaralarala, liguiliguiliguiliguilguilgui, hafta pay, hafta pay

—What?

—Nothing.

—Nothing, nono, zeno, zoro, nudo.

José grabbed her breasts, bit each brown nipple, each long spout, and went down with his tongue, down over her navel (a navel like Raquel Welch, son of a bitch this woman's sexy, fuuuuuuck), he came to her lips, thick and inflamed, he left his head there, as if it were a pillow. And went to sleep, with Rosa running her fingers through his hair.

He woke up hungry. Breathed in the smell of her sex next to him. The smell of past love. He'd been there, had already finished himself off, and she was ready to go at it again. There was lots of time left, "till death do us part." That was the smell of a fuck that would never be repeated; this was love. Not a single reminder of the past fuck, but always another one ahead, that's what to look forward to.

(Rosa's ass was brown, not white, I remember a white ass, right in front of me)

—Are you going to work?

—No.

—They'll fire you.

—They can go fuck themselves.

—But you'll lose your job.

—With no job I can spend all day here in bed. Fucking.

—Don't talk like that.

—Like what?

—You know.

—Fuck?

—Um-hum.

—Why?

—It's ugly.

—Fuck, screw, ball, red hot cunt.

—Shut up!

(Go on, say it, say more, say everything)

—Stop being silly.

—But honey, we got married to make things right, to have a nice life.

—Nice cunt.

—Cut it out, come on!

Rosa stretched out for an hour, José between her thighs, two o'clock, the two of them rolling around, at three, kissing and biting, at four, tongues in each other's mouths, at five, her dark ass, her pink hole, at six, lemonade and cookies, seven, him kissing Rosa's feet, her kissing his, eight, soft-boiled eggs, nine, José underneath, José on top, Rosa sideways, Rosa backward, ten, and ten more, twenty, twenty-four hours, a used and abused teabag, cheese sandwiches and a light headache, José's stomach muscles aching, tongue, thighs, cock, box, burning, their hands, mouths, toes, fatigue, and twenty-four added to twenty-four more, over and over, enough! we've already done everything, enough for a lifetime, no, we haven't done anything yet, wait and see what's next, what could be next, if we've done it all (and I'm a whore, just like all the rest, not worth a damn, and you're going to leave me because I let you do everything, but I wanted to, I knew all this existed, I read, heard, got around—no, I didn't *do* it, that was a lie, I just knew people did these things, things men do).

Six days and seven nights they stayed in bed. José wanted to get up and put a sign on the door:

> WORLD RECORD FOR FUCKING
> COME TO THE NUPTIAL CEREMONIES
> SPECIAL PRICE FOR ENGAGEDS AND
>   NEWLYWEDS
> 120 DAYS WITHOUT GETTING OUT OF BED

—You'd have the nerve to do that?

—Sure.

—To *do* it, in front of people?

—I don't know.

—Oh, sweetheart, let's do it again.

—I can't.

—Just once more.

—Not even once. I'm taking a shower, I stink.

—It's a good smell.

—Don't say that.

Poft, paft, pla, pla, pla, pla, pla, pla, aaaaiii, ai, ai, ai, stop, speak up (even that, say it), say whatever you want, do whatever you want.

Seven o'clock, Tonico and Tinoco stop singing and sign off, promising to be back tomorrow.

Trade bulletin: market price of bananas,
long-grain rice
corn

ON THE THIRD DAY HE WENT
TO HEAVEN

Behind the hotel there is a casino—closed. The last game over, the hotel remained, giant among the trees, no noise, no movement. Only these old women who meet on the terrace, afternoons before dinner, hair done, jewels on, looking at magazines, pictures of astronauts. "So brave, so handsome," they murmur. The astronauts smile, imbecilic faces on the covers of magazines, all the magazines of the world this week. The old men turn pages, come to the photos of the earth taken from space, and say, "It's a crazy world, people wanting to leave the earth for the moon—the moon is God's. God put us here, and here we should stay." I went upstairs to my room, first floor, facing the woods. Rosa was reading Delly, she'd crammed her suitcases with magazines and true romances. She didn't even look at me, reclining in her underwear, her tits hanging out.

ON THE SEVENTH DAY GOD RESTED

José, at the mirror. Seven days and seven nights without eating well. The exertion. Rosa, so fleshy, so soft. He started up again. Went for the face till the blood ran. He looked and saw the blood and tried to scratch some more. Chest, arms, legs, wherever his nails could reach. Hate, for the José in the mirror. A slap in the face, boxed ears, a sock in the nose. When we want to hurt ourselves we lack the strength, what a bunch of shit. Sexy-legged Rosa, a long scratch under her eye, a cut. Sassy Rosa (hard little buns, 20 years old, shit!) a nail scratch on that ass, slaps, plaft, plaft. Rosa, my woman, life-long companion, snatch always open for my cock, her husband's cock, the wife's duty, poft, poft, rrr, tooth and nail. José (Rosa) fell bleeding (dark, fleshy

Rosa) bleeding on the floor (I hate Rosa) still in convulsions (I love Rosa) and crying (while Rosa slept).

SMALL CRAFT WARNINGS

There are no small craft warnings.

SESQUICENTENNIAL

They stroll in the woods, on the paths, between the fountains and the hotel, mugs in hand, liters of sulphurous water; they're sluggish, trembling, blue or white robes over their flabby skin.

INSCRIPTION IN THE PRIVY
(graffiti)

In this lonely place
every conqueror stoops
every he-man grunts
every hero poops

EVERY BRIDE'S DREAM

In the woods behind the hotel there were packed dirt tennis courts, basketball hoops, asphalt for roller-skating, and a thatched shed for bocci. At the far end of the bocci run there were abandoned bathrooms—rotted grass roofing, blocked-up toilets, rusty pipes. Rosa and I went inside. There was a tiny stained-glass window. Once in a while horses came by carrying rheumatic old people along the path through the woods. I tweaked Rosa's nipples, playing around. It was something she'd liked ever since those little nips had been born—

—they were born and pronto she called the boys to come see and to suck and she'd been thrown out of the movies ten times for opening her blouse and giving one breast to each boy so they could play with the spouting tips as they grew—

—her nipples were enormous, jutting out from a dark ring, the sight of them got me so excited. The large brownish ring and that nipple getting hard so fast, while she went crazy with pleasure.

111

The spider came down from the ceiling on a thread. It went up and down, ugly, hairy. We were right underneath. Me, with the turbines of my cock all heated up. I just had to push up her dress and slip in. It was so easy to put it in her standing up. Rosa would open her legs, the way only she knew how, and magnetize my cock, sucking it, pressing it and letting go. The milk and honey I drank every day, morning and evening. What came from inside her was like the Cataracts of Ituabu, a flood of water rushing down from between rock legs. I knew from the first day I discovered it that this waterfall of Rosa's was a tourist attraction which should have been exploited by the Secretary of Tourism. A giant billboard, in color, to show off that bursting mound—

—her mother wouldn't let Rosa wear a swimsuit without fringe or a little skirt in front, because of the way it would show, making her the poolside attraction for all the boys—

I adored Rosa for her fat, healthy cunt, because I like things fleshy and abundant, overflowing. Things you can divide up, dole out, handle, heap the world on top of.

The spider would drop down slowly and then back up a bit, a deadly yo-yo with us underneath. Rosa was paralyzed, not even aware that I was thrusting inside her, violently. I could tell something was wrong but I didn't stop— even though it surprised me, since we've been so good together since the first day.[1] Neither of us had any scruples, or qualms, or thought anything was abnormal.[2] If we were on the field, it was to play, and in this game there were no rules, the same way there can't be rules in life. And we were going to win because everything was worth something to us, even the world blowing up. Sometimes she would yell: explode, baby, make it all explode along with us. What was wrong that day was this: my rhythm was off. The rhythm was the spider's. It went up and down leisurely and set the cadence of the place. So I started to rub back and forth slowly, letting it come all the way out, so I could dive back into that deep well which was asking for a three-way bomb to blow out everything from inside. And while I was diving, Rosa started sighing and twisting her head. She was twisting and I couldn't manage to kiss her and I liked to end

---

[1] José's lying. It was hard for them to get in gear at first.

[2] And Rosa was full of preconceptions; she thought everything was abnormal, and she always took a while to accept things.

112

up kissing at the same time. Rosa forgot all about the spider and coiled around me, scraping her feet on the ground, uprooting the moss. And from the uprooted moss came the smell of wet earth, rotting leaves, a smell of the stable—like the one in the nativity scene. We two, there on foot, also formed a nativity. Simple: two people, us playing all the parts, Bethlehem, the spider as the star, me bringing Rosa my gift, the greatest I could give. The spider hung over her head as she twisted with pleasure. She bit her hands to keep from screaming—there's never been a woman who enjoyed screwing as much as she does (never among those I've known, though my experience is limited to two women who liked me and dozens of automatic ones). Rosa watched the spider come down as I withdrew, slowly, in the same rhythm. I stopped, waiting for it to climb back up before I went inside again, but it kept on descending and landed on Rosa's face. She screamed then, I pushed everything out of the way, and she screamed again (a mixture of fear and pleasure), wrenching herself away from me just as I was coming, and we fell on the ground, little white jets shooting out from inside me, falling on top of her, and the spider was dropping further and faster, letting out thread from inside. Rosa didn't even grab her undies. She left at a run.

THOUGHT FOR THE DAY:
It's better to lose a minute in life
than to lose your life in a minute.

IT'S A GOOD THING THEY'RE LOOKING OUT FOR ME

Rosa came out of the changing room in her white bikini, ready to stretch out her mat in the sun.

—Madam, will you please come along with me.

—Come along? Where?

—To the inspection room.

José looked at the inspector in his yellow and khaki cotton uniform, black leggings, an MCI badge. From Moral and Civic Inspection, a Catholic-Protestant-Spiritualist-Baptist-Faith-healer-Jewish-Mormom-Seventh-Day-Adventist organization, advisor to the government on subjects of morality.

—What's wrong?

—The bikini.

—What about it?

—They're not allowed anymore.

—What?

—Since the tenth of this month. Women who expose their bodies provoke licentious and lustful feelings.

—How could this be? said Rosa.

—That's the way it is. First offense, a ticket; after that, prison.

—I can't believe it!

—While we're on the subject, are you two married?

—Yes, we are.

—Do you have the proper civil and religious certificates, the declaration of twelve witnesses, approval of your parents, a report from your police precinct that you got married of free will and not because you had had sexual relations beforehand?

FRACTIONS OF THE DAILY MELODRAMA

—Research done by A. de Carvalho shows that maintenance of armed forces costs $9.10 per person in Argentina, $18.53 in Portugal, $24.60 in Italy, $31.12 in Cuba, $75.52 in Switzerland, $79.45 in England, and $327.25 in the United States.

—What's that got to do with me?

"Oh, what does it matter to me! she murmured. How could he talk about such useless things when he could see the immense pain on that face, that face washed by fervent tears? Her sensibilities revolted. She took a few steps backward and asked, with an undisguised coldness . . ."

The Past
by M. Delly
(Les Ombres)

Tall, thin, pale-skinned Esmeralda Claudino, twenty-two years of

News Report from "Eleventh Hour"

age, told how her brother Aparecido was assassinated:

—It was 11 o'clock when the three men came up to him in the bar and asked for a cigarette. He didn't have one, because he doesn't smoke, and so they began hitting him. He went unconscious, I took him to the town's first aid station, and when I went back later, he was gone—no one knows what happened to him.

''Regina, who was nearby, sweetly clasped her friend's slightly tense hand.

Soul in Bloom
by M. Delly
*(La Jeune Fille
Emmurée)*

—Oh, poor dear! We understand very well that you're unhappy, that your grandmother treated you very severely . . .

Anabel's lips curled, opening into an ironic smile.

—Oh no . . . no, you who love, who take care to make other people happy, you can't possibly understand my life. My life! All alone these thirteen years, always alone.

Her voice became muffled, quivering a little. The pain was visible in her trembling face.

—Oh, poor dear! said Regina again.''

Her name was Djanira. She lived in Natal, Rio Grande do Norte, as a domestic. One day her employers realized they had been feeling uneasy about her.

''Up to the Minute''

—Listen, don't you think Djanira's voice has been a little deep lately?

From then on, they noticed more and more masculine features, and

115

after a month no one had any doubt: Djanira was a man.

The case was brought to the attention of the hospital clinic. They operated on Djanira, who has now become Djanílson.

Within a month Djanílson will be able to exercise male sexual functions, doctors have declared. He can even sire a family.

"The countess, dressed with almost monastic simplicity, seemed constantly to be tired; she was getting visibly and prematurely older, but there was remarkable energy in her eyes, and Marísia, staring at her, always had the impression that an unbreakable will sustained her, galvanizing that delicate body. The children seemed to take a fancy to their teachers to the extent that their preconceptions about caste allowed them. Marísia had had moments of intimacy with Guntran and Helena, in particular, which gave her hope that one day she would penetrate those youngsters' hearts, which she guessed to be noble and good."

The Golden Misery
by M. Delly
(Une Misère Dorée)

LUNCHEON MARKS OPENING OF FIFTH WORLDWIDE WEEK OF THE POOR. Invited guests and national and international authorities appeared at a luncheon held in the ghetto for the opening of the "Week of the Poor." The conference will concern itself with the problems of man's misery in the world. The menu included shrimp salad, fillet of fish, chicken

116

breasts, french rolls, and ice cream for dessert.

—Honey, you really ought to get some insurance, you know—settle our future. Lots of men are doing it, to guarantee their family's future.

Every Saturday José and Rosa go to the club, "The 23rd of May."

In the afternoon Rosa goes to the beauty parlor to have her hair done up in a bee-hive with lots of hairspray.

—Honey, put a little *glostora* on your hair, I like the smell.

She brought him the bottle.

Families with more than ten children will receive prizes from the government: they will ride free on city buses and suburban trains.

And so they would dance. José's not a bad dancer, in spite of his leg. He'd been to dancing school.

—Want to dance over there, in the middle of that crowd of people?

—No, I don't need to hide anymore. Let everybody see. I know I can do it.

José believed in himself. A cripple who had risen above his handicap.[1]

An anti-pill technique is now being used: they put a drug in large city reservoirs which neutralizes the effect of the pill.

—Stop looking at the girls.

—I'm not.

—You are too.

—Am not.

—I want to go home.

Outbursts of jealousy. Saturday after Saturday passing, let them, life can go fuck itself. There had been a time when José wanted to do something, but he doesn't know what it was. So he spends his days tormented, a pain in the chest, his head splitting. He'd sit in the same spot for hours, without getting up, afraid of going forward or backward, stiff as a statue.

(Batista, we've got to examine this kid)

---

[1] He should send his story to *Reader's Digest*.

—Another cuba libre.

—You've already had quite a few.

—No I haven't.

—You have too.

—Have not.

—I want to go home.

Daily drinking sprees

Where will José go?

(José, what a nice name, José(ph), the father of the Holy family, José(ph) who fled to Egypt, what nice names you women give your children)

They danced and danced. Rosa asked to stop, the sky was clearing, they were dancing in the street.

Dancing and singing (in the rain)

Why are you singing, José?

One day he sang for twenty-four hours straight, closeted in his room at the boardinghouse. Rosa wasn't home, they broke down the door, he was lying in bed, singing. He lost his voice, couldn't talk for a week.

—I want a little house of my own. Our own. So I can fix it up pretty. After all, why did we get married? The other day my father wrote me a letter asking if we'd moved yet, they want to come spend a Sunday with us.

Sunday with the in-laws: all they needed now was children . . .

(So, are the grandchildren on the way? Our little grandchildren.)

Sunday, a picnic by the roadside, at government picnic tables, yellow and black. A tablecloth, roast chicken, mixed drinks, bread, and afterward he'd lie down in the shade of the little forest, long live Sunday, the peace, the nation aaaaaaaaaaaaaaaaaaaaaaaaaaaaaaaaaaaaaaaaaaaaaaah, shit on everything!!!!

THOUGHT FOR THE DAY:
She who gets married wants a house.

SCRAPBOOK

The room tinged yellow, and not from the weak boardinghouse light. José, safe on the bed, so he won't black out. Rosa cutting up magazines and carefully pasting photos and song lyrics in a brown album. José smells shit, for just a second, and notices that everything on the stove is burning.

And he gets up and pisses all over her scrapbook. Rosa has the scissors pointed at his prick, red with anger, yellow (what's this yellow? I'd stopped having it, I thought it was over). Clic-clic-clic-clic, you don't know how lucky you are, the only reason I didn't cut you is that your prick is so pretty, the most beautiful I've seen. (So you've seen others?)

—You've got to stop this, Rosa, I mean it.

—Stop what?

—This cutting and pasting, collecting, for Christ's sake. I swear I'll kill you if you don't stop collecting things.

—Pfffffuuuuuuttttt. (She made a fart sound with her mouth)

Plaft, plaft, ploft, pacatum, pacatum, pimba, pimba, pimba, plaft, ploft.

—You son of a bitch, I'm going home to my parents.

—Go, you whore, horny bitch, fucking piece of shit—

—I'm going home tomorrow for sure.

—The sooner the better. Why not right now?

—No, not today, they don't have a TV.

THOUGHT
The outlaw refuses to surrender.
He's going to kill himself with a
    silver bullet.
The Death Squad wants to get him first.

A DOCUMINT FER THE AUTORITIES

They sealed off the entrance to Boqueirão. Inspection with a fine tooth comb. House by house, alley by alley, hole by hole. They were looking for hiding places, trap doors, secret entrances, tunnels. The place was crawling with a group connected to the Death Squad. The Death Squad itself was no longer a clandestine organization that killed people and phoned newspapers to announce the locale. After the article in *Life Magazine*, they were set up with a headquarters, special cars, uniforms covered with gold braid, medals, high boots, military caps. On their collar they wore the shiny initials DS. What power, and they didn't have to answer to anyone.

—On your feet, everybody. Up against the wall. Come on, faaaaast.

Atila dropped his pool cue, Zé ran for the door, Hero stood gaping. And that still left Clever Bull, Easy Lips, Furious Orlando, the Woodpecker, and the Human Wheel. They had been playing *Vida*, which had been declared illegal (Revolutionary Government Resolution 467), like all games with the exception of soccer (which, however, had to be played in long pants so as not to offend the morals of the women spectators). Boqueirão had never had police raids before because it was a tourist attraction which the police made money on, and the Squad too, and all the politicians. That's why "Celestial Billiards" existed: the largest poolhall in the world, with 3,200 tables. The only thing bigger than this billiard and amusement palace was the sky (for whoever can reach it).

But today the Squad was going around asking people to show all the documents they were required to carry by Resolution 789796: identity card, voter registration, work permit, police record slip, references, proof of residency, school diplomas, health form (vaccinations for yellow fever, malaria, polio), receipts for contributions to religious organizations (everyone should belong to at least one, there are 65,746 in the country), income tax receipts, conjugal conduct card, assistance to parents, old people, school tax, church tax, life insurance, certificate of sexual self-control, and so on.

José ended up being taken to the precinct. He was missing one document: proof of children's school attendance.

—But I don't have any children.

—You're married, aren't you?

—Yes, but not for that long . . .

—And your wife's been on the pill, am I right?

—Well, yes.

—It's illegal.

(Resolution for the Growth of the National Family, No. 7896578)

—So?

—Two months in jail for both of you.

In the penitentiary José met a man with a life sentence

120

for allegedly killing his son.[1] They talked, small talk.

—It's pretty tough out there, huh?

—Yeah.

Or they didn't talk. After he'd served his time, José stopped by the women's prison to get Rosa, and they went home.

And screwed.

—I screwed in jail, you know, said Rosa.

—You did? How?

—There was a woman there who liked women. So I let her.

—Was it good?

(Liar, I didn't get screwed at all. The woman sang to me, she sang, and I gave her a punch in the nose.)

ET IN PAX

—Those people you work with . . . it's embarrassing. I can't even tell anyone where you work. You're my husband, I want to be proud of you. But I just can't. My friends talk about their husbands, about their salaries, and promotions. They have good jobs in banks, stores, offices. They talk about their plans, and we don't *have* any plans, or a life together, we don't have anything. You live up to your neck in garbage, the world's garbage. In shit, I mean it, just plain shit.

José hit her with the backs of his hands.

—Garbage, garbage, who are you calling garbage? Normal people, that's who's garbage, and shit.

Rosa kneed him between the legs.

—Why don't you get a decent job? Give your family some security.

Once more, with the backs of his hands. Fingers in the eyes.

—Security, huh? Look, go screw yourself with your security, you and your little friends, you and your family.

Rosa slapped him across the face.

—Don't you talk about my family. Family's sacred.

(Sacred Family)

Slugs and kicks, jabs, José with a belt, Rosa with a shoe.

—Look, sweetheart, get this straight, I like where I work

---

[1]Could it be Carlos Lopes?

and I'm not leaving. Those people are really okay, they're people.

—It's them or me.

—Them.

—Then we'll be one, big, happy family.

They hit each other for two more hours. Then, exhausted, they went to sleep.

OFFICIAL NEWSFLASH

A drum roll. The herald went up to his station. In urban areas there were platforms every kilometer where heralds made public proclamations. The government also used television, radio, ad agencies, etc. (all anxious to get on the right side of the fence). The President gave a dinner for media people and directors of ad agencies. After dinner he asked those assembled to salute him. They did, smiling: Oh, what a joker. Ta, ta, ta, ta, ta, one salute after another. Then the President made them kiss his boots. What an incorrigible joker, they thought, sure we'll do it, on a lark, it's good for a laugh. You first. No, please, after you. No, I think the biggest agencies should go first. So the men from the North American firms bent down gracefully and kissed the tip of the President's boot. Just like that, one by one. Until it came to the biggest figurehead of foreign business in the country. He knelt down and looked at the glossy boot, shined it up a little, kissed the toe, and bit into it, throwing himself on the floor, asking to be walked on.

The government used newspapers and billboards, too. But it was decided that direct, sympathetic communication was best. The President adored old Hollywood films. He was an Errol Flynn and Douglas Fairbanks, Jr., fan, and his favorite movie was ''Robin Hood.'' He remembered that in those old movies there was always a herald who delivered the king's proclamations to the people.

And so the herald proclaimed:

My dear people. May the blessing of God the Omnipotent be upon you. In an effort to combat superfluous spending and luxury, to establish general equality in the nation, and with the objective of eliminating jealousy, rancor, and hate between brothers, we, your government, have entered into an agreement with all domestic shoe factories, whereby just one type of shoe will be produced from this day forward for the entire country, male and female. It will be a closed-toed, simple design, and will be available only in the discreet and attractive color black.

HERE I AM, LORD, DO WHAT YOU WILL

Independent Insurance Company

Medical Examination: this exam should be done in private, without the presence of an agent or third person.

Investigate whether the patient's immediate or distant ancestors had tuberculosis, syphilis, malignant tumors, gout, diabetes, alcoholism, nervous or mental ailments.

Family History

Please list age, cause of death, and duration of last disease for:

Paternal grandfather

Paternal grandmother

Maternal grandfather

Maternal grandmother

Father

Mother

Brothers

Sisters

Spouse

List the illnesses suffered since infancy.

Has the patient contracted any venereal diseases? Which, and how long did the condition(s) last?

Has he had, or does he presently have, syphilis?

When was it contracted?

Do you note sternalgia or tibialgia?

Has the wife of the insured had any abortions?

Has the insured undergone any surgical procedures?

Does he have a cough?

Is there blood in the spittle?

Does he have regular bowel movements?

Does he have pain when urinating?

Does he urinate frequently during the night?

Does he suffer from hemorrhoids?

Does he live with anyone who has tuberculosis?

Does he smoke? Indicate how many cigarettes or cigars per day.

Is the spleen noticeable under the ribcage?

Does he have anal fistulas?
Does he have static or active ataxia?

JOSÉ ANSWERS 180 QUESTIONS

—Is that all, doctor?
—Yes, for now.
—Can I ask a question?
—Of course.
—Why don't you go fuck yourself?
(END OF JOSÉ'S CLINICAL EXAM)

> BETTER TO SUFFER
> OR BE UNDER THE SOD
> THAN TO SIN AGAINST GOD

She was always in white. The apron from the Revolving Restaurant. Rosa wore it night and day and José thought of her as something white. And that got him excited. White, a dark girl inside white.
—Come on, let's go to the parade.
—I don't like parades.
—Honey, we've got to go.
—I'm not going.
—You'll get in trouble.
—So, you go, and take my card.
—That won't work. You need to go yourself.
There was a flag hung from the window. A plastic flag from the stationery store—purchased at a fancy price, since it's Patriot's Day.

Citizen,
Patriotism must exist inside each and every one of us. We must truly love our country. You and I and everyone must honor our national standard. May we be worthy of it. On Patriot's Day, put a flag in your window and participate in the festivities.
—I'd like a flag, please.
—One large and one small?
—Look, I only asked for one.
—You have to take two.
—Why?
—One for the house, the other for the parade.

124

—I don't go to parades.

—You have to go. Holy Resolution No. 7.

—That's news to me.

—The notice came with the Altitude Tax.

—I didn't even look at mine, I never look at those stupid pieces of paper. There are so many. My wife takes care of them.

Holidays: Patriot's Day, Soldier's Day, Proclamation Day, the President's birthday, the President's wife's birthday, the birthday of the goat who is mascot for regiment 11, a heroic group in the war.

The parades go on forever. The crowd, arranged in order of height, watches and applauds, spied on by the Special Police Militia. Lots of clapping and flag waving. José, 5'6", and Rosa, only 5' tall, are separated. In their pockets they carry their Parade Attendance Books. Properly stamped.

(An unstamped book can lead to tickets, jail terms from ten days to a month, ineligibility to leave the country, and difficulty in finding employment.)

José was sleepy, he'd been out late last night in Boqueirão. When the soldiers passed and a group started booing, he booed along with them. The police came out slugging and collecting Parade Books. Once a Parade Book has been collected, it is never returned. Your life turns to zero. José ran for it. He waited for Rosa at home, but she didn't show up.

GETTING READY FOR A
SUBLIME MISSION

—I really like him a lot.

Ermelinda, who is fifty-six, is talking about Malevil, a twenty-one-year-old student who lives in the room across from José and Rosa. Malevil is a friend of José's. With all the schools occupied by the military, Malevil has nothing to do these days. Rosa is expecting. Fat and happy. Always wearing the white apron from the restaurant, her Cuban sandals, dirty hair, her eyes smeared with make-up from last Saturday (Saturday is pizza and beer day and she leaves her make-up on all week).

The Practical Guide for Modern Mothers, 10 volumes. A fat woman with blond hair and green glasses and a pipe knocked at the door and sold her the entire set. (Duda Barreto, the most formidable salesperson of encyclopedias for pregnant women, wins first prize from the publisher.) Rosa bought something from every traveling salesmen who came along.

The baby's layette, his first days of life, following your child's development,

tangos, boleros, M. Delly,

breastfeeding, the general rules of nutrition, the regimens of diet and the collaboration between doctor and mother,

"when the halo of light reached him, Madel could see it more clearly, he had the impression that he was facing a moral and intellectual force which was imposing itself on him. A monumental interior energy must govern man's soul, purifying it."

—Rosa, I've read every single one.

—I'm just finishing this one.

—Is it good?

—Lovely, I adore these books.

"They talked at length about Bargenac, the grandmothers, and the people of Japanese heritage. There was intense emotion in Bernardo's eyes. Madel felt that his eyes were alive, felt that they knew, without her speaking to them, about the afflictions of her soul, about the solitude of her heart at the paternal hearth, rising up against Christ's law. Once in a while they would keep silent, as if immersed in profound meditation."

It was so sad, Rosa cried. And Ermelinda cried, too, thinking about Malevil.

Volume number three also discussed the child, his physical development, details relative to nutrition, hygiene, toys, and physical exercises. *The Practical Guide for Modern Mothers.*

—What do you think we could name him, honey?

—I haven't thought about it.

—You haven't thought about your own child?

—I've thought about him, just not about names.

(Do I really want a child?)

—But you've got to think about it.

—Let's leave him without a name.

—What?

—He doesn't need a name. When he grows up, he can pick one.

(I, for example, don't really like being José. I'd rather be

126

Hermano, Anibal, Marlon, Harry, Charles, Francis, Nero, Pascal, Lionel, Gazagumba, Metiolato, Viamit, Jadithe, Hepavitan, Hydrocortisone, Calcium Cetalyn, Aesthetic, Vaticano, Pentagona, Cowl, Callus, Shacko, Sarapui, any one of them would be fine. Pretty, nice-sounding names.)

—Are you going nuts?

—No, I really think it's a good idea. The kid will grow up and one day he decides—I'll call myself Windsor, Bragantina, Ripoff, Josefa, whatever he wants. He'll be grateful to us, you'll see.

THINGS GO BETTER WITH COKE

The mass was so long, I sat there on the pew feeling sick, I threw up the Host and everything, my mother hysterical, vomit all over the place, "Look out for the consecrated Host," the priest yelled to the Daughters of Mary and the Association of the Heart of Jesus, and they knelt down in the mess, they lit a candle (white, so white), the sexton came with a cloth, a bucket, and a squeegie, he cleaned up the consecrated vomit, he took the bucket to the baptistry, the priest followed behind him praying out loud, they threw the vomit in the tank where the holy water goes after it's been passed over the children's heads, everything was yellow, I needed to pee and I looked for the bathroom but churches don't have bathrooms.

Conversation in a taxi:

Malevil got a job at a nightclub in Boqueirão.

—What's new?

—I'm going to the States.

—Wow, just one month at work and already they're sending you on a trip!

—Lucky, huh? I'm supposed to pick up some tapes. We need to bring this country's music up to date.

LOVE IS BLIND,
SEES NOTHING

Catapim, catapum, pucutum, plaft, plaft.

—Security, huh? You fat cow, go find yourself some shitty security.

127

Bam, bam, bam, bam.

(I love you, I adore you)

—Go make your goddamned father secure, that SOB.

Rosa's getting knocked around again. She smiles, contented. Then she bites José, leans her head against his chest. José smiles, contented. They go on fighting, rolling around, they yell, they fall on the bed, on the floor, they get up, they break the room apart. José and Rosa are passionately in love.

A PRIZE IN EVERY BOTTLECAP

"Thanks to a strong armed forces, we are safe not only at home, but the most humble citizen is respected anywhere he wants to do business." (*Manuel Du Gradé de Cavalerie a l'usage des sous-officiers, Brigadiers et Éleves Brigadiers*, Paris, Siècle XIX.)

END OF THE YEAR: JOSÉ

"I don't think the last day of the year is sad because it's last, or because I see people happy and I'm not. I'm sad because I don't have any plans—so I'm going to the New Year's race. What kind of shithead gets off watching people run?"[1]

ROSA:

I've had this headache for days. And the sensation that I'm about to find something out. Who knows what. It's like having a word on the tip of your tongue and it just won't come out. You get so upset, crazy to spit it out. It makes you want to throw up, run, scream. The headache starts when José walks in the door. I'm almost positive

Those two are going to kill each other some day / I should call the police and get it over with / Go on, Malevil, go break it up, you're their friend / How could she be happy, poor thing, with a husband like that / He works in that horrible place, full of strange people, outlaws / The government should close that place down / Yeah / Let's call the police / Those two

---

[1]Like that phrase? Then it's yours.

he's hiding something from me. Or not even that. Maybe it's something he doesn't even know about, something that's going to happen to him.

need to learn to live like people.

JOSÉ:

I don't really like her that much. I mean it. I want to break up, but I never seem to be able to. I always think: today I'll end it. Then when I get home, we talk a little bit and I realize it's just the opposite. She laughs, I like it; she talks nonsense, I laugh at her nonsense; she kisses me, I like the kisses. I came home ready to break it off and suddenly I'm sure she's the woman I need, or like, I forget my doubts. There's some kind of valve in her head. Once in a while she tunes in to my wavelength. No kidding, it's strange, it's not just love.

MALEVIL:

Malevil is the world's first case of reanimation. Malevil spent ten years of his life frozen. When they froze his body he was nearly dead from an unidentified disease. They kept him in the hospital, frozen, and watched over him. In the meantime, his parents were killed in an accident and the relatives pounced on the fortune and forgot all about Malevil. One day, the doctors thawed him out, operated, and he came back to life. The newspapers devoted big spreads to his story, he was in all the scientific journals, they eulogized national scientific progress (Europe curtsied). Two things: Malevil doesn't remember a thing about his previous life and he can't eat anything which is either extremely cold or extremely hot, not even vegetables. For some time his nickname was Reanimo. But he was soon forgotten—along came brain transplants, the doctors always have some novelty to think about.[1]

---

[1] At least this is what Atila told José.

WARTIME

The truth was that world-famous Boqueirão had swallowed the entire northern and eastern parts of the city. A hundred roads went in, two hundred came out. Every house had a luminary, an attraction. The human oddities arrived, rented houses, and exploited themselves. The people who had started Boqueirão had lost control. They saw the attractions brought to television. The best of them were leaving, like the singing dwarf, and the perfumed opossum, the four-hundred-year-old chicken, and the woman with the face of a rabbit. But still more swarmed in to take their places, from all over the country, from all the Americas. And after the arrival of the normal man, people had started coming who had no oddity at all. That is to say they weren't abnormal, weren't monsters, they weren't even deformed. They were just sick, hungry, malnourished, miserable families with too many children. And the abnormal people were leaving, moving downtown or to other cities with their families; now that they had children who were also abnormal, a new race was being formed. The abnormals were leaving town. Every time an abnormal moved his family of little monsters into a new neighborhood, the families there, traditional and respectable, called the police, sabotaged their new neighbor, broke windows, made a lot of noise at night, and generally made life rough for them. So they'd move again. And the abnormals began to live in empty blocks and didn't associate with other people. Soon even more arrived, from Boqueirão, or the North, or the South, or from whatever country on the continent. Sometimes they took over whole cities, provoking an exodus, the streets clogged with cars, moving vans, traffic backed up as if it were wartime. It was.

THE CHAIN LETTER

—Sweetie, can I have ninety cruzeiros?

—Again?

—Who knows, honey, maybe we'll get rich.

—Oh, go to hell with your

This is the prayer: "I trust in God with all my heart to remove misfortune from my path. I place all confidence in Him." Attention Please! This is not a joke. Do not keep this letter. Copy it, enchain letters. There's one every week. I don't have the money to spend on this shit.

—Yeah, and what about the house?

—We're doing okay, aren't we?

—No. No, we're not.

—You wanna tell me why?

—You know why. Have you ever heard of anyone getting married and not buying a house? I want to take care of my house, my beds, my kitchen.

close ten cruzeiros, and send it to nine friends. It needs to be nine. Do this within 72 hours. This prayer has already been around the world four times and has brought luck to many people. Mr. Roger Karman became a millionaire after joining this chain letter. Mr. Demetrius Letera died in a mysterious explosion after breaking the chain.

—You knew what I was like when you married me. I don't care about stuff like that.

—You're going to have to change, then. This is no life, you've got to do something.

—Lay off.

—You need to set up your family.

—Fuck, I ran away from my family, what a bunch of shit.

—Don't talk like that.

Plaft, plaft, plaft.

—You can hit me all you want—today it won't work. Really. No way. I want my little house, all white and pretty, so my friends can come visit.

—You've got friends?

—Sure, the other waitresses are always saying: Rosa, when can we stop by your house for a beer? I want to invite my friends over—you bring yours around.

—Fucking shit. They call this life?

He closed the manhole cover, disappointed one more time.
What is it you're looking for?
José wasn't finding it.
(They probably don't even exist)
But they do.

SPECIAL, FOR EXECUTIVES WHO WANT TO GET OUT OF A RUT: WE OFFER COMPUTER SERVICES—ACCOUNTING, CHECKING PRIVILEGES WITH A RUNNING BALANCE, GUARANTEED FUNDS, PAYROLL STATEMENTS—AT A PRICE YOU CAN AFFORD.

—Zé, where did this photo come from?
—Oh, that. It's old. Belonged to my father.
—Your father kept pictures of naked women?
—This one he did.
—How come?
—He liked it. He liked it a lot. He was always looking at that photo.
—Odd. A naked woman without a head.
There was a stove in the background. The woman was standing at a door, with her head tilted backward. Her body was lit up, the face disappearing in shadow. As if it cut off her head.
José heard rumors that the Communs had surfaced in a neighborhood some distance away. Machine guns in hand, they were assaulting banks, armored cars, factories.
Rumor had it they helped people in need. Gave them money, brought medicine, managed to find doctors.[1]
—Gê? Gê goes around curing the world's sick people.

THOUGHT FOR THE DAY:
Charity begins at home.

Conversation in a taxi:
—Well, we really don't understand the stock market completely, but we're learning. It's a good way to make a little money.
—What do you do for a living?
—I'm a cabinetmaker.
—You play the market by yourself?
—No, there's twenty-five of us in on it.
—How much do you earn a month?
—Five hundred.
—Is there any left over?

---

[1] Legendary heroes always have romantic images.

132

—I put aside twenty to play the market.

—And it works?

—Yeah, it's beginning to. I'm getting the hang of it. I do okay.

—Really?

—Look, in one year shares of the Banco Principal appreciated 674 percent. Belga Metalworks went up 157.3 percent. The trick is to buy stocks in several companies.

—How many kids do you have?

—Six.

—What time do you get up?

—Four o'clock. So I can get to work by seven.

—How many years have you been working?

—Twenty-one.

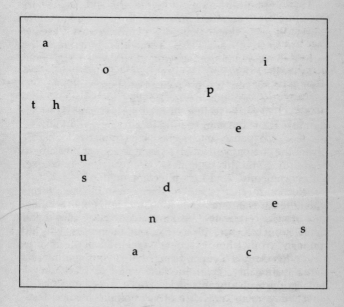

HOUSEWIVES WANT HOUSES

—You'd like to buy a house? Certainly, sir. Then we'll help you buy an excellent house. One of the very best.

The realtor was wearing a suit (Buy your suit here and get

all this free: extra pants, a key chain, a chance to win a trip). Talkative, ingratiating, syrupy, repulsive. (A PR man.)

José sat down. The seat was extremely low. The realtor looked down at him from his desk.

—We have sensational plans. Everything made easy. Not much money down. Great credit terms. You know, sir, our organization promotes the well-being of the family. More than twenty thousand people just like yourself have come to us already. But (a long pause, a smile, a finger pointed at José) you were one of the chosen ones, one of the ones selected from the twenty thousand. Congratulations, José. Our criteria of selection is rigorous, perfected, inexorable; we choose only the best of the best. We enjoy the confidence of the people. Of the government. Of the banks. Of the Residential Cooperative, which is the official organ created at an opportune moment by the firm and decisive action of our very dignified president. But as I said (another pause, the same finger pointing, a smile, greasy Vaseline hair, the smell of Aqua Velva, a smooth-skinned face, the perfect shave—with this shaving cream you could even shave with a hatchet), you're here because you were chosen. I envy you. It is my pleasure to personally, *me* personally, give you this news. I'd like to be—you know what?—I'd like to be feeling the happiness you must be feeling now. Heart pulsing, beating for joy. But, you know—I feel good, too (pause, an absorbed, contemplative look: rule 7 from the company manual)—yes, it is a great pleasure to be affording you this happiness. Not really me, of course, but my company. And I am my company.

(Selection means: papers to sign, questionnaires, forms with little boxes, financial situation, religion, political affiliation, fitness certificate, residential certificate, ideological certificate, work card, please list four references, why do you want to buy a house? what do you think of the government's Residential Cooperative? what is your age, marital status, nationality, color [declare white or black only—mulatto, brown, and mixed blood are considered black], voter registration, certificate of vaccination, medical testimony.)

I passed. That means I passed. This whole pile of shit, just to be selected. Like the college boards—an enormous crock of shit, an exam, which I passed—but I was excessed. No more spaces at the university, sorry. After I'd already passed. The third time it happened I told them to go fuck themselves. If they've got this crap of excessing here, I'll break the bastard's face.

—Fine, you're ready for the final phase now. From here on it's easy. A snap. The Cooperative was created to make you feel secure. We just need to take care of the paperwork. Read these pamphlets. Everything you need to know. Everything, everything. If you have any questions, come back and see us. Would you like to go see the houses first? Personally, if you want my opinion, I wouldn't bother. You don't need to see them. The photos are there on the wall. The blueprints are over here. You can choose your ready-made house from the plans. Make yourself comfortable, take your time.

The plans were all the same. Identical. Three hundred pages, ten floor plans per page. Not a variation. The company man, impatient, José looking over them plan by plan. He asked for a ruler, made measurements. Asked for paper, did some figuring. He chose the next to last one.

—All right, let's get this settled.

—What do I do?

—Do you already have financing?

—No, not yet. That's what I've got to take care of now.

—Good. I should tell you a few things. Financing can be arranged in various ways. Yes, indeed. Through the Savings and Loan Association, or through the Real Estate Credit Society. Four hundred minimum salaries is the legal limit of financing for a piece of real estate valued at less than five hundred minimum salaries. Or, you can arrange it through a public bank. That way the legal limit is twenty minimum salaries for a piece of real estate valued at less than four hundred minimum salaries.

—I know, I know . . .

—In any case, financing will depend on the family income. If you earn less, you can arrange financing which corresponds to a monthly percentage of 20% of your income. If you earn more, it can go as high as 30%. Let's say you and your family members earn five hundred cruzeiros per month, the financing should be calculated so that the monthly payment is between one hundred and one hundred twenty-five. That's the way it works, so that your payments are based on a realistic assessment of your income, without the least bit of sacrifice.

135

José chose the next to last house plan.

—A good choice, yes, a fine choice, it feels good to sell to someone who knows how to buy, to choose well. I'm very pleased. Remember, my name is Eloy, I'm at your service. If you'll excuse me. We hope to count on your confidence in the future. It's been a pleasure. Let's have a beer together after the closing, huh? Blah, blah, blah, blah. Atta boy. Toodle-loo.

A house of our own. A little house just for the two of us. Oh, darling, it's terrific. I've dreamt about it for so long. It even has a room for the kids. Let me see. Oh, it'll be pretty, I'm sure. We'll paint it light blue with dark blue trim. Whitewash the garden wall. Oh, wait till I tell Mrs. Conceição, she'll die of envy. Stay right here, honey, I'll be right back.

Rosa ran through the boardinghouse from room to room. José watched her: flip-flops, hair in pincurls, a white kerchief around her head. He remembered that it was Saturday, she'd want to go out, downtown, see a movie (if there's one with Sarita Montiel, so much the better), they'd have pizza and a few beers. Later, when it was time to go home, Rosa would buy bags of pumpkin seeds, cashews, chocolate-covered peanuts, and a couple of Arab sweets. The night table in their room was always full of little sacks. Saturday was her day to stock up. Weeknights, she nibbled and read M. Delly.

—I'm going to rent an iron so I can press my dress. Tonight we'll celebrate.

Rosa went to iron her clothes (two cruzeiros to rent the iron). José looked over the pamphlets from the Residential Cooperative.

"Attention. Pencil and paper in hand. If you want, call in the whole family. This is how you figure out how much of your income you can spend on buying your own home. The first step is to compare income and expenditures on a monthly or annual basis."

THOUGHT FOR THE DAY

But, shit, why should I own my own house? Who says we need all this? Why don't I just break it off with this woman? Why don't I kill her? Oh, I'm not going to break up with her, or kill her, either. Every time I see her knees, every

136

time she moans, embarrassed (but wanting) to moan, lying there in bed, I know I won't leave her. If I let her go, there wouldn't be anyone else. If Rosa wants her own house, her own hair dryer, her own can of shit for that matter, I'll manage it somehow, that's the truth. I'm not going to agonize over it or ask myself a lot of ridiculous questions. That's the way it's going to be, period.

For three days he thought about it.

The following three he meditated.

Then three more days of hard logic.

And finally: money. Money. Where's the money going to come from?

There isn't enough money.

Sure there is. Somewhere there is.

But where? In strongboxes, banks, investment houses, pension funds. In a thousand places, in guarded safes. For other people.

Why don't they divide up the money among everyone? There would be more than enough to go around.

Boy, are you stupid, Zé Gonçalves. Stupid, that's your middle name. Divide it up. Ah, ha, ha haha heeeeee hoo. Until he had an idea.

If I don't have any money. And if I don't have a job to earn some money. I rob it. For sure. I rob it, it's that simple.

AH, WHAT A TASTE FOR CRAZINESS YOU GET FROM AN ORGANIZED LIFE

Yes, fine, but come back in a few days. Interviews, exams. José stands in line, ten, thirteen hours, a line that goes around the block. And the lines are getting longer. The newspapers say it's the unemployment, the politics of debate. Industry and commerce aren't hiring, they're firing.

Interviewer on TV: why aren't there more jobs?

Manufacturer: it's not our fault, we've got a rope around our necks, the banks aren't financing, the government isn't lending, there are new production taxes, we have to support the fight against communism inside the church, we pay our share to the leagues to defend democracy, morals, patriotism, we have to spend money on flags, banners for company cars with civic sayings, "Your country—love it or leave it," etc., etc., etc., etc., etc.[1]

Hunger. Beggars and peddlers coming from everywhere. Fancy-talking lawyers selling yo-yos which glow in the dark, mice on a string, petrified fish, executive pens (three for a thousand), bags of limes (a dozen for only fifty centavos), religious figurines, helium balloons, cigarette lighters, homemade goodies, cheap perfume, banned books, key chains, socks, rings, eyeglasses, medallions, kaleidoscopes, potato peelers, rulers, pencils, erasers. Doctors selling pennants from door to door. Agriculturalists washing cars. Architects supervising the construction of huts in shantytown.

The lines for social services were growing by the day. There were fights every night in front of the cheapest hotels, under viaducts, bridges, around the doors to office buildings, doors to churches (the strongest taking over and selling a spot to the weakest for a cigarette, a go at the ass, or a shot of brandy, and the priests arriving with the police: away with you peddlers, out of the house of the Lord) : a place to sleep.

Beggars, vagabonds, the unemployed, hordes of people going through the city's trash cans, in every city. Houses invaded, thieves arrested for robbing pantries, corner stores and supermarkets protected by contingents of police. Everyone wanting to go to jail where at least they won't starve.

Couple grazing alongside creek attacks fellow grazers with bared teeth.

Employees dismissed. Dismissed employees killing their bosses.

Priests praying, begging: My children, trust in God and He will feed you.

NEWS

Extremely well-armed soldiers are guarding the banks in the northern sector. Their weapons consist of: .45 caliber INA machine guns, .22 caliber long-range rifles, .38 caliber Taurus revolvers, tear gas bombs.

---

[1] Interview subsequently condemned by the censors and interviewee arrested.

eight at night / streets / stadium doors, open / lights out / grass gone, earth dug up : they're re-doing the lawn drainage / a car goes by / ten minutes later, another / pissed-on flights of stairs, the streets above and below / big houses, mansions / closed: doors, windows, gates / nobody / a black guy watering the plants, the smell of damp earth / a station wagon turns the corner, the screech of tires / an ancient garden—rosebushes, dahlias, zinnias, snapdragons, mums, flashes of light in the middle of the flowers / maids carrying on in the bushes / houses closed up tight / signs: 1936.

—Hand over all your money. And make it fast.

Waving the toy revolver in the guy's face. He had been about to put the Galaxy in the garage, but instead got out. José acting like he's talking with some friend.

—Come on, the money, hurry. I want all of it.

The man, in his fifties, with a rotting face. He took out his black leather wallet (I hate wallets, if I had a real gun I'd kill this guy just for using a wallet). The man opened the wallet, removed some small bills. He handed them over, and showed the empty wallet. José grabbed it, took out the documents—I.D., credit cards, bank identification.

—Not the documents, please, leave them with me. You can keep the money.

—Got any more? Sure, you must have some more here someplace. You give it to me and I'll give you back your papers.

José twisted his mouth to one side, as if he were going to spit. His cold sore was bothering him. Like it always did when he was nervous. The victim stared at him, trying to memorize his face.[1] So José spit in his eye.

—Come on, where's the money?

The man stuck his hand in his pocket and took out a thin bankroll.

—The rest of it, and fast. I want it all.

José tore up one of the credit cards. The man reached into the glove compartment and took out another stack of bills.[2]

Then he leaned on the horn.

----

[1] For the police drawing.

[2] These rich guys cheat on their income tax, you can just imagine.

José bashed him in his rotting face, but the plastic gun didn't do much damage. He took off—and the man ran after him. José stopped, opened a gate and dashed into a yard. He climbed the garden wall and ran through the next house out to the street. He saw the man talking with a group of people. They all went inside. José got in the Galaxy and sped off.[1]

PROCEEDS FROM THE ASSAULT

Money from wallet	$	210.00
Money from pocket	$	150.00
Money from glove compartment	$	700.00
Total	$	1,060.00

The next day José went to a bank and opened an account, taking advantage of their offer: *Deposit your money with us—The only safe place to save money is in the bank—We make it easy for you!* He bought a newspaper, the man had reported the incident but hadn't recognized the assailant. José was pleased. (It's best to wait 'til you're twenty-five to start pulling robberies, you have a cooler head.)

Here are some precepts José came up with on the basis of his accumulated experience from several assaults:

1) Stage a series of robberies every day in the same area, then change course completely and do only one. Keep it varied.

2) Avoid letting the victim get a good look at your face.

3) Use cunning: pretend to limp a little.

4) Breathe like an asthmatic.

5) Pretend to have a hacking cough.

6) Pretend to have poor eyesight; bring the money right up to your face for inspection.

7) Throw in a few words in Spanish, la plata, caramba, etc.

8) Spit out of the side of your mouth a lot.

9) Wear heavy shoes.

10) Dress well for a while, then dress poorly, wear an ac-

---

[1] Incredible how easy it is to pull off a heist these days. Any days.

cessory which calls attention to itself for a couple of days, then change it.

11) Don't pull any jobs for a few days, then start up again, quit once more, do two in a row, go a whole month without doing any.

12) Always put the money in the bank. Withdraw it little by little and keep putting it back in. Make friends with the manager. Request a loan. Keep the payments up to date. Keep making deposits.

TO WHOM IT MAY CONCERN: New York (UPI)—Safecrackers these days are taking advantage of the latest technology. Most recently, they have been discovered using a tool made for construction and repair work, called a "Thermal Bar," which is sold in any hardware store and reaches temperatures between 2,500 and 5,000 degrees centigrade. In less than ten minutes, the "Thermal Bar" is capable of opening a hole five centimeters in diameter in iron or steel a full meter thick. Police are not hiding their concern about the availability of this tool to any thief—it's cheap, too—because it can even neutralize an alarm system.

PROCEEDS FROM RECENT ASSAULTS:
JOSÉ'S MEMORANDUM

Guy in car on Bresser Street .... $	34.10
Woman coming out of bank .... $	100.00
Badly dressed man on Paulista Avenue .... $	23.00
Turk's residence (the one who didn't speak Portuguese) .... $	3,000.00
Miscellaneous (watchman, rich boys, etc.) .... $	350.00
Old balance .... $	1,060.00
Total .... $	4,567.10

Observation: I've come to the conclusion that I should be careful assaulting women. The ones considered honest always scream; the whores carry razor blades in their purses, and are not easily intimidated (let's just hope they don't find Sonia's body).

TO WHOM IT CONCERNS MAY: Members of the military, directors of banks, and representatives of police groups who attended a demonstration of American-made bullet-proof vests the other day left somewhat confused. One of the bullets from an INA machine gun penetrated the vest, injuring the model. But the Army vest's efficiency was also demonstrated. It is made of steel, weighs twenty-eight pounds, and was used with great success by the most elite North American troops in Vietnam.

Hands over your heads / everybody in the bathroom / this robbery is now in progress / machine guns in hand / tellers taken by surprise / bills / coins / stick-up men leaping the counter / fearless hearts / We're not subversives / Then who are you? / How will we ever be able to identify three mulattos? / the search for the mysterious owner of the car / the money in sacks / people in the bathroom / lower your hands now: you could be a little more polite.

Robbery number ten.

(This is going awfully slow. No kidding, in this city nobody carries money anymore. Everybody's robbing people these days, the competition is heavy. Only people who really need to should steal. The way things are going, just wait and see, pretty soon everybody will need to. The other day I decided to try robbing a cab driver. When I got in and gave him the address, on a really long street, he opened the glove compartment, pulled out a gun, and laid it on the seat next to him. And on the mat, within easy reach, he had a lead pipe. I figured I better not take any chances. Plus, the guy had two strategically placed mirrors and was watching my every move. I did my smooth, upper-class routine, really genteel, to distract his attention, but it didn't work. He told me he'd been assaulted twice by well-dressed men, one was supposedly a banker and the other a teacher—wonder if they really were?)

Ten o'clock at night. José ducked under the overpass. He walked down the street near the old funicular station—old whores—hooligans—boardinghouses—a tire shop—auto parts—a dancing school with a green door—the soccer field where soldiers from the National Guard play—he hears women behind peeling doors: come on in, come on—dingy bars—an inner courtyard, a bus terminal with drums of black oil—a modern, tiled chapel—walls with writing on them: "Post no Bills," "Down with Imperialism"—"Hard

Times Kill Hard Workers''—parked cars—a house with wide open windows—cardboard valises stacked on top of a wardrobe with mirrors on the doors—night watchmen—display windows with thousands of tires (*it was during the war, I was eight years old and I was rolling a rubber hoop along the street when a man from City Hall came and said I had to give up my hoop, my ball, everything I had that was made of rubber, because of the war, that I'd be helping the soldiers, but I didn't want to, I didn't care about the soldiers or any old war*)—a white shack—glass doors showing off a model of a building under construction (easy installment plan, buy your apartment now).

A samba group practicing, the music drifted out into the street. All he could do now was wait. Ten o'clock. Any minute now the man should arrive with the package. For two weeks José had been following the numbers runner. He always goes out at three p.m. to make his rounds, from the back seat of the same 1938 taxi, black. The clients know the car. It's the one that double-parks, and they ask: You free? If no one asks, it means the coast isn't clear, police nearby, and the car pulls off. When the numbers runner is done for the day (between ten and eleven), his driver drops him off at the tenement, a tottering three-story building (condemned as illegal construction), which is home to a few miserable families and a hide-out for several local cat-burglars. He goes up to the third floor and closes himself in. He stays there, with the lights out, for several hours and then leaves, nothing in his hands.

The man was coming out now, and got on his bus. José went along, too, as far as Water Park. The man stayed on the bus. The smell of cowshit came from the direction of the park, some exposition of animals. José got off and took a bus back. He had a guava ice cream (homemade, the best around) and went on to the tenement. There were bums sprawling in doorways, a drunk throwing up, children rummaging through the trash, a night watchman taking a piss while his sweetheart waited; there on the corner a car was blazing, people crowded around trying to get a look at the driver trapped inside. Constant yelping from a pack of dogs. José went up the stairs (washed by piss, vomit, booze). No lights. The rooms were all open, for ventilation. Children crying, chickens clucking on the stairs. People gathering—all the neighbors in one room—to watch televi-

143

sion (VIA SATELLITE): the astronauts landing on the moon, the legs of the module releasing slowly in space: a silvery spider—astronauts' footprints in moondust—silence—the silver spacesuits—the absence of wind—images without brightness—another astronaut twirled in the sky.

José stood at the door—
(I'm standing on a point on the earth which appears on the screen. What a ridiculous lie, the earth doesn't exist, I don't exist, nothing exists, it's all imagination. All of a sudden I don't feel like stealing, I don't feel like doing anything, I want to throw up everything inside me, stomach, heart, lungs, spleen, liver, intestines, kidney, bladder, pancreas, glands. Empty myself completely, and swallow that dry, hollow moon made of plaster.)

THE ASTRONAUT IS READ-ING THE BIBLE
(It's hard to see clearly, there are two areas, one black and the other white; the white is the soil on the moon, the black is the sky, and these two men walking in awkward jumps and us here below finding it hard to imagine that they're thousands of miles away, in another world. It makes me feel weird—as if nothing matters. Or everything is even more important than I thought. These men are not alone, they're being followed by a billion pair of eyes. Such immensity, without anyone. Now I'm sure something is happening. Changing. It must be, it's not possible.)

144

The show's over (NETWORK SIGNING OFF), women shouting, someone singing boleros, one, two, cha-cha-cha, rah-ta-ta-ta, ta*bum*-pah. On the top floor, José got out a hair-pin and turned it in the keyhole delicately, as if he were inserting his finger in a pussy. And the door opened, like a woman opening her legs, and José went in, worried, a little nervous, electric. He entered the darkness. Alert for what he was looking for, without knowing what he would find, like a prick against the vaginal membranes, going in and pulsing and moving everything around. (And suddenly he felt a bright yellow like a thousand yellow flashes and it was just for a second and then the desire to steal came back, and also to kill and to set off bombs and to make the earth fly, blue, in a thousand pieces, the splinters getting lost all over the universe, going into orbit; and even though the earth will be smashed to pieces, in the pieces there will be plenty of people, or pieces of people, and these people, or pieces of people, will reproduce, and there'll be not one but a thousand blue earths peopled with people, or pieces of people.) José turned on the light: a chest, boxes, newspapers piled up to the ceiling, a safe with a quart of milk souring on top of it, eggshells, a figurine, an oil painting, a bottle with an appendix floating in liquid, old shirts, a blender with the brown leavings of an old milkshake, old '78's. José toppled the pile of newspapers and found a hole in the wall and, behind it, a telephone. He picked up the receiver. It was connected. (They must call in their bets from here.) He made a note of the number, and changed the record. Bienvenido Granda, singing "Angustia." He kicked over the rest of the newspapers and found some pornographic pictures, a pair of underpants, and a shiny red coffee table. (Son-of-a-bitch, there's no money in here!) Then he remembered the movies he'd seen and the books in the "Yellow Detective Series" and started looking under the floorboards. (Once more, life imitates art.) There was a loose plank, and a packet of money underneath. (These people who play the numbers play for low stakes and with old bills.) He closed the door behind him, leaving the record player on.

At the door to the boardinghouse—four thugs.

—Hey, kid. Time to give us a rundown, don't you think?

These guys were big. What did they want, who were they?

—We followed you from over there. So this is your hide-out.

145

—What hide-out? (Who were they, who were they?)

—Upstairs here. Not bad. Not a bad fucking job you did, either. How'd you pull it off?

(Uh-oh, now what do I do? What do they want?)

—Come with us, fella.

There was a car at the curb, a Volkswagon (real life, but just like in the movies, turn the page, tune in next week, don't miss the next installment of our thrilling police story).

WHO CAN THESE FOUR MYSTERIOUS CHARACTERS BE?

PLEASE

Human Solidarity Service: we have a man here who left his ass in a taxi and can't shit anymore. He would be grateful to whoever finds it. Please don't eat it.

BETRAYED: A SENTIMENTAL MELODRAMA

—But they need it. It's "gold for the good of the country."

—Give them something else, Mom. Not your wedding ring.

—They need the money to fight communism, son.

—They're lying, Mom! It'll just go into their pockets.

—Dear God, help me, what a lack of faith. If the priests are asking, it's because they need it.

—Okay then, give it to them, give them your wedding ring.

HOLY RESOLUTION

The herald proclaimed: from this day forward, men shall take only black taxicabs, and women shall take the yellow ones.

MOBILIZATION TO CAPTURE THE CRAZY DONKEY

The police are recruiting cowboys to assist in capturing a donkey who has gone crazy. The animal attacks women who go to do their laundry at Italiaño stream. Veterinarians say the donkey is suffering from encephalomyelitis, which

146

is common in herbivorous animals and consists of simultaneous inflammation of both the encephalon and the medulla, provoking disturbances which are difficult to cure owing to the seriousness of the wound.

—Hi, nice to meet you, I'm Atila, and I'm pretty good with a lasso.

—My pleasure. I'm a bullfighter, they call me El Matador.

THE PAPERS TO GET THE HOUSE

The realty agent approved the papers. The secretary typed up the contract. José signed. More papers appeared, José kept signing. Five hours later, he was finished.

—You are now the lucky owner of a house in Jardim Assunção, the biggest and best residential unit in the country. Only a government as active and dynamic as this one could handle the housing problem this efficiently.

> OFFICIAL NEWSFLASH
> Record companies have until one month from today to liquidate their stock of profane music. After this thirty day period, only sacred or patriotic music will be allowed.
> *Holy Resolution no.* 5463789 j78a

Rosa dropped the Alka Seltzer into the cup, it bubbled, and she lifted the cup to her chin: "to make it tickle, it feels so good."

The Alka Seltzer went on tickling her, Rosa went on laughing.

—Come on, Rosa.

—No. Not tonight, I don't feel like it.

—Come on.

—No, I don't want to.

Plaft, plaft, plaft.

—You son of a bitch. I'll cut off your prick.

—Come on, you cow. Come fuck your husband.

—No.

Pimba, catapim, catapam.

—Ah, ah-ha, ha, ha, ha, ah . . .

José took out his cock. Rosa closed her eyes.

—Come here, kneel down over here.

—You're a pervert, a degenerate, I'm going to report you.

—Let's see a piece of your little ass.

(He doesn't know it, but I put out a lot of ass when I was young.)

—No. *No, no, no* . . .

—Give it to me.

(I'll take a chance. If she goes for it, I've got it.)[1]

ROSA GETS A PRESENT

The station wagon cut across white streets, passed white houses, identical, identical lamp posts and telephone poles. Incredible traffic, as if it were a national exposition. Women in the streets gesticulating wildly, laughing, yelling, chattering, hens clucking hysterically at their chicks. Happy owners of their own homes, no more rent or landlord or late payments. They kissed the garden walls, they knelt down in front of the gates, they fondled the walls of their houses, they squealed, laughed, sang at the windows. Station wagons went by with loud-speakers: the government is happy that you're happy. There were banners, colorful flags, music. Rosa was beside herself.

—Do you think our house will be as pretty as the others?

—Should be.

(Why shouldn't it be, since they're all prefabricated from the same molds, sizes, prices, comforts, coziness?)

A festival of domestic joy everywhere you looked. They passed one corner where a housewife had thrown herself on the ground, kissing the threshold, her arms extended like a Muslim inclined toward Mecca, praying.

—It's this one, said the agent (consulting a little map with letters and numbers).

ROSA PENETRATES THE HOUSE

Rosa brushed her hand over the gate ("It's already dusty, we'll have to clean it"), leaned on the door ("Mine, mine, all mine"), and turned the key, overjoyed (a satisfied customer) to see the newly painted house, white in the sun (a white light that hurts your eyes), windows shining, cheap

---

[1]Which goes to show: there's got to be dialogue.

oil-base paint, the house: impeccable, smiling, satisfied, like a shoe polished up right before being sold, too perfect, too shiny. The house offered itself to Rosa, letting her penetrate it, Rosa's pleasure and the house's pleasure, the smell of fresh paint, sanded floors, varnish, turpentine. José went behind her, pushing the door open, welcome, the house is small but the heart is large, the house is made of rocks and the hearth of love and tenderness, I'm the man but my wife's the one who gives the orders, God protect my home (José beginning to vomit).

AND NOW, THE WAR: JOSÉ BOMBARDED

Don't you need a working blender, with a plastic cup you can throw out the window from ten stories up and it still won't break, because it's made out of the same plastic used in the cockpits of American rocket ships?

Don't you want to buy some gorgeous furniture, with classic styling—it's just fabulous—in dignified mahogany?

Couldn't you use a dual-drive dishwasher which does the whole job in just four minutes?

Don't you want to own this electric knife set?

WHAT IS IT

—Full during the day, empty at night.
—I dunno.
—A shoe.
—They work together, but never meet.
—The wheels of a car.

Many Thanks
TO THE BABY JESUS OF PRAGA
For grace received
Yolanda

Rosa went up to Yellow Square, there was a line in front

of the corner grocery, it was the only one in the development: one market for four thousand houses.

—Now, this is how I can make some money.

—I'll buy your magazine, sure I'll buy it.

—I'm going to sell it in bus and train stations, at soccer games, in lobbies of movie theaters. People like riddles.

—Yeah, I like it, I'll take one.

Malevil, his little notebook in hand, wandered the neighborhood all day, collecting riddles for his magazine.

"Left to right, I'm like Othello,
plain and easy to see;
but you have to spell me backward
to get inside me."[1]

Gigantic billboards filled the square around the grocery, looming in vacant lots, on the sides of buildings, wherever there was space.

Rosa lugged her bags full of canned goods, felt a pang in her head. She had been shortchanged, the cashier must have made a mistake.[2] Rosa stood in the middle of Yellow Square.[3]

She was looking for transportation, a bus, a taxi, anything. But she saw only cackling women, making friends, neighbor to neighbor.

"Come to the Sanctuary of Charity."[4]

Not one car, nothing. And her headache was getting worse.

"When you enter the sanctuary you will be soothed."

The women were smiling at her, looking for complicity.

"Come receive light from on high, come, sister."

A station wagon with a loud-speaker turned into the lane. Paraguayan harp music. At the microphone, a man with his mouth dripping saliva was shouting in an ardent voice: "It's time to think, brothers. It's now or never. There will

---

[1] Moor / room.

[2] Don't kid yourself. She did it on purpose.

[3] The Residential Cooperative intends, in the near future, to build more squares in various colors, according to presidential guidelines, dividing the neighborhood into social classes.

[4] The Sanctuary of Charity charges an admission fee for the faithful to enter and be soothed. Inside, they sell candles, indulgences, relics, and good luck charms.

be no second chance. Come, join us. Leave your worldly affairs behind, light a candle and your prayers will rise with the radio waves right up close to God, carrying with them your worries, your needs, your requests.''

Rosa just stood there in the middle of the square. Her eyesight blurred, she tilted forward, about to fall. A man saw her and grabbed her by the arm. Rosa wanted to go home. Was it the second or the third block? Maybe she would recognize the corner. No, they were all the same. Not one point of reference, just white houses all in a row. It should be down one block. It wasn't. Ten blocks, looking and looking. Maybe she'd recognize a neighbor. She didn't. Empty blocks. She was in the heart of the development, the sun beating down on the white houses, hurting her eyes. She asked directions, other women opened their eyes in surprise.

One of these houses is mine. She marched up and down, she turned, she doubled back, around and around, twisted this way and that. Sidewalks of gray cement, cement paving stones, the yards all so many feet wide, blue windows, yard-high fences: like an infinite mirror in which the development was reproduced a thousand times.

Then she saw two women. Where can my house be? they each asked her. And the two became ten, then a group of twenty, soon a hundred clucking women, shouting, laughing, wide-eyed: bzzzzzzzzzzzzz, they murmured. Where's my little house? and how much butter do you put in? and my street? how much Jell-O? where did that street go? and my flowerpots! Does it call for evaporated milk? They walked up and down, they ran up and down, beat well in the blender: two whole eggs and two yolks. They spun around, they got acquainted, a tablespoon of brandy, one cup of flour, sifted, then you put all the ingredients for the dough into the blender, there's a doormat in front of my house, so pretty, all green, it matches the blue, and now where is it? Where's my house? Chopped onion, green pepper, one chopped pickle, and the women who always stay inside at their doors and windows, afraid to go out, run upstairs to the roof, from where they can see a desert of roofs, red roofs, red sun beating down, sun, nus, uns, INSTRUCTIONS: cut open the packet of Jell-O, and the women at the windows run inside, frightened of being swallowed by the multitude/maze/labyrinth-without-end, and the clucking women, laughing, yelling, running around in circles, then put the dough in cold water, white houses in the sun, streets crossing and countercrossing, one house, a thousand identical houses, a thread for the maze, foolish women: they're like crazed ants the day the warrior ants grow wings, all afternoon looking for their houses/hearths /home-sweet-homes. Serves six.

THE BOMBS EXPLODE NEARBY, REACHING JOSÉ

Don't you want to buy a transistorized, battery-operated TV and an electronic tape recorder-record player-crystal set-transmitter-and-receiver?

Wouldn't you like to buy a shiny new silver faucet that sterilizes polluted water?

Don't you think you could use a gas-electric-wood-atomic stove?

Wouldn't you like to buy a refrigerator which keeps food for up to ten years?

Or Eternal Lazer lamps?[1]

YIPEEAAAY, YIPPEOOOOHH

In those green fields live cheerful herdsmen, frontier farm hands with Brazilian Indian blood.

HERE COME THE PATROLLERS OF THE NIGHT

Modern man is well-informed—Nakedness with no more secrets—Live the good life, shave with Endless Blades—with Philishave—the cadaver went to the morgue and the criminal to detention—the Pope smiled when the synod contested his authority: the church should be governed by committee?

Bam, a violent blow from the back.

—Documents, your DOCUMENTS.

José showed his papers. The soldier was almost a kid. Two-foot-long club in his hand, machine gun slung over his shoulder. He was bent over from the weight of it. He made a terrible face and shouted.

(He must be enjoying himself).

—Go on, go, GET OUT OF HERE.

---

[1]Eternal, nothing. After two years they burn out.

The Northern Patrol Operation in action. Little kids just barely of draft age, proud of their authority, full of their power, vain about their machine guns, bold, they patrolled with impunity. They had responded to the ads which promised weapons, vehicles, prizes for the number of people apprehended.

That's how they had gotten Malevil. They burst into his apartment, threw the books on the floor, planted a gun on the shelf, took some pictures, and put the handcuffs on. Malevil was in for two months.

José stood there with his documents in his hands. He was shaking. From nervousness, from rage. When they come at you, you can't think about anything, even whether or not the train is going to hit you or turn off to the side.

He slept all curled up in a tight ball. He tossed and turned violently in his sleep. Rosa complained: you're always kicking, it's like you're being attacked. He always woke up with a headache, he needed exercise. Twist to the right, left, front, back. He had lower back pain, he woke up with a bad crick in his neck. One night he wet the bed.

Someone threw an egg out the window of an apartment building and it landed on a patroller's head. They shut down the building, arrested all the tenants, old people, children, sick people, everybody.

Who threw the egg?

Then they closed down all TV and radio stations. Just two channels and two official transmissions were left. Official communications came over the TV at 9 p.m. A tape, some sort of registering machine, marked whether or not a given set was on. It was better to have it on, even if no one listened. But it was better to listen. Suddenly they might knock on the door, round up the whole family, and give them a test on the latest official pronouncement. When you least expected it they would come check the tape. If you missed one day:

Penalty of one to six years in jail; no trial.

At nine o'clock the whole country stopped dead, people sat down in front of the TV, notepads in hand.

People without television listened to the radio. People without radios were supposed to go to their neighbors, or to the park whenever the herald made his appearance.

MEANS OF COMMUNICATION

Once upon a time there was a master of ceremonies . . .
Once upon a time there was a man without legs (to be continued).

BOMBARDMENT

Wouldn't you like to own a typewriter with seventeen different typefaces?
Don't you deserve a brand new car, with a big fat zero on the odometer?
Wouldn't you like to buy a Readjustable Treasury Bond?
Don't you think you ought to buy television insurance?

ROSA LOSES HER APPETITE

When Rosa isn't hungry, she doesn't feel like sleeping with José. One day she lost her appetite completely. José called his mother-in-law. "It's normal, don't worry. It's happened ever since she was little. She'll get hungry again, it's just a 'stage.' " It took a week. Her appetite came back with her period. And for José, that meant another week doing without. "No, José, not now, it's too sickening." And when it was over she wanted to wait a few days more, until everything was all cleaned out. She spent half her time at the bidet, washing herself. She hated blood, she thought it was a punishment.[1] Until the day she was finally ready and waiting in bed. Uneasy, thinking it was a sin, after all, while he manipulated her, and she watched it grow, she put it into her mouth, swallowed it whole. And the moment she swallowed it she calmed down, as if the act itself somehow bestowed absolution. José was so silent tonight, she wanted him to talk, she wanted him to talk without stopping. Rosa had a special way of moving the muscles in her vagina. It was as if she were a virgin, sucking him in for the first time. José kissed her red mouth, smeared with lipstick. And how she yelled, that fleshy, gorgeous thing.

---

[1] In this day and age, how could she think such things?

TEMPERATURE UNSTABLE, SUBJECT TO RAIN AND THUNDERSTORMS

Denounce a terrorist or a subversive, and you get a point on your card. Points will be tallied and counted toward job promotions, priority in official bank loans, purchase of houses and apartments, credit availability, discounts, income tax, half-price admission to theaters and movies. Those who have a lot of points when they are arrested will have special privileges such as private rooms, lawyers, *habeas corpus*, better food. The execution of prostitutes began yesterday at six o'clock in the major cities of the nation. It is part of a campaign to exterminate vice, announced the Minister of Social Well-Being. In an interview he emphasized that this does not reflect an inhumane attitude, since all of the women have a chance to reform and be converted. If they accept, they will be set free and trained to work as nurses or social workers, but they will be required to confess and take communion once a week, at which time the priest will stamp the cards they must present every three months at the police station nearest their homes. Prostitutes who refuse reform and conversion will be shot. The great majority are not going for it. So the whores die at dawn. This law concerning prostitutes is even more comprehensive: clients who are caught in the act shall be arrested and brought to trial. The married offenders will be shot for adultery, while the single ones will be sentenced to from ten to twenty years in prison for vice.

WHAT IS IT

1—I have hands, but no fingers;
   no bed, but lots of ticks.
2—Newlyweds' favorite salad.
3—You ought to keep it—
   after you've given it away.
   (Answers in the following pages)

FRAGMENTS FROM THE BOMBARDMENT OF JOSÉ

Wouldn't you like to buy a table which has nothing exceptional about it?

Wouldn't you like to own a collection of books full of blank pages? That way you wouldn't have to read them.

Couldn't we interest you in an anatomical quilt?

Wouldn't you like to buy a fork which carries the food to your mouth without your having to lift a finger?

THE REVELATION ABOUT HERO

I can't take any more of Luzia Bullet's parties.

Luzia Bullet was shot twice. They never found out who did it. For years she bragged about the shooting, saved the bullets. She showed them to her lovers, and one of them stuck them up her ass, so for a while she was called Luzia Bullet-up-the-Ass. She had a habit of organizing parties at other people's houses. She'd call up and tell one person to bring a pizza, another a bottle of whiskey, someone else Coca-Cola and ice, and so on. Luzia knew El Matador. El Matador knew Atila. And Atila was the one who had the idea.[1] He decided that they should inaugurate José and Rosa's already inaugurated new house.

José was right there when the cheese got smashed. Later, El Matador had to scrape off a piece of papaya which stained the wall yellow. Beans, rice, pieces of meat, a wedge of pie. Everything went flying. At the kitchen door stood Hero, tall, dark, with a Mexican mustache, throwing food at everybody. Like a gag on TV with banana cream pie.

—Uh-oh, Hero is on the warpath again. It's been a while since he had a fit.

—A fit of what?

—He has a heroism neurosis. There are people with war neurosis, you know. He has a heroism neurosis.

The story went like this: "Before the coup that overthrew the last liberal government, even Hero was a good guy, and talented. He wrote well, he composed songs. There was one song people were singing all year. Hero went all over the country organizing centers of popular culture. He got a whole bunch of them started, too. Then there was the coup, and everything got all fucked up, remember that crazy time, everyone fled or went into hiding, waiting to see what would happen next. Then we got the news: Hero had been shot. Executed. Shit, was that a shock. In those days, beat-

---

[1]Things are much simpler than we imagine.

ings and arrests were common, sure, but this life of death—executions, torture, disappearances—that hadn't started yet—Ah, Spain, Portugal, Greece, Russia, the U.S., Czechoslovakia, Algeria, Argentina, Colombia, Bolivia. Executions were something new, were too much. So everybody considered the guy a hero. They talked about him a lot, he became a sort of local Guevara. Really. Today it's comical, but in those days everybody considered the guy a hero. A martyr. A legend. The girls who'd gone out with him went into mourning. It was an honor. The guys told stories: 'the day Hero came to dinner,' 'that night we were talking, I just knew he was going to die a violent death,' 'Hero had been coordinating guerrillas for the whole continent, you know—he was going to be commander of terrorism.' Until one day Hero turned up. He came back, full of himself, to the places he had frequented. The wave of jailings had passed—that first period, at least—people were coming out of the woodwork. It was months later, and it was something, I'll tell you. Like being run over by a tractor. What deception! It was too much. Here was some guy in a bar bragging that he'd been in the same gang in the old days, telling how Hero had resisted arrest, had been tortured and shot, and the character suddenly appears on the spot. Hero wasn't a hero! It was really depressing. Hero had run so far away, had hidden so well, that no one found him. And he hadn't even seen the papers. So when he came back and went around looking for his old pals, people got sullen, shit, *furious*, they gave him the cold shoulder. He didn't expect it. I guess it was kind of shitty of them, but the gang needed a myth, people are romantic. (It's only now they're changing.) And Hero could sense their disappointment, he found out about the whole story, the execution, his glorious legend. And he wanted to kill himself, he wanted to die or turn himself in. They were still calling him Hero but now it was a joke. The unrealized Hero. It was all downhill from there, he just couldn't bring himself to do anything, he started getting violent, aggressive, pushing people around. Like this business of opening the refrigerator and throwing food at everybody in sight. He loves to throw food at people when he's having a fit.''

WHAT IS IT (answers)

1—A clock.
2—Lettuce alone.
3—A promise.

BOMBARDMENT

If your family deserves strawberries, they deserve strawberries with A & B milk.

Don't you need a camera to capture all those happy moments as they go by?

Buy a heater, an exhaust fan, buy a window fan, buy a trash can, buy a cake-mixer, a magic circuit-breaker which turns on the lights without your fingers touching it, buy a C & G television antenna, buy all new lamps, buy furniture, sheets, lawn mowers, towels, buy silverware, buy a shower curtain, carpeting, buy everything that has no use at all.

Atta boy, atta boy, walk for Daddy, come get the candy.

A SHORT SOCIAL CALL

Good morning, Madam. I'm from the Political Police. Here is a card you and your husband should fill out. Then staple on two 3 x 4 photos. This little plastic bag is for a copy of the key to your house. The brown envelope contains a Judicial Order for the police to enter your house legally at any moment. Make sure you don't lose or misplace it. When one of the agents needs to come in, he will knock, ask for the court order, and only afterward come inside. Thank you. Oh. If you lose the court order, the penalty is three months in prison before you can get a second copy. Have a good day, Madam. Respects to your husband. And God bless.

FREE ASSOCIATION

I stole pens and notebooks and erasers from Navega's stationery store and he didn't suspect anything—we'd say, Mr. Navega, can I see that pencil? and he'd turn his back to get it and all we had to do was stick a hand on the shelf and grab something, until one day his brother-in-law was spying from a hole behind the book rack and saw who it was snitching things and went to the high school principal, and me and Amaury almost got expelled but I got detention instead, every afternoon I had to sit on the porch during recess, I'd watch the line of girls leave class and cross the porch on their way to chapel to pray and by the time chapel was over so was the afternoon, night had fallen and only then did they let me go home. My father talking to the principal and my mother dying of embarrassment, I was a scholarship student because she was a friend of the principal, the two of them had sung in chorus together, and I was afraid to even look at my one-year-old brother because he didn't make any trouble at all, wasn't a little thief and didn't make everybody ashamed of him, he wasn't going to be expelled or get punished on the porch or be looked at by the girls as they left class on their way to say their rosaries, ah, I really liked that Marilene Vierira, she was so pretty and she had lots of scrapbooks.

FACTS

They trail in, trail in like cattle with their wagons, freightcars coming down from the plateau, their clothes are permeated with copper dust, they're old at forty, undernourished, sick, withered, and with their withered wives and famished children they fill the immigration rooms.

UNDERGOURND (And not underground)

—I'm Juan, I wanna talk to Gê.

—Gêêêêêê, the Puruvian, Juan, is here.

Gê and Juan shake hands (The Americas united, united they will win). Juan's great-grandfather and great-great-grandfather were shot in the Plaza das Armas, they didn't live to see independence in 1821, but they fought for it.

Juan: greetings, friend. (He shakes Gê's hand.) Juan: a creole from Piura, whose father had just one piece of advice: Put one foot forward only when you've got the other planted firmly behind.

Juan: from a family of miners, mined copper for Cerro de Pasco (an American company); his father retired at 35, lungs full of copper, from working twenty-five years in the mines.

BLISS

We were married and couldn't care less about anything else. We'd take walks, drink coffee in dirty, smelly bars, eat sandwiches in sordid taverns. We'd sit and watch people come out of the fancy-shmancy snack bars, going to the movies and strutting up and down. We hated the movies, those fake figures moving across the screen speaking rehearsed lines. We'd look at the posters and we'd think: actors must be awfully unhappy living lives that weren't theirs, suffering suffering that wasn't theirs, loving people they didn't love, pretending to be happy about things that don't make you happy. We were so happy-go-lucky, Rosa and me, walking the streets without worrying about anything. If we ended up a long way from home, we'd take a taxi and we'd be all over each other in the back seat and the driver would get grossed out and ask us to leave. We weren't embarrassed, the world could go fuck itself.

OFFICIAL NEWSFLASH

The government has the great honor of announcing that nothing abnormal is going on. The people need not worry. The Americans have asked permission to install a military base up north which will give them access to all Latíndia America. This base will be a so-called trampoline for the actions of the "New Alliance for Help to the Latíndio People" and will be very important, because the North Americans will pay in dollars and bring up the exchange rate. Calm down, everyone,[1] don't think of this as an invasion or even an appropriation of territory, but just a little help from our friends.

The Americas United, united they will win.

SONG

Rocket ship, rocket / an ultra-legal mission on the docket / and the cosmonauts / watch the ceremony / Rock it, ship / linking the moon and our patrimony / the moon and our

---

[1] The President to his aides: Anyone who doesn't calm down, wipe them out.

patrimony / linking all humanity in the ceremony / and the child with no face / a rat ate the child's face / it's the first case / the very first case / and the rabbits / little rabbits / big rabbits / they gave them cigarettes / filled with narcotics / rabbit shit cigarettes / narcotics / naaaarrcotixxxxxxx.

DOCUMENTARY

—Would you tell us, please, why you broke windows and started stealing things?

—No, sir, it wasn't me who broke the window. When I got there it was already broken. Smashed. All busted up. So I went in. But I didn't steal anything, no sir. I just carried a few things home. Things I needed.

—What did you take?

—A cake-mixer, a blender, a toaster, and a hair-dryer.

—Do you make cakes often at home?

—No, sir, I don't. Because to make a cake you need milk, eggs, and butter.

—And the hair-dryer? Why did you take that?

—Well, you know . . . it makes a sort of hot wind, I really like it. On a cold day you can turn it on and point the wind at yourself to get warm.

—You said before that you didn't steal anything, you just "carried a few things home." But if you take something that isn't yours, isn't that stealing?

—Well, those things weren't exactly mine, no. But let me tell you something. About a year ago when that store opened, everybody in the neighborhood bought stuff—on the "easy credit plan," they called it. I bought a blender because my wife wanted one real bad. She'd seen some ads, and really liked them. I also bought a TV so we could have a little entertainment at home. And then comes this problem of the bad unemployment we're in. I still got no job. So, anyway, I missed two monthly payments and I went down there to explain why. But they didn't want to hear about it, they came and took the television and the blender and everything. And they didn't even give back the eight payments I made. No job and no TV. So I figured they owed me something, and I was just being, like, compensated. But I only took what I thought was fair.

—Thank you, my friend. This is Maltone, here, your roving reporter from Team 2300, with the most complete coverage on the airwaves.

ENTERTAINMENT

—Wanna go watch the races?

—Shit, again? Every night, the same old thing. It's a drag. No one's gotten killed for over a week. Let's find something else to do.

—You find something else. After eleven, that's it, the clock chimes and nobody even wants to think about going out.

—The *cruisers* do. That's why I like them.

—So, let's give it a shot tonight. The cops said they were going to give 'em hell.

There was an eleven p.m. curfew. Sirens would scream all over the city, and anyone seen on the street was arrested, or gunned down. The cops didn't bother to ask questions.

All because of the Communs: one night a Shell gas station exploded in the suburbs; ten minutes later, dynamite blew open a bank; at the other end of town a police station was taken over, prisoners released, cops taken prisoner, guns liberated; at the same instant, the sentries at a military base were shot, their rifles and machine guns stolen. And there was also a fire in some public building every night. You never knew where the fire would be. The government didn't have enough manpower to cover the city. No one wanted to go out on neighborhood patrols anymore. The bases received notes: send out your men and we'll shoot them down. After eleven, anything that moved was fair game.

The Communs distributed pamphlets, put up posters, spray-painted walls. They had a mark, a sign, which identified the group (were they a group or a platoon or a batallion or a whole army?). It was a small, horizontal line with four legs.

After eleven, people got together at home and gambled. In three months of curfew, private casinos had grown a hundred-fold. José and Rosa had been invited dozens of times to an eleven o'clock gaming date in the neighborhood. The bars were actually small hotels where the customers drank as late as they wanted and afterwards slept

162

right there. Each building had at least one apartment with prostitutes.

The *cruisers* cruised the brand new streets without intersections. The police were right on their tails but didn't do anything, just watched. The *cruisers* were sons of judges, lawyers, military men, sons of the rich, of people in government. They were saying: we want to have a good time. Just driving around wasn't enough. The real fun was in the roulette game they played on the viaducts over the streets. One gang raced, another group stood above the viaducts. The ones overhead would calculate time and distance and when the cars passed underneath they dropped rocks, trying to smash the windshields below. The thrill for the drivers was this: at the instant the windshield shattered, to maintain control of the car, keep a cool head.

> The Secretary of Health reports: every night
> a million cockroaches die in this city.

Atta boy, atta boy, walk for Daddy, come get the candy. The shot didn't make a sound.

OFFICIAL NEWSFLASH

My dear ladies and gentlemen!
The herald farted. He had a big pot belly which wrecked his otherwise fine physique—the result of years of vigorous exercise. But he had cirrhosis and farted a lot. The herald was up on a platform in front of a microphone. The microphone was hooked up to loud-speakers installed in all city parks and transmitted simultaneously to the interior as well. The same thing on all the airwaves. The fart heard 'round the world.

My good people!
Everyone knows, yes, everyone knows, that we are the nation which spends least on its armed forces in the whole world! What do you think? Aren't you pleased to hear that?
He farted again, silently this time.
Each citizen contributes just two and a half dollars a year toward defense costs.
My good citizens, you can see that this is not right. It's just not right. That's why we are an undefended nation, at the mercy of anyone who might want to attack us.

163

Your government cares about this. Cares about all of us. And is therefore preparing a formidable defense plan, which will cost us a little more, each and every one of us.

From now on every citizen will contribute ten dollars annually for the maintenance of the armed forces.

Another fart was on the way, but he held it until he got to his car, where he relieved himself noisily four times.

NO HALF MEASURES

One of the officials of the Batallion of Morality grabbed Rosa by the arm, while the other measured the length of her skirt with a ruler.

—How do you explain this? It's two centimeters shorter than the law permits.

—The seamstress must have made a mistake.

—Are you sure?

—I gave her the right measurements, the ones in the decree.

—We'll see about that.

The seamstress showed the order form for the skirt.

—I did it according to the paper.

—You knew it was against the law.

—But the order form is stamped by Post #16 of the Public Decency Department.

One of the officials made a note of this. He arrested the seamstress. They went along to Post #16 and arrested the person responsible there. And they took all three to Headquarters 145 where, as a warning, they were kept for two hours naked under a cold shower.

Exclusive in this issue—
Emotion, violence, the supernatural:
What strange things are going on
  in the cemetery?
DON'T MISS IT! A TRUE STORY:
The Bandit of the Yellow Rose

OPEN THE WORLD,
I WANT TO COME IN

I stuck the gun in the guy's face. He was walking along, I was standing under a telephone pole, and all of a sudden I yelled. He thought it was a mugging. He raised his hands

164

and waited for me to say what to do. I just thought: "He's a piece of shit." One straight shot. His face opened up, but the blood didn't start flowing right away. You could see the hole in his temple, the skin ripped open, broken bone, brains.[1] Then the blood was running, filling his face, and the man fell. I wasn't even scared. I shot him and stood there watching. I knew I was going to remember this. It was my first time and I'd promised myself that I'd watch carefully. Then I blew on the barrel of the gun. I didn't really mean to, but I felt like it, so I blew on it. Like in the movies.

CHECKUP

An explosion, as if I had been shot with a thousand little bullets. The world roared, filling with rays of light, a yellow so intense I couldn't look. Even with my eyes closed I could see the yellow. Inside of me. My body leaped with the shot, heart racing, pulse soaring to 180, I felt my left toe going numb.[2] And my vision expanded. I could see 360 degrees. Just what I was looking for. The shot also made me vomit. Not from the stomach, but from the head, from what was in the memory, deep in the cerebrum. Memories stampeding. Me, in front of the cadaver, without a past or a present.[3]

IT WAS FASCINATION, I KNOW

A certificate. You get one when you complete a course. Now I had one. Mine had a picture of the man's head with the hole in it, skin ripped open, broken bone, brains. I really didn't deserve the certificate until a month later. I kept wondering whether it had been a mistake to expose myself like that, under the light. But the street lights were so weak that no one could have recognized me.[4] Finally, after about a month went by, I gained the composure of a man who kills with impunity. I tried to go back to the exact spot where I'd killed the man,[5] but never could find the street.

---

[1]José didn't actually see any of this. He was shitting in his pants.
[2]Which toe on the left foot? It's not clear.
[3]What does that mean?
[4]Nowadays they have mercury vapor lamps.
[5]The criminal always returns to the scene of the crime. I don't want to be an exception.

The way the plots had been secretly parceled out, the neighborhoods got all confused, there were no maps or anything.

STAND UP AND FIGHT

I've been standing here in the same place for days. Rosa's off visiting her mother in the interior. I don't have the energy to take a step. I want to, but I don't want to move. I'm not moving. I'll probably be like this for about three days.

MEANS OF COMMUNICATION

The master of ceremonies was smiling . . .
The man without legs was unemployed (to be continued).

THE PROGRESS OF SCIENCE

"Our team of scientists has discovered that the happiest chickens lay the best-tasting eggs."
(We interrupt this note for an official message.)

TEMPERATURE UNSTABLE, SUBJECT TO SHOWERS AND THUNDERSTORMS

The nation is calm.
The congress has been closed. One hundred state and federal representatives have been imprisoned. The military's gains are increasing. Police have received a new type of foreign gas for use during repression.
Book burning continues every night in the main squares of all cities, to the strains of religious hymns.

THE PROGRESS OF SCIENCE

In addition to supplying the chickens with a special diet, the scientists left them in the open air, scratching here and there in search of worms or whatever food most appeals to them. They are happier this way, and lay better-tasting eggs, compared to those laid by chickens . . .

FORGIVE ME, SOMETHING JUST OCCURRED TO ME

José asked himself what the motive for his crime was. And what if there wasn't one? José's problem is a lack of clear-headedness.

THE PROGRESS OF SCIENCE

. . . as we were saying, compared to those laid by chickens which have been confined in chicken coops.

The loud-speaker on the van repeated the message every five minutes. After a little while, the van stopped in the square and riflemen made sure the line was kept orderly.

It was chicken day.

Every week they brought a van full of chickens and gave out one to a family. Thus the people would have a steady supply of eggs, and they were allowed to kill and eat one chicken per week.

Nutritionists had arrived at the conclusion that the people needed to eat chicken rationally.

Everything was part of a great plan to save us from malnutrition.

There was chicken day
lettuce day
pasta day
meat day
milk and cheese day
and vitamin and protein day.[1]

THE WOMAN WHO LOOKED BEFORE SHE DIED

He got off the trolley behind her. Then he walked ahead, turned the corner, and glued himself to a tree.[2] The woman approached. He took a shot. In the neck. She had enough

---

[1]But José hated eggs and vegetables, he only liked meat—bloody, rare meat, with very little seasoning. And he could only eat meat once a week—which isn't much. His quota at the butcher was the minimum: 300 grams.

[2] He'd seen it in the movies, the bandit or the tough guy would do this.

167

time to turn and look in his direction. He shot her again. He wasn't seeing the woman herself, just a shape. He emptied the gun and leaned against the wall. Walked away slowly (I hope they get me), returning to the bus stop. There was an old woman there waiting. She was black and very wrinkled. José got on and stayed on until the last stop. He could see the whole city from up there (someday I'll get down from here and conquer the world—but I just didn't know what I wanted, and I still don't, I'm trying to figure it out).

In American spy pictures the agents use silencers. The shot goes pffftt, like a metalic plug. Impressive. In the movies it's easy to get a silencer. In real life they're illegal. I've been to all the gunshops in town. They look at you funny. These days to buy a gun you have to register, leave your identity card, bring along your police record, get your picture taken, a thousand things.

> Whole city blocks taken over by machines / debris / houses falling down one on top of the other / concrete viaducts passing overhead / super-highways, airways / seven in the morning, a Japanese going out to the street to buy oranges / the 7:30 news team / fair weather / viaduct ERZ-0 / radial viaduct / marginal viaduct 1 / viaduct p-12 / cloverleaf above the construction / cloverleaf in front of the green house / cloverleaf over the railroad tracks / cloverleaf in Vila Prudente / steak and french fries / the bus at the curve, near a vacant lot, a kid kicks a goal / people with rotten teeth getting on / my balls itch / gas stations and more gas stations / a small varicose vein in my leg / it hurts a lot / heat like this makes you feel sick / Atta boy, atta boy, walk for Daddy, come get the candy. The boy fell, José stood watching /.

JOSÉ, COMING AND GOING

He ran up and down the white halls. Corridors with no way out. Last time there was a hole opening in the wall, where's the hole? (Why do they always put me in here?) He was deaf—he'd been listening to Rosa and suddenly he couldn't hear anything anymore. A spool of thread. With a spool of thread, I'll find my way out. Nah, I don't need to, I'm on my way out already, there I am leaving, I'm coming in, arriving at my meeting. But I've already been here, here I am again. I gesture to myself: Go away, pal, this is no place to be.

—I'm worried about you, sweetie. You should see a doctor.

—What for?

—It must be fatigue. You work too much. And then at night you go out . . .

—I go out?

—Sure you go out.

—Last night I didn't.

—Yeah? Then who walked in the door just a minute ago?

He closed his eyes. Yellow light filtered through his eyelids. All he needed to do was close his eyes and he saw the corridors, the wrinkled black woman, the symbol of the Communs, Rosa lying on her back. Pieces of Rosa.

—You never say you love me.

—But I don't.

—Then why did you marry me?

—I like to fuck you.

—That's all?

—Isn't that enough?

—Do you think it's enough, do you think a woman likes to hear her husband say that?[1]

—Shit on what women like.

Atta boy, atta boy, walk for Daddy, come get the candy. The boy fell with one shot, one shot in the face.

OFFICIAL NEWSFLASH

The herald announced:

From this day forward, all couples will be required to have a certain number of children, under penalty of imprisonment. The number will be assigned in accordance with social conditions. Statistics will be furnished by the Ministry of Planning. Abortion will be considered a crime, punishable by life imprisonment for the woman and death by firing squad for the doctor.

---

[1] Clearly a preconception.

NEWS REPORT

Boqueirão has been dismantled. In what could be called a fine-tooth operation, police have brought in all suspects, convicts, and accessories. First, all the women were rounded up, and then they took care of the gambling casinos. The next stage was to close down the animal curiosities which were considered "too much,"[1] the abortions of nature.[2] Boqueirão is virtually empty; only exhibits of chickens with four feet, pigs with two tails, and things like that are still authorized. The mass of newly-unemployed are traipsing through the city, begging on viaducts, in front of churches, parks, and movie theaters. Police have been beating and arresting them. Deformed bodies have reportedly been found in local rivers. The unfortunate misfits don't know who to turn to. There isn't anyone.

THE INITIATE

Paulo brings the last punch cards to the computer. His shift is over. He leaves the air-conditioned room, goes through inspection. Midnight. He's got to hurry, or the old woman won't be able to perform the ritual. The Ebó. Today's the day. When he left this morning, Didu-Beré already had the ingredients prepared. Transportation is tough at this hour, and Paulo needs to take two different buses. When he becomes a technician at IBM he'll go home by taxi, or in his own car. But Pauol is just beginning his career as assistant in the Ebós of the Spirits.

A YELLOW GARDEN
AT THE BANDIT'S TOMB
A rosebush has sprouted at the bandit's tomb, and as it grew it produced yellow flowers. A month later there were three rosebushes. And they kept on spreading. Today, the tomb is a yellow garden.

---

[1] Too much for the government. The animals considered themselves normal.

[2] *Author's* preconception.

LIFE AND TIMES OF JOSÉ

When the President's face appeared on the screen, on a news program, the entire audience booed. It didn't happen very often, but that day the image of their beloved leader didn't please them one bit. They stamped their feet on the floor the whole time he was inaugurating this, that, and the other thing, shaking hands with army men, priests, and government ministers. In fact, they booed for as long as the show lasted. In the end, 578 spectators were arrested for disrespect. Penalty: one month in jail.

José 1: I'm just too nervous, I can't stand to go home, I'm gonna stay in the streets until I collapse from sleepiness or drunkenness[1] and then I'll start home from wherever I am but at this point I don't even know where I am I didn't even know these neighborhoods existed, such low houses little alleys no sidewalks drainwater running in the streets. One day nine o'clock in the morning I fell head first into a puddle of foul water and the only reason I didn't die is that some people who lived nearby lifted my head out of the water.[2] They took me inside a house and put me on a sofa and when I woke up the first thing I saw was the symbol of the Communs. But they got me out of there fast.

A weekly magazine (which was always right on top of the news) had the President on the cover, as usual. People would go to the newsstands, buy the magazine, and rip it up. The Repressive Patrols, in plainclothes, began to hang around the newsstands. Anyone who ripped up the magazine was arrested. Penalty: one month in jail.

José 2: All I had to do was stick out my hand, grab something, and drop it in the sack. The supermarket was deserted at two in the morning. I had knocked the guard over the head and tied him up in the bathroom but I had to be careful grabbing things—there might be people passing in the street—canned goods paté sardines ham sausages Néstles milk peaches in syrup pineapples oranges figs pears applies strawberries all in cans fish cheese cornflakes tea sugar coffee (they might as well be brothers) toilet paper

[1]José has been drinking a lot lately.
[2]From that time on, José had a strange illness: his head lost its firmness, and tended to fall forward as if he were sleeping on his feet.

peas cookies detergent enough to last a week if only my liver wasn't still bothering me it would be easier to survive all this I could even eat weeds, that way I'd be in training to live *really* tight eating any old shit because some day they're going to be on my tail . . .

The government has decided to get involved in comic books. They have created new characters, like Corporal Deodato who has a magic bayonet. All he needs to do is sit on it and he turns into Super-Corporal, oppressor of the poor.

José 3: Boy Rosa really hated it when I'd grab her in the back seat of a cab and the driver would stop all grossed out and make us get out, she'd get mad and wouldn't talk to me for days—You pervert you're a sex monster but I wasn't I'm normal and in those days probably less than normal because I was worrying about Boqueirão and it wasn't just Boqueirão it was something else I don't know what, Rosa in her greasy white apron she never took it off I don't know why she didn't lose her job she smelled and I accepted that I even liked her sweaty smell I put up with everything everything that came along I didn't even exist to myself and now that I exist I'm not sure anymore. When we'd fight we'd fight a little (or a lot?) then I'd put on a record that really irritated me, that way I'd be able to fight more and get mad enough to beat her up, I've got to pull her out of the apathy she's in, she doesn't care about anything.

Who is it that doesn't care about anything?

It's you, José.

Super-Corporal Deodato has asked for a change of plan. His bum is all cut up from the bayonet.

JOSÉ, ALONE IN OLIVEIRA'S GARDEN, PONDERS

Outside the city there was a garden, in the French style, which belonged to the Oliveiras, an extinct Portuguese family. The last Oliveira donated the garden as a national park. José discovered that weekdays there was no one there; it was a good place to go to be alone. There aren't just human beings around, there's something else, someone who's trying to communicate with us. But we're afraid. Earth men! We're scared of each other, never mind someone from another planet. I'd like to contact them so they could protect me with their force. I'd like to have a flying saucer, atomic

172

weapons, laser rays, the ability to disappear. I'd like to have known Doctor Jessup, the scientist from Philadelphia whose experiments in 1943 succeeded in making ships and sailors invisible for a few instants. Oh, we could have done incredible things together, but Dr. Jessup went and died, *they killed him* or he killed himself. I need help, and lots of it. I think the Repressive Patrol is out looking for me because *I killed two people yesterday, it was really something to shoot at the two of them*, a gun in each hand, a shot in each temple, surprise. I feel better when I kill someone from the patrols or the police than when I shoot at someone I don't know. If only I could get some help. I need some *outside* help. But I can't trust *anyone on earth*. Because they're just like me and I never trusted myself. I keep thinking I'll meet up with them some night (where do I get the idea that they only show up at night or in deserted places like Oliveira's garden?). For a while they were making appearances in the mining regions. I think they've tried to reveal themselves to me: that night the picture fell off the wall; the times I got soft and couldn't screw Rosa; when I'd get the sensation that someone was in the house; the yellow rose appearing on the table and the yellow bandit peeking out from the bookshelf; the lights going on and off by themselves. It was them, *wanting to talk to me*. And I was so scared (stupid ass), I was panic-stricken. It was something physical, but it was more than that, too. I was uneasy, I felt I could do lots of things which normally weren't within my reach. I just needed the key which would release me from myself, I needed to be more out of control. They came and saw that I was ready to react. They saw *inside* me; they went in and out of me. But I refused to talk to them. All that seething and boiling and I was scared. An earthly fear, idiotic. I'm so small, so mediocre, so full of bullshit. I lost my chance. They got tired and went away without making contact. Because I didn't let myself help.

OFFICIAL NEWSFLASH

The heralds climbed up to their platforms and the trumpet sounded. Government decisions:

The observance of Carnival will be permitted once again.

173

Official departments of the government, in communion with the Holy Mother Church,[1] have resolved that:

Every citizen will receive a card (green for men, red for women, blue for children) which will be stamped by their local parish priest after every one-hour visit to the Most Holy Sacrament. Entrance to clubs, carnival balls, and parties will be denied anyone who does not have a properly stamped card. Citizens must be attired decently and suitably or they will not be admitted to the area. This precludes skimpy costumes for women and transvestite outfits for men. In addition, contact between the sexes will not be permitted: the halls will be segregated by sex in order to avoid seductions, scandals, and immorality.

Penalty for infringements: from one month to twelve years in prison. In more serious cases, castration.

BYE, BYE

Hélio Borba, the scientist arrested for experimenting with artificial insemination and the creation of test-tube babies, left the country yesterday, accepting an invitation extended by the University of Moscow. Professor Borba's work has had world-wide repercussions, despite being illegal in our country.

EXTRA HELP BRINGING UP JOSÉ

The women were making communion wafers, get your hand out of there, boy, his mother was in charge of the group, Thursday afternoons, the women mixed flour and water, filling the elongated forms, and José would gobble up the leftovers while he listened to his mother sing, sweet hummingbird hovers over the flowers in the garden bower, there's a song in your murmur, there's a kiss in your song, hummingbird, hummingbird.

ROSA'S ILLNESS

—I'll borrow a station wagon and bring back a drum of water.

---

[1]In spite of the great schism, the conservative wing of the church still retains the majority of power and is linked to the government.

—No, never mind, it'll come back on soon.

—But what about the smell, Rosa, I can't take it anymore.

—I put creolina in the bowl every day. It doesn't smell that bad.

The toilet was full, the water black, and Rosa would still sit on the bidet all day reading M. Delly, waiting for José to come home so they could go out and get something (anything) to eat. There she sat, surrounded by that putrid smell, the smell of everything that had passed through their bodies. It had been part of them and they had given it back and now it rotted and reeked. Rosa sat there and breathed it all in.

21 DAYS WITHOUT WATER

A neighbor:

—She's not well, José. Not a bit.

—What happened today?

—She ate Mrs. Cota's yellow chicken.

—What's so bad about that?

—She ate it live. The whole thing, José, feathers and all.

22 DAYS WITHOUT WATER

Another neighbor:

—José, I need to talk to you. It's important.

—What is it today?

—She was standing there at the gate in just her panties and bra, yelling that the house was full of Martians. She said they climbed out of their flying saucer and asked her for some water. That's why she ran out and stood at the gate, she didn't even care about the gang of boys watching from the sidewalk. We had to hit them to get them to leave and stop looking at her, it was indecent.

(I've got to set a bomb under this neighborhood. Blow up the whole place. I'll burn every one of these houses to the ground.)

28 DAYS WITHOUT WATER

Another kind-hearted neighbor:

Knock, knock, knock.

(Those tightwads could put in a doorbell at least, they've got some nice ones on the market.)[1]
—What did she do this time?
—Ayyyyyy, what she did, and how she did it.

31 DAYS WITHOUT WATER

José disappeared for a week. From the first to the eighth of August.
Neighbor: Yoo-hoo, Mr. Joséeee.
Second neighbor: Something has to be done.
Third neighbor: It's for her own good.
Fourth neighbor: Poor José.
And so forth.
The neighbors among themselves:
—That guy is a jerk.
—She's really putting one over on him. Have you heard?
—Why doesn't he put her in a hospital?
—Could he really like her all that much?
—He's a worthless good for nothing. She's the one who calls the shots, and uncalls them.
—But she's a lousy housekeeper, that's for sure.

THE SOLUTION

—Leave it to me. I know jus' what she needs.
—Who sent you?
—I jus' come. I knew you need me here. It was HIM.[2]

(I know this woman from somewhere, I'm sure of it. I've seen her a couple of times . . .) An old black woman, real black and real old.

When he was living in the warehouse and didn't have running water, José would shit on a newspaper, roll it up, and leave it by the edge of the sidewalk. Then he'd wait for someone to kick it and get their foot all dirty.

The water was black and full of mosquitos, and the smell was taking over the whole house, you couldn't even walk in the door. Rosa was turning yellow, swollen, dirty, and she asked José to bring her some Dorly soap, that brand that

[1]Bring the sound of Big Ben to your house: Bell's Bells. And don't forget, we offer Qwik-credit.
[2]Some neighbor knew this black woman and called her, that's all. It wasn't HIM, or anything like that. Who's HIM, anyway?

doesn't exist anymore, nothing exists anymore, period. My life with her isn't heaven, and it isn't hell, my life with her just isn't. Why do people meet, and couple up, it doesn't make any sense.

MEETING WITH GÊ

José opened the door, the man came in. He didn't say a word, he just walked in. He looked at José for a second and sat himself down on the sofa. Skinny, bearded, dressed in red. He looked strong in spite of his thinness. But it was the look in his eyes that impressed José. It was unflinching. A blade. It was because of his look that José opened the door and knew: this man needs to come in and take a rest.

Rosa was in the bathroom and the putrid smell wafted through the house, as if they lived in a gas chamber. The man sniffed the air, and went to sleep. José felt like taking off Gê's boots—the kind the military wear.

Late at night, the man woke up. José brought him some bread and coffee. This man simply made you feel like doing things for him. He would do it for you if you needed it.

—Did I sleep long?

—Two days.

He had an accent as if he knew a thousand languages and didn't speak any of them well but could speak them all at once. He put his hand on José's shoulder. His face looked tired but peaceful. It was something rare, this calmness, this serenity. Everyone else, everywhere, was full of uncertainty.

—You know that I am Gê.

(I knew, but I didn't want to admit it to myself, I was afraid.)

—I am not worthy for you to enter my house.

Rosa opened the bathroom door, the smell spread through the house and disappeared. Rosa came in and tapped Gê on the shoulder. He started and turned quickly. He smiled.

(Say just one word and she will be saved.)

When Gê took Rosa's hand, she drew back and vanished into the bedroom.

—She's suffering from an abulic crisis. You should take her to a doctor, a psychiatrist.

—An abulic crisis?

—Yes. Abulia is when a person loses his or her will, becomes apathetic. Nothing makes any difference to them. There are abulics who spend days and days literally standing still.

José wanted to ask more questions. To know what could be done for Rosa. But Gê left, slapping him on the back.

In the following month José heard more about Gê. His picture was in the newspapers and on posters the government put up in bars, bus and train stations, banks, movie theaters, gas stations, churches, poolrooms, and stadiums. From time to time, he was on television: *Make your contribution toward peace in our country—Denounce this man to the authorities—He has assassinated family men—He has robbed the National Treasury—He preaches subversion.*

They talked about the Communs, who they said wanted to overthrow the dictatorship. He'd never paid attention, before.

READY FOR THEM TO RECEIVE ME

José thought: I can't live like this anymore.

But what could he do?

He tried to find a Commun.

But how?

After all, they were in hiding. Spread out all over the city. He wandered everywhere, by bus, on foot, by cab. Through all the suburbs, woods, lakes.

He knew they were hiding underground. Under the streets, like the Vietcong. They went out at night, set off bombs in police stations, barracks, official's houses, shot military men.

Where do you find the underground?

Night after night in the streets. Hoping for a manhole cover to open and a Commun to pop out. Then he'd try to go up and talk to him. Gê was his friend, right?

Would Gê remember him?

They were kidnapping people, demanding freedom for political prisoners.

What if the Communs accept me, will I be ready for them?

Then one day, José woke up and saw the symbol on his door:

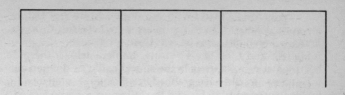

OFFICIAL NEWSFLASH

The herald announced:

As of eleven p.m. yesterday, the city of Luislândia, head-quarters of the Communs, has been condemned to death. The government is facilitating the general suicide. At this very moment, pills are being furnished to every inhabitant. Tomorrow the city will be razed and the ground leveled so the sea can reclaim it.

COMPULSION

After we fucked I just lay there (it tired me out). The woman left. On the way out she looked at the gun lying on the table. She hadn't seen it when she came in. She left quietly. After collecting her money. I like whores, because if you want to you can go hours without them saying anything (as long as you're paying). Not a word. Or, they'll talk a lot. I wasn't going out again. The man was dead. I didn't even want to know who he was. I saw him coming out of the base, he got in a taxi. He got out, the taxi drove off. He was slow to open the door of the building. I waited for him to go in and close it. There was light in the hall behind him. I could see his shape in the glass and I shot at it. The man fell. I got in the car and left, lights off so no one could see the plates, which I later changed in a parking garage. (It wasn't a bad idea to break into the Registry and steal all those plates off the old cars. I got more than twenty.) I wonder if he was a military or civilian guard. Who knows. I took a good look at his face so I would recognize the pictures in the papers tomorrow. I buy them all, I like to read every bit. I keep wondering all night if someone saw me, took my picture (or something like that); I worry that this might be my last night of freedom (I don't think so), or that they're going to kill me, too. What if he wasn't an army man? Well, then I'll only enjoy it half as much. It doesn't really turn me on to kill a civilian. The man fell: dead, or just wounded? Dead, for sure. I know where the heart is, where the liver is. That's where I got him, he was dead for sure.

He fell, and I felt like screwing. Immediately. If there'd been someone right there in the street I could've jumped on top of her. I would have grabbed her, I really wanted it bad. I walked around until I found the little number who looked at the gun and said nothing.

THE TRACTOR

The tractor treads were half buried. Too much mud. People said: the Communs meet at a place where the ground is being leveled. There were lots of places on the outskirts of the city which were being leveled. So José and Atila ran around like crazy. (Atila came along for the ride, drunk.) They didn't find a thing—except for two Repressive Guards. José shot at them. One dead, one wounded. They climbed up on the tractor. The man was stretched out on the ground, he could see the lights coming toward him, the mud churning. He tried to move. José jumped off, leaving Atila alone on the tractor, and he heard, or thought he heard, the sound of the bones being crushed, but he wasn't sure, because of the noise of the motor, the rain, the mud.

LADY LUCK

(This guy scares me, I should waste him right now.) The cabdriver was speeding along, José took aim. A foot hit the brake, the car lurched, José was thrown into the front seat. The driver was about to pull a weapon (knife, club, gun), but José got him in the temple first. Luck, pure luck. Stand up and fight. Raquel Welch, what thighs, whoooooeey, deeky-deeky dum, spend those greenbacks, pretty soon even whores will be paying income tax.

INSTRUCTIONS FOR THOSE WHO WANT TO KILL

Locate the subject. Do not study his habits or go anywhere near his house, and do not make friends in the neighborhood. Just find the person, go there and shoot him (or stab him or hit him over the head). If there's anyone around, don't hesitate: kill them too. What's the difference between killing one person and killing two? Just don't leave anyone alive to identify you. Keep a cool head. If it's someone you hate, it's good to wait a little while, to let the hate out. So you can be absolutely lucid. When the time comes, take a cold shower, shave, dress carefully, check your weapon, and go. It's best to shoot for the middle of the temple. Or, if you're sure you won't miss, go straight for the heart. It's also a good idea to change weapons occasionally and to vary the technique. Heart, neck, forehead, ear, mouth, liver, balls. No kinkiness. (Sounds kinky to me.) Kill as if you're doing someone a favor.

BITS AND PIECES AT DAWN

The car exploded at 5:30 a.m. and woke José. He looked out the window, black smoke puffing up. He went downstairs, people were running, police all around. There were pieces of people all over, pieces of car, blood, ears, fingers, the bloody trunk of a man, leaflets. That's what it means to explode. José threw up from the smell of gunpowder, the burned flesh, the fear that this would happen to him someday.

LIVE AND LEARN

—Here's one that just arrived, Gê.

—Is it the Livingstone?

—I don't know.

/ "Today no one even considers getting into gunrunning anymore. The small-time gangsters have almost completely disappeared in the face of competition from gigantic monopolies. And with all that's going on, from Algeria to Biafra, from Pakistan to Yemen, from Colombia to Bolivia, and from Vietnam to . . . Vietnam, they don't get a moment's rest, or suffer from unemployment." From a news report /

—Do you carry the Mitchell Livingstone pistol?

—Nope, you need to buy that direct.

—How do I do that?

—I don't know, that's another department entirely. I don't even want to know about it.

/ The Mitchell is the most powerful pistol in the world (it has a miniature launching pad which fires a .50 caliber rocket). It pulverizes your adversary. /

ENTERTAINMENT

Atta boy, atta boy, walk for Daddy, come get the candy. The shot caught him in the mouth, threw him several yards backward. But it wasn't for the . . .

And now, what's left of Boqueirão: aged dancers doing striptease acts. The only thing the least bit entertaining is that they take off all their clothes. Even so, the audience is small. Besides the dancers, there's just the Gorilla Woman. Atila spends hours in front of her cage, he wants to run away with her. She's only a girl of twenty, with red marks on her enormous thighs. The marks stand out because her thighs are so white.

No more single roses are appearing on the bandit's tomb. It's two per night now. The cemetery caretaker has been keeping watch, but has been unable to discover who puts them there.

Does somebody really put them there?

—There's no point coming here any more, pal. Boqueirão is finished.

José walked around the little theater (a tent with an improvised stage, wooden benches, a half-a-dozen spotlights). Behind the stage, there was a large space full of cages, dressing rooms, everything abandoned, bums sleeping on the benches.

Atta boy, atta boy, walk for Daddy, come get the candy. It wasn't for the boy, it was for his father. But the shot got the boy. I shot the father, I shot the son. It wasn't supposed to be the kid, no, not him, never. The father stood there looking. So I shot him too.

The fire started in the Gorilla Woman's cage. Atila ran to

182

save her, but she had left, and was already appearing down near the bus station. The fire spread from the cage to the tent to the house next door (old houses, dry, rotten wood, easy to catch fire) to the bar to the ancient porno theater to the poolhall to the illegal casinos to the whorehouse to the shady hotels. There was no one there. Boqueirão was an emptiness in the middle of the city. And I wanted to get rid of that emptiness. The one out there (and this one in here). The fire was consuming everything, the firemen were called but didn't come, it wasn't worth it. If I'd known it wasn't worth it, I wouldn't have set fire to anything.

$$\frac{\text{Man}}{\text{Animal}} = \text{EQUATION OF EQUILIBRIUM}$$

I couldn't get up. I woke up shaking. A whiteness in my head. No memory. Trembling and cold. I grabbed for a blanket, my skin was cold as a snake's. I lay there on the floor, scratching for pool cues with my nails. Every single muscle was trembling. My lips parted and I sat there listening to my teeth chatter. A rooster crowed. Intolerable pain. I tried to get up, I fell. I wasn't in control of my body. I threw up. And then there wasn't anything else to come up, just a bitter taste. I lay there, surrounded by that stink, and lifted the gun, and started shooting—and the people in the rows of seats applauded and yelled and clacked their teeth. I woke up and had a sudden urge to eat hay. My mouth watered at the thought of green pastures. But my teeth hurt and I knew I wouldn't be able to eat. And from the bathroom came the smell of stale piss.

INTERVIEW

—Where are they, where are the Communs?
There were people all around, hanging on crosses. It was the field of crucifixions.
—He's a Commun? Crucify him.

CRUCIFY HIM	CRUCIFY HIM
CRUCIFY HIM	CRUCIFY HIM
shouted the multitude.	shouted the multitude.

Whichever company ended up getting the bid for the crosses was undoubtedly making a bundle, there were a lot of them. Simple, made of iron, with holes for the screws which went through the hands. Saturdays, Sundays, holidays, Holy days: the people would come with picnic baskets and watch the men (and women) die.

In hoc signo vinces.

FREE ASSOCIATION

At the washtub, mother washing clothes and singing: Mr. Sunday, Mr. Sunday, why are you here? / To seek a fortune for me and my dear.

If you've got a mother / you've got it all / if you don't / you've got nothing.

Oh Sailor / good sailor / Pull hard on your oars / Your wife and dear children / are waiting on shore.

THE LONG AWAITED ONE

The gun didn't take up much space. He carried it everywhere.

What if I started shooting at the people hurrying to work?

What if I stood on the corner, with the gun aimed, and shouted at them not to go to their jobs? No more punching in, no more typewriters, paperwork, pens, computer cards, offices, cash registers, department heads, managers, no more production (let's manufacture anti-progress), no more of the same work every day, always doing what other people tell us to. That's what they're waiting for: a leader. For someone to organize Operation Salvation, an association for the prevention of mechanical work. (I've got to do it, I've simply got to, and right now: look at these people's faces, they're asking me, begging me to do it. If they had time and if it wouldn't make them late for work, they'd get down on their knees and say: go on, go stand on the corner and lead our movement. Lift up your gun and we will follow you, the long awaited one, savior of men.)

An ant was climbing up his white shirt. Just as it reached his neck he made one quick swipe, and there was the ant in his hand, black, miniscule. José let it drop to the hood of a parked Volkswagon. And stood there, choosing his corner. A strategic point, jammed with people. Crowds walking by:

a girl in green rolled her eyes and squinted at him, a mustachioed fat man was tapping his ears as he walked along, a washed-out blond drew her lips back, showing her teeth, a guy rearranged his balls, someone walked two steps forward and spun around, two more steps and spun around, one man carried his briefcase on his head, another wasn't wearing any pants, one person barefoot, the next crawling by on all fours, a woman with four pocketbooks, a guy with an earring in his nose, a naked boy, a person carrying a bow and arrow.

The people.

WHO LOOKS, FINDS (I)

—I know Gê passed by here. Which way did he go? asked José.

—Gê?

They were suspicious of this guy who came every day looking for Gê.

(Who is he, anyway, an agent? or one of us?)

Whoever he was, times were such that you couldn't trust anybody. He better just keep looking.

—You looking for Gê?

—Yeah!

—Then come with us.

IN PLACE OF GOOSEBERRY JUICE, GÊ SUBSTITUTES WINE

And so it became known; whether it was by word of mouth or through underground pamphlets, the story was told: the daughter of one of Gê's men was going to get married. The man was very poor, he had virtually nothing, like the majority of Gê's followers. But the girl wanted a party, because a wedding is a wedding, once-in-a-lifetime. (Or at least if it happens more than once you don't get a party, nothing.) So, neighbors, relatives, and friends were coming to the house. And there was no wine, or beer, or any alcoholic beverage to be had, just water and gooseberry juice, with some shaved ice. And the bride was sad, because the poorer you are the bigger your wedding party should be. The bride's father said to Gê:

—There's no beer or nothing.

185

—What can I do?

Gê went to investigate. Pails full of water, gooseberry juice, and sugar in the back room. So he jumped behind the wheel of somebody's jeep, knocked at a wine merchant's, and when he opened up, Gê pointed a gun in the man's face. He arrived back in no time with three casks of fine wine, and left them in place of the gooseberry juice.

In this way, Gê revealed his nature, and his disciples believed in him.

José thought: what a pretty word, really, it sounds like a bird's song. I walk by the marquee just to see the word. Tystnaden. I haven't see the movie, they say it's lousy. I don't want to see it. I'd rather have a beer. Two large drafts cost the same amount as a movie. Tystnaden.

QUOTE OF THE DAY

"If they have no bread, let them eat styrofoam. It's soft and white and, when sliced, looks just like Wonder Bread."(Presidential Declaration)

WHO LOOKS, FINDS (II)

They drove around in a white Corcel. They brought him downtown to an old building, renovated, with a yellow vestibule full of dark brown doors. They put José in a bare room. The windows were nailed shut. They left.

A long time passed. They turned off the light.

They turned it back on.

José waited. The light went off again.

He got hungry, thirsty, he needed to piss, his belly was writhing.

They turned on the light. José relieved himself in a corner of the room. A man came in, furious, and hit him on the head: clean it up, clean it up, *now*.

—With what?

—I don't know, I don't care, I don't even want to hear about it.

José took off his shirt, cleaned up the mess, and stood there with the shirt in his hand, full of piss and shit.

—What do I do with this?

—I don't know, I don't care, I don't even want to hear about it.

They turned off the light.

He got hungry, he got thirsty, his belly was shrinking.

José waited. They turned on the light. The yellow walls ran together. He was on the floor, his back hurt. The walls of his stomach grated against each other. When they turned off the light, the room stayed yellow. Rap, rap. Rap, rap. BLAM. *I left my heart in San Francisco,* chickachickachicka-chicka, bam, *Buona Sera Mrs. Campbell,* beeee-beep, the bombs rain down from miracles (myriads) of airplanes and fall, like drizzle, the people waiting, the sirens screaming, nnnrrreeeeeeeeeeeeeeee, the joy of hand finding hand, study your catechism my son, God it was cold, I was reading *The Treasure of Youth,* I'd borrowed it from Nena next door, she was rich compared to us, her father worked for the electric company. It was so cold. I was shivering, and so were my brothers, we weren't sleepy, none of us, the bed was like ice, how could you sleep? Then my father came with some rum. He filled the cup and had each of us take a drink. Then came the warmth and, with it, sleep. Just like that, every night after dinner, gluglugluglugluglugluglug, heat, and then sleep. No one felt the cold. It felt good, and I'd go to sleep memorizing *The Book of Whys.* Because yes, because no, because yes.

They turned on the light, the room stayed dark.

The Man should have taught me to put up with hunger and thirst.

It makes me mad to lower myself, like an animal reduced to begging for his food.

Hunting in the forest that has no animals, looking for water in a dry place, no rivers to be seen, just marks—squares, circles, buttocks, thighs, clouds of spermatozoans swimming, swimming, all my children who died at the orgies we had at Bidêt Farm, glip, glip, there go the babies down the glass bowl. My God, what the devil, all the saints, all the demons, yeah, demons, demons of every day, look at the leopard leap, she's on top of me, me on top of her, a double leap, like sixty-nine,[1] the trapeze of life, her mouth open, my mouth open, the leopard leaping into my mouth, me leaping into hers. She's inside me, I'm inside her: something singular (man-animal-animal-man) and then I remember the day I ended up in the alley full of cars, me coming in

---

[1] Even delirious, you can have vulgar images in your head.

and me coming out. Here I am! Inside this yellow leopard stomach, God I hate yellow.

except for the pallid yellow of Gê's face.

he's the one who can save me
from all these doubts
of mine,
this indecision, this
staying here.

RIGHT YOU ARE, IF YOU THINK YOU ARE

José didn't notice being taken to another room. They threw water in his face.[1] They gave him water to drink.[2] There was an aroma of food in the room. It was extremely clean. When he came to, José saw a man seated in front of him in a designer armchair. José himself sat in a fancy model, compliments of Sergio Bernardes, the architect. They offered him a cigarette. An impeccably dressed waiter carried in a steak sandwich and a pineapple milk shake, to restore his strength. Jack Jones, Sinatra, Aretha Franklin, playing softly on the stereo. The man said he was sorry to have to talk about unpleasant things.[3] What was unpleasant was the stench of this filthy room, the light in his face, his unbearable thirst, the hard bench they made him sit on when what he felt like doing was falling over backward just letting his body go. The man gave him more water to drink. It was brackish, José vomited, and they started beating him. The smell of shit, shit and mold mixed together, in a room that hadn't seen fresh air for a long time. From outside came the sound of a squeezebox, playing a lively jig.

(1) That's what they do in the movies.
(2) Incredible!

(3) Here's where José came out of his numbness and delirium.

188

A man came in, and the first one left (or was *he* the first?). The second stayed a little while, went out (leaving José alone), a third arrived (or was it the first?), smacked José, and left, counting: one, two, three, four, five, six, seven, eight, nine, ten, one hundred and twenty. The first one came back (or was it the second?), yelling as if possessed, and punched José in the face, knocking out a few teeth, laughing and laughing.[4] The accordian music ended, and then started up again, the same song. A priest came in (or was it a man dressed like a priest?) and said: Confess, my son, confess everything to the Lord God our Savior. José struggled to his feet, bashed the priest over the head with the bench, and the priest keeled over without a word.[5] José jumped on top of his stomach and danced a jig. Then he sat down on the bench and waited. They would be back to avenge the priest.

And

suddenly,[6]

they actually did arrive.

What now?

There were four[7] of them, big, strong, silent types, dressed in green uniforms,[8] with high boots, stainless steel helmets, and dark glasses.[9] One held José down while the other hit him with brass knuckles. The two others stood watching. Then they changed places and took turns beating him, leaving him bloody. One of them said: "Away with such a fellow from the earth! For he ought not to live."[10]

Then they let him go.

(4) Are all police sadists?

(5) What could he say?

(6) Suddenly, nothing. They were due back a long time ago.
(7) It could have been five or fifteen, it doesn't matter. They're just numbers.
(8) Uniforms of the National Institute of Repression & Inquisition: N.I.R.I.
(9) In the movies the S.S. and Gestapo always wear dark glasses.
(10) *Acts of the Apostles* 22:22

189

Observation: Nothing was ever brought to light about José's arrest and interrogation. It could as easily have been Gê's people, suspicious of him, as the N.I.R.I.

SHOCK

Rosa is in the hospital. The doctor said she's had a bad shock. It will be some time, a month at the minimum, before she recovers.

FREE ASSOCIATION

The skinny, yellow canary with jet black eyes, the day of mother's burial, my youngest brother yelling out the window: Auntie, can my bird come too? Mother had been poisoned by the medicines, murdered by the doctors . . .

THE SILENCER

José is looking for a Dutchman who smuggles silencers. The guy has links to the Mafia, or the CIA, or gangsters.

WHAT DO YOU WANT, JOSÉ

He didn't need to look in any more manhole covers or sewage pipes. There he was with Gê. They were under the city in a cement room which had ducts in the walls, common in the underground. The Communs had built narrow cement tunnels, just wide enough for two thin men, or one, if he was in a hurry. Incomprehensible labyrinths winding this way and that, straight hallways which suddenly ended, doors opening into two other halls, the one on the right forming a square and leading to another hall (the same one?). A door into a room with two more doors, corridors zig-zagging back and forth. Niches every so many yards, with electric outlets, networks of wires (telephone connections?), meters. José suddenly understood: the Communs would control the city from underneath. They had infiltrated through the wiring: water, lights, gas, telephone. During the fifteen years of the dictatorship they had been working, preparing for this. Now they must be ready, or almost ready.

—I've heard about you, said Gê.

—About me?

—About your little robberies and killings.

—And?

—Why?

—Why what?

—Maybe you're one of us?

—I don't want to be.

—Why not?

—I don't know what you want. I don't want leaders. I don't want anybody telling me what to do. I just want to be . . . me.

—What you say is meaningless. You don't really know what you want.

—You need me?

—You're pretty good. You shoot well, you've got nerve. You do amateurish jobs, that's what saves you.

(But I'm scared to be one of them.)

Then Gê said:

"Thus was I envious of the arrogant, when I saw the prosperity of their wickedness. For they have no pangs; their bodies are sound and sleek. Nor are they troubled or stricken as other men are; their pride is their necklace; violence envelops them like a garment. Their eyes swell with fatness; their hearts are wellsprings of foolishness. They scoff and talk maliciously; they speak of oppression with magnanimity. They turn their mouths against heaven and their tongues travel the earth. Therefore, the people turn and praise them and they are as founts from which to take generous draughts. For behold, thus are the wicked; always tranquilly increasing in riches. All in vain have I kept my heart pure and washed my hands in innocence. For I am tormented the day long, and chastened at the morn."[1]

And José, referring to himself, answered:

"You will find in my depths neither rancor nor bitterness nor spite. Evil can only inspire in me sadness and piety. Evil alone inflames me to hate. Because to hate evil is to love goodness, and to be angry with evil is divine enthusiasm."[2]

And Gê, also referring to himself, in this two-man monologue, said:

"In this soul, so many times wounded and so many times

---

[1] *Psalms*, 73:3–14
[2] *Oration to the Boys*, Ruy Barbosa.

transgressed, there is no hostility, nor calumny, nor ingratitude, nor persecution, nor betrayal, nor does there remain the smallest vestige of vindictiveness. God is my testimony of all I have pardoned."[1]

José concluded, almost convinced:

"There is nothing more tragic than the inexorable fatality of our destiny, whose swiftness only intensifies its severity."[2]

PATIENCE, IMPATIENCE

I don't know why but today I'm pissed off about the raid on the university. They broke things, burned things, hit people, arrested people, killed people. The same as yesterday and the day before yesterday. The same as a month ago. When I read about this stuff I can't even get a hard-on. There's not a prick that can take it when this kind of stuff is affecting people all around, even if it doesn't affect you. I always wanted the world to be orderly so it wouldn't be able to hurt me. Everything outside concerns me. Suddenly I discover it's we who put the world in order, the way we want it. It needs to be tidied up every day, put back together, reorganized. There's not much comfort in this, or security, or stability, or peace. All those things we're looking for and pretend we're not. I think people are born to aim for a little peace. But if there's war we'll fight it, because if there's war peace doesn't make sense. I've always been a coward, a real chickenshit, scared of other people. One day I got slugged, and even though it didn't hurt, I was still afraid of fights. That made me mad at myself, to think like that, such stupid thoughts. I've been in this room for five days, looking out this window for five days, five days eating crackers, sucking oranges, and cooking eggs on a hot plate, while I wait for the man to come out of the hotel across the street. In five days he hasn't come out once. Two to one he snuck out the back. Here I am, in a fucking police movie, this stinking room is a mess. The place across the street is a wreck, too, and that's where the general is. With his pals. He was the last one in. I was over there trying to get a room, me and this little tart I found peddling it on the

---

[1] *Ibid.*
[2] *Ibid.*

street. They didn't even let me stay in the lobby, if you can call it that. A narrow, smelly hall, with a dilapidated counter. That's where "Sixteen" was hanging around, the bandit everybody's talking about, the one who stole sixteen cars in one month, got sixteen years for car theft and other offenses, and ended up paying his way out of jail. Now he sells pot and works as a doorman. "Sixteen" told me he couldn't get me a room, strict orders from the big guy, who was keeping an eye on him. I asked him if he knew what was going on up there.

—Nope. And I never will. I don't want to get mixed up with guys like them, they got a big, well-oiled machine behind them.

I went back to my room, and it was a good thing, because soon the street was teeming with soldiers arresting people. Two cops came up to my room and asked to see my I.D. They wanted to know what I was doing and they looked over my documents carefully. They stared at the girl but didn't say anything about her, just told me I should be careful, I don't know about what. I took a good look at their faces, and managed to get their plate number when they went down, because there's no way I'm going to leave the two of them alive now that they've seen me. Good thing they didn't search the room or they would have found the gun and the rifle. Then I'd really be fucked! Five whole days, of course you think about this kind of stuff. Five days, and I'm already sick of this whore and she's sick of me. I'm a real bore. I don't talk (I don't like to talk), that was always my problem. I just don't like to talk, so I keep quiet, everything locked up tight inside, until the thing ruptures, I don't want anything to do with it, so it breaks wide open. What a bunch of shit, today I'm thinking the dumbest crap. All because of these five days. I can't stand to look at this room anymore with its filthy curtains. I've had enough of this little whore: she only puts out when I pay, and—big deal—she gives me a reduction for the off hours. She sits around listening to the radio and complaining that she'd be making more money out on the street.

But I've decided: she's going to die too. This morning I couldn't get it up so I grabbed the rifle and stuck it in her. She laughed like crazy, the barrel was so cold. I kept moving it around and all of a sudden she came all over it. She started laughing again and kissed the gun, said it was a real man because it never gets soft, the best man she ever had. She asked me to put it in her again, the whole thing, gunsight and all, she said she was hot for the cold gun, that bitch. The barrel was over forty centimeters long, I felt like shoving the whole thing inside her. She wanted to know why I had the rifle and what I was doing holed up in the hotel room. I told her the city is full of people with guns, it's just that everyone else carries revolvers. Must be something different about me, 'cause I had a rifle. Maybe I was going to go around killing people left and right. She got scared, then, but I said I was just kidding around. That I was staying in the hotel while I visited local merchants, selling my medicines.

I showed her the suitcase full of first-aid stuff I'm always using, and it has everything, because you can never tell when you'll get hit, not a deadly shot or anything, say the bullet just grazes you, something you could treat yourself.

—Know what I saw the other day?

And she told me:

I was downtown, coming out of a movie at four in the afternoon (which is a good time for a whore to go to the movies, cause you don't miss many johns at that hour). Anyway, she said she saw two guys facing each other across a vacant lot. Cars were stopped, everybody was watching. They started walking toward each other and at about two meters they drew their guns and shot. One fell, the other turned and got in a taxi and left. People stopped hanging around, continued on their way. An ambulance came, with a cop, to pick up the body.

My little girlfriend, here, went into a record store. Then she went home and I met her on the street, she came upstairs with me to the hotel. And now she's fed up because all I do is stand at the window and peek out. And there are those guys over on the other side, trying to figure out how to screw people even better in this town. No joke. They were: the chief of police, such and such a general, the chief of the secret police, of the political police, the T.I.S. (Torture and Interrogation Squad), and some federal agents. "Sixteen" had told me all about it. One of these days I'd need to take care of Sixteen, too. You get mixed up with a guy like that and one day he's not satisfied with just money anymore.

194

Jesus, Mary, and Joseph, my soul is yours.

If the plan I've got up my sleeve comes off today (now this little tart has started praying, for Christ's sake), it will be my masterpiece, a gorgeous piece of work, definitely worth a medal. If this were a sport, I'd walk away with the gold. I know which room they're in, but I'm in a tight spot, there's not much I can do. If I shoot through the window I might not get anyone, or maybe I'd just get one, and the others would get me. That goddamned hotel doesn't have a back exit, I'd have to climb the roof or run back out to the street. Of course I'm not stupid enough to run out to the street and right into their hands. And the roof's no good, I already checked it out, I'd have to jump some four meters across to the building next door. And probably fall through the rotten roof tiles. This whole neighborhood's falling apart. The thing to do is to have another go at my little sweetheart and think about it for a while, maybe I'll come up with a solution (what if I land on my back on the roof and get the wind knocked out of me?). If there's a way to figure it out, fine; if not, tough luck. Before I would have gotten freaked out in a situation like this, but I don't care anymore, I learned to sit tight and be patient, that's the way to keep them from getting you. But shit, these feds piss me off. I don't know why, it's everything all put together, but I'll get them, and soon, soon enough. *Our next complete station identification will be at 5:30 p.m., on New Flag Radio, and now, another sports update . . .*

CIVICS

—Your car doesn't have a flag, or a slogan.
Arrested on the spot.
—Madam, there are no flags in your windows.
Off to jail.
Until every day was a festival of national colors, flags everywhere, love, faith, and pride for this land of your birth, there will never be another country like this one.

THE SCREAM

Maaaa, where's your head, where is it, Mama, I can't see it, I don't remember, where are you, Mama, no, that's not your head, that ugly yellow thing, don't take me away, take me, take me away, I don't want to see that thing, I want my mother's head.

MEANS OF COMMUNICATION

The master of ceremonies was wearing a big smile, because he owned a big company that sold things to the poor, and he was really rich . . .
The man without legs just needed to earn some money . . .
(Will this turn out to be the story of good and evil, of the bad rich man and the virtuous poor man?)

THE WRONG PHOTOGRAPH

Rosa had gone to her parents' house. She was hemorrhaging, and José hadn't been home for two weeks. While she was gone, the police raided the house /
"Good day, my dear sir. I am a patriot. You've no doubt heard of me. I volunteered for the first platoon of firing squads. I want to put a stop to subversion and terror and unpeacefulness, I want democracy in this country. I've noticed strange activities in the house next door. The guy who lives there is never home, strangers arrive and stay a day or two, then leave, the wife is ill, he doesn't even care, he disappears. I'm sure I've seen guns, and if I'm not mistaken there's someone on the police posters who looks like him, it would be good to check on it, don't you think? Just to see. It's been nice talking to you. Glory to the Fatherland."
/ and ransacked the books and searched for guns and pamphlets. They didn't find anything, except an envelope of pictures inside one of the books. They showed it to the neighbors who said: yes, it must be him, a little younger, maybe. At least it looks like him. And they had the photos put on posters in movie theaters, bars, stores, bus stations, train stations, police stations, barracks.

Conversation in a taxi:
—But I need some money, to live on.
—What for? You eat and drink gratis.
—It's always good to have a little money.

—The money is for the cause. We make sure it goes to the right place.

WEATHER FORECAST

Sunday at dawn people run to the newsstands for the morning paper. El Matador bought one printed in blue: "People have been gathering at a house in Vila Branca to witness the miracle of José Luis, the boy with music in his belly, and to be blessed. José Luis's father reports that the music consists of trumpets and drums, specifically Joshua's trumpets before the battle of Jericho. Many people have searched, but no one has discovered hidden wires or recording equipment in the shack."

TO BE DECLAIMED

Only someone who knows the terror of an organized home—

the tranquility of a house that functions, with clean, pressed laundry, the aroma of home-cooked food, no dust—

weekdays of dinner, television, sleep, wake, work—

meetings on Sunday, Saturday night plans, the tedium of Monday—

—tomb, mausoleum of life, flat country.

THE SIEGE OF THE SOLITARY SHARPSHOOTER

On the same day that the papal airplane arrived, bringing (along with His Holiness's blessing) four thousand kilos of presents for "our brothers in Christ," the first shot rang out. Nine-thirty a.m. The dum-dum bullet exploded in the chest of an eighteen-year-old salesgirl, poor, engaged to be married.[1] It happened in a downtown square, in the center of which there was a statue of a man on horseback, hero of grammar school primers and history lessons. A radio patrol came along. As soon as the policeman got out, another shot. It happened so fast that his body stood there without a head, the neck torn wide open. His partner didn't even

---

[1] Melodrama once again imitates life.

197

have time to get out of the car. His belly exploded, intestines flying all over a nearby display of bras and underpants. They discovered that the gunman was up on the statue at the horse's feet. He had a case of ammunition and several firearms, and dislodging him was complicated by the fact that the statue was taller than the buildings surrounding it. Gunfire shattered streetlamps and plate glass windows. Between 9:30 and 10:00, four people were shot dead. At ten-thirty, eight radio-patrols and a car from the Repressive Forces arrived, with Neco Collisione in charge. He was the biggest and strongest of all the agents, extremely violent, not much talk and a lot of action, known for shooting first and asking questions later. They tell the story (on the inside, among the cops, so it can't be confirmed because it would be considered slander, or envy) that at the beginning of his career, when he was twenty, he was raped by a big, black dude in the slums. Anyway, Neco went to the square to lead the attack, machine gun in hand, yelling, taking aim, the superman of the police. (He even believed in the "closed body.")[1] But the solitary sharpshooter got him between the legs. Neco bellowed and sprayed a round of machine gun fire into a display of lingerie.

No one could even get out of their vehicles. The solitary sharpshooter was fast. It seemed as if he could cover all 360 degrees. And he didn't allow anything to move down below. They hid inside stores, behind trees and telephone poles. "Terrorist," they yelled, and they trembled, wanting to be *him*, there, up high, omnipotent, with the power of death over those below. So much confusion, cars screeching to a halt, a traffic jam, horns, screams, sirens, shattered windshields. An army truck showed up. The commander was dead as soon as his foot hit the running board. Then a horizontal line opened up, absolutely straight, in the tarp across the back of the truck. A row of holes, all the same size. The soldiers who were sitting along the bench, their backs to the tarp, fell like dominoes, and the others threw themselves to the floor and refused to get out.

At one p.m. reinforcements arrived: the Special Repressive Troops, two battalions of the Anti-Terror Army, four tanks, four armored trucks with sand hoses, and eight ar-

---

[1]Having a "closed body" means that, as a result of a macumba (or voodoo) ritual, you are completely protected from all bodily harm.

mored cars with 4.2 inch mortars[1] and 66mm M-72 extra-light (five pound) rocket launchers.[2] They were set up in tactical positions under the direction of a logistics expert.[3] Unfortunately, some of the men were hit while setting them up, and instantly transformed from men into photos for the heroes gallery on the walls of police stations, barracks, corporations, etc., to be honored from year to year.

Whenever anyone would fire from the ground the man above would respond. Bullets ricocheted off the bronze statue like a bell chiming at a church festival. As the strength of fire from below increased gradually, the man answered back slowly, regularly, methodically. Flame-throwers[4] reached halfway up the statue, which seemed to be enveloped in fire: an ancient hero on horseback, rising out of the flames of battle. The man at his feet kept shooting. Anyone approaching with flamethrowers was mowed down, and the others retreated. Back to their machine guns, rifles with long distance gunsights, mortars.

And of course the TV crews came too, to film a special for the eleven o'clock news, cameramen and radio people, and the newspaper reporters, all excited because it was like a war, without the danger of war. Intelligence agents were on the roofs taking pictures with telephoto lenses, they developed their photos right on live television / this program sponsored by Brick's Tomato Juice, the reddest, the family favorite / revealing the solitary sharpshooter as a man around thirty with graying hair and a five o'clock shadow.

José had gone up to the seventh floor to work his way down again. Four apartments on each floor, all the doors open. Through each of the doors he could see a narrow hall where whores sat waiting for business. Two per apartment. It was hot, they were fanning themselves with magazines, fans, waving their hands in the air. The building was called The Pigeon Loft; it was always jammed full of people. Whenever he went there José would go to the top floor and work his way down, more to look at the people going up and down than because he felt like screwing. The building

---

[1] Used in Vietnam.
[2] A gift from friendly governments.
[3] An official (retired from Korea and Vietnam) on loan for temporary action (as an advisor) in Latíndia-America.
[4] Sanctioned in the extinct Vietnam war.

had an aroma of disinfectant—garbage—beer—sweat—stale sperm. He went into a room on the fourth floor with a dark-skinned woman named Madalena and heard the racket outside. By this time the solitary sharpshooter had been up on the statue a half hour. José went to the window. He wondered whether Gê would show up. There was his symbol on the corner of a door, that horizontal mark with four shorter vertical slashes: the sign of the Communs. (Was Madalena a Commun?) She nudged him and pointed out the window at the TV truck. José followed her into the bedroom. Maybe there was time for a quickie, as long as Gê hadn't arrived yet. Would Gê come at all—with all the police and confusion, and that maniac there on the statue? What's he up to, anyway? Deep down inside José probably knew. The solitary sharpshooter didn't stand a chance, but he would stage a grand finale. Apotheosis. José felt like applauding, right then and there. But he couldn't look even look out the window, the camera was there, sweeping the building with its telephoto lens. Later, in intelligence, they would examine each face at the window, each face in the multitude, trying to discover Communs, terrorists, subversives, criminals. These photo identification sessions were a daily event, and they brought results. It was best to give up, Gê wasn't coming.

In the square below, the battle plan was unfolding. Battalions on their knees, rifles aimed. Tanks with 88mm cannons. Heavy-duty machine guns, M-60's (OTAN), 7.62 caliber, six hundred shots per minute, ammunition in a continuous tape, plus it had an adjustable barrel for use with or without tripod. The surrounding streets were closed off. The Expert was giving orders over a walkie-talkie. It was his first big mission here and he wanted it to come off well. He gave interviews to the newspapers, talked to television correspondents, was filmed by the networks. The Department of Public Relations had already distributed his mimeographed bio notes, listing battles he'd won in Korea, Vietnam, at popular uprisings in various Middle Eastern countries, outlining his participation in the Six Day War.

—The problem is we need some of those German-made M642-59 machine guns, which fire twice as fast as the M-60.

The solitary sharpshooter fired a round and hid. With each round he cut down one or two of the opposition. Meanwhile, machine guns were eating away at the foot of

200

the statue, bullets ricocheted off the horse's hooves. They had called in the country's best marksmen, to study the layout and angle the shot so the bullet would ricochet and hit him in the back. But at that distance they would need an extremely powerful weapon and bullets tough enough to penetrate bronze.

At two p.m. the Commander-in-Chief of the Repressive Forces, accompanied by high military, civilian, and ecclesiastical authorities, visited the square. "They're destroying the statue of a great national hero," he complained. The pedestal was full of bullet holes. "No—no, you can't use grenades, nothing like that." They were considering bringing in the Laser Ray to saw open the pedestal so the whole thing would collapse to the ground, and they promised to erect the statue again afterward. Permission denied.

The Expert was getting irritated, (shit, what do I care about some national hero?); he was trying to come up with a plan and not succeeding. He was used to the jungle, to a hidden enemy. But this guy was right there, visible. He touched his necklace for luck. It was a bunch of human ears strung on a nylon thread. Tiny, shriveled ears, like raisins. Just as cowboy heroes marked each victim by notching their gunbelts, or wartime fliers displayed flags in the cockpit, he too kept score. He wanted the solitary sharpshooter's ear. But he didn't see how he was going to get it.

In fact, he was (almost) beginning to regret the day he got the telephone call from ex-major Allistair Wicks, from Baker Street. He had been at the Zambesi Club, in London, when he got the call: a mission. In Latíndia-America. After Vietnam, the Expert had considered going to Africa, India, anywhere they needed mercenaries. Maybe the Middle East, Egypt, Israel. Incredible, this work wasn't easy. He didn't understand what was going on in the world, but one thing was for sure: Latíndia-America was still an open book. Who knew what would happen. The Expert knew jungle antiguerilla tactics inside out, so he accepted the contract: a thousand dollars a month, ten thousand dollars in case of death (who to send the money to?) or debilitating injury.

The Expert had worked with the Belgian, Col. Jean Schramme, and Bob Denard, the Frenchman, and had spent many years in Africa involved with Tshombe. No one knew the Expert's real name; maybe he himself had forgotten, he was so used to the nickname. Fifty years old, he had always lived with a weapon in his hand, and in peacetime he hung out with guys he knew just as little about, not that they didn't have references. One an ex-S.S. man, another from the Gestapo, one from the O.A.S., another from the C.I.A. He'd been intimate with exiled politicians, failed politicians, idealists, mercenaries, deserters, guerillas, Cubans, Germans, Greeks, Algerians, Africans, adventurers: a clandestine network of ambition and personal advancement. He had buddies who were today heads of state of small nations sustained by the U.S. or the Russians or the Chinese or the French. On the plane to Latíndia-America he'd met Bimns and Craig, and Delgay and Bukuvu, dressed as journalists, cultural attachés, businessmen, communications experts (the governments of Latíndia-America wanted to install color television). Three of them were C.I.A. agents, and the other was working for a more obscure but nevertheless powerful organ of the U.S. It was good to know that they would be on the same continent, there was always the possibility of working together again, making some extra money.

But he'd made a discovery: he hadn't been sent to the jungle after all. And he didn't understand anything about cities, didn't want to. He hated the city, that's where he'd got shot the only time in his career. Furious, in Harlem, looking for some blacks who were shooting from rooftops and windows, he had run out into the middle of the street yelling for them to come down and "fight like a man"; he'd almost lost an ear, a shoulder, a finger, a foot. He left the same night, flew straight to London, anxious to get back to work in the jungle, looking for Major Wicks and waiting for a call.

They had said that in Latíndia-America there were jungles, rivers, Indians, ferocious animals, mosquitos, heat, waterfalls, palm trees, music, mustachioed men, sombreros, siestas, carnival, and dark women who gave themselves to Americans, Englishmen, Germans—because they liked strong, blond men, and the native men were thin, sickly, malnourished, and died alone; it would be easy to make a thousand dollars a month, and enjoy it.

But here he was trying to dislodge a maniac from the foot of a statue. Neco had guaranteed that he would solve the problem, and look what had happened to him. The Commander didn't want the civil police involved. Now the armored trucks were spraying sand and water at the statue. The machine-gunners, protected by steel shields, were advancing. You could hear the sharpshooter's bullets pinging off the shields. The Commander had evacuated the buildings surrounding the statue and stationed marksmen at the windows. (But the hooves and tail of the horse blocked their view.) He was directing the attack through a megaphone. Bullets were coming from all sides; from underneath, the fire from the flame-throwers rose higher, the spray of sand made a compact cloud. And the solitary sharpshooter, indifferent to the ruckus, to the insupportable heat, to the bullets, was cutting down policemen.

—But what for? asked Gê. It doesn't accomplish anything. There he is, blasting away, killing people, all for no reason.

—I understand him, said José. It's the only thing we can do.

—If you want to do that, join us.

—I thought about it. But I don't believe in the things you and your group stand for.

—For awhile, it will be enough that you're angry. In time you'll learn who we are, you'll like us, you'll like fighting with us.

—No, I'm staying on my own. My fight is mine alone.

—But that's silly. You're just angry, and when the anger passes, it's over. It won't amount to anything. Whatever you do alone doesn't amount to anything.

—And whatever you do with other people doesn't amount to anything, either. Alone, I risk less. A man alone knows himself, knows his weaknesses, can get to know his own nature. It's easier that way.

—More comfortable.

—A group brings problems, suspicions, jealousy. Is everyone strong and courageous to the same degree? That's a good question. And to what point does someone endure torture to protect the others? When one falls, they all fall.

—No. There's always someone left to continue the fight. Alone, you fall and it's all over.

—Once I'm gone, what do I care?

—That's egotism. But you're a good guy, we know what you've done. Just to do it. Without any purpose. You could be useful.

—No, it's not egotism, no. Everyone is his own person.

That may not be news, but I didn't come here to say original things. I only wanted to say that I'm me. I can't imagine a "we." It's not my fault, I was born that way.

—No, I just don't buy it, José. You are what you make of yourself.

—Look, Gê, you're never going to understand. A group, for me, is a house of cards. If one on the bottom teeters, everything ends up on the floor.

/ I came to set fire to the earth, so much the better if it's already flaming /

Gê left and went down the street dressed like a woman, made up like a whore, in a blond wig. The TV camera didn't notice him. He slipped into the crowd.

By three-thirty the police, the militias, the Commander, the Expert were all hysterical, screaming at each other, picking up the dead and wounded. The Commander put in an urgent request, and minutes later helicopters surrounded the square. Ten meters above the statue the machine guns went into action. They were in the belly of the machine, they spilled out bullets like rain. Six thousand per minute. In a few seconds, the horse was without a head, the national hero had lost his legs and his sword. Then, at the instant the machine-gunners took a second's rest, the sharpshooter made a hit on the pilot, exactly like James Bond in the movies.

—He's my brother. I don't know what he's doing up there, he must have gone nuts. Completely nuts. I knew it, I knew it would happen someday, but I didn't think it would be this soon. Adamastor's only twenty-five.

Television and radio reporters, newspapers, had surrounded the mild-looking man wearing round glasses. He had seen the reports on TV. He had come running, and managed to push through the crowd, helped by a cop. He was a cabdriver, dressed in ragged clothes.

—The only thing Adamastor thought about was winning in life. He vowed that someday he would be somebody. No one who knew him had any doubt about that. He started college preparatory courses, but had to stop. It was too expensive. And he just didn't have the money to go to the university. The preparatory course he took would have guaranteed him a place in college but it was really, really expensive. So Adamastor had to give up. He's been a little crazy ever since. He worked here and there but didn't stay at any one job, he thought they were all worthless. He went to work for a consortium or whatever you call it, and ended up getting mixed up with the police; then he worked for some investment company, it was a big deal, everybody getting rich. Except Adamastor. Things just got worse and worse. He and his fiancée had a fight—because he was acting "strange," she said. But it wasn't anything like that, nothing to worry about, he just wanted to win at something, to succeed in life. If they'd only let him have a decent car, a house, maybe a little country place, a pretty wife, some money in the bank, the stuff that makes people happy . . . he would've been okay. Now he's going to die up there under a horse.

There was a sudden roar of an airplane, and the tanks withdrew. The militias dispersed the people watching from below. Megaphones asked that all buildings be evacuated as fast as possible. By five o'clock there was no one left. And the airplane came back. It flew over the square. And froze dead above the statue. Just for a second. The belly of the plane opened and the bomb sank down. (The familiar drone you've heard in the movies.) Then everything shuddered and shook. Pedestal, horse, and sharpshooter flew upward, stopped in mid-air, and disintegrated in a dust of cement and rock and bronze and bones and blood and iron. Not a building was left standing, not only the square, but for blocks and blocks around. Just one enormous crater. And by 7:00 City Hall was already preparing to reconstruct the square. The Historical and Geographical Institute ordered a new statue of the national hero, and the city arranged for billboards: *One of this administration's newest projects—to be completed on this site in 180 days.*

FREE ASSOCIATION

This child Rosa wants—it just can't be born. I want it, too, but I don't know, there is no today, no tomorrow. Nothing but a few moments. A life shouldn't be moments, a life is *everything*, and here everything is death, tomorrow (this prison): no way for my child to become something, live, love, grow, study (they'd kill him in school), get a job, have children. Fear. Mine, Rosa's, the neighbors'. General fear. Fear that is dread. Terror.

—What are we going to do if this child is born?

MEANS OF COMMUNICATION

At eleven o'clock, as he does every night, the President appeared on television, interrupting a soccer game. Tall, with shining eyes, a paternal air, like a grandfather, so well-behaved, such a calm, leisurely voice (what a good man, what a good man, what a good man: fractions of a second, the lettering flickers across the screen: subliminal).

At 11:04 the benevolent, magnanimous, liberal president raised his right hand and blessed his people, the whole nation of them (you must love him): ''Sleep well, my good people.'' The populace made the sign of the cross and thanked him.

EJACULATORY PRAYER: Sweet heart of Mary bring us your salvation. (300 days of indulgences)

THE INVINCIBLE ROSE

They cordoned off the tomb of the bandit of the yellow rose. Nobody could pick the flowers anymore. The manufacturers of the potion weren't allowed in the cemetery. But the rosebushes kept on growing; they were putting down roots under other tombstones, taking over the whole cemetery. The city brought in special crews with spades and torches. It didn't do any good, the roses kept on growing. People said it was because of Our Lady. Government botanists said it was because they were plastic. Crowds lined up in front of the cemetery: we want roses, they shouted. The police came and broke up the disruption with fire hoses and sand cannons.

ALMANAC

Many years ago wax candles were discovered, the most important invention after the electric light.

MESSAGE

José, you already have the answer to your problem. Now all you have to do is move on it.[1]

THE BOY WITH MUSIC IN HIS BELLY

One morning José woke up feeling strange in his own house, strange with Rosa there by his side, and found a note: "The boy with music in his belly is Gê's son. We must protect him."

PREDICAMENT

. . . afraid to argue with a cab driver, afraid of being attacked, murdered, he read absurd things in the news, people getting killed over small change for busfare or a shot of rum in a bar or an accidental encounter or a fender-bender . . .

If he saw someone coming toward him in the street, begging or asking for directions, he was suspicious, nerves on edge, ready to run . . .

ANNOUNCEMENT

Now available in all participating stores: people's uniforms, in the full range of colors established by the government in accordance with social classes and professions. The uniforms are cheap, yes, affordable. Those who cannot pay cash can buy them on time, with government financing. To do this you need: residency certificate, receipts for gas and electric bills, work card, identity card, official newsflash attendance card, proof of good conduct, references, police record, and credit history. Within two months the entire population is expected to be in uniform.

---

[1] He who offers advice offers friendship.

REPORT

In re: operations presumably directed by Gê, the leader of the Communs, with the probable participation of an individual who is slightly lame, called Zé (probably a nickname), and a tall individual with a black mustache (probably fake), who is called Hero (obviously a nickname). Also participating were two Japanese, two blond girls (perhaps wigs?), and fourteen other individuals, nine of whom have been identified as having previous records in the Robbery, Homicide, & Morals Division.

(A conservative journalist's commentary: "The terrorists are making use of the worst elements in the criminal community, common thieves, assailants, sexual offenders . . . in other words, the dregs of society, individuals of the lowest moral standards. Of course this appropriately reveals who they themselves are and what they represent.")

To date:
1) Thieves armed with machine guns and revolvers assault a bank in Chora Menino and take all money from the safe, the cash drawers, and the depositors present at the time.

(Gê's instructions before the job: only money from the bank, not from the customers.)

2) Armed with machine guns and 7.62 FN rifles, five men assault a railroad paymaster and get away with millions. One killed. Crime attributed to Gê.

(Detective Dores, chief of the Murder Squad, comments: "It wasn't Gê. He doesn't use a 7.62 rifle. But so what.")

3) Gê or José or Hero or another member of the Communs who is called Avila, or something like that, is probably the man who fled in the following heist:

For the purpose of the bank robbery, five men stole a Willys from a judge. But a friend of the judge's saw them with the car, became suspicious, and telephoned the police. The men entered a bank near the judge's home and overpowered employees and customers, again demanding all cash on the premises. When they attempted to leave they were met by police who had surrounded the bank. A five-minute shoot-out ensued, during which the suspects ran out of ammunition. Four were killed, receiving a total of forty-two bullet wounds, various blows and stab wounds, and one fled. No policemen injured.

Bomb activity:
1) Seventh Regiment: dynamite. Four dead. Assailants' car sprayed with machine-gun fire. Presently checking all hospitals and first aid stations for leads.

(The nation's most famous surgeon, who is known largely for his transplants, was abducted and taken to an apartment somewhere in the city, where, at gunpoint, he was obliged to perform operations on two men, one age twenty and the other around forty-five. "If they die, you do, too. And your wife and kids." A phone call was made to his home so he could hear his panic-stricken wife: "Yes, they're here with me." Two days later, when the patients were out of danger, the physician was released on the steps of the Fifth Precinct.)

2) Homemade bomb set off at Federal Police Headquarters. One killed.

3) Seventy-five (75) sticks of dynamite robbed from a quarry.

4) Five simultaneous bombings, identical technique: at the Stock Exchange; offices of a newspaper loyal to the government; Detective Dores' home; the U.S. Consulate; and the Czechoslovakian Consulate. One dead.

5) New Legislative Assembly bombed, totally destroying the main entrance.

(José: No, Gê, I don't want anything to do with bombs. I don't even want to be in on these jobs at the bases. I already told you, this business of group participation isn't for me. Not even with my pals. I want to work alone. Find me some solitary jobs.)

THE SPLENDID CRADLE

After walking east for a long while you come to an uninhabited plains region where there are only minimal possibilities for human life. Nevertheless, many kinds of vegetation from around Latíndia-America are found there. Trees from Peru. Brazilian jacaranda. Uruguayan cedar. Varieties from Colombia, Guatemala, Chile, Paraguay, Bolivia, all the Central American forests.

Legend has it that thousands of years ago there was only one people in all America, a great civilization, which settled in this region. But one day the rivers inundated the land and an immense swamp was formed. The game disappeared; the trees stopped bearing fruit; the people's very subsistence was threatened. So the big chief ordered his subchiefs to disperse, taking along seeds and provisions. They were to explore other regions and find places to rebuild their civilization. When the best place was found, the others would join them. So they went off and established new clans. Which grew. They grew, though they grew poor in a rich land. And, meanwhile, their native land became utterly worthless, an uninhabitable jungle. It is to this region that the militias nowadays bring criminals, assassins, subversives, terrorists, and guerillas, and abandon them. There are thousands of people buried here. Those who know why they died and those who don't. Some of them died for something, knowing they were in the cradle of this miserable continent, beaten, oppressed, broken. But united in the earth. And maybe they will be born again. Americans reborn for the fight that will surely take a long time.

THOUGHT FOR THE DAY:
"Granada / Tierra sonanda por mi"

VARIOUS TONES OF VOICE

It was easy to look at death and revolution at the movies, in photographs, and history books. Now, José, you see it all right in front of you. Death is real; blood is really blood; the revolution marches on. And you're in it, whether you want to be or not. There's no way out. You're so cowardly, so timid, so resigned. Think about it: from now on the wounds are going to hurt, and people are going to suffer because of you, just like you're going to suffer because of them. No, José, no more fun and games with a play gun, hands up, come on boy, bang-bang you're dead. Now it's for real,[1] accept the challenge, win or lose. You have to try to win.

Read this passage in the following tones of voice:

A) like a sermon, in a monotonous voice
B) like advice, in a serious voice
C) like a prayer, in a sorrowful voice
D) like a warning, with the voice of the arbiter of truth
E) like a prankster, in a falsetto voice

DRINK MORE COFFEE

In accordance with the plans sealed in the envelope,[2] José and his pals left for the job. The plans had been delivered by Sweet Tooth Chico, whom the police had listed as dead six months ago, so he was able to operate freely. The eight of them pulled up in front of the bank, got out, went inside, and aimed their guns. The employees held their hands over their heads[3] and the cashier began to take out the money[4] and shovel it into the plastic bag[5] Atila held open for him.

—Open the safe, said Chico.

—We can't, said the assistant manager.[6] The manager has the key.

—Where's the manager?

—Out for coffee.

—Shit on a stick.

---

[1]José thinks it's boring to play serious all the time.

[2]Obviously.

[3]Bank Policy #7 from the *Manual of Behavior During Robberies* (for employees' eyes only).

[4]*Ibid.*, Bank Policy #10.

[5]A really ugly bag, with gaudy flowers. Industrial design (at least for this type of bag) is going to the dogs.

[6]In the absence of the manager, the assistant manager is responsible for the bank. From the *Manual of Behavior*.

—He'll be right back. Why don't you have a seat.

They took the employees into the bathroom. It could hardly fit everyone, but Hero kept kicking the attendant (last one in) and somehow they managed to close the door. They locked it and waited for the manager.

When the manager arrived, Chico greeted him and said: This is a stick-up. Open the safe.

—Is this a regular time for a coffee break? asked José.

El Matador was nervous (I should get the fuck rid of this guy, thought Sweet Tooth) and missed the bag, spilling a stack of bills all over the floor. The blond wig, the mustache, everything was giving him trouble.

They left.

After they had gone the guard managed to break down the bathroom door. He ran to the bank van parked at the entrance.

—Follow those cars.

—Where's your transport requisition? asked the driver.

—I don't have one.

—Then I can't go.

—But the bank was just robbed!

—Well, you really should have requisitions all filled out in advance for these occasions.

The guard went back inside and got a requisition, but the getaway cars were long gone by the time it was signed and ready.

They revised the manual: "Drivers are authorized, immediately after assaults, to leave in pursuit of the thieves without a requisition. Afterward they should send a memorandum justifying their actions, signed by the manager of the branch which was assaulted, to the Central Agency."

The story of Sweet Tooth, even though he only appears this once: In June, six months before the assault in question, a man driving a Volkswagon hit a truck. When a cop attempted to come to his aid, the man jumped out of the car shooting, and fled in a taxi whose driver had ducked into a bar for a quick drink. The cop and a Repressive Guard pursued the guy, there was a shoot-out, and the man was killed. Homicide investigators identified the man as Sweet Tooth Chico (he was crazy for cotton candy), twenty-nine years old, a thief with fifty-six previous arrests. The real Sweet Tooth Chico was alive, but very smart: he had his family claim the body and bury it amid torrents of tears. And he blithely continued his life of crime.

INTERVIEW (not recorded)

Gê: It's my life. And I like it this way, I wouldn't want it any different. I'm used to being chased. If they stopped chasing me one day it would be strange; I'd have to adapt all over again. Understand: you only adapt to what you want to, or accept. Living clandestinely doesn't mean anything in and of itself. But it puts you on your guard, permanently. In the underground I've developed my instinct for self-preservation a thousand times over. It's exciting, it doesn't allow me to get comfortable. Sure we're scared. But when you cross the street you can be scared, or when you foresee an increase in your income tax, or when you think about the lousy salary you make which doesn't even cover your debts, or when you realize that not only don't you have a house but you don't know if you'll ever have one, or when it dawns on you that you could be arrested all of a sudden (it happens to innocent people, too), or tortured or killed, or when you don't trust your neighbors, your friends, people you meet in the street, when you feel millions of fears like these you're more scared than I am. Don't forget that.

José: But wouldn't you like to have a peaceful life, to be happy?

Gê: Above and beyond everything else, I am happy. I'm not sad, I don't dramatize my problems or get all depressed about them. There's no time for that. Seriously.

I'm happy. I'm doing what I want to be doing, the way I think is right. You can count on one hand the number of people who can say that these days. When it's time to die, if I know that I'm dying, I'll be sad, sure. First, because of course I like being alive and, secondly, because dying means being cut off from something to which I could have given more and more.

José: What about violence, and pain?

Gê: You know, I'm terrified of suffering. Of just that: pain. I'm afraid of being tortured, of them making me go crazy.

José: Sounds like fun.

/ end of José's mawkish interview with Gê /

THE MAN WHO PUT OUT
THE MILK BOTTLE

Mr. Carlos Alberto Fernandes finished dinner and turned on the television. It didn't work.

—Virginia, let's go to the movies.

She was beside herself, it was like a party. It had been twenty years since they'd gone to the movies. Since before they bought their first TV set. Virginia loved movies. The last film she'd seen was a revival of an Esther Williams movie in which she reigned over the pool in a yellow maillot.

Lights down, the short had already started. It was a local piece about a man who had tried to break the world's record for fasting. On the screen a kid was being interviewed. He was eating a sandwich and waving it in the direction of the fakir. He was looking right into the camera, laughing and eating. Mr. Carlos Alberto Fernandes was about to fall asleep when this scene started. (He only liked films from abroad, he liked subtitles.) This movie must have been really old, he thought, because the women were wearing short dresses. It must date back to the Era of Degradation, which had ended fifteen years ago.

—It's him, it's him!

—Keep your voice down, said his wife. It's who?

—The assassin. I'm sure of it. I opened the door to put the milk bottle on the stoop, as I have every night for twenty-two years. I put the bottle in the box for the milkman to exchange in the morning, and I heard a shot. I looked up. The door of the building across the street was shattered. This kid in the movie was pumping shots into a shadow behind the glass. The shadow fell. The kid blew on the barrel of the gun and left. It was Colonel Camilo he'd just killed, a good man who took care of his obligations and had never gotten mixed up in politics or anything.

The film was confiscated, the director was interrogated: "I didn't even know the guy, he was just there, he was a strange character, ironic. He left all of a sudden, in a hurry, he had a slight limp. Uh-huh, he was limping, I'm sure of it. I never saw him again." Photographs were sent to newspapers, television stations, law enforcement agencies, police informants. Posters went up all over the city.

DENOUNCE THIS MAN—HE COULD ASSASSINATE YOUR FAMILY NEXT—IT'S EVERYONE'S DUTY TO DENOUNCE SUBVERSIVES.

ROSES WITH MOON DUST

It came to a fight. The people vs. the police. Crowds of people had managed to get into the cemetery and entrench themselves among the tombstones. They attacked the police with slingshots, and the cops shot back with guns. The government decided: anyone found with yellow roses would be condemned to from five to nine years in prison. Commandos were sent in to destroy the plantings. Protesters were dealt with harshly. (Imagine, all this because of some yellow roses.)

The rose garden kept growing. Branches scaled the walls and crossed the street. Plants twined up the white walls of buildings.

—This has nothing to do with God, it's a curse, announced the heralds.

But the people thought it was a manifestation of the Lord. And they wanted the roses. Those who managed to get more than one sold the others. A black market for yellow roses. Some people went so far as to make fake ones out of paper and plastic. The police confiscated these, too.

Members of the government had a meeting on the subject. They concluded:

As long as these roses are getting people's attention they forget about their problems. Let's take advantage of this chance to tighten things up a little more. There's still way too much freedom. Let's feed this thing.

The roses didn't even slow down. Some people said they were sent from Mars. Prophets walked the streets yelling:

Infidels, oh ye infidels, punishment at last. We never should have gone to the moon. This is the Lord's punishment. These roses are fed on moon dust.

José found a yellow rose on top of his dresser.

—Where did this come from?

—The backyard. I planted a cutting.

—Don't you know they're illegal?

—I know, but I'm the one who planted it, a long time ago, before this whole business. And besides, this is the first flower. It's pretty, just leave it at that.

Suddenly the whole room was yellow, José felt giddy. He leaned against the wall and saw an open well, very deep. It was triangular.

B.P. JORGE APPEARS (ONE TIME ONLY)

Baggy Pants Jorge, or B.P. Jorge, as he was called, was a permanent candidate, a professional left-over. He had been taking the college entrance exam for six years, and passing, but there were never enough openings at the university.

His nickname dates back to childhood. The only pants Jorge owned were his brother's, and his brother was five years older than he was, so they were much too big. According to the psychologists who interviewed him, two things had made him a marginal character: being consistently left over and not having his own pants. So that explains why Jorge attempted to rob the Ducal Department Store and got arrested. Since it was his first offense he got a suspended sentence. And now he was wanted for throwing molotov cocktails at university buildings: ''Jorge or nobody'' was his motto.

THE JOB

There were seven of them: José, Hero, El Matador, Malevil, Atila, Barrel Chest, and B.P. Jorge. They had gotten hold of a Willys; inside, they found two machine guns,

216

the floor plan of a bank, and a street map. The entrance, the exit, the times of heaviest and lightest business, the schedule for when the guards changed, when the armored car arrived (it's lunacy to attack an armored car, this isn't an American movie), the location of the bathrooms, the safe, the back door. It seemed like everything was already set up.

This job shouldn't take more than a few minutes, everything should be timed perfectly (synchronize watches). Hero calls the moves. B.P. Jorge will go in with José and Atila. El Matador will stand lookout. Malevil will cover them from the second getaway car.

The plans were complete. Carefully explained, written out in detail, mimeographed, and distributed:

1) notes on exterior of locale
2) notes on interior of locale
3) floor plan of bank
4) street map
5) analysis of traffic problems, stop signs in the area, duration of red lights, exit options, etc.
6) descriptive plan of assault: enter, guns aimed. Say: "this is a stick-up, everybody's hands over their heads." Take employees to bathroom, find the manager, collect the money, and get out of there. No unnecessary shooting, no running in the street.
7) disguises to be used: lighten hair, wear wigs, glasses, mustaches, false teeth, speak ungrammatically, pronounce names wrong, yell made-up nicknames, use a little Spanish, *muchacho, hijo de una puta, la gaita.*

They read and reread the plans, they memorized them, they went to check out the bank. Drove by a few times. Looked over the guards standing there with machine guns in hand. Observed daily business. Confirmed the information in the reports. All set.

They left for their first job together.

Creeeeeeennnnch, the tires screeched as they braked. Doors slammed. B.P. Jorge ran toward the bank, lugar in hand. The others were advancing slowly, cautiously; Jorge was calling attention to himself. The guards raised their machine guns. It was time for Malevil to raise his and yell: Hold it right there. Malevil lost his voice,[1] he couldn't say a

---

[1]Malevil didn't lose his voice. I just can't believe that. Later you'll find out why.

word. So the guards opened fire on B.P. Jorge. The bullets picked him up as if he were flying and landed him on the curb, cut to ribbons. By this time, José and Atila were inside the bank. They put their guns away fast. They took a deep breath and went up to the counter. Stuck their hands in their pockets. Took out thirty cruzeiros apiece and said to the panic-stricken teller:

—We'd like to make a deposit.

LESSON NUMBER ONE
(practical instruction)

He would leave the cup under the faucet and try to go to sleep, listening to the plink, plink of the water. He knew there was a Chinese torture like this, to make a person go crazy. He needed to practice, so he could endure it if necessary. But he could never get to sleep, he kept counting the plinks until he'd get so enraged that he'd spring out of bed and run to take the cup away, so worked up sometimes that he would tear the whole kitchen apart.

THOUGHT FOR THE DAY:
Nine out of ten starlets prefer Lux Soap.

VISION

A little blonde in a miniskirt, flower vendors, boys, girls, sleeping in doorways, whores discreetly climbing into automobiles.

THE MAN ON THE POSTER

Wanted: These individuals commit robbery and kill family men. Attention! If you recognize one of these men, denounce him to the nearest policeman.

José stood next to the poster with his picture on it. A grainy photograph. People passed, glanced at the poster, looked at José. And walked on by. He went up to a cop.

—Mr. Policeman, I saw a guy over there who looked just like the one on the poster.

—Where?

—Near that book stall.

The policeman looked suspicious.

—Was he alone?

—I think there were two of them.

—I bet they're setting a bomb . . .

—Shit, you better go arrest them!

—I will. In a minute. Keep an eye out while I make a phone call.

The policeman disappeared.

End of José's first experiment.

THE QUESTION

—Oh, policeman, sir, where's Maria Antonia Street?

—That's quite a ways from here. You'd have to take a bus.

—Oh, wow, how am I going to get there? There aren't any buses this late.

—What's the problem?

—Well, my friend's mother died, I have to go let him know.

—Hey, maybe we can take you out there. Yeah, why not.

So the policemen gave José a lift in the patrol car, and he had a lively chat with them about terrorism, the climate of crime in the city, and those sons-of-bitches the Communs.

—Gee, thanks an awful lot for the ride.

—Aw, don't mention it, son.

End of second experiment.

EJACULATORY PRAYER: Who can do more, weeps less. (500 days of indulgences)

THROWING IN THE TOWEL

—Here he is, chief, he says he's got some information.

—He does, does he.

A nod of the head. (That must be the detective who commands the Death Squad, the Anti-Terror organization. An immense man, wide-shouldered, with the blue eyes of a baby.[1])

—How much will you pay?

—That depends on the information.

—Give me an idea at least.

—Robber or terrorist?

—It's all the same thing, isn't it?

—Not really. You know, money's tight . . . we're not paying top dollar here. Just look at all the leads we've got already today. All hot, maybe a hundred of them. Everybody's looking for a little extra cash.

(Mother-fucking competition.)

—I got some good stuff. On a guy you're looking for. His picture's in all the bus stations, bars, and movie houses.

—Good, we can arrest you, hook up the wires, and you'll start talking without us paying a dime.

He laughed. Out of fear and at his own stupidity.

—Thirty dollars, said the detective.

—Thirty?

—Not too bad, huh? In real dollars, too.

—This is worth a lot more, but . . . I'll take what I can get.

—Okay, go on.

He walked over to the poster behind the detective's desk. Pointed out José.

—Aw, he's not worth much.

—That's what you think. He's worth a lot. He knows Gê.

—Gê is dead. Dead and buried.

—Another trick.

—What trick? I was in on that operation myself.

—From what I hear, that wasn't Gê. You buried somebody else.

—Who?

—Some guy who looked like Gê. What I heard was that the Repressive Forces got the tip and took off after Gê, but he'd been warned at the last minute by one of the women. Who hid him. There was a guy in the group, shy, practically Gê's double, who offered to stay in his place. The poor fucker was a manic-depressive. Always in the pits. He was scared to death of robberies, bombs, scared of everything.

---

[1]Eyes are not the portrait of the soul.

220

That was the only day he was brave. Cornered, but brave. You guys killed him, thinking he was Gê. Nobody saw Gê slip off with the women, wrapped in a kerchief.

—How do you know all this?

—I'm a friend of José, José's a friend of Gê.

—There must be more to it than that. Maybe you're one of the Communs, huh?

There were three greenbacks exploding in the detective's hand.

—Okay, here's the thirty. If we get Gê, you'll pick up three hundred.

—You'll get the whole bunch of them. Atila, Hero . . .

—Who are they?

—Guys from José's group.

—Never heard of them.

—They just joined a little while ago. Before they were just drunks and troublemakers.

—When will it be?

—Day after tomorrow, Sunday. They're going out to Vila Branca to look for the kid with music in his belly.

—That kid who's in the papers all the time?

—Yeah, he disappeared.

—That so.

—And he's Gê's son.

—What?

—Disappeared. José's gang is supposed to find him. He's somewhere in Vila Branca.

—So how do we proceed?

—Well let's see . . .

(The detective thinks: this José character is no big deal.)

—He'll be there with his wife. When she's standing next to him, I'll go up and kiss her. You take care of the rest.

(What a riot, this guy will get the group together and we'll bust them all, him included.)

Not a bad idea, detective.

OFFICIAL NEWSFLASH

. . . expulsion of professors who have been trying to destroy the national university . . . making the change from paving stones to asphalt in all cities: in the most recent demonstrations students have been prying up the stones to

221

make barricades . . . police just purchased fifty million tons of anti-personnel gas to be used to put down uprisings. Released in a spray, this gas provokes a loud buzzing in the ears as well as an acutely upset stomach . . .

MAKE LOVE, MAKE WAR

(War is love)
—What's wrong, Zé?
—Nothing.
—You're not after me like you always used to be.
. . .
—Is there someone else?
. . .
—Has it ever occurred to you that I like you, that I need you?
. . .
—Talk to me!
(There's a big job tomorrow. I don't like these group jobs. If I were on my own, maybe I'd manage to do the thing right. And when I pull a job, I want at least some of the cash for myself. Gê says: it's for the struggle, political ends. I don't have anything to do with that. I want what's mine, to do things my way. Like the other day, those guys kidnapped the Ambassador. That's what it's all about, kidnapping, making demands. That's smart. Down with the government.)
—Don't you like me anymore, honey? . . . Yeah, I can tell what you're thinking. But you're just as guilty as I am.
. . .
—Talk, for God's sake, talk to me.
. . .
—It's not what we wanted, Zé. But it happened. I didn't know what I was doing. Neither did you.
. . .
—Remember? You must have been drunk, or high, or whacked out, I don't know . . . I don't remember. I blacked it all out. Everything.
. . .
—But I've already got my punishment, Zé. A constant headache, this discharge, whatever it is, every other day . . .

(Sometimes I feel suddenly light. Gravity disappears, and I float upward a few centimeters. It starts with a drunken sort of feeling, then I lose my sense of direction, and finally I feel light, like I'm floating on air. Two seconds. That's what it was like after I smelled the pit.)

> THOUGHT FOR THE DAY:
> We're not the biggest
> so we've got to be the best:
> Come to Atlantic for Grade A service.

SWEATY FEET?

Use Sonsock, and eliminate foot odor fast! (Available in all drugstores.)

A BLESSING FROM THE FRANCISCANS

Sometimes when José was screwing, he would get up and go run cool water over his wrists, letting his body cool off a little, and then he'd go back to bed with a vengeance, making the woman moan, scream, howl. Afterward, he went to get a blessing from the Franciscans—which, according to popular belief, repels bad luck and brings health, good fortune in business, and happiness in love.

PRECAUTION

A good terrorist never leaves cartridges around. Prevention.

JOHNSON'S BABY

According to Rosa's mother, old newspapers testify to the fact that Rosa was the Johnson's Baby contest winner in such and such a year, rosy-cheeked and robust.

GOVERNMENT ENACTS TEN COMMANDMENTS FOR WOMEN

1. The hems of thy skirts shall be lowered.
2. Thou shalt not wear low-necked dresses.
3. Thou shalt wear long gloves.
4. Thou shalt not leave the house.
5. Thou shalt not participate in profane entertainments.
6. Thou shalt not dance erotic dances.
7. Thou shalt not frequent swimming pools.
8. Thou shalt learn to play the piano, to embroider, to sew, and to cook.
9. Thou shalt learn to take care of children.
10. Thou shalt be always pious.

LETTER TO THE EDITOR

". . . I had finished painting my house just the day before, so I was very upset to see that it already had a bunch of slogans written all over it by some frustrated defeatist who thinks he can overthrow the government with a brush and paint. Something better be done about this, because law-abiding citizens like myself are sick and tired of spending money on improvements and progress just to have these communists come and ruin everything."

Signed, Carlos Mueller.

PERCEPTION

You may have noticed that so far José hasn't himself been wounded; in fact, he hasn't got a scratch on him. Not because he's a super-hero. On the contrary, he's a sub-hero, and goes by unnoticed, unattacked, unappreciated.

CARELESSNESS

Detective Dores called a press conference to declare that due to carelessness the banks have not been sufficiently cooperative in the area of security problems. They lack special rooms for large deposits and withdrawals. The alarm systems are ancient and defective. They have not invested in closed-circuit TV cameras to film whatever incidents regretfully occur.

CONFIDENTIAL

The eminent Detective Dores, to a friend: I think the banks must be collaborating. They're unhappy with the economic policies of the government so they want to overthrow the regime, I'm sure of it.

THE BOY WITH MUSIC IN HIS BELLY

Hero proclaimed: I want to see this kid. I've got an idea for a song, I'll enter it in the Festival Competition, I've even got the title: *How I Went to a Poor Neighborhood and Met Misery and Saw Unhappiness.* Or: *The Belly's Empty But There's Music Inside.*

Conversation in a taxi:
—You were visiting in the interior that day, Rosa.
—No I wasn't, you're wrong. I went to the First Aid Station.
—Really?
—Uh-huh, I was hemorrhaging, losing a lot of blood.
—Where was José?
—Oh, out somewhere.
—What did you do?
—I almost died of the abortion. I lost a lot of blood. It was only afterward that I went to visit my parents. A friend of José's took me.
—That husband of yours!
—They found José at home, days later. Out cold on the floor. He'd bitten his tongue, his head was all bruised.
—Leave me on the corner, please. I'm going to go buy a bra.

THE SEARCH

For three days the old Ige-Sha's assistants have been walking the city, looking for the Chosen One. They're sure they'll see a sign. They're walking in the right direction, they're already in the neighborhood. For the day is fast approaching and the Chosen One (does she really exist?) is about to arrive.

LESSON NUMBER ONE
(repetition)

He left the cup under the faucet and tried to go to sleep, listening to the plink, plink of the water. He knew there was a Chinese torture like this, to make a person go crazy. So he needed to practice to be able to endure it when the day came. But he couldn't fall asleep, he kept counting the plinks, until he got so enraged that he jumped out of bed and ran to take the cup away, so worked up that he tore the whole kitchen apart.

ESCALATION

The Chief of Police informed
the Chief of Political Police and the Chief of Political Police informed
the Chief of Super-Security and the Chief of Super-Security informed
the Chief of the Repressive Political Council on Terror and Subversion for the Cohesive Maintenance of Order in the Nation (RPCTSCMON), who, in turn, informed
the Chief of General National Order, who, in turn, informed
the Chief of the Repressive Militias, who, in turn, informed
the President, who, in turn, informed
whoever has the final say.
And so, whoever has the final say decided. And after deciding, consulted with his advisor. Consulted just for the sake of consulting; he had his own ideas, immutable, fixed, definitive.

The decision thus ratified, the President was informed and gave the order:

"Kill all children in Vila Branca on Sunday. Gê's son will be among them."[1]

---

[1]Which proves: history repeats itself.

MEANS OF COMMUNICATION
(Tribalization)

When I killed the master of ceremonies I should have sat on the throne of the Most Hated For A Day. I was walking behind him. He turned, I limped a little, he thought I was a fan. So he hurried on ahead, thinking I wanted to ask him a favor or something. I know, because when I got closer he smiled and said: "Please, I'm really very tired. I spent the whole day choosing people for my program, I listened to more than four hundred sob stories and had to choose ten. So, please, my friend, if you want to talk to me, come see me next Friday morning, not now." He talked to me as if I were a TV camera. He was smiling the enormous smile of someone who has always won in life, a rich man. He was smiling like that when I shot him right in the temple.

THERE ARE DAYS WHEN YOU FEEL
LIKE SOMEONE WHO WENT AWAY, OR DIED

Seven-thirty, they get on the bus. El Matador is looking at Rosa, crazy to ball her. José, drunk, says to Hero:
—My life is just like Scott Fitzgerald's. Tragic, and mixed up with a crazy woman.
—Oh, come on, don't start getting depressed.
—I'm a fuck-up, aren't I?
—Yeah, but you should fight it.
—Tomorrow. Today I'm not in the mood.
The bus winds along, following the river. They see firemen pulling a decapitated body out of the water.
—Must have been the Death Squad.

LESSON NUMBER ONE
(listening to the recording)

Plinkplink, plink, plink, plink, plink, plink, plink, plink, plink, plink / 16 in 50 seconds.
Plink, plink, plink, plink, plink, plink, plink, plink, plink, plink, plink, plink, plink / 32 in 95 seconds (1 minute and 35 seconds).
Four hours and ten minutes: plinkplinkplinkplinkplink-plinkplinkplinkplink—plink praaaaaaararaaaaa, preem,

pra, crash, treen, trock, trock, trock, trock, pam, plaaarim,
plim.

VISION

Signs—total cost
of this project: 2 billion.
Paper bags / truck
carcasses / grass / viaducts /
entrances to developments /
detours / more trucks / gas stations /
tire repairs / oil /
garbage / house foundations /
trade in your old battery
for a new one / asphalt
factories / cement
mixers / striped trucks /
tropical monuments.

LAST STOP

The girl next to Rosa with the old face, tired eyes, was listening to the radio: "Let's ask our Father in heaven to put
an end to all wars. We pray that He may extend His hand to
us and that all men may extend theirs to Him."

Last stop. Directions from the ticket-taker:

You take the first street to the left, and you'll come out in
a little square with a maracock tree. Look for the stucco
house where they sell macumba stuff, and walk a little ways
until you get to the shack made of tin cans. Ask there, and
they'll tell you.

HOME SWEET HOME

parents and children arguing about the filth, the garbage,
the city's rotten leftovers heaped up in mountains, vultures
and trash-pickers sorting and selecting, the smell of de-
cay . . .

THE RENDEZVOUS

They found the house and met the father of the boy with
music in his belly.

—Welcome, brothers, welcome. My house belongs to the world, the house of God, the house of the Spirit.

He was in his forties, skinny as a rail, and had only two front teeth. He spit when he talked. He offered José a Coke, José said no. Rosa asked for a Fanta.

—Ice cold Coke, or catuaba tea, sister. That's all we have.

They went around back in the tiny yard to wait. It was hot in the sun. The walls of the house were cracked. They could hear soft music coming from inside.

—Could it really be from the boy's belly?

—It's a hoax, it's gotta be a hoax, just wait and see, said El Matador. I came prepared.

He was excited, happy, even; he looked at the others self-importantly.

(I never liked that superior look of his, thought Rosa.)

The door to the shack was closed, chained and locked. They wandered around the yard, the other door in back was closed up tight, padlocked. Stones, leaves, paper, bottles, wood, leftover food. A scabby dog tied on a chain. A clothesline, with bags full of rags hanging on it, faded Lee jeans, and two skirts. The shack was perched high on the hill. Two hundred meters below: the woods, the river, chimneys, factories under construction, factories already churning out things for people to buy.

—This city stinks, said Zé Scott.

—This city is completely colorless, said Hero.

(Hero always thinks he's so original, thought José.)

WAIT

—We want to see the boy!

—Not right now. He's with Joshua, his captain. You'll have to wait.

—How long?

—An hour and a half, two hours.

—Two hours? What do we do till then?

—You know the Family?

—What family?

—The Family. That's all I can say. If you don't know what I mean . . .

—What family you talking about? Speak up.

—No, forget it, I really can't say. But stick around, this will be worth the wait . . . it's terrific, really.

—Look, we want to know about this family, whoever they are.

—I'm not saying any more. 'Cause Vampire doesn't want me to . . . Look for Black Brit, he'll show you the way.

—Yeah, sure, and who's Black Brit?

—The black dude with a little market down below.

—Bunch of shit. Let's get out of here.

—Not me, said Atila.

José and El Matador took off. The air was filled with a samba beat, tamborines and frying pans.

> LIQUIDATION / SALE
> repressive militias have acquired at rock-bottom prices the entire stock of napalm bombs for use on Christmas, the first of May, and other important dates

SMOKING, I HOPE

Blam, pleck-pleck, proom, blaaaaant, vrooooom: machines, excavators, opening holes in the ground. Men digging the earth like ants. They pulled out trees, knocked down houses, planted iron stakes, filled gaping holes with iron and concrete: the subway.

Two hours later:

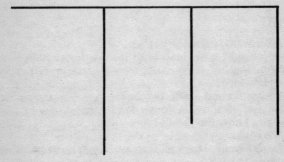

—Look how they're cutting down the trees all along the river. They're destroying the only greenery in the city, said Malevil.

230

(Malevil has a profound civic sense.)

Asphalt jungle—inhuman metropolis—insatiable city—devourer of people—cave of neurotics—glass tomb—cement forest—the world's fastest-growing city—locomotive hauling freight cars & dining cars—the biggest industrial complex in Latíndia-America.

Two hours later:
—It's a trick.
—What should we do, hang around or leave?
—For now, let's wait.
—This kid doesn't exist.
—They're suspicious, that's all. They've got to be careful, they've got to keep him hidden, if the kid is Gê's son.
—But they can't hide him now that everybody knows about the music in his belly.

Atila looked at Rosa.

(I'd like to screw that one.)

Rosa was sitting on an upside-down oil drum. She scratched her thighs violently: mosquitos.[1]

An hour later:
A group of boys were walking along rattling tamborines, banging pots and pans together, beating out their samba rhythm on anything they could get their hands on. They curved around the side of a hill and disappeared, but the samba beat remained.
—Sun's hot.
—What have you got to eat?
—Mortadella, bread, guava jam, rum.
—Any beer?
—Only in cans. No ice. Today's Sunday, we're cleaned out.

Mortadella cut in thick slices, a fatty smell in the air, dry scraps on a plate: linguiça in vinegar, hot dogs, skinny meat pies.
—You folks got business in the neighborhood?
—We came to see the boy with music in his belly.
—Don't waste your money. Kid's a hoax.
—Nah, we heard lots of people come to see him.

---

[1] To lend a tropical setting.

—Yeah, sure . . . his father's a regular flimflam man, always got something going. Everybody around here knows him.

—A little more mortadella, please.

EUROPE CURTSIES

Mr. Raphael Luiz Junqueira Tomaz, the country's one-hundredth heart transplant patient, has been out of the hospital four months and is doing very well at home. . . . In fact, he is the only heart recipient still alive in the world today.

—More mortadella.

—That's the last of it. And I got to close up soon. We've got a soccer game this afternoon.

José had eaten the whole mortadella. Now he wrapped the last piece to go. El Matador took along the bottle of rum. The man closed up shop.

—Son-of-a-bitch Sunday.

—Let's find this kid, whatever it takes.

—I'm already lost, aren't you?

The alleys climbed up and down, dividing and subdividing. Empty streets. Everything closed. The sound of tamborines and pots and pans in the air.

VISION

Graffiti on the shacks: "Down with the Government," "Death to the Death Squads," "Long Live the Communs," "Every dead policeman should be paid for with twenty dead terrorists," the symbol:

FREE ASSOCIATION

That attack José had on our honeymoon in São Pedro Springs—he was unconscious twenty-four hours. When he came to, he looked at me so strangely, and then he got up and walked away! Wanted to take a stroll by himself, he said, but I followed him. He went into the bushes and just looked down at them, all confused. He just stood there staring at the bushes, the grass.

—Where's the stream?

—What stream?

—Yesterday there was a stream here.

—There was never any stream here, that's the trouble with São Pedro Springs: no water.

—But I was here. Yesterday.

—You were in a stupor yesterday.

Ever since then, José has been looking at me strangely. Once he even told me I was crazy, completely nuts. And he asked me about the old folks (my parents?), and the "crime," and I said what are you talking about, there hasn't been any crime.

Or has there?

BLACK BRIT

They walked across the balding soccer field, full of holes, bounded by warped goal posts. At the other end, there was a bar. Skinny kids playing with a mouse on a string. And a cat, also tied on a string. One kid held the mouse's string, another one held the cat's, and they'd give both animals some slack so the mouse would run from the cat and the boys could control the strings.

(No, this didn't remind José of his childhood, or even of the time he spent catching mice in the movie theater.)

—Where do we find Black Brit?

—Straight ahead. When you see the Coca-Cola, you're there.

It was a Coke bottle seven feet tall. Black Brit ran a little market. The stall was made out of labels from cans, advertising mar-

When the Queen of England visited this country, the government constructed immense panels, with gardens and pretty houses, buildings and factories, painted on them, and they were set up in front of all the slums and poor neighborhoods. But a resident of one of these run-down sections, who happened to be extremely dark-skinned, had his heart set on seeing the queen. He knew that the royal car would pass by the panel in front of his shack, and though the police were enforcing the rule that poor people stay in their houses that day, he managed to sneak

garine, oil, beer, Fanta, Pepsi.

He winked at Rosa. He was very black, slim, handsome, well built. He had a big smile on his face, and wore a red linen shirt with an alligator print.

(No, he's never played soccer, or even been in a samba club, he was just very black.)

Rosa laughed at him.

out and hide near the panel. Just as the queen was passing in front of him, he slit the canvas open with a razor and burst through yelling: "Tank you, tank you." From then on he was known as Black Brit.

—Do you have guava jam?

—What brand do you want: Cica or Peixe?

—Cica.

—All right! The little lady's talkin' passwords. You here to see the Family?

—Family?

—Yeah.

Black Brit ducked his head out of the stall and called to Hero.

—Who sent you people? The Astronaut?

—What are you talking about?

—If you say "Cica," it means you want to see the Family.

—What Family?

—She coming too?

—Uh-huh.

—It's pretty strong stuff . . .

(What kind of shit will this turn out to be?)

—That's okay, she's a whore.

—Son of a bitch.

HOME SWEET HOME

His Mom and Dad agreed with him and they kissed him good-bye He said he'd rather kill himself than fall into the Death Squad's clutches He was just a boy, a twenty-year-old burglar, the terror of the neighborhood He killed himself with a shot to the head, having taken care first to sit himself down on a bench

BLACK POWER

—Hoorse! Hoorse! Oh, Hoorsey . . .

Sun on the walls. A house opened up, an old black

woman came out, followed by a younger black woman, and a girl, and finally the smallest girl, wearing a white dress with the red letters "Peace" on her chest, and a veil and white gloves, and she carried a fancy candle in her hand. Then out came an old black man, and a younger man, and a boy, and two very little boys.

—On your way already, Dona Arminda? Gee, the little girl has some fancy dress! Whyn't you stop by later and have a couple, on me.

The blacks marched off down the street.

—Come on now, horse, come here . . . hoooorse, hey hooooorrsse . . .

—What do we do now? asked Rosa.

—I don't know.

—Hey Brit, should we wait or come back in a little while?

—That rotten horse. He disappeared.

VISION

there was a fight: one kicked the other in the face and got shot for it

HEROIC

Rosa and Hero started walking. The black family had gone into a tiled house right where the street forked into four narrow alleys, subdividing again and again, all crooked. At the first main fork, there was a little square with a spigot in the middle of it.

Dona Arminda "makes little angels," which means she does abortions. She's got a room downtown and usually does about ten a day. The police don't bother her (she pays them well), and she makes a steady income.

The spigot was on. A guy nearby was taking a piss. A group of girls watched from the house across the street. Rosa was watching too.

—Let me shake it for you!

HOME SWEET HOME

my father has a liver disease my mother is epileptic no one wants to give me a job because I'm old enough to be drafted that's why I steal things

235

THUD

The street split into four alleys, each of them subdividing into more crooked alleys, and the new ones branching into narrow paths. The grocery was called *What Love, Ltd.* The owner was a wizened old man from the interior . . . probably from up north. It was the kind of grocery that has a greasy counter.

—Shot of rum please.

—One for the lady, too?

—No, just one.

Hero looked at the kid sitting on a sack of beans. Skinny, ragged clothes, a shirt with a patch on the side. He had a heavy beard and his arm was in a sling.

—I know you, don't I? What's your name?

—Journalist.

—Journalist?

—Yeah.

—No, what's your name?

—Journalist.

—His name is Bernardo. But ever since the gang dubbed him the Journalist that's what he's called. He's sort of whacko. Some days he's okay, other days he's really out of it, said the old guy.

—How do we get a bus around here?

—Going where?

—Out of here. Downtown.

—For a bus downtown, you go straight up to the Association, turn left and keep going 'til you get to Sandro the chicken farmer's place. Go around back of the coop (all stolen chickens) and down the steps. Then you take the whores' shortcut, straight ahead, and you'll end up at Marginal, the stop is two hundred meters further.

—The whores' shortcut?

—Yeah, the neighborhood whores go there at night, they call it home. Anybody who wants one just shows up and waits.

VISION

he shot the woman and shoved her under the car and ran her over he was a dope dealer and the police were after him the squad had him on their list

Old Ige-Sha's chosen ones stopped under the pole strung with high tension wires and listened to the hum and buzz. Four bars of wood nailed across each pole to hold up the wires, and the sun beat down from one side, casting this shadow on the ground: a horizontal line with four vertical crosspieces.

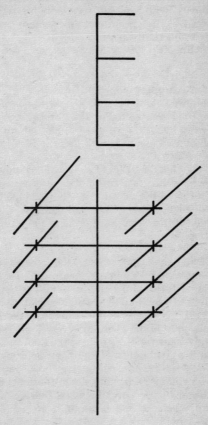

I'VE GOT A BLACK MULE

clup, clop, cluppety clop
nei-ei-ei-eigh

—Whitey, hey whitey, nei-ei-ei-eigh. Yoo-hoo, hey you with the girl . . .

A heavyset guy with dark hair was calling. He was all harnessed up, with saddlebags and partial blinders on, he even had a bit in his mouth. And hanging from his ass was a black tail, real horse-hair. He wore boots made to look like horse hooves, with wooden heels. In his right hand, a whip. He was in continuous movement, pawing the ground with his right "hoof."

—Black Brit says everything's all set. You can come now . . .

nie-ei-ei-eigh

clup, clop, cluppety clop

They followed along behind. Rosa with her mouth hanging open. The horse trotted up the slope quickly. He would actually whip himself, continue on, hesitate for a moment, and whip himself again. He led them to Black Brit's.

scritch, scratch

Horse got a little handful of sugar and sat down in a corner, munching the grass and looking at Rosa and Hero.

—You're back! It's all set up. The Family's ready and waiting, just let the horse have a little chow, then you can follow him. Or I'm sure he'd be glad to carry you if you want to hop on.

—Who *is* this guy?

—Can't you see? He's Horse. Don't worry, completely tame. Every once in a while he rears, or bites someone a little. That's all. He thinks he's a horse. They even made a barn for him to sleep in. He just ambles around here, delivers messages, hauls carts home from the market, gives kids rides. And, pardon the expression . . . look, miss, if I say this it's only 'cause you're going to see the Family, I mean I know you're a good girl and don't have anything to do with all this . . . well, the horse even screwed a couple of mares they got in Vampire's pasture down there near the dairy. There's this ravine, see, and the mares that are hot shoulder up to him when he comes around, so he fucks them. Whoooey—yow!

—What do we do now?

—Where did everybody go? We're going to miss seeing that kid.

—What's this Family we're supposed to be looking for?

—Who knows.

The blacks went by in a line down below. All in white, high-quality linen. As they passed, red stains appeared in the air behind them.

HOME SWEET HOME

mother stabs son in the middle of the street at three in the afternoon and son asks mother's blessing before he dies

THE RENOVATION OF THE OLD WOMEN

José and El Matador saw the red stains.
—Where did everybody go?
They entered the square where the crooked alleys met. The alleys subdivided and formed other little squares, with yellow-green houses, an Anacin sign, a billboard of a man eating a cow. *He makes an open pass to Parada, Parada returns it to Eduardo. Eduardo fakes and loses the ball to Paulo Henrique who kicks it into midfield . . . and now a brilliant header by Dirceu Alves!* José stood still and looked in the window. A radio in a wooden case, a magic eye, transmitting the game to a group of fat women in blue satin dresses, strings of pearls around their necks, red lipstick. They ran their tongues across their lips, slowly.
—Hey, handsome. Come on inside.
An old woman straddling a gold footstool, panting like a tired dog, her tongue hanging out. Thighs crisscrossed with varicose veins, no underpants, her half-bald privates exposed.
José got excited just looking at her.
—How about it, handsome, yes or no?
(Should I go in?)
—If not, keep on moving.
The team got a goal, they laughed a laugh without sound. Some of them had no teeth. From inside the house came the smell of yesterday's bad breath, dirty feet, sweat bottled up in the armpits (no deodorant), poorly washed cunts, stomachs boiling and letting off gas, releasing farts slowly so the smell lingered in the folds of their clothes.
One of the women threw up all over her dress and the others ran off, fanning themselves madly. José walked away from the window. A man grabbed his arm.
—Did you go in there?

—No.

—Good thing. All the women are sick. There's better places.

—I'm really not interested.

—You son-of-a-bitch! the woman yelled from the window, shaking her yellow and green fan streaming colored ribbons. Son-of-a-bitch Vampire, get the hell outta here! Stop ruining business!

The man twisted up his mouth and spit at her. The spittle flew up in the air but missed. She spit back at him.

—Stop screwing around with our business, I tell you. If you don't like it, there's folks who do. Who need it.

—Only if they need it real bad, to go to your asylum of paraplegics.

—So's your mother.

—Come with me, said the man.

José didn't know what to do. El Matador was in the middle of the square whistling patriotic hymns. El Matador adored patriotic hymns.

—You watch yourself with that guy, handsome, I mean it! the woman screamed after them.

—You should come visit the Family.

—What Family?

—A model family. Don't worry, you'll like them.

—I don't understand.

—Just come with me. You can pay later. Trust me.

—What are you talking about? I don't understand a thing you're saying.

—Trust me, kid. I'm president of the Neighborhood Association. I'm an honest guy, straightforward.

—Petty politician! Thief! Assassin! Scoundrel!

—I'll have you arrested someday, you old bag!

—Yeah. You would do a thing like that.

—No, even better, I'll have you evicted. For licentious behavior. You and all the other sickies. Syphilitics.

—So's your mother, creep.

—Come on, kid, let's go see the Family. Don't pay any attention to the old hag. Live and let live, that's my advice. She's the oldest whore in the neighborhood . . . in the country. She taught the girls everything they know, maybe their grandmothers too.

The red stains moved along in the air. The white mass

240

had disappeared. José shaded his eyes from the sun. The stains seemed to be moving with the wind.

(I wonder what that is down below.)

—So. There's a session at four-thirty, how about it?

(This guy is beginning to get on my nerves.)

—Four-thirty . . . then it's still early. Let me think about it. How do I get there, if I decide to go?

El Matador was whistling the strains of the national anthem. He was thinking about the alleys that divided and subdivided.

(What are we looking for, in the middle of this fucking confusion?)

—Do whatever you have to do. I'll send someone for you at four-thirty sharp.

—Sure. I'll be with some friends, they'll probably come too.

—Okay. See you later . . .

José went up to the whores' window again. The oldest one was sitting on her gold footstool, waving her yellow-green fan. The one who vomited had changed her dress. She was sucking in air (like a glutton) through an asthma device. Her pulpy gums showed, her dentures were falling out.

—Come on in, sonny. Aparecida, open the door!

Two houses down a gate opened. A Japanese woman came out and motioned to José. He followed her through the yard full of primroses, dahlias, marigolds, snapdragons, hydrangeas.

HABITS AND CUSTOMS

the government has been requested to establish gallows and guillotines and electric chairs and gas chambers in addition to the firing squads and lynch mobs

FIRST COMMUNION

The little girls continued up the hill while the grown-ups went inside a wooden shed which had been all done up with crepe-paper flowers, streamers, palm leaves, and little flags.

As the girls approached the large stone cross and kneeled down in front of it, the catechism teachers clapped their hands. The girls sang: *My heart belongs to Jesus alone, my joy is the Holy Cross.* They prayed for the soul of a girl who had died in an accident, as the teacher called it, but the girls near where Atila was standing murmured *accident, what accident, she got raped by the Blind Rooster Gang.*

The girls arranged their dresses, set their piety in order, and started back. Except for one small black girl who stayed behind. She walked around the fence and over behind a tree stump.

The other girls went into the shed with the crepe-paper streamers. Almost immediately, an old black woman came outside, with a man and two little boys. They peered all around, obviously looking for someone.

Atila went off in the direction of the stump.

(The girl must have gone over there to pee.)

She wasn't there. He continued on until he came to a lot full of tin cans, between two houses painted black and red. The girl was standing in the middle of the lot surrounded by a gang of boys.

They were taking turns running up to her and jumping in puddles, splattering her white dress with mud and dirty water. She tried to run. The boys made sure that whenever she came near a puddle (there were a lot of them) someone would jump into it, splat, and up flew the mud. Then they started throwing horse manure at her, trying to hit the red letters, "Peace," on her chest.

—Help me, mister!

Atila picked up a piece of horseshit and joined the fun. The boys laughed and jumped up and down.

—Hey, I've got an idea . . . that priest wouldn't let *us* make first communion, let's throw turds at him, too.

—Yeah, he only likes girls, let's ruin the bastard's little party.

As soon as they got close to the church they started heaving the stuff at the white walls. They screamed like demons: *we want chocolate, we want chocolate!* They circled the church throwing turds and yelling. They ran for refills and approached the shed, their hands full. The women were still inside but some of the men were just coming out, taking off their jackets. The boys plastered them with shit and disappeared into the crooked alleys that divided and subdivided.

HOME SWEET HOME

soldier tries to violate girl and is lynched by father mother brothers and other relatives

DEFENDING THE FAMILY

The banners were brilliant, the girls were circling around, and the men with the clipboards were impatient.

—A bunch of illiterates around here.

—Take a look at that first list of signatures! Call Maurice . . . he knows how to do a thousand different signatures. The person can just give his address and approve and Maurice will sign. It's easy. The thing is to get signatures. The more the better. We've got to hurry, got the whole neighborhood to do yet.

The marchers raised the banners in the air. Atila was feeling the sun, he was half giddy. Hunger. Houses on one side, the river on the other, wide and dirty. A motionless excavator, half in the water, a drain pipe sticking out from the edge. Thick mud ran out of it, liquid shit.

(Where did everybody go?)

Sign here! Let's go, everybody sign!

They were like a mob. Sweeping the area, one with a red banner, another with a clipboard, papers, and pens. They walked with their backs straight, chests thrust forward. In sharply pressed gray suits and dark ties. The banners had gold lettering, shining in the sunlight, and the people carrying them seemed to be drawing an army along behind them. Onward into battle. Even the shortest and slightest among them becoming (they thought) tall and fearless warriors.

—Sign here, kid! Sign this petition against communist infiltration in the church! Come on, let's go!

They were pushing people around. The priest leaned out the window of the shed, calling to each and every one. Sending them to the young men with the clipboards.

—That's the way, let's go, everybody.

—What for?

—You've got to sign. We're defending the family.

—But I'm not married.

243

AS-pir-in, AS-pir-in,
it makes you feel better
and that's no sin!

clup, clop, cluppety clop
nei-ei-ei-ei-eigh, nei-ei-ei-gh
cluppety clop, cluppety clop

Leaning against a wall, no ambition to go anywhere, Atila just listened to the cluppety clop.

The horse trotted past him, harness and all.

—You there . . . hey you, come here . . . Shit, this guy's crazy!

The horse stopped.

—Hey, you know the kid with music in his belly? Where's he live?

—What will you pay?

—Shit, I don't know . . . how much do you want?

Atila stuck his hand in his pocket looking for small change.

—No, not money. Oats.

—Sure . . . okay.

The horse trotted up the street and through the alleys. Atila had to run and still he couldn't keep up. Weak legs. The horse galloped on at an even pace, whinnying without even looking back. Atila's feet hurt. His head was spinning, his stomach grumbled, he was getting cramps in his calves.

HOME SWEET HOME

lesbian kills homosexual accusing him of lesbianism: she found him in bed with her woman

They paraded by like a samba school. Shaking tambourines, beating pots and pans, whistling. The ragamuffin boys. Who had a lot of rhythm. The ones in front didn't even have instruments, they just danced the samba. They marched along past Rosa and Hero, making a devilish noise.

HABITS AND CUSTOMS

the thirty-sixth victim of the Squad has been found: riddled with sixty-five bullets and wearing only his underpants

—Documents please.

Rosa and Hero showed their papers.

—What are you doing in this neighborhood?

—We came to see the boy with music in his belly.

—Ah, mmmmmmm . . .

The sound of sirens. From where they were standing, way up high, you could see the alleys down below. Full of black and yellow patrol cars (the new police colors). There were an awful lot of them. They were honking, they had their sirens on, and you could hear shooting.

VISION

cadavers mounting up in the National Medical Institute and there's no more room so doctors proclaim the collapse of the N.M.I. and go home

THE NECESSITY OF POLITICS

—Well, son, he calls the shots around here. The big guys from downtown support him. He takes care of things. Makes sure the neighborhood has money in the cash box. The Association's cash box, that is. Now he's going to be city councilman. Hell, I'll even vote for him, he's not all that bad. He stirs things up a little, but he's a good guy underneath. Got his problems like everyone else. Me, you, these old girls.

The old girls were fanning themselves with their ancient fans. Some of them went out and came back with Pai João. The smell of his meat-smoking business followed him into the room. Out in the street the sun beat down fiercely. José was sleepy. El Matador was still hanging around the square, whistling.

—Why don't we go to bed, huh? Me and you and a couple of the girls. We'll tell you Vampire's whole story. And you'll like the things we know how to do.

(Secular experience, a thousand years old. The rites of love, handed down from the Greeks and the Egyptians. Maybe from even earlier. These immoral courtesans spending their art and wisdom on the dregs of the neighborhood.)

(What could it be that these women know how to do?)

(With their wrinkled thighs and varicose veins, their flaccid breasts, nipples that will never be hard again, never.

Generations have sucked at those breasts, drained them of every last drop. Empty. Used up. Dog-tired.)

(What am I thinking? Fucking shit. Intellectualizing a bunch of old whores.)

—Don't you want to go in the bedroom yet? Well, maybe a little later. Oh, that Vampire. He's president of the Neighborhood Association. Has been for over ten years. Just try to get him out of there. A real SOB, that guy. A shameless thief. We've gotta pay him to keep the house open, that's right . . . and meanwhile he's got his own stable of girls, right nearby. Sixteen years old, the whole crew. Sure. Didn't he invite you to visit the Family? Yeah. I bet that makes him a pile of dough.

(Ah, I'd forgotten about the Family.)

—Do you have anything to eat here? Or to drink?

—Mortadella sandwich. And beer. But it's expensive. This is a house of women, not food, you know. So it ain't cheap, no kidding. Adelma! Bring the man a healthy sandwich!

—So, what were you saying about this guy Vampire?

—Like I said, he calls the shots. Protects the con men, sells stolen merchandise, pays off the police so they won't bust anybody around here.

—Why's he called Vampire?

—Jesus, I don't remember! Let's see . . . his real name's Caluda, but he's gone by the nickname for so long now. He used to fight it, though, boy did he ever. Killed someone over it in the beginning. I mean no one proved it was him . . .

(El Matador was talking with some guy in the square. Strange, the guy's wearing a harness. That bit really shines in the sun.)

—When Vampire was twenty he worked in the Emergency Room. But he always had a lot of money, nobody could figure it out. Until they discovered he also worked in another hospital, a private one for rich people. And he robbed blood from the lab. Substituted bottles of dog blood, horse blood, stuff like that. Then there was some trouble, I don't know . . . Vampire disappeared for a while. He came back years later, changed. Older. Even more of a scoundrel. The police know all about him, they don't pay no attention. The guy's mysterious.

(El Matador is trying to signal to me. What? He's getting

on that guy's shoulders, the guy with the harness, ha, now he's using the whip.)

ENTERTAINMENT: PANES ET CIRCENSES

—Dive again, said the man.

—No, Dad, no more. I'm so tired.

—Go on, just one more time.

—But I've got a headache. No more, Dad, please.

—One more time, son. Let's go!

A tiny yard behind a shack. A mulatto with gray hair, could be forty or fifty, or thirty, looking at a deep trough of dirty water. A skinny boy was in the trough, he could have been twelve, fifteen, eighteen, or twenty. He was breathing hard, gasping at the edge, looking at his father.

—Come on, boy, one more time. You're not gonna win that way, giving up.

—But I don't wanna win, Dad, I'm scared.

—Don't give me that scared business. Dive! I'm counting . . .

The skinny boy went under. Rosa leaned against a pine tree. Stink bugs ran along the limb with their brightly painted backs. Hero killed one, smeared the awful smell all over his hand, and Rosa laughed and laughed. (Perfect: city boy never even heard of stink bugs, ha ha.)

The boy's head popped out of the water, gasping.

—I can't do no more today, Dad.

—You got to.

—No, I can't, I'm gonna die. Jus' like Zé. An' then Pedro.

—No you're not gonna die. I'm watching, aren't I? Go on, once more.

—No, Daddy, you gotta let me stop!

—Boy, if you die it'll be because I kill you. Don't you know we need the money?

—I know, Dad, I know. But I just can't today, no more.

clup, clop, cluppety clop
nei-ei-ei-ei-eigh

—You got the youngest one in training, Mister Zé?

—Hey there, Horse. Yeah, but he don't want to. My own son, knows how bad off we are and everything . . .

—You already killed the others, Zé. You're gonna kill him too.

—No, not this time. This time we win the prize. Jatniel's got some lungs, that boy is strong. He's almost up to five and a half minutes now.

—That's not good enough anymore, Zé. Friday a guy stayed under for six minutes!

—Son of a bitch.

—Some guy from Vila Gumercindo. With a chest this big.

—If I lose this time . . .

—It's tough, Zé, that guy Friday was something.

—Ten million. Boy do I need ten million. I get that prize money and I'm out of here.

—Give it up, Zé. They say the network doesn't even pay.

—Sure they pay, don't kid yourself. I saw the greenbacks in Mrs. Ele's hand, the one who did the interview. They paid the guy, one bill on top of another. And this year they'll be paying me, Mr. Horse.

—Nei-ei-eigh. Pay, nothing. Gonna kill your kid, just like you did the others. One less mouth to feed, that it?

—Jatniel's gonna win for me, Horse.

—He's gonna win a hole in the ground, that's what. Nei-eigh.

cluppety clop, cluppety clop

THE CHOSEN ONE

There she was in the neighborhood, but no one recognized her. Even she didn't know who she was. She didn't know she'd find her way into a purification ritual. Maybe the last Ebó old Ige-Sha would ever do. Because that old woman, that didu-beré's mission, would be complete. And her spirit must go back to Africa (what's going on in Africa?).

THE CRUSADERS REACH JERUSALEM

—Look, I really have to go now, ma'am.

—Oh what's your hurry. Just another minute.

(El Matador disappeared, riding that crazy guy. And now this old bag.)

—I've really got to go. I have an appointment.

—You going to see the Family, huh? You can't fool me, I know that's where you're off to.

—The family?

—Everybody comes up here to see the Family. Sure, it's the big attraction.

—What *is* this family anyway?

The woman who vomited spread her legs and started pissing on the floor. Her urine was dark as Coca-Cola. The woman herself was yellow.

—Oh just look at that one. She gets worse every day, can't even work anymore.

—I'm getting out of here, lady.

—Cripes, what ingratitude. Boys are like that. We've been here in this house twenty-five years. From mother to daughter. A tradition. All the girls started here. Since they were kids they came to class with us. Take that one, the one who just pissed all over herself. She always did like to open her legs, ha ha. She'd take the guy's face and put it right up there. The girls loved her. All the young toughs came to us first: Seven-and-a-half, Little Wirey, Potto, Transistor, the Match, Mister Votes. The police killed so many of them . . .

—I've got to go. Really.

—Yeah, well, you've got lousy manners. No consideration. Taking up our time like this. The whole time we've been talking, I could have been working. There's always customers.

—Excuse me, ladies, said a clean-cut looking young man.

—Yes?

—We're collecting signatures against the Communist infiltration of the Church. In defense of the family, of tradition and propriety.

—Come on, girls. Let's defend the Church against Communism.

—That's it, exactly. Very good, thank you, ladies.

—What nice boys.

The oldest woman signed. She passed the clipboard around to the others, and they all added their signatures.

José took advantage of the distraction. He wandered through the kitchen looking for the back door. The yellow one who had pissed saw him leaving.

—Wait a minute, dearie, yoo-hoo!

—Yeah, come back here and sign this, the least you could do, said the one in charge.

The man held out the clipboard. José signed quickly, without looking at what it said.

—Okay, come in the other room, sweeties, come on in and collect some more signatures. Adelma! Open the door. Go on, call your friends, honey.

José followed Adelma and slipped out into the street. The boys with the red and gold flames on their lapels were streaming into the house.

(What now? Where did El Matador go?)

José went back inside.

—Where's that kid who was collecting signatures?

They pointed. He was with a woman who had a face like a sick monkey. José saw the clipboard sitting on the footstool. He tore out the page with his name on it. The boy with the red and gold flame on his lapel leaped up and punched José in the face. José socked him in the stomach. Another guy joined in, José got hit in the ear, a fist in the side of the head, the neck, he got kicked in the chest, the nose. He bled. He fell down, they kicked him again, in the stomach, between the legs. He went unconscious. They kept beating him. The old women looked on. "You can bet this one's a Communist," they said. The boys just kept on hitting him.

cluppety clop, cluppety clop

They dumped José, still unconscious, in the middle of the empty square.

The horse galloped up to him.

HABITS AND CUSTOMS

{ factory worker kills boss who didn't want to approve a raise and gets killed by security guard in the factory where there hasn't been a raise in five years

THE STAR SHOWS THE WAY

Hero and Rosa walked up and down the alleys. They met a boy selling goat's milk.

—Do you know where the Family lives?

—Follow the star.

—What star?

—Down there. See where the star is pointing? It's the blue house.

The narrow street wound down the hill toward a star made of wood and colored lightbulbs. A sign for Xram Grocery. They followed the star all the way to the blue house. Vampire was there waiting.

VISION

thieves shoot at flying saucer which appears in a vacant lot: they say they thought it was police in disguise.

WHEN HORSES TREMBLE

—Horse was going to take you, but he ran off.

—He got a look at a mare in somebody's back yard. Threw me right on the ground.

José and El Matador had turned into the first alley. The tambourines were getting further away the more they walked. The rhythm seemed to be following along behind them as the alleys divided and subdivided. It was hard to know where you were. They came to a soccer field, ragged nets flapping in the wind, a field full of mud and holes. A boy squatted in the middle taking a shit. José called to him and he ran off.

cluppety clop, cluppety clop
nei-ei-ei-eigh, nei-ei-eigh

—Climb on, you guys.

—Both of us?

—Sure.

They got on. But it was hard to stay on. Horse was strong; he galloped up the hill. Then all of a sudden he threw himself into a doorway and stood there trembling.

—What's wrong?

—It's the Squad. If they get us, we're screwed. They come every Sunday afternoon. A clean-up operation they call it. Last Sunday they killed six people. Right in the street, in front of everybody. In the old days they did their killing in secret, but no more. Nobody even pays attention. They come, do their business, and they're on their way. The cops around here protect them. Doesn't pay to be a bandit any more, too hot. Police kill them and they kill each other. Nei-ei-eigh, eieieieigh.

The men had disappeared. Horse came out of the shadow, sweating and trembling. He spit and farted, a strong smell of grass.

—You're going to have to go on alone.

—I'm getting out of here, said Zé.

—Yeah, I've had it with this shit, said El Matador.

WEATHER REPORT
(or, homage and thanks to Ernesto Cardenal)

"el hombre que está en el poder / el gobernante gordo lleno de condecoraciones / y se ríe y cree que no morirá nunca / y no sabe que es como esos animales / sentenciados a morir el día de la Fiesta."

NIPPING IT IN THE BUD

They came in force:
the Repressive Militias, with white steel helmets;
the Death Squads, in gray suits;
the Crusaders for Democracy, carrying bright red banners;
the Defenders of Tradition, white pants and blue ribbons around their necks;
the Champions of the Family, wearing red ribbons and black suits.
They came. And they had in their hands:
revolvers,
rifles (Korean War surplus, contributed by a friendly government),
machine guns (brand new, from the Forces of the Allied Nations),
bayonets (from the proud national steel industry),
and daggers.

The operation was simple. They had the neighborhood completely surrounded. All probable and possible exits sealed. They had trucks, jeeps, cars, buses, tanks, point-fifty machine guns, bazookas. Like a siege of a medieval city, warriors encamped, the city beleaguered, destined to die or give up, walls, moats, stairways, caldrons of boiling oil. Except that the city was already theirs.

They went door to door in groups.

—Any children in this house?

—Yes.

—What ages and how many?

—One. A year old. Why?

—Bring him here.

A Champion picked up the child and a Crusader pierced him through the heart with a dagger. That simple. Just like an experienced farmhand killing a pig. Except it was a child. And it screamed.

They handed the child back to its parents and knocked at the next door. Thus many screams were heard that Sunday afternoon in Vila Branca.

And all the screams merged into one. From hundreds of bloodied houses, the clamor rose up in the Sunday afternoon air.

YOU CAN'T ALWAYS GET WHAT YOU WANT

Rosa ran, the men ran after her. She turned, went into a narrow lane, turned again, and entered another. The alleys twisted up and down, the vista of the far-off city had disappeared, and with it any feeling of security. Identical houses, one after the other. She kept running, the men kept running too. They reached the square, somehow she had gotten herself surrounded. The terrain was steeply sloped, she lost her balance, landed on a shack's low roof below, and rolled to the ground.

Rosa ran, the men ran after her. She headed down the hill toward the fetid smell of the river. Reached the bottom and ran along the edge, maybe she would meet someone.

Rosa ran, the men ran faster. One of them grabbed her by the neck. She stopped. He let her go.

—What do you want?

The men laughed. Rosa laughed with them.

—Come with us, honey.

—No.

(They just want to screw me, right?)

—Come here, I said.

He hit her in the face. Again. She bit her tongue, there was blood, thick as paste, in her mouth. Another punch, in the nose this time. Pain, blood running down, darkening her blouse. But before it could even soak in, they hit her again, a ringing in her ears, shutting out the fetid (and good) smell of the nearby river.

(Mother of God, they're going to kill me.)

Before everything went black she felt herself fall face down on the ground, her face in a tuft of grass. Someone had taken a shit close by, she could smell the rotting turd.

PREPARATIONS

Paulo brings the last punch cards to the computer. His shift is over. He leaves the air-conditioned room, goes through inspection. It's midnight, he's got to hurry. If he doesn't, the old woman won't be able to perform the ritual. The Ebó. Today is the day. When he left this morning the ingredients were already prepared, and the woman was ready. He needs to get there on time. Transportation is tough, though, at this hour. When he becomes a technician at IBM he'll go by taxi or buy his own car. But now Paulo is just beginning his career. At IBM and with old Ige-Sha.

THE FLIGHT TO EGYPT

All José remembers is a man with a hammer, nailing up a sign.

—If you're here to see the Family, forget it.

—How come?

—The cops were here, so they took off. Father, mother, kids. Packed up the cart and took everything, stripped the whole shack.

—Where'd they go?

(I don't even know who they were or what they did, what I'm interested in is where they went.)

—To Vila Egypt. About two hundred kilometers from here. But they won't be able to do it anymore.

—Do what?

—The united fuck.

—No kidding. What's that?

—You know, the whole family at once. Boy, did that bring in a lot of dough.

Rosa started running and José saw some men turn the corner, running after her. So José ran too.

SALUTATIONS

Ige-Sha nodded her head slowly: yes. She had examined the stone of Xangô, the Thunder God. It was pure, legitimate. She thanked Obá-Ol-Orun, Lord of the Sky. Paulo, her chief assistant, said yes, they had taken the dark, heavyset girl inside and laid her on the white surgical table, a gift from the followers. For the Ebó, the transference of the evil spirit. Very good.

THE LEAP

José had to run. He had to get out of there, out of the city, out of the world. And now he could. If he ran without stopping he'd be able to leap into space. He wanted to rise up, enter the orbit of the moon, and never come back. Earth was impossible, life wasn't worth living. He'd get there and see that the moon was grayish, dead, made of plaster. But the earth was more dead even than the moon. Maybe the earth seemed blue, but that was a lie. He'd walk around looking at the earth far, far away. José and everyone spinning, in orbit, around the earth. Each one spinning within his own life, never landing. Astromen, dead in space, twirling.

FREE ASSOCIATION

a white ass and a yellow ass, the white ass turning yellow, the smell of asses, the fat white yellow getting continually fatter, filling everything, flowing to the river, to the sea, the sea filling the bed, the body swallowed in the sea, she's drowning, I've got to save her, but it makes me sick, how can I stick my hands in the sea/bed and pull her out of there when the sea smells of sewage, maybe I'll get a fever, she's dying, it's because of me, because of my fear, I'm afraid to pull her out of the bed/sea

BESAME MUCHO

José was standing next to the Caçula Hotdog Stand. Atila watched the cars peal out, horns blasting: a holiday. José felt dizzy, the rotten smell from the pit, he closed his eyes and Rosa was at his side looking for something in the bottom of the well, there was something down there. José knew that it was his. He had forgotten what it was but it was something he had made, or created, or cared about a great deal, and now it didn't exist anymore.

Someone tapped him on the shoulder. He opened his eyes. It was Malevil.

—Hey, man, everything okay?

—Yeah.

—I'm fucking hungry.

José saw eight men walking toward them.

JOSÉ IS ARRESTED - I

They were still eating when they saw the eight men come toward them with machine guns, revolvers, one-and-a-half foot clubs. Rosa grabbed José's arm. Malevil had told the eight: I'll go up to him, tap him on the shoulder, and say: Hey, man, everything okay?

JOSÉ IS ARRESTED - II

Malevil had told the eight: I'll go up to him, tap him on the shoulder and say: Hey, man, everything okay? Then you arrest him. That will be José.

Malevil walked over to him.

—Hi, gang, boy did I get lost.

He came up and kissed Rosa on the cheek.

—What's up, Malevil? asked José.

At that, the eight arrested José. Atila pulled his gun and took a quick shot, shearing off one of their ears. José said: Forget it, pal, we're fucked. And you don't have anything to do with it. You guys just came along for the ride. (And you, José, what are you doing here?)

The guy who'd lost his ear wanted to kill Atila on the spot. José kept on talking.

—This was bound to happen, pal. What's bound to happen happens. I could have asked for help and Gê would have come with a dozen batallions of Communs. But it wasn't meant to be that way.[1]

---

[1] I've never understood this acquiescence of José's. He doesn't raise a finger, even to stay alive. Or else he's misleading us.

REFLECTION

José thinks: This is for shit. It's suicide. I should have made a run for it at least. But I just stand here gassing. I fucked myself in the national tradition.

WHAT COMES IN AND WHAT GOES OUT

Running, José has yellow eyes and the taste of salt in his mouth. Running, he realizes that the alleys and lanes of Vila Branca are his body, like the time it was projected on the Man's tent. Alleys he couldn't enter, even though they were inside him; alleys he couldn't leave, even though he wanted to. Lanes, alleys, shortcuts, he just couldn't understand. A maze. José: inside, wanting to get out. Like the day he went in (the forbidden door) and saw himself coming out. That's me, José. Two of them. One: me, myself, coming out of myself. The other: me, myself, going into myself. The two of them cohabiting. One denying the other. Divorced. Separate beds, the same body. I don't know which one is more me. I go in and out all the time. I go out, but when I do, I meet myself coming back in. The one coming back in wants to stop the one leaving from going out. The one going out doesn't want the one coming in to come in. I'd like to feel alone for a moment, without: one or the other. Empty. That moment could be the moment of my death. I don't want the two of them to be opposites.

Conversation in a taxi:
Shit, Zé, don't start with the lectures, don't preach to me. My life is mine and I'll do what I want with it. Which happens to be nothing. Zilch. I want to waste my life. Just that. I want to sit around doing nothing, watching life pass me by. It can go fuck itself. I'm wasting time, getting old, that's exactly what I want: to forget about time, to die, to fuck myself. You've got such a mania, you and those people. To *do* something, build something. I'm no stonemason, I don't want to build anything.

257

ASSAULT: WHICH WAY OUT?

On the walls of tar paper shacks: "The Death Squad is coming," "Last chance for robbers," "Down with the Commies," "Long live the government," "Down with poverty."

Blood stains, hand prints on the walls, a skull and crossbones.

They were standing right in front of the graffiti: a small black guy, a nervous white guy, and a Japanese. They were laughing.

—We want your money, mister, hand it over.

—I don't have any.

(I really don't.)

Brass knuckles in the face.

—Your money, white boy. Don't be stingy.

Another punch in the mouth, broken teeth, El Matador felt splinters of tooth mixed with blood, a thick paste forming in his mouth. Another blow, cracking the bone in his nose, what pain, blood running down, darkening his shirt. But before it could even soak in he was struck again, a loud ringing in his ears, shutting out all other noise.

Before everything went black, he felt like he was falling face forward onto a soft mattress. And there was a strong smell of asphalt. The mattress closed around him like an embrace. He felt protected, soothed. He could go to sleep.

LIGHT FROM THE STONE OF XANGÔ

As soon as they arrived, the men saw the light in the stone, light from the lamp post reflected in her ring. They breathed in the rotten smell of shit and they knew: she was the one, ready for the Ebó, already anesthetized. It was a ring made from the stone of Xangô, the Thunder God, the ring of Saint Barbara. The blacks thought: she has been lucky, blessed, her whole life long. And still is. She is the Chosen One, everything is reserved and ready for her. Stones of Saint Barbara fall during heavy rains and thunderstorms. They sink seven fathoms into the earth and rise to the surface seven years later. Whoever finds one is specially favored.

258

JUDGMENT AND SENTENCE

This campaign has been going on a long time, we've been looking for you nonstop, stoolpigeons blabbing making phone calls pointing fingers: *here they are* but "they" didn't show up because "they" is really only you, it's you we were looking for all along without knowing it until one day one of our men discovered it was you but we couldn't figure you out, you didn't even have a face, didn't need one except that you were mixed up with those subversive sons-of-bitches, we kept following you it's strange you spent months and months doing nothing we could grab you for red-handed no fights no robberies no killings and just when we were going to give up some stoolie says it's really you, right in the middle of this terrorist business, son-of-a-bitch I *thought* he was with those fucking Communs, you'll see we'll get him *and* the others and we checked out this guy you killed but he didn't have anything to do with anything not even with you, like that day you shot a guy in the face and walked away calmly, you went to the movies a comedy and died laughing and we wanted to know what kind of lunatic this was walking around killing here and there you weren't crazy or anything, remember that fat guy with the mustache who lived in the Trufo Bar, the French guy who sold speed, we knew you offed him but we didn't manage to grab you because you're a slippery fish that's your nickname with the cops, without our even knowing your face or what you were like but we left the case to the feds we thought it was a job for them after that colonel you killed and then later all the soldiers and the informer who'd given us so many good tips and the detective on the Squad and the guy who was in charge of the anticommunism forces, you sons-of-bitches, you piece of shit, I'd like to break your face, before I kill you I want to make you suffer bastard walk all over your face we'll drill you with fifty slugs but first the chief's gonna give it to you in the eye with a .45 and he'll make sure your head's beaten to a pulp brains and all you Communist bandit son-of-a-bitch.

THOUGHT FOR THE DAY:
Is this an underdeveloped country? Bunk.
Visit our Automobile Showroom.

NON-EXECUTION

—Look, Skeleton, do me a favor and shut up.

He talks nonstop. He goes on and on, even while the chief is telling him to keep quiet. Skeleton's got a full head of hair, with a part down the middle. He shakes a lot, his mouth gets all twisted up, the words are mangled, as if they're all fighting to come out at the same time.

—Shut up, I said, *can* it.

—Aw, let him talk, chief, he's only brave when he's talking.

They're going to kill me. I'm scared. I'm cold. I shouldn't be scared, I knew it would happen like this, I knew someday they'd get me. But I can't help thinking: they're going to kill me . . . and I don't want to die. I just don't want to die. I used to wonder what I'd be thinking when they got me but I'm not thinking anything, I'm just scared. If only it would be over fast, but they'll torture me first, I know it. They'll want me to tell them things, I don't even know what. I can't figure it out. That Skeleton babbling to himself, he can't wait to get down to business. All you have to do is look at them: eight mental retards. Waiting for an orgasm. Each one with his rifle, revolver, shotgun, a belt full of bullets across his chest like a banner: Miss Violence, Miss Assassin, Miss Blood, Miss Torture, Miss Agony, Miss Beating, Miss Mutilation, Miss Executioner.

Did my violence accomplish anything?

Yes. You've got to spit instead of swallowing the snot and getting poisoned. Spit in the eye or the mouth of whoever it is that wants to walk on you. Give back the change. Instead of owing something. What I did I did so I wouldn't suffocate, so I could yell. One minute of mine is an eternity to them. I lived a hundred thirty years, Mom, that's it, *salvation, my son, save your soul*, that's what you told me, surrounded by candles and incense and flowers and saints. I lived a hundred and thirty years in front of each man I pointed my gun at.

COUPLING WITH THE DEVIL (The Ebó)

earth orbit insertion   get 00 - 11 - 53
                                  cdt 08 - 43 A.M.

The area around the launching pad has been completely evacuated and the security tests are under way.

Howls moans hissing screams feet stamping hands clapping candles rum sweat incense. Rosa's hands and feet were tied. The old black woman stooped down and blew smoke in her eyes, nose, ears, and mouth. Rosa closed her eyes, she heard barking and quiet murmuring, wind in the pasture. *She was running and the farmhand was chasing her, the wind cut like a knife, then a shot caught him in the neck and he fell covered with blood and she never told anyone about it but from then on she had been sure: she was protected, somehow, enclosed.*

Apocintio
The day Rosa was born the midwife rushed her to the Emergency Room where they sucked the badness out of her ears, nose, and mouth, badness attracting badness. And they tossed the whole mess into a copper pail . . .

Countdown
. . . and there were cherries in it, and a sparrow egg, and a copy of the prayer of St. Agatha with every other line missing. With Ige-Sha here puffing on her cigar Rosa remembered that day—she'd been born just twelve hours earlier—knowing that a girl from Emergency had taken the pail to the stream so the water would carry it to the river and the river to the sea, the great father, the sea which would watch over Rosa's life and spirit.

Preliminary Check-out
Rosa felt a hot hand passing over her face. Dizzy, she opened her eyes. There were people on all sides of her. Shouts, claps, whistles, howls, moans, hissing. The sounds were coming from loud-speakers. The people were silent, seated on benches against the wall, leaving the middle of the room for the people in charge. Then the loud-speakers fell silent.

Rosa was sleepy, she could hardly keep her eyes open. It was pleasant here, she could stay a lifetime (but what about the others? where could they be, what was José up to?). The old woman had a face of black soapstone. She was dancing, moving closer, then farther away, she took sips of something from a large bottle, she shook an iron pole with four crossbars, dangling chains—medallions—crosses—moons—suns—stars—circles with barbs around the edges—triangles—pieces of tin—cymbals—nails—tiny balls—screws—metal disks—little figurines—nuts and bolts—paper clips—bottlecaps—teeth—glass disks—plastic bags full of hair.

Then Rosa saw that there was another table, and stretched out and bound to it was a naked girl. Her whole body was spotted with blood, little spurts which ran from tiny cuts, all the same size. The old woman stopped dancing and picked up a round glass container (like they had in the old days in bars, for bullets). She came over to Rosa and opened the container. There was nothing inside. The old woman shook the chains again and stood transfixed. The people watching began to moan and murmur in a low monotone:

A orêrê aiê orixá iomam
ia, ochê Egbêji orêrê, aiê

Nothing in the world is hidden from God, muffled voices, African words all jumbled, the sounds swallowed and mispronounced. (What am I doing here?) Rosa was exhausted, she felt like a bag of cement, heavy, dumped on the table, no will . . . just curiosity.

A dark-skinned boy stood up in a corner of the room (she was fascinated with his beauty). He had shiny, straight hair and blue eyes which sparkled in the dim brightness of the forty candles in the room. *A orêrê aiê orixá iomam.* The boy approached her and put his hand on her stomach. Her muscles contracted involuntarily, her intestines began to empty. She was ashamed. (To shit like that, all of a sudden. But it was his fault. I wanted him to lie down on top of me.) The boy kept his hand on her stomach as her intestines expelled everything. An empty feeling, then just the pain of tired muscles. The hand moved lower and her kidneys emptied too. It came back up to rest on her stomach and she began to vomit. The heaving was painful and she was getting herself all dirty. Ige-Sha came over and kissed the boy on the mouth. He put both hands on Rosa's chest, right over her lungs, she felt all the air being sucked out of them, she was suffocating. Ige-Sha puffed her cigar and the smoked curled inside Rosa. She blacked out.

Atetu, cadê olônã

Rosa came to. The boy's hand was on her heart, it beat fast. Then he withdrew, saying:

—She's ready, she's pure. She is yours.

The record started again, people were dancing, circling around her, moaning, twirling, praying, hitting themselves, whipping each other, dragging their feet, weeping, whistling, murmuring, shaking their heads yes, yes, spitting over the left shoulder. The girl stained with blood raised her head. She had enormous eyes. It was as if she had died of shock, with her face fixed in the anguished expression of someone trying to understand. She was pretty, very thin, and pale. (Where did everybody go?)

The old woman brought a Coca-Cola bottle, family size, full of green liquid, and began to sprinkle it over Rosa. A sickening smell. The nausea returned. Ige-Sha held the bottle up to Rosa's mouth, she wanted her to drink. She was insistent. Rosa turned her face away (the girl on the other table was watching her every move). Rosa refused the bottle. Two men came over, dressed in blue, with green and red buttons.

The old woman touched Rosa on the head. Pain spread through her body, reached her fingertips, and stayed there. The men in blue pushed her head back and Ige-Sha poured the green liquid down her throat. It was viscous and evil-smelling, but didn't taste bad. Rosa recognized anis, wormwood, and parsley (but it also contained euphorbia, rue, manguava, and eugenia leaves).

The two men disappeared. The music was turned off. They put out the lights, leaving just one candle inside a glass surrounded by red paper.

The spectators sat down, the woman came over carrying a tin can with a yellow fruit inside. She offered it to Rosa.

—*Ofé ogum:* you want to eat?

Rosa just looked at her.

—*Echô aguá:* good fruit. *Echô ocô.*

It was a yellow quince. What would be inside it? Rosa began to feel more and more light-headed.

4, 3, 2, 1, 0

Rosa drifted free. She saw the woman in her true shape: black wood, varnished smooth and shiny: strong jacaranda from Bahia. Rosa's father was sitting on the smooth, black tree trunk, at the right hand of God the Father Almighty. And José was there too: a blue frog, just like the day he had the attack in São Pedro Springs. Rosa was suspended above the table, another body underneath hers. It looked like her. Rosa had lost all gravity and saw that people had been transformed: stones, animals, flowers, iron, crystals, water, tongues of flame, paper, coins, silver, clay, stars, electric lights, food. The room extended, the walls moved back and fell away, the roof flew up and down, circling around the black tree trunk where José and her father were sitting.

.00 h 02 m: the crew begins a rest period

Kinin kan nbelódo
irê irêninje ô irê

Rosa floated up and down, she saw the stars shining, the moon, then the sun, too, lights burning, the earth spinning, getting smaller and smaller, and she could see the earth the sun and the moon all together, it wasn't night or day, day or night.

José, standing under a streetlight, shooting at someone. He looked around. He blew on the gun, he was leaving but at the same time he was standing in front of the mirror, scratching his face till the blood ran.

Correct bearings, verify all instrumentation
Giant crystals flashing brightly, reflecting her life, the toad opened his mouth but no sound came out. The jacaranda tree was splitting into pieces like a cell dividing, it got smoother each time, Rosa wanted to slide down the black trunk.
Obá-ol-orun: God, King, Lord of heaven.
Omulu, Omulu. Omulu, the devil is darkness (God)
Umofé, OMULU, Ofé, Obá-ol-orun
The crystals were getting darker, the roof was the sky, the sky was getting darker, it was four in the afternoon and she walked and walked until she got to a square building with rows and rows of men hanging from metal grates, they were spitting and swearing, and the building rose above the endless desert. The room darkened. The sky darkened, and

264

she saw that one of the men hanging from the grates was looking straight at her but she turned away.

Now she was a captive on the roof and one of the crystal stones down below was square and covered with little marks that looked like tiny windows but it was so far away and she felt too heavy to go down and look, it was so nice up here . . .

The Devil is Goodness
God is Evil
The Devil is Love
God is Hate
The Devil is kindness
God is Malice
    Happiness
    Unhappiness
    Abundance
    Misery and Hunger
    Peace
    War

She fell, the toad opened his mouth, the blue face of the toad, the light in the man's face, the man who was calling from the grates, José pulling a job, the driver's fear, and José pointing the gun, and José's fear even greater than the driver's, and the driver with his foot on the brake, José thrown to the front, seeing that he's going to die, and pressing his hands against the windshield, and fear, so much fear, more than fear, now the driver is going to kill José but José manages to shoot first . . .

Onicá orxagui guannaigê êranexi
Oni cá odolôrã coninge aracutã
Atetú cadê olônã

The police were knocking at the door and her mother and father had come to visit during her lying-in but there hadn't been a lying-in and her mother opening the door and the police going from room to room searching for what and Rosa saying that he hadn't done anything and the sergeant saying if it wasn't him who was it and why was his face on the wanted posters and neither mother or father not even Rosa knew that he was on the posters and if he was then what did he do I'm not here to explain anything you're all lying don't want to collaborate with the police because he robbed stores and killed people and deflowered a girl and set bombs and killed soldiers and stole money from the church and dressed up like the pope and robbed banks banks banks savings and loans finance companies armored cars no no it's a lie he's out of town and even if he lived a long time said the old man who was objective he couldn't have done all those things he's being framed no he's not out of town he's in hiding and the sergeant picked up Rosa's and her mother's dresses and took a long look.

—Come down, daughter, said Ige-Sha.

The flowers were withering and she didn't want them to they were pretty but losing their color getting gray and white and the crystals grew larger swallowing the animals, stones growing and growing and now the animals were inside them solidified, the stones were swallowing the crystals and rays of light crossed the atmosphere like a windstorm forming swirls and eddies enveloping Rosa completely . . .

—I invoke the power of the stones of Cevar. The complete and total power of Cevar's paired stones.

The old woman disappeared into a corner of the house, a deep, dark closet. She brought out a wooden box: which had another box inside: and three more inside that: until at last there was a tiny wooden case. There inside was a pair of stones, absolutely identical. The old woman returned to Rosa.

Rays of light crossed her body and seemed to be coming from two small stone fountains which sat on top of a smooth black stone. The toad had disappeared. In his place there was an enormous yellow stain.

—May the ritual be sound, *kinin kan nbelódo, irê irêninjê ô irê,* and may the demon leave her, leave our virgin and come to inhabit this stained and impure body, this house of filth.

Everything began to blow, the wilted flowers were bent over by the force of the wind, leaning toward the floor, stones, crystals, animals, began to spin, swirled into motion by the eddies of air. It started to get dark again and Rosa felt so heavy.

The whole neighborhood staring at her as she scrubbed and scrubbed trying to remove that threatening and ominous symbol which had attracted the police, José was nailing a man to a cross and when the man was almost dead José took him down and wrapped him in sheets and threw

266

him into an immense pit in the ground, he was listening to the Beatles singing *carry that weight* and she saw the pit full of men some dead some alive some rotten and she saw Malevil come up to José and embrace him . . .

Suddenly there was a noise so loud she couldn't stand it, she put her hands over her ears to shut it out, her hands covered her head and she was buried in the bottom of the stone, she couldn't see anything, it felt like they were opening a hole in her brain and stuffing something soft inside, it dissolved and took over her body, she wasn't herself anymore. And the stone expelled her.

Horses running, their shoes striking the paving stones and setting off sparks, morning and afternoon, and in the morning Dad was making coffee and waiting for José to go to school . . .

Rosa went back out to space transformed into a membrane: fine, soft, and yellow, and José would tie a rope around the cats' necks and swing them against the wall, his technique so refined that only the cat's head would hit the wall and it would be killed instantly . . .

She was flying, the world was chasing after her, the city disappeared and Rosa flew over the fields, above the sun . . .

Ground Control: (17 h 23 m): "According to flight plans, the coupling should occur ten minutes from now."

—Through the power of Satan, may the spirit inhabitant enter this initiate chosen by the Stone of Xangô, and may he leave on my command.

Rosa saw the wind. She didn't feel it, she saw it: a set of transparent rollers moving forward automatically, a continuous motor above a limitless conveyor belt. The air kept moving, the wind pushed Rosa along, making her run toward endless space. She felt so heavy.

José lying in the sun on top of a mountain of armed men . . .

Until an unbearable anguish came over her. So that she wanted to burst open, *carry that weight,* and she exploded. Rosa: exploded into a yellow cloud, bursting into a million pieces which soared into outer space. Rosa: divided into pieces, and whole in each individual piece. Thousands of particles falling down to earth . . .

Horses rearing and José falling under their hooves, his head opening up. Horses in pastures and yellow-rose particles falling on top of them, they were stained yellow and running fast, both at the same time, Rosa, in pieces, riding the backs of hundreds of horses who neighed and shook her off, Rosa, in pieces, falling, a storm of Rosa drenching the earth, soaking into the ground, feeling the hot, suffocating earth close around her. She dove deep, finding stones, roots, worms. Until she dissolved. Merged with the soil once again. In the interior of the earth peace reigned, happiness, silence, no anguish at all, no fear, no memory. Way down deep, one piece of Rosa had landed on a seed, and the seed swallowed the yellow drop, closing itself around her, preparing to germinate.

NON-EXECUTION (II)

Right now I feel like shitting in my hand and throwing it in their faces, all eight of them, so they can see how good it is to eat shit. The shit they make me (and everybody else) eat out of their hands.

—Dump him in the ravine, quick, you're taking too long.

The first shot zinged past his ear. A near miss. What about when the bullets hit me? How will it feel?

They served *adum* a sort of African corn fritter, to everyone. The assistants didn't touch it, because of the onion-shrimp sauce. Old Ige-Sha ate two portions.

NON-EXECUTION (III)

If I was high, this would be easy. I just need to think. I've got to think real hard until I can't even see these guys.

One of them came toward him. A punch in the ribs. Another. A flurry of them. He's got his eyes closed. He opens them. The man stayed where he was. All eight of them lined up, weapons raised. They fire. José sees blood where the shots have hit him. No pain. He just feels a little weak. Another shot. Now a kick, and he falls. He tries to prop himself up but finds only the emptiness of the ravine. His arm feels like it's going to come off. José thinks he's going to black out.

He falls into the stream and the water wakes him. The men above him are shouting. They shine their lanterns down into the ravine. He lies completely still, he knows he can survive. The shooting stops. They're climbing down into the ravine for the coup de grace. Now what? José creeps painfully along. He wants to live. A light hits him in the face and stays there, while bullets splinter branches and ricochet back and forth off the rocks (ah, those bang-bang movies, Sunday matinees at the Odeon, the girls' heads bobbing up and down in the balcony, girlfriends and non-girlfriends, and ping, piiiing, the hero escapes).

José sees that the stream suddenly comes to an end, swallowed by a cement pipe. He crawls into the pipe on all fours, it's on an incline, he feels a rancid breeze, which proves one thing at least: there must be a way out.

Right?

AFFECTIVE MEMORY

Ige-Sha was eleven years old when her father took her to Lagos (Nigeria) and left her with the man who would be her husband. He had been a stoker on a British ship and when he came back from sea he was one of the first people in the village of Abeokuta to have a cotton gin. They say Ige-Sha's husband was closely related to Alfa Cyprian Akinosho Tairu, chief of Abeokuta, and that he had conferred on him the title Morope de Ake. Alfa taught him to show money to the new moon so that he would never lack material goods; owing to the moon, Ige-Sha always lived comfortably, until the day her husband left for America to publish a journal called *Wasu*.

COOKING ON A LOW FLAME

From the chief of POPO (Political Police) to the chief of FEPO (Federal Police):

"Responding to your CI confidential report of the thirty-first of this month, I must inform you that no prisoners have been tortured in the cells of this department since the beginning of the new government. All those detained have been well-treated. The only inconvenience is the diminishing number of cells available for the large quantity of prisoners. Sincerely yours, etc. . . .''

Note one detail: the phrase "tortured in the cells of this department." True, no torture took place in the cells. They have special rooms for that.

From the chief of FEPO to the chief of SUPO (Supersecurity Police):
"Close down all newspapers that accuse the POPO of torture. And prosecute them."
An ironic question I definitely wouldn't ask the chief of FEPO:
Prosecute them for what?

From the chief of POPO to Detective Dores:
"Stall a little, it's kind of a strange situation. They say there's some international commission in the country to investigate torture."

Detective Dores:
"Shit on the international commission. No gringo's coming into my precinct."

From Detective Dores to Investigator Ternurinha:
"Turn down the heat a little. Only beat them once a day." Observation: Ternurinha will be focused on next.

Order to investigators, interrogators, marksmen, and all participants in anti-terrorist, anti-Commun operations:
"Low flame."

APOCINTIO

TCHEW-tchew, TCHEW-tchew, TCHEW-tchew
BLAM, BLAM
Saws and pile-drivers, all sorts of machinery. But even with the noise, she could hear the screams.

wrrrrwoosh-shoooo
wrrrrrrwoosh-shoooo
And the applause. As if there were a large auditorium
nearby. Screams and applause.
Blam, blam, blam, blam, BLAM, BLAM, BLAM
Chookachooka, CHOOKachooka
And she heard howling, human howls and animal howls.
Rosa couldn't see them, but all around the shack there
were:
gigantic searchlights, floodlights, spotlights, vapor and
mercury lamps.
It was light as day.
Blam-BLAM, blam-BLAM, blam-BLAM
ssssshhuuuuuu
tatatatatatatata, ta, ta
rackatacka, rackatacka

aaaaaaaaiiii, aai, aaaaaaaaaaaaaaaaaiii
It was a human scream. A woman. In pain. It pierced the
air. It pierced through the walls and through Rosa (where
am I?), echoing off the machines outside. Yellow machines
at work behind a boarded-up construction site. (What am I
doing here, why am I tied up?) The planks had signs on
them:

DANGER: CONSTRUCTION UNDERWAY
CITY SUBWAY
Completion time: 5 years

rrrrrrooon, rrrrrrroooooon, bambambambambambambam.
Motors spinning, compressors, cement mixers, earth-

271

movers, generators, pile-drivers, cranes, pulleys, shovels, backhoes, electric saws, whistles.

The whole neighborhood trying to lean away from the hole—huts, tents, shacks made of wood, tin, cardboard, and plaster: Vila Branca. Men with brightly colored hardhats (yellow, red, blue, green, white) looked over blueprints, pushed hand trucks or wheelbarrows, carried picks and hammers. They were sawing boards, bending iron, operating machines. The gigantic pile-drivers made the earth shake

Blam-BLAM, blam-BLAM

rhythmically.

The shacks trembled and swayed, the zinc roofs vibrated, and whatever was on top rolled off: rocks, wood, tiles, glass, cardboard cartons, pieces of metal, tin cans.

wrrshooo, wrrrshooo, wrrshooo, rackatacka BLAM

COUNTDOWN

steam

the pile-drivers pounding

An excavator digging, digging, lumbering and powerful, like a prehistoric animal

throwing tons of earth into dump trucks

Ohhh, aaaaaaiiii, AAAAAAAIIII

That scream, the same one, a silent scalpel doing its job. The screams seemed to come from the other room. Rosa didn't want to open her eyes. She was giddy from the incense and smoke.

BLAM

jreeeeee, jjjreeeeeeeeeeeeeeeeee

ta,ta, ta, ta, ta, ta, taaa

Leaning down right next to Rosa's ear, Ige-Sha, the old woman, beré, whispered:

The useful (she puffed on her cigar) *are called to carry the weight. There are signs for you to read* (another puff), *signs and symbols.*

Rosa saw a telephone pole through the smoke, sliced into four pieces. The four stages of life: before, beginning, during, and after.

Zzzzzzzzzzzzzzzzzzzzz

She heard a ringing sound, nearby. But it could just as well have come from outside, there was so much noise.

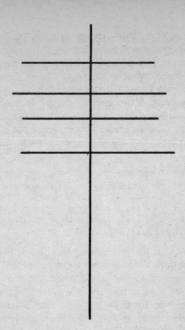

It felt as though they were passing a hand across her face, a hot hand. She opened her eyes, still giddy. Nauseous. Tired. Scared. The old woman: *beré, ogofá*, one-hundred-and-twenty-year-old woman (some say one hundred and forty, who knows?). Mute, cigar in her mouth, clouds of smoke circling her head, her back straight as a rail. She shot a look at one of the assistants. There were two of them (one was Paulo, the Watu, initiate in the Ebó), they were dressed in blue, prepared for the Ebó of the demon, good, pure, and brave. The old woman, *beré, ogofá*, had chosen them years ago, when the stone of Xangô was first discovered. The two assistants, small and tense, were waiting, eyes wide.

A orêrê aiê orixá ioman
ia, ochê Egbêji orêrê, aiê

Rosa ate the wild yellow quince. It had been cooked for two hours in coconut water from a coconut palm which was fifteen meters tall. Cooked in water from the dimba plant,

273

with vines, a chicken heart from a chicken born in May, and a little kava, a plant from the Orient of which only three exist. The quince was cooked two consecutive nights, an hour each time. Then it was wrapped, still hot, in cocoa leaves from Bolivia. It was getting harder and harder to get the cocoa, because the police wanted money from whoever carried it into the country. The Ebó was getting expensive, almost impossible these days. Not like in the days of *beré*'s grandmother, *Meuá, messan meuá,* nine hundred years old. And her mother, and her great-grandmother's mother, all of them spokeswomen for *abáol-orun,* god of heaven and earth and moons and stars, master of goodness.

CORRECT BEARINGS, VERIFY ALL INSTRUMENTATION

The important thing was that the Ebó of the demon was almost complete. People who were possessed by the good demon preferred to keep him inside. *Beré, ogofá,* Ige-Sha didn't like walking in the city, it was too big for her. Not because of her age, for to be *ogofá* is to be old and yet young; her legs were firmer and stronger than many assistants, the young *ocoré-adaquadés.* But Ige-Sha was so sensitive to the demons in other people that she would shiver all over, she'd get dizzy, she'd get a bitter taste in her mouth when there was a dark demon nearby. A bad demon would misbehave, bringing unhappiness and bad luck. The host would get dizzy and feel like misbehaving too, just for the fun of it. The bad devil knew the old woman and tried to upset her so she'd go away, so she wouldn't perform the Ebó to bring the good devil, the one the world needed so badly.

Ige-Sha didn't like the city because it was infested with demons, thousands of them, hiding in people and houses, making them worthless without themselves being exorcised. The city was a carnival of beelzebubs. She could actually see them. They tooled down the sidewalks, slithering like cobras, they were crafty, they followed people, dashed in and out windows, from one house to another, sounding like an infernal party with their blind screeching. They were like bats, blind, but smart and subtle, and they had unfailing instincts. Demons with bodies, anti-bodies, no bodies, gyrating around people's shoulders, necks, heads, pockets, mouth, feet, and hands, glued to the controls: big devils, little devils, a concentration of thoughts and desires, people walking around without noticing what they were doing and how the demons made use of them.

The lost city, so big, *olu-lilá*, that city which the *beré, ogofá*, couldn't understand. And to think that she was more than a hundred years old—ancient, for a common person, but not for a *beré* like her. In the *olu-lilá* there was lots of smoke, noise, people, cars, machines, buildings, shop windows, bright light. Everything under control. Ige-Sha felt weak and powerless in the face of so large an evil. Whatever possessed the city was very strong, people wanted it to be this way, nothing would eradicate it, not even a gigantic Ebó. An Ebó for a whole city would need a lot of blood, a waterfall of blood filling the *olu-lilá*, a storm of fresh, pure blood from chosen ones who had the special mark on their knees and possessed the stone of Xangô. *Oru. Oru-didu.* Night. A black night. Many years ago. An *oru-didu* of meditation. *Oba-ol-orun* had said: someone must go out and look for the pair of twins with my mark. There are many of them, they are in contact with each other. They must be sacrificed for the city. The daughter will know when she is in *olu-lilá* that she needs to perform the Ebó, to save humanity and to create another people, another time, another, more human, world.

Make a circle around the whole city. Within the circle, 434 meters apart, the chosen ones must be crucified: without heart, kidneys, liver, bladder, or suprarenals. After being crucified they should be taken down and thrown to the dogs who will crisscross the city from end to end, dripping blood through the streets. Wherever just one drop falls, that place will be completely purified for two centuries to come.

LUNAR ORBIT INSERTION*

Oguá lê, oguá lê

Ige-Sha was in the back yard. Sitting under the rue was a pitcher made of old porcelain which had belonged to her great-great-grandmother, who had brought it with her from the black land far away. It had originally belonged to a queen. Had her great-great-grandmother been a slave to this dazzling black queen who reigned over a city as large as this one, this *olu-lilá*? Who had poured from this pitcher to drink, or used it to wash themselves? Where was it made? Ige-Sha didn't know. The pitcher had come to her from great-great-grandmother to great-grandmother to grandmother to mother to daughter. There was still some dried blood on a corner of it from when her grandmother had been killed in Palmares . . . or had she been wounded while fleeing?

Unidentified voices: we are raising the pressure in the cabin.

Now the pitcher was full of greenish water, *umi*, made from roots of the pipi plant, a hallucinogenic herb, and moira. It had been sitting under the rue four nights, taking the dew. Good, said the woman. All clean. Ige-Sha transferred the *umi* in the pitcher to a Coca-Cola bottle. There was no wind. If it had been windy, it would have made things much more difficult. The wind brings the angels of the Lord, *omodê-orun*, enemies of the demons, since the angels' goodness had caused the demons to fall in the eyes of God. (Ige-Sha preferred the demons because they had revolted, which means rebelling against something that isn't good. The demons were the first rebels, the first of the first.) When it's windy, a demon won't leave the body it inhabits, even to enter the strong and well-prepared twin that awaits him. Ige-Sha took the bottle to her chosen one, the *amanda*, maiden, to drink. What if she wasn't an *amanda*? She had no ring of manly power, she was *amanda*: strong, healthy, good, with a full face, a well-formed head, the perfect place to receive the spirit taken from the one possessed. She needed to receive it in order to disseminate it, and she must be wide awake for the entire ritual. Smooth hair. The woman passed her hand over the girl's face. She was the one Ige-Sha had been waiting for all these years, the one to plant the seed in the world. It was twenty years ago Ige-Sha had received the message, the revelation that she needed to hurry, that the twins had been born, one for the demon to nurture and the other to receive and transmit it later. Strong twins for the demon to inhabit. *Omulu* needs a lot of meat for his sons and followers. They will appear after the *oiô*, three days without wind. A quiet day after much terrible noise. *Umi* under the rue: two days, three, and the girl, *amanda*, in the kitchen with the mark on her knee.

They served *adum* to everyone. The assistants didn't

276

touch it because of the onion-shrimp sauce. Ige-Sha ate two portions.

> INDEED, THE HOUR IS COMING
> WHEN WHOEVER KILLS YOU WILL
> THINK HE IS OFFERING SERVICE
> TO GOD.   (John 16:2)

AN OUNCE OF PREVENTION IS WORTH A POUND OF CURE

Carpenters were hurriedly nailing planks around the sides of open trucks. A boy stood and watched. When they were done, the trucks would look just like army support vehicles; it would be easy to drive right into the base and load up with weapons. And they would use them for bank robberies, too.

José came back from the security check. He'd been mounting an alarm system: cans full of little stones suspended by vines. They had sharpened stakes and hid them among the camouflage branches: to stumble would mean being pierced through the breast.

The carpenters were mixing paint now. Gê's lieutenant, Pedro, was matching the color to ''army green.'' When he noticed the boy watching, he said: ''Go away, go on, get out of here. You could hurt yourself.'' The boy didn't budge.

—You still have a lot to learn, José.

—I know plenty.

—You don't know anything. What you did on your own, with no objective in mind, doesn't count. It only accomplished one thing—you're on the wanted posters, we need to get you some bogus documents and a new face.

After crawling out of the pipe, José had gone home. Automatically. When he got there and saw Gê and four other men waiting for him, he realized that it could just as easily have been the police.

—You're only an asset to me because of your courage, your anger. Otherwise, you're an amateur in need of some solid training.

(And what if I ask about the story of his death? They say

Gê died. What if I ask about the guy who died in his place? Or the two women who went at night to get the body and wrap it in sheets?)

José had then gone straight to the Commun headquarters in the country, a little farm. Tired and wounded, all he wanted to do was sleep. But Gê wouldn't let him. Instead, they hit the road in a stolen Volkswagon. José would nod off, his head falling to his chest . . . he was flying over Spain in a plastic balloon, and he didn't want to get out of the balloon, there were people shooting down below, any minute they might puncture the plastic and the air would rush out with a whistle . . .

. . . he was on a tiled patio across from a boarded-up house, planting banana plants because he had lost his legs . . .

. . . he was tied up on top of a brazier with soldiers basting him and turning the spit. The fire wasn't too bad, but the oil and pepper were really getting to him . . .

. . . at a roadblock a cop stopped them, José sat waiting, holding a can of acid. When the guard leaned down to talk to them, José threw the acid in his face. His features melted before their very eyes, eaten away, Gê hit the gas . . .

At a roadblock a cop stopped them, José sat waiting, holding a container of yogurt nervously in his hands. When the cop leaned down to talk to them, José felt like throwing the yogurt in his face. The cop said they could go. Gê hit the gas.

They had gone to work in a nearby orchard, cutting camouflage branches for the stolen trucks. José spent the entire day sucking oranges.

—This is your first kidnapping, but you'll just be a lookout, that's all. We need you to keep alert.

—But I want to participate.

—In time you will. Wait till the time comes.

DIALOGUE IS NOT COMMUNICATION

Enter two of Gê's guerillas:

—I don't trust that guy, there's just something about him . . . like maybe he's a cop or something.

—Yeah, I don't understand why Gê spends so much time on him.

—Who knows.

—Did you notice that Gê didn't take him out to the target range? And he really didn't get much of a tour of the rural headquarters.

—You know what I think? He's probably testing the guy.

BASIC TRAINING

—No, you're not training with Camarga. He's got nothing to do with this cell. I don't know anything about him, only what the papers say, but I don't believe them of course. There are lots of things you'll go to your grave without finding out about, like the other guerillas, other groups, their objectives. What's important is this: accomplish *your* group's objective. There he is now, that's the man who'll be training you. Trainer Number Two.

Trainer Number Two had a kind of vacant look about him. As if hate had immobilized his eyes: their steady shine told you he was a determined man. His name was Carlos Lopes and the only thing anyone knew about him was that you could trust him. When I told Gê I didn't trust people and that I was scared of group actions he said: everybody is. Shit, man, we've got bellies, assholes, stomachs, just like everybody else. But we've got one thing they don't: an idea. And an idea can work on you like a drug.

My opinion of him fell when he said that. So, they needed drugs? Not me. Then I remembered where my early bravery had come from. In the beginning, because I had more hate inside, I was more blind, I threw myself into things without thinking. For these men, throwing yourself into something was suicide. It was precipitous. "Precipitousness and impatience are death." That was in the mini-manual, a xeroxed booklet Gê brought me one afternoon. "I never go by rules and regulations," I told him. "I don't want anything to do with them."

"But if you're going to live in a group," said Gê, "you need to learn the rules for survival. If you don't, you'll die."

"I think I'd rather die," I answered. (Maybe I'm here because I'd rather die. I've already lived long enough following mini-manuals.)

The whole movement was under wraps. All groups linked to Gê had withdrawn to their hideouts, on farms, in apartments, and in safe houses. It was not a good time for

279

staging actions. The army, the repressive militias, and all the specialist organizations had gone on the offensive lately.

Then one day I ran into the Mexican again. In the Santana Bar, where we used to go for coffee in the morning. He was still a radio man, working on his transistors. He recognized me because of his remarkable memory. He photographed everything mentally and kept it there in the back of his head. He had a memory like a computer, Gê said. He was the one who "photographed" banks and streets before jobs. Always letter-perfect, his machinery well-greased with tequila. Which, in itself, demonstrated the group's incredible organization. The tequila made its way down through a clandestine network all the way from Mexico.

The Mexican swore that his father and his grandfather had fought with Pancho Villa, and that an uncle of his had been in Emiliano Zapata's group (hey, remember that flick with Marlon Brando and Jean Peters—or was it Susan Peters?—boy, was that good, I got so sad when they killed him, and the cowardly way they did it . . .) The Mexican swore he belonged to a family of nothing but revolutionaries, that was why he had to emigrate. They would have killed him if he stayed in Mexico. "Ha, don't worry," said José. "They'll kill you here if they get you, too." But he didn't seem too worried: "At least here something's happening, that's what I like. In Mexico everything's at a standstill. Down here is where it's hot. The last good fight in Mexico was in that stupid Brigitte Bardot movie." "The movie may have been stupid," said José, "but not Brigitte Bardot." And the Mexican agreed with him and they talked about Bardot and Raquel Welch and Maria Felix and Libertad Lamarque and Ninon Sevilha and Maria Antonieta Pons, the goddesses of rhumba and mambo and cha-cha-cha, and their fat legs, and José told how he'd go to the movies with a bunch of pals and have a contest to see who'd get off first. And the Mexican talked about Trotsky, and how his father had known him in Mexico, before he was assassinated.

At the end of the first week, a van arrived. With a man who was blindfolded. Three days later they led the man back to the van and drove off, and José heard someone say: "They gave back the ambassador." José had learned not to ask questions. Even if he had, no one would answer. They were united, but it was as if each person was still alone; one didn't exist for the other.

Gê disappeared for one or two days and returned with more trucks, cars, supplies. They painted the cars, changed the license plates, unloaded packages. The next time it was the captain's turn. Only the captain never returned.

José was walking along a high hedge of cedars that enclosed the farm. He found a cement slab with an iron handle, it was disguised under some recently cut orange branches.

(I know this slab from somewhere, I know this place . . . that's impossible, I've never been here before. But I know there's a pit down there, and I've seen them throw people in.)

He stood there and looked at it. He wanted to open it and peek inside, but he knew he shouldn't. He moved a little closer. (What if it's not meant to be opened?) He pushed hard, the slab was heavy. He pulled on the handle, he stuck a piece of wood in the crack. He needed to look inside.

CARLOS LOPES'S DEPOSITION

''. . . he was in the same cell with me and told me about it. Just at the beginning, though. Later he cut out part of his tongue so he wouldn't be able to talk when they tortured him. He said the shocks hurt a lot at first. They jangle every muscle in your body. Then you sort of get used to it. You just have to try to take it and not go crazy before your body gets a chance to get used to it. I admired the hell out of the guy. If it had been me I would have been dead, completely crazy, I would have killed myself like that priest.[1] Who could have imagined things like this could happen? I hope I get my hands on those cops someday. He never even told me his name. They called him Crato. He was from up north, a valiant son-of-a-bitch. Really. They would take him out of the cell at night and he'd be back in the morning, no teeth, all bloody. He couldn't walk, the soles of his feet were like raw meat. Picked at with needles. He just wouldn't talk. I knew they were going to kill him, but the guy just wouldn't talk. He spent the daytime in the cell, terrified of what would happen at night. They were always inventing some-

---

[1] Carlos Lopes is mistaken. The priest only *tried* to kill himself; he wasn't successful.

thing new. Inventing, no. Applying. They were profession-
als. One of the interrogators, the worst of them, was always
saying: 'I leave my stomach at home when I come to work,
because I just can't stomach Communists, and I might
throw up. At night I kiss the wife goodnight and in the
morning when I go home I wash real good, use mouth-
wash, brush my teeth—because I talked to Communists and
I might've got contaminated. I wanna put all the fucking
terrorists, every single subversive, every last Commun on
the rack, that's the only way I'll be able to look my children
in the eye, my wife, my friends. That's the only way I can
take communion on Sunday.'

"That guy was the one responsible for the priest's suicide.
They almost succeeded in covering it up. But word got out.
A letter the priest wrote was smuggled out of jail and released to the foreign papers. Anyway, they finally took my
cellmate to the 'perch.' 'All right, talk: names, hideouts, future plans. This is your last chance.' The interrogator had
his hands clasped as if in prayer. He was begging. Crato
was dangling, quiet, naked, electric wires connected to his
balls. His balls, his prick, his ass, all live meat. They got the
razors out, made fine cuts, a hair's width, all over his body.
Blood in tiny spurts. They threw salty water on him, then
ice water. The interrogator cried: 'For the love of God, this
is painful, I don't want to do this. Be nice to me, don't be
like this, you have no right.' They brought him to another
room: there were his wife and kids, the youngest one four
months old. 'Talk.' Crato was silent. He couldn't talk if he
wanted to, he didn't have a tongue. They took off his wife's
clothes. They screwed her, right there in front of him. Six
bulls. They fucked her in the ass, they came in her mouth,
they beat her. 'Talk, come on, talk, now you're gonna talk,'
Crato said nothing. They hooked the wires up again, to his
ears, nose, mouth, his fingers, up his urethra. They were
maniacs, they shouted as if they were having an orgasm.
They took the infant and gave him a jolt. He cried. They
gave him a stronger one and he died, charred black. The
woman couldn't stop screaming, she went crazy right on
the spot. 'Here we are killing your family one by one and
you won't say a goddamned thing, you son-of-a-bitch.'
They beat up the other kids. Nothing worked. They connected the last of the wires. Crato was electrocuted. Worse
than if he'd touched a high-tension wire, his body black and

almost entirely disintegrated. They disappeared with the wife, children, everything.''

DON'T SHAKE LIKE THAT, JOSÉ.
HOW MUCH WILL YOU BE ABLE TO TAKE?
BECAUSE IT'S NO JOKE ANYMORE.

DIALOGUE IS PART OF COMMUNICATION

—Tell me something, Gê. Is it power you want?

—No, José, I don't want power. I already told you a hundred times . . .

—Well then, what's all this for?

—Look. Maybe what I do is come up with a formula for power. I don't know. I exist and they know I'm watching them. Every squeeze of the tourniquet and I set off another bomb, assassinate someone important, pull off a big heist.

—So?

—So they have to think twice before they tighten the screws.

—But they do it anyway.

—Yes, but they're scared.

—Shit, man, they do it anyway. So what difference does it make?

—The difference is that they're always nervous, they can't relax for an instant. The threat of terror allows me to demand certain things.

—They're going to get you, you know.

—Well, I'll keep it up until they do. We're about to begin a big escalation.

—What big escalation?

CONFIDENTIAL

President: I want to do as I ask. You'll kidnap a diplomat. My administration will refuse the demands, and then you'll set the diplomat free. This little scenario will make the Communs look bad, they'll lose points. If it's a diplomat from some small country that wouldn't create too many problems, we could even let him be killed off, to show the firmness of the government's resistance to terrorist blackmail.

Ministers: What if the O.A.S. tries to intervene?

President: It's not strong enough, that organization can't do a thing. It hardly even exists, I don't even know what O.A.S. means, and I don't even care, no one's coming in here to snoop around.

Chief of POPO: All right, then, the plan is set. I have your protection?

President: Right.

(Protection, nothing.)

Chief of POPO: Fine. It shall be done. I take you at your word.

THOUGHT FOR THE DAY

I'd like to be sure.
If someone could just convince me
that Gê is right, that this is the path.
Somehow I'd like to believe
that if the whole thing exploded
it would start up again from scratch.

BYE, BYE

Harold Limeira has left for France, where he will continue his work on lateral vision radar. The departure of this well-known scientist had a humorous side to it because at the last moment friends had to protect him from his landlord, who was hysterically trying to demand an extra year's rent, right there in the airport.

RETURN

After a week, Gê returned to camp.

ROSA COMES BACK DOWN TO EARTH: ROSA IS THE EARTH

They brought in the heavyset brunette and undressed her. Ige-Sha took a taste; the meat was tough. The Second Assistant (the smaller one) shaved off her hair and tied her up with a rope which had been left for forty-seven days at the bottom of a hundred-year-old well.

They put the record on again, the music blended with the sound of the wind, animals, screams, frogs croaking, car horns, factory whistles, bells, buzzers, pile-drivers, steam-rollers, stone-crushers. The sound grew and grew, people threw themselves on the floor, rolling around, hitting each other, kissing each other, some curled up as if they were fetuses in the womb.

The assistants carried in gigantic old mirrors, the silver almost gone. They hung the mirrors all around the room and the room multiplied, as did the multitude of people. The old woman was chanting and manipulating the ropes: Rosa was suspended above the table where the skinny girl, her mouth foaming, her body punctured and covered with blood, was struggling to get free.

blam-BLAM, blam-BLAM, blam-BLAM

sssssshhuuuuuuuuu, chookachooka

The sounds from the subway construction site rose and fell—saws hammering, tractors, cement mixers, trucks.

When Ige-Sha had managed to center Rosa directly above the other girl, she pulled on the ropes, lowering her until there was only three feet between the two. The assistant worked rapidly on the ceiling, tearing away a part of the roof. Milky sky appeared. Since the house was high up on a hill, tilted in the direction of the slope, the opening in the roof revealed the city below, lights, a gigantic clock, an enormous Coca-Cola sign with bubbly liquid pouring out endlessly.

rum, rum, rum, rum, rum, rum, rummmm

ding, ding, ding, ding,
chee chee chee chee chee chee chee chee chee chee
The old woman let go of the ropes, Rosa descended until

ner body rested on the skinny girl. The record turned, slowed to the wrong speed, the beat stretched out, elongated.

oh oh oh oh oh oh
ioom, ioom, ioom, ioom, ioom
—Rise and spirit yourself away, demon.
ooooiiioooioioiooooooooo
BLAM
BLAM BLAM BLAM BLAM B L A M B L A M
The old woman put down her cigar, went into a closet, and brought out a wooden box; from inside the box she took another, and three more, until there was just a tiny silver case. Inside there were two identical stones, a matched pair. She walked back to the table. The pulleys were spinning and whirring, Rosa flew up and down and whirled around, resting on the skinny girl and then flying up into the air again. The assistants, larger and smaller, brought the daggers. Paulo Watu was chosen by Ige-Sha's pointing finger. And he
plunged the dagger into Rosa's foot,
the pulleys whirred;
he plunged it into one of her eyes,
the pulleys whirred again;
he plunged it into the other eye,
a whirring and whining;
into her navel, her back,
into her temple;
the contraption hummed and shook;
into her breasts, belly, buttocks, sides, knees, shins, toes, every part of her body, making small holes from which blood spurted, spilling onto the skinny girl underneath;
and blood mixed with blood, from the holes in one body to the holes in the other,
until Rosa was a piece of meat, suspended by ropes . . .
The old woman checked her dead eyes, dead heart, dead lungs.
—Ready.
The assistants took her down from the ropes and placed her on top of the surgical table once more. Ige-Sha cut off a tiny piece of thigh, put it in her mouth, and chewed. The people watching drew in closer, slowly, purposefully, and stood around the bloody meat. The toothless old woman sucked on her morsel. The assistants cut more slices from

Rosa's arms, breasts, belly, and passed them around. The people ate leisurely, some using the meat to garnish what was left of the *adum*.

The assistants proceeded to cut Rosa up into little pieces. Now she would fit into the plastic pails. Boned like a chicken. The old woman picked up one pail. She was still very strong, as strong as her ancestors who had been field slaves. The assistants picked up the other pail, and everyone left. They walked up and down the alleys. There was no one working on the subway, it was three a.m.

The crowd straggled along in a disorderly way. Ige-Sha held Rosa's heart in her hand as she walked, and she moaned softly. She stopped when she came to a yellow tractor. One of the assistants opened the oil tank and Ige-Sha dropped the heart inside. Then she pointed toward the partly excavated earth and the assistants bent down with little shovels, digging and digging, placing the little pieces of Rosa into the earth. They also threw a few pieces into the holes made for the subway. The burial took an hour. It was dawn by the time they got back.

More *adum* for everyone. The assistants didn't touch it, because of the onion-shrimp sauce. The old Ige-Sha ate a double portion.

HONORABLE TREATMENT—
AS EVERY CITIZEN DESERVES

Conversation between guard and interrogator:

"No problem, we know how to take care of things, without leaving a mark."

"Okay, but you've gotta be careful . . ."

"Careful, nothing, we're the ones in charge around here, the government's on our side, everyone else can go fuck themselves."

The torturers applied technique number one: Atila was shut up in a dark cell. Black walls, black ceiling, black floor. Not a chink of light.

Motive: In a little over a week the blackness would be engraved on the retina, totally debilitating the prisoner and destroying whatever resistance he had left.

—Okay, talk.

—What do you want me to say?

—Everything, everything.

—Everything about what?

—Plans, hideouts, weapons.

—What plans, what hideouts, what weapons?

—Shit, man, think a little harder. Up till now we haven't laid a hand on you, but things are about to change.

—But I don't know anything.

—Who was your leader?

—Leader? I don't have any. I don't know what you're talking about.

—There was a leader who gave you orders. Think, man.

—I don't know. I was always with José.

—José?

They looked through the mug shots and wanted posters.

—This him?

It was a pretty good likeness.

—Yeah.

—Okay, then, start talking.

—About what?

They kept at it for a whole hour. Ternurinha was patient. (His nickname was Mr. T.L.C.) He started his interrogation tenderly, kindly, trying to catch the prisoner in a contradiction; and meanwhile he spoke eloquently, he was clever with words. But Ternurinha was intransigent about one thing: he set a time limit for the detainee to begin talking. After that, he applied the ''methods.''

Atila wasn't telling him anything of use. He didn't know a thing, even though he accompanied José on some of the assaults. He went along just to go along. He didn't have a job, he needed to do something. Ternurinha was dying of laughter. When the time limit was up, Atila was brought back to his cell. On the way they took him through a room where music was being played at top volume. He heard moans from some of the other cells. In the middle of the night a guard brought another prisoner, a student, age twenty-one, accused of participating in a kidnapping. In the morning, Atila tried to talk with him, but he wouldn't say a word. Atila persisted, but the guy just looked at him, his eyes open wide, a terrified expression on his face. By late afternoon Atila gave up and went back into his own corner. That's when the kid motioned from across the cell. Opened his mouth and showed Atila that half his tongue was missing. Self-inflicted, so he couldn't give away any information. The boy cried all night long, and in the morning he

288

tried to hang himself with the bedsheet. Atila wouldn't let him. Then the guard came back and took the student away.

Atila was in front of Ternurinha, naked, standing on two upside-down tin cans. They told him to hold out his arms, palms up, and placed a telephone book in each hand. For a few minutes Atila found he could support them with no problem.

Eight minutes went by, and Atila's hands fell to his sides, the telephone books landed on the floor. Ternurinha attached wires to Atila's feet (one to the big toe and another to the smallest, so the current wouldn't go directly to the heart). He flipped the switch and Atila howled. Ternurinha told him to hold his arms up and they put the phone books back in place.

—Every time you lower your arms you're going to get a shock. You may die here, but you'll talk.

(This is what it is to die. How pleasant, thought Atila after the first hour—which seemed more like days, weeks, months, years, centuries, fucking son-of-a-bitch.)

—Okay. Back to his cell. I don't know why I'm being so nice.

They passed through the room with the loud music. His cell was empty. The corridor was silent, until the guards began bringing in new prisoners; their moans and cries and screams echoed off the stones (where the hell am I?).

Conversation between two cops:

"I'm not so sure it's true, but I heard the Squad already picked up this guy Zé. Bet they sent him to No Exit."

"If the chief of SUPO knew that, he'd have the Squad taken out and shot."

"Yeah, they're looking for a fight, for sure."

"Everybody wants to bring in the big fish, you get a promotion."

There were three companions in the cell with Atila. One died during the afternoon. His left eye had been torn out. Atila had a loose tooth. (Ternurinha had started getting heavy-handed.) Guards walked back and forth in the hall. Keeping an eye on things, Winchesters in hand. This cell had a window, but it was so high on the wall you couldn't look out. The window let in a yellow glow. A trickle of water ran down from the sill.

(Where's José? Where's the gang?)

No one came to take away the guy who had died until

evening. Atila didn't even look up, it had nothing to do with him (something strange is happening to me). They left him his dinner in a rusty tin can. He cleaned out the urinal, ate the dirty water with beans and hunks of bread floating in it, and waited for it to be time to face Ternurinha. He was terrified when he saw what they had waiting for him.

(Why don't they kill me once and for all. If I knew what they wanted, I'd tell them. Anybody would. But I don't know anything, I just hung out and messed around with Zé, there wasn't anything else to do.)

They hung Atila on the "perch": With cloth wrapped around his wrists and his hands bound together, they made him get in a sitting position, his hands behind his knees. Then they stuck a broom handle between his knee joints and wrists. They propped the broom handle between two chairs. Left it there for a few minutes, took it down. After a while Atila felt like he was suffocating. He needed air, the blood was rushing to his head.

They hung him up and took him down. Until he fainted. He woke up in his cell the next day, still tied up. Alone. Above him, the dim yellow light from the window. (What time is it there outside?) He asked the guard. The answer: "It's a hot time in the old town tonight. Yes, sir. Already got all your pals, every last one. Shot 'em at dawn. Too bad you were asleep, you could have watched. They crapped in their pants, begged forgiveness, pissed all over themselves. They're all shit, like you. Soon's it gets hot, just a bunch of cowards."

Atila wept.

Conversation between the President and the Chief of National Security:

"Look, our image abroad isn't very pretty. They say we're dictators, that this is a terrorist regime. Just look at this list of interrogation methods and people tortured or missing."

"Mr. President, our regime has many enemies, you have to remember that. These lists are lies, what it amounts to is slander. No one is being tortured. No one has died."

"This French newspaper says we open up the bellies of pregnant women."

"Lies, lies on top of lies. That's why we need censorship,

290

surveillance, we've got to keep a tight grip on things, we've got to guard against distorted images like this."

"Then tighten the grip, if you think it's necessary."

The President thinks (but doesn't say): we've *got* to use torture, we've *got* to do away with our enemies.

The Chief of Security thinks (but doesn't say): this president is a jerk. I'm the one running the country, and anyone who doesn't like it better watch out.

Phone call from the President to the Minister of Justice:

"Prepare a press release denying all rumors of torture and political assassination. Say a panel of inquiry has been convened."

Aiiiiiiiiiiiiiiiiiiiiiiiiiiiiiiiiiiiiiiiiiiiiiiiiiiiiiiiiiiiiiiiiiiiiiiiiiiiiiiiiiiiiiiiiiiiiiiiii

THE LITTLE BARBEQUE: a technique of torture which is a slight variation on the perch. The prisoner is hung on the apparatus in the normal way, only they burn newspapers underneath him.

Atila was dragged back to his cell with first-degree burns on his ass and back.

Eleven students were marched down the hall (arrested in police raids). Every day two or three cadavers went by. The music room kept functioning nonstop, volume at the highest decibel level possible, old time singers (*I dreamed that you were so pretty*) and young singers and good singers and bad singers, and then water dripping, plink, plink, plink, plink, plink, plink, plink, plink, plink.

—You'll be set free tomorrow.

And tomorrow never came. They cut off his hair with a razor, making enormous slashes in his scalp in the process, letting the blood flow. Then they tied him up and Ternurinha directed two husky men to hold him upside down and dunk his head into a big kerosene can full of shit and piss. They held his head inside the can.

They dunked him in and out.

And in and out and out and in. Push, pull, push, pull, pushpull, pushpullpushpullpushpullpushpullpush.

His lungs were full of shit.

But Ternurinha decided that it wasn't quite time yet for Atila to die. Atila was strong, he wasn't saying a word. If he doesn't talk, he'll die, it's in Holy Resolution #768, the chapter on repression. But what if he knows everything and has been trained to resist? Ternurinha had learned in Police School that there were rural and urban training centers for guerillas.

It seemed like the foul smell was permanently inside Atila, in his nose, his mouth, in his stomach. He vomited and vomited and when there wasn't anything left to vomit he hurled himself at Ternurinha with every bit of his remaining strength. Two militiamen knocked him down with a few karate chops. Unconscious, he was dragged to his cell.

How long can a man resist? As long as he wants to, that's what Atila decided when he saw what it was like to confront intense pain. Because he didn't want to die. Even if he didn't have any more strength left, if he could still hold onto the will to live. But Atila didn't want to be beaten anymore, he didn't want to endure a "manicure" (needles under the fingernails) or a game of "scare-the-horse" (gunshots right next to the ear, bursting the eardrum), like the two who had been led past his cell yesterday.

Postmortem:

"They say the number of political prisoners has hit fifteen thousand."

"I heard it was eighteen."

"Someone told me ten."

"Well, at least ten thousand have been killed outright."

"That labor leader who escaped said that in FEPO alone they've killed more than five hundred, so imagine if you totaled the rest of the country."

"There must be some three million dead."

Observation: where there's smoke, there's fire.

—Telephone, for you.

Ternurinha handed the phone to Atila.

Atila grabbed it mechanically. A telephone, a cannon, or a locomotive, it didn't matter anymore. Ternurinha helped him put the receiver up to his ear. He heard only a busy signal. He left the phone there and waited. Ternurinha placed another phone on Atila's other ear, wrapping adhesive tape around his head to hold both of them in place. The receivers

were now glued to his ears, with the busy signal, bleep-bleep, bleep-bleep, bleep-bleep, bleep-bleep, bleep-bleep, bleep-bleep, bleep-bleep, bleep-bleep, bleep-bleep
> bleep-bleep
> bleep-bleep
> bleep-bleep

for twenty minutes. Atila blacked out.
—You going to talk?
—Yes or no?
—Tell us everything.
—Everything.
—And stop repeating what I say.

Ternurinha went to lunch. He was dying for a steak and french fries. When there was someone to torture, Ternurinha was happy. It gave him a big appetite. Even when there wasn't anything to do at the station before lunch, he'd drop by just to have a look around. For quite a while the work had been especially brutal. Extra hours, crazy schedules. In the old days the place was calm, really quiet. He had straightforward cases to deal with: robbers, stolen cars, dope dealers, a murder or two. People who opened up fast with a smashed hand or a shattered sternum. Nowadays the majority of these people let themselves be crippled; they just wouldn't open their mouths, this bomb-setting contingent, robbing banks and weapons depots. (Shit, what the fuck do they want?) The thing was that Ternurinha was afraid of being shot. These guys were intelligent, the administration ought to crack down on these Communs before they finished off the country completely, or the whole goddamned human race.

Operation Hot Embers:
Those who could walk, walked; those who couldn't, crawled; those who were totally disabled were dragged. Outside, across the runway to the fat-bellied plane which was ready and waiting. Atila was one of the ones who crawled.[1]

---

[1]The reconstruction of Atila's story is obviously not perfect, because the testimony given was confused, contradictory, and in some cases just too fantastic. We have provided a rough account of the narrative, eliminating as much as possible the elements of fantasy and exaggeration which could change fact into fiction.

A NOCHE, A NOCHE SONE CONTIGO
QUE COSA MARAVILHOSA,
AL COSITA LINDA

Gê and José:
—We're going to kidnap diplomats and make their release contingent on our demands.
—What if they don't accept your conditions?
—We'll be forced to kill the diplomats. Which may create international incidents.
—But what if they realize this is a tactic, and refuse to create incidents?
—Then whoever accepts a post as ambassador or consul in this country will inherit the problem. If they want to play a different game, we will too. Say we just assassinate diplomats outright. Not too many people will want to risk their necks being posted here.
—They'll come down really hard on us. Talk about repression . . .
—They've been coming down hard on us and everybody else for ages, it's about time we give them some of their own medicine.
—It will be war.
—It's already war.
—You've got a hundred men. Against cannons, machine guns, tanks, trained armies, bombs, international funding, supplies, and support. From everywhere.
—But we know who they are and they don't know who we are. And we do our sabotaging and bombing all in the dark, that's our advantage.
—Where will it all end?
(Where *will* it all end? I'm not sure this is the right road. Maybe I'll die without ever really knowing. But, more than ever, I need to keep my head on straight, so I can see, and analyze, and take action.)

AFFECTIVE MEMORY

It was a deep pit just like under the cement slab or the water tank back home and José had hit the man in the head and when he opened the slab the smell of decomposing bodies rushed out and José didn't know if he had thrown other

294

people in there, was this man a sadistic interrogator from the police? it didn't matter, why should it, José had been asked to do it, the Communs told him to, and it was necessary to do what they asked, and the trench was the well and there was water reflecting his face and Rosa's and his face contemplated himself as if José was going in the same time he was going out and José wondered if he should push Rosa in the well, because of the baby at the bottom.

TRICKING THE WORLD[1]

The President called the Supreme Commander of the Repressive Armed Forces:

—Clean up the prisons. Hide or kill the prisoners. Arrange for subversives willing to collaborate, have them sign declarations in our favor. Fill the hospitals with our people and say they were wounded by terrorists.

Months later, the U.N. received the following communication:

OUR PRISONS ARE OPEN FOR INSPECTION BY THE INTERNATIONAL COMMISSION ON TORTURE AND POLITICAL PRISONERS WHICH WILL NO DOUBT VERIFY THE FALSEHOOD OF THE NOTICES WHICH HAVE RECENTLY BEEN DEFAMING THIS NATION ABROAD. WE ARE A GOOD, PEACEFUL, DEMOCRATIC PEOPLE, OPPOSED TO ALL VIOLENCE.

GÊ TO JOSÉ:
—In this day and age you've got to be made of iron.[2]

HOLY RESOLUTIONS

''From this day forward, all vehicles must bear a flag and a plastic sticker with patriotic slogans. Any car lacking these

---

[1] My friend Alcides always used to say: you can only trick the world when the world wants to be tricked.

[2] This revolutionary saying is from an old Errol Flynn movie about the Norwegians' resistance to Nazi occupation.

visible manifestations of loyalty will be apprehended and the owner will be detained for six months."[1]

(Underground leaflet: be careful during distribution. Verify the recipient carefully as genuine and trustworthy. Be wary of informers.)

DEPOSITION

"They touched a wire to my tongue and my mouth exploded, it filled up with something awful tasting trying to slip down my throat and suffocate me and it was fire and ashes and shit and blood and dirt and loose teeth all together. You're going to find out what hell really is, the guy said to me, lieutenant, sergeant, captain, whatever he was. And don't think you'll get out of this alive, you'll crack like all the rest, there won't be a bone left unbroken in your body, get ready for this. It was at night. They left me in a cold cell full of roaches and ants, I don't know where the ants came from. I slept on the tiled floor, well, I didn't really sleep because I kept thinking about what was going to happen the next day. The cell was damp, no light at all, and it smelled bad, mold shit stale sperm blood fear. I don't know what time it was they came to get me, they led me through the halls lit by fluorescent lights, hurt my eyes, no idea if it was day or night. They put me in a room with a table, a chair, and the famous perch, plus six guys waiting very calmly to punch me as hard as they could in the stomach, they put the telephones to my ears, and I couldn't hear anything, I just watched their lips moving, nothing, and then they started beating me again. Suddenly they stopped and were gone, I sat down, walked around, tried to rest, I was alone, I didn't know how many hours or days had passed. Until they came back and put me on the perch. Wired up my feet and hands and started with the shocks. The little man who flipped the switch on and off furiously was saying talk, talk, talk, tell us everything you Communist son-of-a-bitch, tell us about the hideouts, we want names, we want

[1]A colonel owned the business which manufactured the flags and stickers: he became a millionaire.

296

the addresses of the priests, those shitty priests, god-damned fairies, everybody knows they don't like women. Then the wires were on my balls, on the soles of my feet, talk, you asshole, tell us everything you piece of shit, and me frgsthfhtryg rufjutifjur itid narerad mertardstr frsgrtuio-kilo. And now you're going to find out why they call me Joe Nice Guy said the colonel as he threaded a wire up my cock and turned on the juice and I flew into another world, so much pain I didn't even feel pain, it seemed like my cock had been torn off and I didn't even feel it anymore, I thought: I'll never screw again, not even if there's a thousand luscious cunts in front of me. And Joe Nice Guy rammed a stick up my ass and connected the wire to a magnet on the stick and flipped the switch and the shit came running out, down my legs, those guys were dying of laughter, they said I should eat it off the floor because I had made such a mess and the general commandant didn't like messes. A shit to end all shits, when they flipped the switch all my muscles started shaking at once, that was the worst, I couldn't take it anymore, ukjitgfyjghtyaaoirsgrt groitsgruio groatrareasresreaa dfrees dgrefregstrfncgui cracrecrecrei-crocru, lick the floor, you shitty commie, mother-fucking bandit, lick it up with your tongue, clean up the mess so the general won't see, turds aren't all that bad now are they, kind of like baby cereal, and the sergeant suggested that they have me piss so there'd be a drink to accompany lunch. I remember that little sergeant's face, he had a crooked nose and a big scar on his chin. I ate the meal off the floor, what choice did I have, I ate what had already passed through me once before and they hung sharpened hooks on my ears and pulled and pulled until the right ear was cut off and they threw the ear in the middle of the mess and told me to try the feijoada again, what's bean stew without a hog's ear, they roared, and the world rose up again and disappeared and when it came back there were rats and cockroaches on top of me, licking me, nibbling at the wound where my ear used to be and I struggled to get away from them and my whole body hurt, the roaches were frightened off but there were still shit-eating beetles walking all over me and ants (shit, where did these fucking ants come from, they're biting me) and the light in the ceiling went out, sleep, a little sleep, but wake up, hey, wake up, the interrogation is about to begin, they dumped cans of

cold water over me, no, no, there isn't going to be an interrogation, what they'll do today at sunrise is to shoot you, ha
ha, me, looking up at the little window, looking, waiting for
the sun to rise (you son-of-a-bitch, don't come up, don't).
And the sun coming up and me sleeping, sleeping, forgetting, forgotten, until they were beating me on the back with
a whip, hard, they mounted me like a horse and there was
one who wanted to ass-fuck me for christ's sake, my macho
ass, no, please, so up went another electrical wire, a little
feather, and they put the feather in my asshole and wiggled
it around (some feather: a stick with little needles around
the end), and they tore me to pieces in there, the camp doctor is still trying to patch me up, start talking, confess,
names, addresses, who was at whose house, telephone
numbers, meetings, start talking, creeeeee, regstruij,
grfareeueieol   mjhuyirofgetgfuietruio,   freererrerere,
aaiiiiiiiii, FUCK! No cursing! Prisoners aren't allowed to talk
dirty, kiss the flag, kneel down and pray, confess to the
priest, you're going to be taken out and shot, come on,
YELL, say it: I betrayed my country, I repent, or else we're
going to kill your father, every last one of your relatives,
look at the rifle, aimed and ready to fiiiiiiiire. I fell asleep, I
woke up, I dropped off again, I woke up on the perch, more
jolts, I blacked out, then I was back in solitary, a bright light
that wouldn't let me sleep, I tore up my shirt for a blindfold,
ten minutes of sleep, awake again, sleep-awake-sleep.
You're a bastard, fucking asshole, too bad we can't do anything about this, you're going to take a bath, get cleaned
up, new clothes, put on a good face, eat hearty, your
name's on some goddamned list, you must be important
and you didn't tell us a fucking thing, if we could have you
one more day you'd crack, if it wasn't for that stupid-ass
consul, piece of shit, I'd say let them kill the jerk, you'd be
staying with us, behind bars where you belong, you'd rot
your ass here, no bone left unbroken, you'd be ground to
powder, terrorist flour, shitty commie. Fuck your mother.

CAREFUL, CHILDREN

The boy was looking straight at the man who said for the
second time: "Get out of here, go on." The boy didn't
budge. The man pushed him. He yelled, but didn't move.
So the man shoved him a few more times and the boy ran

off. To tell his mother. Dona Osvaldinha was outraged: "This is the last straw, this time they've gone too far. Those people are always doing something to bother me, for years it's been like that. But hitting the boy—that's too much." Dona Osvaldinha called her husband and the two of them marched down the street to settle accounts. But when they got close, they saw the trucks being painted, and they saw that the men were armed. So Dona Osvaldinha and her husband went running to Corporal Omar, and told him all about it, and the corporal came to see for himself. And he saw. And immediately called in a detachment—officers, trucks, soldiers, the works: you're under arrest! And the men painting the trucks looked up. And the soldiers discharged their weapons.

THE SOUND AND THE FURY

Stop, look, & listen: take 30% off your income tax / with real estate bonds / Attention! It is prohibited to be poor / This is the epoch of money, producing and reproducing / Poor / Shmoor / Your / More / You can't lose with our financial advice: we know the market / Looking for something? / We have it all: credit, financing and investment / new savings certificates with interest compounded monthly / Get one now / It's easier / It's easier / a camel to pass / don't pass us by / for a camel to pass / through / keep your eye on us / the eye of a needle / than for a rich man / Rich / Switch / Quick / Get the Itch / to enter the kingdom / Join the Millionaire's Club / of heaven / Be one of us: You've got some savings, right? / but you don't know where or how to invest, right? / Value Stocks return your investment threefold / Want your money to stand up and be counted? / Millionaires are created equal / Sequel / Ah, the wish to enter the kingdom / of heaven / Heavens / So invest in the Bank, ah-ha! / in the "no worry" Finance Group: letters of exchange to the bearer, monthly return guaranteed / This means you / Mr. João da Silva Gomes / Mr. Anonymous / You should both apply / apply / ply / pli/pli/plink/plink/ Plunk yourself down and enjoy your real estate investments / The government pays you to buy a piece of the action: take advantage of this special offer / Invest in Progress / our motto / And see if you don't learn / earn / don't learn that money / Money that isn't growing can only be shrinking / inking / in / come on in / Join the club / The Money Club / the Pires Germano Money Club / remember / prospective members / Remember that money under the mattress / What's it doing? / Put your money to work for you / You should know / Starting tomorrow there could be 18 million people / the working capacity of the nation / working / working for you: Biafra Finance Co. / a secular tradition in / Security / Investment / and Participation / Move up in life / Moving up to the 2nd floor shop at 67 Fifteenth Ave. / Corretora Brokers / Don't delay

DON'T CUT OFF A FUNERAL PROCESSION— IT'S BAD LUCK

Finally the shooting stopped. The place fell silent. The soldiers moved in and collected the prisoners. The wounded. The dead. They found José (drugged) in a pantry with a kitchen knife in his hand, murmuring: she killed the baby, she killed him.

Why did she do that (or didn't she)?

And he was scratching himself violently.

THE JOURNEY TO THE SPLENDID CRADLE

Hands chained behind his back. His entire body hurting from the beatings. A vacant look in his eyes. Fear. Three times Atila had been in front of the firing squad. Three times they used blanks.

One by one they were put on the airplane, two hundred of them all together. It was a journey to the heart of America.

They were piled on top of each other. Atila found it hard to take: the awful smell of sweat, dirty bodies wallowing in blood and shit.

A STATUE FOR EL MATADOR

Because it was an odd case (and picturesque, if it weren't for the fact that a man died), the newspapers and television and radio and magazine and film crews came to see and photograph and film, and they told it like this:

An unidentified man apparently had a few too many drinks and decided to take a rest in a vacant lot in Vila

Branca, next to the new street that's being constructed in the neighborhood. He sat down right on top of a heap of tar that had been dumped in the lot, not noticing that the stuff was still soft.

As he sank in comfortably, the mound collapsed under his weight until the tar covered him like a blanket. Since he was drunk or drugged (there are many marijuana dealers in the neighborhood), the man didn't even wake up. Yesterday morning people passing by found a strange sight: the shape of a man, almost seated, with his right leg crossed over his left knee, an elbow balanced there as if, upon feeling sleepy, he had rested his chin in his right hand.

Firemen and police arrived with picks and shovels in an attempt to free him, but the tar had already hardened, transforming the unknown man into a bizarre statue.

THE EGGS FROM THE SILVER BIRD (a legend)

Lying face down, hands tied behind his back. Hard to breathe. José tries to turn his face. He feels the cold wind on every part of his body.

Brrrruuuuuuuuuuuuuuuuuuuuuuuuuuuuummmmmmmmmmm mmmmmmmmmmmmmmmmmmmmmmmmm

The noise over his head, always the same. Monotonous.

The wind warms up a little. There's a glass wall. Behind it, clouds appear.

The wall dissolves, he sees groves of trees. They are motionless in the wind.

chup, chup, chup, chup, chup, chup, chup, chup, chup

Shovels above the glass roof, in slow motion. He turns his head to the side. There are people lying on the ground. Soldiers are cutting the ropes and freeing a bearded man dressed in prison garb. The man goes down a ladder and disappears into thin air.

The wind turns cold again.

They stop. Another man goes down the little rope ladder. They stop.

Twenty-one times.

—Give him an anti-sadness pill.

A little yellow box.

—Come on, man, wake up. Make yourself at home. Be of some use. Just look how much land the government has given you!

(Pills discovered by a team of Polish scientists, Lesbek Krowcsynski, Ryseard Grylewski, and Zoffia Shiffer. They chase away sadness, diminish nervous crises, and then act as a stimulant, enabling the patient to overcome laziness and fatigue.)

José climbs down the rope ladder.

The shovels: chup, chup, chup chupchupchupchup-chup. Fast.

José just sits there. Walking or sitting still, it's the same thing. He looks and sees nothing. It's as if he were sitting above a piece of paper that covered the world. Nothing moving down there. At times, rare times in the last thousand years, something moved. Millimeters, fractions of millimeters. Dust moves imperceptibly, driven by the heat, or intense cold. A fine dust, almost powder, finer than fancy talcum powder, and it lies in layers. When José walks his steps leave deep prints. Dust in a film on boulders. Miles and miles of emptiness. No sound can reach it—not from the forests to the north, or from the meadows to the south, or from the swamps in the middle. This is desolation, a light blue. In the middle of this desolation (José) the silence is total.

HE ASCENDED TO HEAVEN
ON THE THIRD DAY,
THE DEAD ROSE AGAIN

The yellow mass was shifting, swept by the north wind. A dry wind, which threatened to dissolve the explosive gelatin. The mass rolled along, thousands of miles, each time more fine, almost cellophane, while the earth was a blue ball, as the astronauts saw it. A ball surrounded by white clouds, smooth icing, good to eat. ("The world got small and in your hands turned to poison.") The mass was dropping lower, falling, to enter the atmosphere where it would slip in sideways, so as not to explode on contact. Even entering from the side, though, there was danger of friction which might ignite the gelatinous plastic. It slipped into the atmosphere in three layers, falling until it covered the big yellow desert. It lay everywhere, transforming sand, stones, cactus into an even fiercer yellow. The mass had traveled thousands of miles without seeing any living thing. Then suddenly, in the middle of all that immensity, a bright green tree appeared, and the mass converged on top of it. Beneath the tree raged a jungle waterfall.

THE SMELL

Atila understood death. There was permanence in burial. He still had his senses: sight, smell, taste, touch, hearing. Death meant powerlessness against small animals that ran over your body, your mouth already full of earth. It was to feel yourself being eaten. Death, Atila realized, was a smell: bitter, disturbing, excessive, cruel, invincible, unavoidable. A shocking smell which went to the depths of him and came from the depths of him. It seemed as if he had been born at that very moment, inside the smell. Atila was rotting. He was decomposing and he could smell the vile odor of his own body as it decayed. Pungent, extravagant, sharp. The smell cut like scissors cutting cloth, a scalpel slicing skin, the wheels of a train passing over his body, circular saws, like beavers gnawing trees, the smell was cutting him to ribbons like a razor-sharp axe. It was unendurable. Atila wanted to scream. But his voice didn't exist anymore.

Death was just that. Your own destiny, alone, in the dark. No help, no protection. Death is vulnerability, individuality. He wanted to fly, he wanted the decomposition to stop. The more he decayed, the weaker he got. When the smell reached an utterly unimaginable level, beyond the range of toleration, in another world, having gone off like a rocket with the force of 500 thousand locomotives, Atila was only minimally conscious. Many days, weeks, months, had gone by. Each millisecond had seemed like a thousand years, each second, minute, hour, day, month, an immeasurable time. Atila disappeared, and the smell (Atila) remained.

FRACTIONS OF THE DAILY DRAMA

Commun taken prisoner: Bambam BAM. Whap, whap. Plaft, pleft, shit, he's hit in the mouth, all his teeth are knocked out, his nails pulled out one by one, he's been burned, they've drilled a hole in one eye, thrown acid in the other, stuffed a rat in his mouth, razor slashes and briny water, wires stuck in his asshole, shocks, tear him all apart, smash his fingers, his cock, jab him in the stomach, make

303

him eat shit, cut out his tongue, prick his veins, give him an injection in the head,
shred, tear him into a thou

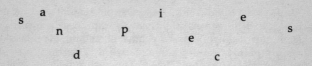

break a leg, arm, head, neck, fingers, bones, nose, ear, heart, eyes, guts, of the Communist's worthless body, son-ofabitchcocksuckingterroristprick.
—Would you like to take communion before you die, my son?
. . .
—You're gonna take communion before you die, buddy.
. . .
—Okay, hit him.
. . .
—Take communion, you shit!

Second terrorist taken prisoner:
—I'll do whatever you want, don't hit me, I'll talk.
They pushed the second terrorist into the cell with the yellow walls. He landed on top of (what was left of) the first terrorist (DEMOLITION: we buy and sell rubbish): blood, piss, shit, guts, stomach, heart, bones, legs, arms, fingers, eyes, nose, teeth, everything scattered around.
They showed the second terrorist a photograph.
—You know this guy?[1]
—No.
—He in your group?
—No.
—But he is a commun, right?[2]
—No.
—What do you mean, no?

---

[1] It was José.
[2] The law now prohibits *commun* from being written with a capital "c."

304

—You already asked me about him. This photo. Nobody knew him.[1]

—Nobody knew him where?

—In our cell.

—You sure?

—Yes.

—Okay boys, rough him up a little bit until he stops lying.[2]

GRRRRRRRRRRRR

That same night, Hero had made a run for it. He and Malevil swallowed a mess of pills to get psyched up. They stole a car and robbed a gas station and three passers-by. They shot at some cops, stole weapons, attacked a barracks, blew away the soldiers on watch, and found a stash of machine guns.

—The world can go fuck itself, shouted Malevil.

—Let's finish off this whole pile of shit, shouted Hero.

Because what they wanted was not to die. They had made their attacks, had slipped away quietly. They had filled the gas tank.

—Too bad we don't have any gelatin dynamite. Then we could set the whole place on fire.

—The military must have some. All we got to do is attack an army base.

—You got it.

—Let's set this fucking city on fire building by building.

—Biggest fire in the world, after Rome and San Francisco.

—Aaaaaaaaahaahahahahaha, uiu iuiuiuiuiui ooooooooooooooooaaaaa ooooaaaaiiiiieeiiaa

—Okay, let's go for broke. There's the base.

Silvana Mangano, out in the rice fields in those black stockings in "Arroz Amargo": me in the balcony

The newspapers have been able to increa se circulation with the introduction of scientific suppleme nts.

---

[1] The members of a cell don't know the members of another cell. Each faction, group, sector, operates in isolation.

[2] The second terrorist wasn't lying.

ARMY BASE 500 METERS AHEAD
REDUCE SPEED

—Step on it.

ARMY BASE 200 METERS AHEAD
REDUCE SPEED

—That's the way!

ARMY BASE
STOP
CARS AT HIGH SPEED WILL BE MA

ratatatatatatatatatatatatatatatatatatatatatatatatatatatatatatatatata

CHINE-GUNNED

(Military Security Policy #187965784653426789J198s)

—They get you?
—Who knows, shiiiiit . . .
—I think I'm hit.
—Look, there's one!
blam, blam, blam
—He's still alive. Back up.
The guard was reeling, trying to find his holster. Hero
shot him again, in the head this time, he fell. Hero emptied
the gun into him. Got out and kicked him. Someone was
watching, Hero shot him, too.

—Okay, let's celebrate.
—You think the cops are already looking for us?
—We'll switch cars.
Volkswagon, Plymouth, taxicab.
—Shit-fuck, we haven't done nothing yet. Nothing that's
really worth it.
Mercury, Kharman Ghia.
—Take it easy, you're pushing it a little.
Malevil was having trouble shifting, and his reflexes were
obviously off. He was driving recklessly.
—What's the matter, you don't like me tonight or some-
thing?
—I never liked you, you can go fuck yourself.
—But the fire . . . shit, let's not forget the fire.

306

—A fucking fire, I want a fucking fire.

An Impala, with a fur coat in it. Malevil ripped out all the car's accessories. Threw them out the window. They passed a gas station, got some gas, stopped in a little square, and set fire to the car. They stood watching. Malevil had put on the fur coat. A police siren. They ran. Climbed a wall, and dashed into a narrow, cement yard. The chickens started making a racket. Hero tried to climb the back wall but it had glass shards imbedded in the top, he cut his hand.

—Son-of-a-bitch motherfucker . . .

The chickens cackled. A man appeared at a window and took a shot at them. Malevil crouched down, he saw the man fire again. Hero was bleeding. He'd been hit in the head, lead shattering bone. Flesh plastered on the wall. The man leaped out the window and Malevil scaled the wall. His hands got all torn up. He ran. Signaled a cab. He wasn't even high anymore. The doorman at Le Masque would get him some more. And did.

There was a bottle of rubbing alcohol in the bathroom. He splashed a little on his face and walked back into the bar, with the bottle. The Blue Devils were playing. Malevil splashed some alcohol under a table and lit a match. Everyone scattered, screaming. Malevil climbed up onto the stage, the fire was spreading. He picked up an electric guitar and tried to play that song he'd heard Merilee Rush sing: *Reach out.*

a helicopter
is flying
over the
fields and
mountains and
lakes and
dense jungles and
swamps—
men with binoculars
are watching

The Literary Battalions had the street closed off. They went into the first building, up to the first floor, to the first apartment. They knocked and entered. They looked around the room. Picked up a calendar with a picture of a woman in a bathing suit. They flipped through all the magazines, confiscating any which had illustrations or ads with nude women, partially nude women, photographs of breasts, thighs, etc. They took an oil painting of a woman wearing a skirt above her knees. Then they went on to the books. They emptied the shelves of all those already known to have swear words, spicy scenes, references to sex, venereal disease, or unseemly situations. They confiscated any with suspicious titles. They skimmed all the others to see if their covers had been changed. They fined the owners of the apartment the equivalent of a year's pay at minimum wage; a second offense would mean arrest and confiscation of the apartment by the government. A third offense: life imprisonment. Then the Literary Battalion went on to the second apartment on the first floor.

THE PRESENCE OF THE RADIO

If only I had it now, glued to my ear, it would be like the good old days at the warehouse, loads of friends and companions talking to me, telling me stuff, singing songs, I wasn't alone. The helicopter came on patrol yesterday, it was up real high. Then it zoomed down, thwack, thwack, thwack, thwack, vroom, the blades beating the wind, what a nice sound.

CONCEPTUALIZING THE GUERILLA

"When active foreign guerillas fall into the hands of the government, they will be subject to all the rigor of domestic repressive legislation," as stipulated in *El Fallo Sobre el Conceptualismo Jurídico Extranjero*, written by the Colombian ambassador Caicedo Castilla. This legislation will be submitted later this year for the approval of the delegates to the Interamerican Judicial Commission.

QUIET PLEASE:

<table>
<tr><td>Attention,
WE ARE NOW TAPING</td></tr>
</table>

—My dear sir. You are the father of José Goncalves, assassin, terrorist, and armed robber. What can you tell us about your son?

The house was closed up tight. The reporter knocked again.

A neighbor stuck his head out the door:

—He moved. A long time ago. Went to Aquarara.

—How long ago?

—Right after the revolt of the priests. He defended the priests against the Bishop. He had to leave.

—Really?

—It was the women, the churchgoers. Not just the super-sanctimonious ones, either, but all the Catholics around here. They picketed his house. Called him on the phone. Sent hate mail. They came and made a racket, called him names, threw rocks at the place, peeked in the windows. They smashed everything all up. The women started it. Then the corner grocer wouldn't sell anything to him anymore. If he had, the other families wouldn't shop there. Same with the butcher, milkman, baker. Life got tough for him, he had to leave town.

The reporter went to Aquarara. A dead city. Empty stores, sleepy salesclerks, a hellish sun, long streets with sawed-off tree trunks in the middle.

(ATTENTION, TAPING)

—I have nothing to say. My son was just my son, his life was his own. He did what he wanted.

—You approved, then?

—I didn't approve or disapprove. He just did what he wanted.

309

—Do you think it's right to rob, kill, torture?

—Did you come here to interview me or to pass judgment?

—I came to do an interview, but your son was an assassin and I want to know what you think about that.

—I already told you.

—Did you know that he denied your very existence? That he said you had died? Did you know that?

—Yes, I knew. He killed me off years ago. He always disapproved of my life.[1] He was really attached to his mother. It was a shock for him when she died. The way she died.

—How did she die?

—Cancer of the intestine. She died defecating. She filled the bed with excrement. I can still smell it, even today, that smell. That room. José thought I was the guilty one, he thought I didn't like her. And I didn't. How can you like someone who dies like that? She shit on me her whole life long, and on José. She was so authoritarian. Moralistic. Religious. I don't know if José admired his mother or if he hated her strength. He wanted to be strong. Strong on the inside, like his mother. But all of a sudden he saw that on the inside his mother was nothing but shit.

—You sound so hard, so cruel, it's easy to understand why your son ended up the way he did.

—Then José started having strange attacks. He'd foam at the mouth and fall down in the street. He'd hurt himself. Afterward he never remembered a thing. José never wanted to kill anyone, he just wanted to kill himself. He wanted to commit suicide, he was sensible, religious.

—Religious! You call that religious?

—He believed in God, in goodness and evil, in heaven and hell. He never talked about it but I know he believed.[2] He read a lot of books. He knew *The Imitation of Christ*, the whole thing, by heart. It's true. He went to church. He took communion. He celebrated Easter. He did his penance.

---

[1] Really? That sounds odd.

[2] Either José's father is given to fantasy or he's just having fun with the reporter. Probably the latter; he liked to trick people, to give out false images of himself and of his son.

—When was it he left home?

—When he was eighteen. He went to the capital to study law. Then he quit. He wrote and said he didn't have the vocation. That he didn't have the vocation to work, period. He'd discovered violence against humankind. He said: "I'm not going to work to make this lousy world advance." He thought it was better, after all, to be a drunk, a bum. Like me.

—You consider yourself a bum?

—That's what *he* thought I was. But I worked hard. Really. I worked *and* I screwed around. José inherited that from me. You know how they say people inherit things from their parents. I don't know . . .

—Heredity, what a traditional idea . . .

I believe in it. I passed it on to my son, all that screwing around. He was right about one thing. He wanted the world to go fuck itself. Not a bad idea. I wanted the same thing. So I screwed around in my profession, I cheated, misrepresented facts, screwed up the legal process, I fucked the rich and the poor, the governors and the governed.

—Are you an anarchist?

—Who, me? No. I don't know. I'm pissed at life, that's all. Like my son. Look, I was proud of him once upon a time.

—Go on, tell me about his childhood, his youth . . .

(END OF TAPE, THE REPORTER DIDN'T NOTICE, BUT THE REEL RAN OUT.)

U.S.A, U.S.A., LAMA SABACTANI

I CRY OUT IN THE NIGHT FROM THE TORTURE
CHAMBER: Psalm 129
*"más que como se cuentam en la prison las horas nocturnas
Mientras nosotros estamos presos en fiesta"* (Cardenal)

By morning the five-hundred-thousand hippies and non-hippies had gone home. Leftovers from the five days remained on the beach: empty bottles, cans, bottlecaps, paper, plastic bags, cups, blankets, pieces of guitars, rubbers, sticks, shoes, dresses, socks, underpants, hair, necklaces, rings, money, fruit peelings, records, teeth, nails, corks, pens, glasses, belts, pocket knives, earrings, chains, bras, pocketbooks, cassettes, daggers, straw, Modess, cardboard boxes, vibrators, door latches, magazines, watches, Pond's cold cream, car parts, newspapers, buttons, film, the smell of seaweed, vomit, piss, shit, rotting leftover food, drinks fermenting in the sun and rain, sperm, marijuana, cigarette butts. And the sun of freedom beat down / in dazzling rays / José had a mouth full of wet sand. No shirt, sunburnt chest. He wanted to stay here / he could like here forever / but he got up and started walking. Without wanting to, without knowing why. Walking / along the flatness, no sound, no wind, no movement / . Empty pockets, no dope / and the desert around him / . Zigzagging in the hot sand / the helicopter overhead / . He fell on his face / beloved land / and the water washed in and out over him / again and again / and there were rivers, waterfalls, mosquitos, dense vegetation, flags waving, buglers, cavalry, tanks advancing / . He swallowed the salty water / binoculars observing him / and saw the black-and-white Ford pull up. Two giants in blue got out. On patrol. They walked in José's direction. José, Joe, Joseph / José had traveled the entire country, he'd seen clean and cheerful skies, the whole showy landscape, seas and forests, no country like this one / . The giants in blue picked him up / Police: beach patrol / like a sack of potatoes / carried him through the air in the virile helicopter, the gigantic eagle taking him to his nest in the head of America / . The giants put Joseph, Joe, in the Ford and drove off, siren screaming, through the streets of Miami, and they threw José in a clean, light, sterilized jail cell. A shiny white cell that smelled of disinfectant, detergent, clean clothes / democracy / and José blacking out, pockets empty, not even one pill left / wait, there *was* one / . Waking up and going under: and everything was clear and light and bright like the white cell, thoughtless, sterilized, hygenized, disinfecticized.

The conversion went like this (now I understand that night in the warehouse): It wasn't fatigue or hunger. It was a revelation. My body paralyzed, numb, the infernal noise, a thousand cars honking out in front of the bar down the street. The deserted street, and the greenish-yellow light

312

from the sign blinking on and off and growing and suddenly I understood the thousand books I had read. Neon light filled the warehouse, it was transformed into a yellowish-green gelatin and I heard a rhythmic song, a thousand voices singing: "Lord, this is the thrice-holy hour, through the fortunate presence of our Lord Jesus, together with our miserable souls. The wound in Your breast, always open, reminds You of the earth and gently obliges You to attend to the supplications and moans that rise up from the wilderness." Supplications and moans that rise up from underground prisons, torture chambers, fresh graves, and from fearful people. And the wound in Gê's breast, and Artigas, and Ché, and Simon Bolivar, and Sucre, and Tiradentes, and Peredo, and Jose Marti, fortunate presences together with our miserable souls, open wounds, looking to tend to us, Latíndio-americans, part of whom came from inside Africa. I felt this, and it gave me strength: I was Latíndio-american, nothing in the eyes of the world. It was destined for us to inherit the stigma that followed the Hebrews for millennia. Persecution and segregation and oppression: transplanted. I realized that it was our turn to be humbled, offended, spit upon, to be human leftovers, dejected, nonexistent flesh on top of nonexistent bone. A cycle was ending in that greenish-yellow moment, the Jew making way for the Latíndio-american, passing on to us the pain and despair of the world. And we were in bad shape to begin with: underdeveloped, malnourished, miserable, diseased. Maybe in a thousand short years we'll become, as they have, strong, something difficult to destroy, and some other group will take our place in the cycle. Meanwhile, we extend our hands, Latíndio-americans, Africans, Asians, not to weep and moan, but to understand and to organize. Brothers in the blood, brothers in the skin, blacks—non-blacks—whites—non-whites, whoever's got a stone in the intestine.

The giants in blue, talking to the chief of police:

—What about that guy?

—Does he have any papers? Identification?

—Nope, nothing. Must have entered illegally. He looks foreign.

—Cuban? Puerto Rican? Panamanian?

—Search me. They're all skinny, dark, with black hair, kind of sick-looking.

—The government should do something about these secret organizations that bring in refugees. The sooner the better.

—So what are we gonna do with him?

—Leave him there in the cell. He looks like he's high on something.

yyyyyyyeeeeeelllllllllllllllllllllloooooooooowwwwwwwwwww
  wwwhhhhhhhhiiiiiiiittttttttte   ttteennnnnnnnnnttttttt
ttt the Maaaaaaaaaaaaaaaaaaaaaaaannnnnnnnnnn

  tttennnnnnnnnn dddaaaayyyyyysssss with

  HIMMMMMMMMMMMMMMMMMMMMMMMMMMMMMM

  Jose hadfooooooorrrrrrrrrrggggggoootttttttttennnnnnnnthe
eeeeeee Maaaaaaaaaannnnnnnnn

  heeeeeeeeeeee's beeeeeennnnnn killlllllllllledcrucified, sh
pppptttttttt, crucified, beeeeeeeattttttennnnnnnn

  charlatan! (was he really?)

innnnthe maaainnnn sssssssssquaaarrrrrrrrrrre

  between twooooo

  terrorists

  terrrrrorrrrrrrrboomboomboombambambambambambam
and the Man wasss yellllllllllinnnnnnnngggg

  the useful will be called on / and the yell

echoed in the cell / and noooowwwwwwwwwwwwwww
innnnnnthe celllll the Maaaannnnnn the Man
was shhhhouuuttttttting

THERE ARE SIGNS FOR YOU TO READ

aaaaantisssseppppppppptiiiiic, clean white cell
eeeeeennnaaammmmellllled tiiiiin: the sign, the symbol
314

José looks: finds:
:four lines, four lives, before
                          beginning
                          during
                          after
                          and as he came nearer,
                          shouting,
he saw: in the triangle: Rosa, in her white uniform, in the
kitchen. Without a face.

                                        pieces of Rosa.
            Zzzzzzzzzzzzzzzzzz: didu-beré.
            a clang of keys, he woke up, he saw the sym-
bol of the communs: there are signs for you.
    They opened the cell:
    —Allll raaaate, come on, fella (they were talking like cow-
boys in the matinee: me in the balcony).
    They took José to another cell / José / . A hallway, a door,
a corridor leading off into two more corridors. The one on
the right forming a square and leading to another corridor.

Hallways zigzagging, one inside the other, cells inside the white hall and José kept walking . . .

GRAND FINALE

. . . until the grandeur of this homeland came to an end—no torrential rivers—no soaring mountains—no verdant jungle waterfalls—not even a scrubby prairie.

The only thing in front of him was space: America ended in isolation, where the child was born, laid in a cradle of rice straw, poppy, peyote, and nightshade / and at his side, the ox and burro watching, without understanding. And ahead of him was the world of rocket ships—satellites—computers—frozen bodies waiting to be revived—underwater civilizations—the ocean conquered by the earth—men inside other men: transplants, the reconstitution of cells, organs made of plastic—earth as food—combustible water—men with gills—talking animals / the maximum in communication: Macluhanluhan III / absolutely no distance between two points—and a new conception of liberty: an earth of love & green seas & forests & wide open fields in flower & a mother country & goodness & hope & the altar AND José, Joe, Joseph, José saw (heard): the covered heaven. Locked shut. An incandescent metal plate. Closed. (Irremediably.) With a cover. The metal formed a ball. And the world was locked up inside it. Metal made of millions of projectiles: bullets from cannons—revolvers—rifles—machine guns—shotguns—rocket ships—bazookas.

> BUT WHAT ABOUT THE HEAD?
> WHERE'S AMERICA'S HEAD?
> I DON'T SEE IT.

> BURN
> BABY
> BURN

And he heard the noise (it was deafening) and the echo of the noise inside the ball of fire: motors, airplanes, armored cars, trucks, tanks, explosions, shouted commands / ready, aim, fire / screams of pain and shouts of laughter and marching boots. And José, Joe, Joseph, José saw reflected in the incandescent metal (screen, TV, mirror) the new order, the chains, the nakedness (finally, all the illegal words), the immobility (finally, all the prohibited gestures), the executed communs, Gê crucified (but I thought Gê fled, I thought he was hidden on a chicken farm, raising chickens and selling eggs, manure, day-old chicks). Did they really get Gê (again?)—they got everyone, and they'll keep on getting everyone until we find a way to fight and organize. And turn things around. And turn things around again. Whoever is right will be wrong, whoever is wrong will be right, whoever—later—will be wrong—today—sure, unsure —whoever will be sure, wrong—later will be right or wrong. And the metal plate hotter than hot, the ball of fire. The earth enclosed, the intrepid sphere.

&
hear the prayer
of this bold people
who don't fear war
but desire peace

GOD SAVE AMERICA.

NEW FROM BARD
DISTINGUISHED MODERN FICTION

CALL IT SLEEP
Henry Roth   **60764-6/$3.95**

One of the great American novels, it tells the story of the immigrant experience in America. First published in 1934 to critical acclaim, it quickly dropped out of sight. But with its 1964 publication it received the recognition it deserved when **The New York Times Book Review** hailed it as "one of the few genuinely distinguished novels written by a 20th-century American."

KONTINENT 4:
Contemporary Russian Writers
George Bailey, Editor   **81182-0/$4.95**

A compelling and provocative collection of 23 articles and short stories from *KONTINENT*, the quarterly journal of Russian and Eastern European dissident writers. These powerful works are written both by emigres from the Soviet Union and her satellite countries as well as by dissidents who must smuggle their manuscripts from behind the Iron Curtain. Filled with courage, defiance and surprising humor, these works afford a unique look at contemporary Russian literary, political and social thought.

DAUGHTER OF NIGHT
Lydia Obukhova,
translated by Mirra Ginsburg   **61192-9/$2.95**

An absorbing fantasy adventure that explores an intriguing possibility: what if human thought were created with the help of alien visitors from technologically advanced planets? "Expertly translated, excites the imagination and should keep a tight grip on any reader...a smashing tale."
Publishers Weekly

QUIN'S SHANGHAI CIRCUS
Edward Whittemore   **61200-3/$3.50**

A surreal, colorful novel of a young man whose search for his lost parents takes him on a wild odyssey through the Orient. Edward Whittemore "has an incredible imagination. His fantasies could be a combination of such as Borges, Pynchon, Nabokov, Fuentes and Barth."
Pittsburgh Post-Gazette

AVON BARD
DISTINGUISHED
LATIN AMERICAN FICTION

■ **By Jorge Amado**

✔DONA FLOR AND HER TWO HUSBANDS	54031-2/$3.95
✔GABRIELA, CLOVE AND CINNAMON	60525-2/$4.95
HOME IS THE SAILOR	45187-5/$2.75
✔SHEPHERDS OF THE NIGHT	58768-8/$3.95
TENT OF MIRACLES	54916-6/$3.95
✔TEREZA BATISTA: Home from the Wars	34645-1/$2.95
✔TIETA	50815-X/$4.95
TWO DEATHS OF QUINCAS WATERYELL	50047-7/$2.50
THE VIOLENT LAND	47696-7/$2.75

■ **By Gabriel García Márquez**

✔THE AUTUMN OF THE PATRIARCH	64204-2/$3.50
✔IN EVIL HOUR	64188-7/$2.95
✔ONE HUNDRED YEARS OF SOLITUDE	62224-6/$3.95

AVON Paperbacks

Available wherever paperbacks are sold or directly from the publisher. Include $1.00 per copy for postage and handling: allow 6-8 weeks for delivery. Avon Books. Dept BP. Box 767. Rte 2. Dresden. TN 38225.

2 Lat Am 6-83

AVON BARD
DISTINGUISHED
LATIN AMERICAN FICTION

CELEBRATION
  Ivan Angelo   78808-X/$2.95
THE DEAD GIRLS
  Jorge Ibargüengoitia   81612-1/$2.95
DON CASMURRO
  Machado de Assis   49668-2/$2.95
EMPEROR OF THE AMAZON
  Marcio Souza   76240-4/$2.75
EPITAPH OF A SMALL WINNER
  Machado De Assis   59659-8/$3.50
THE EYE OF THE HEART: Short Stories
from Latin America
  Barbara Howes, ed.   54346-X/$3.95
THE FAMILY OF PASCUAL DUARTE
  Camil José Cela   60749-2/$2.95
THE GIRL IN THE PHOTOGRAPH
  Lygia Fagundes Telles   80176-0/$3.95
THE GREEN HOUSE
  Mario Vargas Llosa   60533-3/$4.95
HOPSCOTCH
  Julio Cortazar   58701-7/$4.50
THE LOST STEPS
  Alejo Carpentier   46177-3/$2.50
MULATA
  Miguel Angel Asturias   58552-9/$3.50
PHILOSOPHER OR DOG?
  Machado De Assis   58982-6/$3.95
SEVEN SERPENTS AND
SEVEN MOONS
  Demetrio Aquilera-Malta   54767-8/$3.50

AV✦N Paperbacks

Available wherever paperbacks are sold or directly from the publisher. Include $1.00 per copy for postage and handling: allow 6-8 weeks for delivery. Avon Books, Dept BP, Box 767, Rte 2, Dresden, TN 38225.

NEW FROM AVON ⑂BARD
DISTINGUISHED
MODERN FICTION

DR. RAT   63990-4/$3.95
William Kotzwinkle

This chilling fable by the bestselling author of THE FAN MAN
and FATA MORGANA is an unforgettable indictment of man's
inhumanity to man, and to all living things. With macabre
humor and bitter irony, Kotzwinkle uses Dr. Rat as mankind's
apologist in an animal experimentation laboratory gro-
tesquely similar to a Nazi concentration camp.

ON THE WAY HOME   63131-8/$3.50
Robert Bausch

This is the powerful, deeply personal story of a man who came
home from Vietnam and what happened to his family.
"A strong, spare, sad and beautiful novel, exactly what
Hemingway should write, I think, if he'd lived through the
kind of war we make now."   John Gardner
"A brilliant psychological study of an intelligent, close
family in which something has gone terribly and irre-
trievably wrong."   *San Francisco Chronicle*

AGAINST THE STREAM   63693-X/$4.95
James Hanley

"James Hanley is a most remarkable writer....Beneath this
book's calm flow there is such devastating emotion."
The New York Times Book Review
This is the haunting, illuminating novel of a young child
whose arrival at the isolated stone mansion of his mother's
family unleashes their hidden emotions and forces him to
make a devastating choice.

NEW FROM ◢◣ AVON BARD

DISTINGUISHED MODERN FICTION

SENT FOR YOU YESTERDAY
John Edgar Wideman   82644-5/$3.50
In SENT FOR YOU YESTERDAY, John Edgar Wideman, "one of America's premier writers of fiction" (*The New York Times*), tells the passion of ordinary lives, the contradictions, perils, pain and love which are the blood and bone of everybody's America. "Perhaps the most gifted black novelist in his generation." *The Nation*

Also from Avon Bard: **DAMBALLAH** (78519-6/$2.95) and
                                    HIDING PLACE (78501-3/$2.95)

THE LEOPARD'S TOOTH
William Kotzwinkle   62869-4/$2.95
A supernatural tale of a turn-of-the-century archaeological expedition to Africa and the members' breathtaking adventures with the forces of good and evil, by "one of today's most inventive writers." (Playboy).

DREAM CHILDREN
Gail Godwin   62406-0/$3.50
Gail Godwin, the bestselling author of A MOTHER AND TWO DAUGHTERS (61598-3/$3.95), presents piercing, moving, beautifully wrought fiction about women possessed of imagination, fantasy, vision and obsession who live within the labyrinths of their minds. "Godwin is a writer of enormous intelligence, wit and compassion...DREAM CHILDREN is a fine place to start catching up with an extraordinary writer." *Saturday Review*

Available wherever paperbacks are sold or directly from the publisher. Include $1.00 per copy for postage and handling, allow 6-8 weeks for delivery. Avon Books, Dept BP, Box 767, Rte 2, Dresden, TN 38225